WALTON – JUL 2019

WITHDRAWN

Please return this book on or before the date shown above. To renew go to www.essex.gov.uk/libraries, ring 0345 603 7628 or go to any Essex library.

Essex County Council

Valerio Varesi

THE LIZARD STRATEGY

Translated from the Italian by
Joseph Farrell

MACLEHOSE PRESS
QUERCUS · LONDON

First published in the Italian language as *Il commissario Soneri e la strategia della lucertola* by Sperling & Kupfer in 2014

First published in Great Britain in 2018 by MacLehose Press

This paperback edition published in 2019 by

MacLehose Press
An imprint of Quercus Publishing Ltd
Carmelite House
50 Victoria Embankment
London EC4Y 0DZ

An Hachette UK company

A CIP catalogue record for this book is available
from the British Library.

ISBN (MMP) 978 0 85705 615 3
ISBN (Ebook) 978 0 85705 614 6

2 4 6 8 10 9 7 5 3 1

Designed and typeset in Adobe Caslon by Patty Rennie
Printed and bound in Great Britain by Clays Ltd, Elcograf S.p.A.

MIX
Paper from
responsible sources
FSC® C104740

Papers used by MacLehose Press are from well-managed
forests and other responsible sources.

To Christopher MacLehose, his ever-helpful
team of Paul Engles and Katharina Bielenberg,
and to Joseph Farrell, with grateful thanks to all

A Note on the Italian Police System

Italy has three independent, national police forces: the POLIZA DI STATO (state police), who come under the Ministry for the Interior; the arma dei carabinieri (no ready English equivalent or translation), managed by the Ministry of Defence; and the GUARDIA DI FINANZA (Financial Police), answerable to the Ministry for the Economy and Finance.

The first two have de facto the same responsibilities and there have been attempts, so far abortive, to merge them. The Finanza investigate financial crime, fraud, tax evasion and smuggling, which means that they are active in drug offences.

In addition, many local authorities have a force of VIGILI URBANI (municipal police), employed by the city council. They are active in traffic management, but are also involved in enforcing by-laws, dealing with residence permits and so on.

The QUESTURA is the Police H.Q., and the QUESTORE is its chief officer, who co-ordinates enquiries. However, ultimate responsibility for instigating and conducting criminal investigations lies with the PUBBLICO MINISTERIO, a magistrate.

Commissario Soneri is an officer of the polizia, while a MARESCIALLO (more equivalent to a sergeant rather than a marshall) is an officer of the carabinieri. Although the respective hierarchies do not quite match, a commissario would rank higher than a maresciallo.

I

"JUVARA, WHAT WOULD you say if you read that some unfortunate individual had been injured when a roll of cotton wool was tossed from the fourth floor of a building, that someone was at death's door after being struck by a feather, or that someone else had been knocked to the ground by a pigeon shitting on his head?"

"Sorry, what are you on about now?" the inspector asked.

"Nowadays you get the most incredible rubbish in the papers."

Juvara gave Soneri a puzzled look. The commissario walked over to his desk and laid out that morning's paper, bringing his fist down on a headline splashed over five columns: WEEK OFF FOR MAYOR CORBELLINI, and lower down: ON THE PAGANELLA WITH BOYS FROM NAVETTA.

The inspector continued staring at him with the same bewildered expression.

"You see? You don't look aghast. You've been anaesthetised."

"But commissario . . ." Juvara was reduced to stuttering.

"Don't you see the state this city's in? Do you care if the mayor has pushed off to a ski slope? And do we have to be told all about it? However, if everybody reacted the way you do . . . I hope that at least a few folk would get seriously angry."

The inspector shrugged. "It's just another piece of news."

"Yes, I suppose so. Let's forget it."

"Forgive me if I say so, sir. At times, you seem unduly moralistic," Juvara said with a grin. He had long since grown accustomed to the commissario's outbursts, which arrived without any warning.

"If only there were a bit more morality around in this city! There's a putrid, stagnant stench in the air, but anyone who so much as holds his nose is attacked as a hypocritical bigot," Soneri said. "Take all those poor souls who end up here. Sometimes I wonder what right we have to slam them in jail. What are we supposed to blame them for? Yes, alright, every so often they rob a bank and run off with a couple of thousand euros, but don't bankers get away with thieving day after day? How come one lot ends up in jail and the other doesn't?"

"Commissario, we shouldn't be saying things like that. And anyway, that's a right can of worms."

"That's the sort of thing people say when they want to change the subject," Soneri said, somewhat piqued. He got to his feet and marched out of the office.

He strode furiously along Via Repubblica among the rush-hour crowds. It seemed as though the city was being evacuated and a defeated army was careering heedlessly through it. A few centimetres of snow were more than enough to cause an outbreak of madness among Parma's mothers, done up like mountain rescue teams as they went to the aid of their offspring, but also among the fathers, muffled up inside their two-ton four-wheel drives which mounted pavements and flowerbeds to get right up to the school steps. The television channels and the newspapers had gone into overdrive about the dreadful weather and had generated waves of hysteria, contributing to a commotion that irritated Soneri more and more. He remembered his own childhood in the Montanara district: the heavy snowfalls, the sledges on the few slopes, the walk to school, the snowball fights, the search along the way for stretches of virgin snow, the crunching sound underfoot, and his wonder at finding his own footprints still there as he made his way back home. What has it come to when one of the most natural occurrences of winter is seen as an insurmountable obstacle?

Angela had long reproached him about his disquiet, and said he had lost all sense of time. He replied that he did not think of himself as being out of touch, but the whole world had gone to rack and ruin, had become grimy, worn out and unbearably slothful. He found some peace of mind in the silence of Piazzale dei Servi, where he stopped to look at a fir tree whose branches were weighed down with snow. Staring at the tree, he blotted the houses, the people and Parma itself from his view as though he too were on the Paganella. This perspective somehow brought the mayor back to mind.

He had never thought of Corbellini as a skier. Always so elegantly turned out, hair so carefully parted, suits in sober English hues, he seemed to walk on tiptoe as though crossing an ice field. He did not seem in any way the sporty type, and the idea of him with the boys from Navetta, a district on the outskirts of the city once inhabited by poor people crammed into huts but now an estate of social housing colonised by immigrants, its balconies festooned with coloured clothes hung out to dry, was too much. This was a day of strange events: snow, general chaos, phoney excitement, and now Corbellini on a ski-lift.

As he stood contemplating the fir tree, his thoughts jumping about in festive delight on the first real day of winter weather, Angela called him.

"Commissario, be careful you don't go skidding about. The city has turned treacherous."

"Why, did you end up on your arse?"

"You'd love that, wouldn't you? When I was a girl, I used to go ice-skating."

"When you were a girl!"

"What are you getting at? Are you implying I'm past it?"

"No, it's just that memory plays tricks. Like with this city, which seems never to have seen a snowflake before. Want to know something? I'd like to see a metre of snow falling just to annoy all these idiots here."

"Well, I haven't lost my memory. I like the snow, even if it's just for its colour. This world is so grey nowadays!"

"If we ever fall out, *signora avvocato*, at least we'll have one thing in common to hold on to."

"You mean something to slide on."

"It's our mayor who's sliding."

"On a grand scale! They've just arrested a pack of Council officials, the ones closest to him."

"No, he really is sliding about. He's away on a skiing trip to the Paganella."

"The world's going mad. I never expected to see him anywhere except in a theatre foyer or on a sunbed."

Soneri made no reply. Angela's irony was the best solvent for his bad mood.

"Today isn't the first time odd things have happened," she went on.

"I was just thinking the same thing not so long ago. I'm now convinced that normality doesn't exist, that everything seems strange to me because I no longer understand where the world's headed."

"Come on! You're having one of your crises of total rejection, but just hang in there and it'll pass. Listen to this. You remember that elderly colleague of mine, the woman who became one of the first female lawyers in Parma?"

The commissario grunted in agreement.

"Well, she called me this morning to tell me that during the night she keeps hearing ringtones and snatches of tunes."

"So what? That's nothing new. With all the devices people cart about with them, their pockets are like bandstands these days."

"It's not that. She lives in the Montebello district and her house is near the dyke along the Parma river. The ringtones come from there."

"There are piles of toxic waste along the river bed."

"Adelaide is not going off her head," Angela said, raising her voice a little. "She told me because she thinks there's something fishy going on."

"Has she heard anything else? Did she go down to have a look?"

"Don't be silly! She's afraid. She lives alone in that house, and there's open ground down to the embankment."

"A lot of people are afraid nowadays. What does she want me to do?" Soneri asked.

"To drop in for a few minutes. She's a good woman and deserves a bit of attention. She's one of the old school, a bit like you," Angela said, with a touch of mockery in her voice.

"You don't have any younger colleagues who need a bit of cheering up?"

"Plenty, but I doubt they'd be glad to have you hanging around. Do as you please. If need be, I'll go myself."

The traffic was quieter at lunchtime and rays of sunlight brightened the city. Soneri walked down to the Lungoparma, the road along the river where the view opened out onto the sprawling, irregular skyline on the far side. The houses there were huddled together in groups in what had once been the city's working-class district. Snow fell on the river, and the still water resembled a sheet of cast iron. On the other side of the parapet from the road, there was a small urban jungle of poplars and willows which followed the river into the heart of the city and offered cover for the urban wildlife seeking shelter in the comfortable heat bubble of the houses. At the Dattaro bridge, he found himself opposite the Montebello district, dominated now by the appalling Mirror Cube that housed the Post Office. Following the river in the direction of the distant hunchbacks of the Apennines, he ended up at Adelaide's doorway, which he remembered from having been there with Angela. The district, on the other hand, brought to mind a construction scandal in the '70s which had involved a group of Council officials of every political stripe. At that point Parma lost her innocence, and the shamelessness of that episode provided her with an excuse for giving herself to anyone who asked.

"How are you, Adelaide?"

She shrugged her shoulders. "Like a ham hung up to be seasoned."

"You'll become even more desirable," Soneri said.

She threw him a warning glance. "Don't mock me. I really miss my work. Retirement produces more victims than an epidemic, and the worst thing is you were looking forward to it."

"Tell me more about these ringtones."

"I know you'll think I'm off my head or on the bottle. I didn't even want to tell Angela, but then I decided it was better to risk setting off a false alarm and being taken for an old drunkard than just ignoring it. And anyway, I don't care what they think of me anymore."

"Does it only happen at night?"

"Yes, I think they come up along the embankment. Sometimes the sound is like a pop song, but at others it's like classical music. Other times it's just an ordinary ringtone or an electronic buzz."

"When did you first hear it?"

"Three days ago. At first, I paid no heed, but the second time it was obvious it couldn't be someone hiding out down there. No-one could stay on the embankment for long in this cold."

"Did you hear the sound today as well?"

"It's very punctual, at regular intervals, hour after hour."

They looked at each other in silence, engrossed in their little mystery. Meantime, the first traces of darkness seemed to be moving across the slopes down to the river, beyond the embankment. Soneri leaned out and it was then that he noticed the first wisps of mist floating along the river Parma in the direction of the hills. The moisture suspended above the water seemed to be going in the opposite direction to the mist on the riverbanks, the one seeking out the mountains and the other the sea. It was this rebellion against normality which he found delightful in mists. Quite suddenly, the horizon seemed to vanish, and in the grey gloom the croaking of crows fleeing for refuge among the houses rang out.

"This seems to be the boundary between the city and the countryside. You're vaguely aware of an invisible border which separates the one from the other. I love the ambiguity," Soneri said.

"You're near the city centre even if you seem to be far away. Piazza Garibaldi and the Duomo are little more than a kilometre from here," Adelaide said.

"In your opinion, what is it that's ringing over there?"

"If you ask me, it's a mobile. The new models give out different sounds depending on who's calling."

"And how many different tones have you heard?"

"At least four, maybe more. I was wondering, if there's a mobile among the trees, does that mean there's an owner who can't reply?"

"By this time, the stench would've given him away. Anyway, we'll have to wait till morning. The mist has brought down the curtain," he said, watching the mist flowing towards the mountains as though rolling on the wind.

It took only a few minutes for him to walk from the silence of the house by the river to the residences of the wealthy in Viale Solferino, and to proceed from there through the Barriera Farini into the city. Adelaide was quite right: the distances were not great. But the change of scenery seemed like a leap in time. He turned into the botanic gardens and felt the same sensation he had experienced shortly before, but the roar of the traffic and the shouts of the children returning home from school broke the enchantment of that little jungle. To complete the change in atmosphere, his mobile rang.

"Am I disturbing you, sir?" Juvara asked.

Soneri detested that kind of hypocritical premise, and cut him short. "What is it?"

"They've managed to lose a patient at the Villa Clelia care home, and they've been onto us to ask for help."

"What do you mean, lose a patient? It's not like losing a button!"

"The fact is they can't find him."

"What did I say earlier? There's so much rubbish doing the rounds nowadays."

"It's an elderly man with dementia. He seems to have got out of bed and disappeared."

"Are the patrolmen on the job?"

"Yes. They looked in the courtyard, in the garden and in the neighbouring streets. The hospital's security staff are searching too, but they've come up with nothing."

"Has he any family? How old is this man?"

"Do you want me to read out the report?"

"Do what the hell you like," Soneri snapped. "Do you have

to read out a schedule to tell me if he's fat or thin, tall or short?"

"Alfio Romagnoli, eighty-three years old, medium height, slim build, taken into hospital with gastroenteritis, suffering from senile dementia. No known relatives," Juvara said, without missing a beat.

"Does he have problems walking? Is he lame? Arthritic? Does he have a limp?"

"None of the above."

Soneri ended the call and set off for Villa Clelia, passing the Arco del Petitot and the Tardini stadium on his way. The entrance was on Viale Partigiani d'Italia, near San Lazzaro, and he thought to himself how appropriate it was that a care home now filled with old folk dismissed from the public hospitals and sent there to die should be situated in the district which had once been a refuge for people suffering from the plague.

On reaching the hospital, he walked up the stairs and past wards where in the darkness an unconscious, resigned humanity lived in a silence interrupted by isolated howls emitted from the depths of night terrors.

The director, a corpulent individual who was extremely sure of himself, gave his name as Malusardi. In his office, Soneri found two other doctors, one male and one female, waiting for him. The male doctor introduced himself as being in charge of the geriatric ward.

"We cannot understand how it could have happened or where he might have ended up," the director said.

"When did you notice he was missing?" the commissario asked.

"At six o'clock, when the nurses made the rounds with the morning medicines."

"How many people are on night-shift?"

"One or two, in addition to an on-duty doctor, who has to

take care of the medical ward as well. It's on the other side of the staircase."

"The patients in the same room as Romagnoli, did they see anything?"

Malusardi shrugged his shoulders. "They were asleep, but even if they'd been awake . . ."

"Can you show me to the ward?"

The male doctors got to their feet, and the woman, who had not yet opened her mouth, led the way along a corridor where the heat and the smell of medicines caught Soneri by the throat. From the darkness of the various rooms, a litany of the moans, curses, laboured breathing and occasional snores of people intermittently asleep made up a chorus that resembled the death rattle of some large, wounded animal. There were ten rooms on either side of the hallway, with two doors at the far end, one opening onto the staircase and the other onto the emergency exit.

"Is there an alarm on that door?" the commissario asked, pointing to the exit.

"If anyone opens it, a buzzer goes off and flashing lights come on all over the ward."

"So, he must have made his way out among the visitors," Soneri said.

The three doctors remained silent, foreseeing trouble ahead.

"Perhaps someone took him out, pretending he was somebody else. Anyway, the important thing now is to find the old man," the commissario said. This suggestion seemed to cheer Malusardi up. Some half-asleep carers and a couple of elderly ladies who were assisting relatives peeped out from behind doors.

"Are they here overnight as well?" the commissario asked.

"Some of them are," the director replied. "But they often doze off."

Soneri had the impression he was holding something back. "Were you around when Romagnoli disappeared?" he asked the doctor in charge of the ward.

The doctor was about to answer but Malusardi got in first. "No, it was Dr Camelotta's day off. Dr Magni was on duty."

"What did you do when you noticed he was missing?"

The director came in quickly with his reply. "Dr Magni was finishing his shift, but he stayed on to oversee all the procedures – in other words, to inform the ward sister, the medical office, the police, the hospital's security staff and the paramedics."

The commissario gave a grunt. He found it strange that an elderly patient suffering from dementia had managed to outwit all those white coats and the ostentatious efficiency of a private healthcare establishment.

"If he's not under the bed, there's no point in searching in here," Soneri said, making no attempt to hide his annoyance. He got up and left the hospital, but stopped near the stadium to pull out his mobile. He called Pasquariello, the head of the flying squad.

"What can you tell me about the disappearance of this old fellow?"

"We've searched the neighbourhood and spoken to the shopkeepers in the district, but nobody's seen him. A very curious business."

"Did you search the hospital itself?"

"Only the garden, together with their own security men. The directors kept us out. They're convinced he's left the premises."

"It does seem the most obvious conclusion."

"And yet I can't help thinking that if he did get out, we'd have found him by now," Pasquariello said. "Where's an old guy in his pyjamas with no memory going to go?"

"In his pyjamas?"

"The nurses told us that all the clothes he was wearing when he arrived, including his shoes, were still in his cupboard."

The commissario struggled to contain his rage. The case seemed at the same time both extremely simple and desperately complicated. He felt inadequate.

The head of the flying squad advanced a comforting hypothesis. "If he can't be found, there's only one possible explanation. Maybe there was some reason to make him disappear."

"You mean he might have been kidnapped?"

"It doesn't take much to convince someone suffering from dementia. All you have to do is tell him you're taking him home, throw a raincoat over him and pass him off as a relative. From what my men picked up, the security amounts to nothing more than a doorkeeper. But even this idea is hard to credit. The old guy had no relatives and no property. Not a bean. Or else . . ." Pasquariello added, leaving the phrase hanging in the air.

"Or else?"

"Maybe the solution is so obvious that none of us has thought of it. We've got our heads so filled with complexities that we often neglect the most obvious leads."

Soneri muttered, "You're right," in the tones of a sleepwalker, and hung up. A similar thought had shortly before struck him with the strength of an urgent physical need. He turned back towards the hospital as the city was settling down for dinner and the snow was hardening on the roads and pavements. The courtyard of Villa Clelia, covered with a film of ice, shone under the lamplight. Everything appeared as bright and inviting as the entrance to a mountain hut. He rushed up the stairs and burst into the geriatric ward. A couple of nurses pushing the medicine trolley stared at him and tried to stop him. "Excuse me. It's not visiting time."

The commissario paid no heed but marched straight on, hearing at his back the hurried steps of one of the nurses, her

shrill voice shouting out, "Where do you think you're going?"
He reached the emergency exit with the woman still remonstrating behind him, grabbed hold of the handle and pushed. He stood for a few seconds with the door half open onto the freezing walkway, observing the nurse with a triumphant and accusing look. The woman stopped in turn, silent and bemused. The freezing air on his face was an invitation to go forward onto the darkness of the staircase where the service lights seemed to be out of order. He felt like a bloodhound following the scent of a pheasant. He stood on the walkway waiting for his eyes to adapt to the gloom and then it struck him that he had at last found a use for the torch on his mobile. He went down one floor, became aware of the brightness coming from the door of the lower ward, and continued on down. The torchlight went out and he almost tripped. When he switched it back on, he saw him. He seemed so composed as to suggest that he had consigned himself willingly to a gentle death from the cold. He was seated on the third step from the ground floor, his feet on the ground, his body lying back on the stairs and his head reclining serenely on a step as though it was a pillow. He was wearing nothing but his pyjamas, standard issue, rather like overalls, tightened at the wrists and ankles. Soneri stretched out a hand to touch him, but then pulled back as though afraid of waking him. This time his mobile was genuinely useful, allowing him to make a call that would help old Romagnoli escape from his involuntary concealment.

"There's a job for you here at Villa Clelia," the commissario told Nanetti, head of the forensics squad.

Nanetti replied with his mouth full. "You think I'm a nurse?"

"Unfortunately for you, you chose a profession where it's permissible to give you a kick up the arse at any time of the day or night."

"What do you mean, 'chose'?"

"Come on, you love your job really! Your face is always on T.V., and that white coat gives you a certain *je ne sais quoi.*"

"Piss off, commissario! If it was left to me, I'd only put on the white coat to look like a doctor and get to visit the young female patients."

"Tough luck! We're in the geriatric ward."

"What's going on?"

"There's a body on the staircase of the emergency exit. They left it in the fridge."

"You've been imbibing too much Gutturnio, eh?"

"If only! No, he was on the stairs all night and the freezing cold has left him stiff as a board."

"You do pick your time! I was halfway through a dish of *pasta e fagioli.*"

"Please accept my apologies for having interrupted this delightful relationship."

When he had hung up, Soneri sat down on the steps beside the old man and kept watch as he slept.

2

NANETTI ARRIVED WITH two members of his staff and all the necessary paraphernalia. The hospital had been roused from its torpor, and Malusardi, the doctors on the executive and Camelotta, head of the geriatric ward, rushed to the scene. Together they made a lot of useless fuss as they milled about with worried expressions.

"What do you think?" Soneri asked, when his colleague came in from the cold.

"At first sight it seems he froze to death, perhaps after a stroke," Nanetti said, blowing his nose. "There's no trace of blood, the body appears intact with no sign of violence. Then again, maybe they poisoned him."

"That was my verdict too, but this story has taught me not to ignore the most obvious lines of inquiry, which are very often the right ones."

"In the forensics squad, we never ignore them, but for us it is much simpler because physics and chemistry force us to follow the one path. That way we avoid behaving like mental tossers, which is not the case with you intellectuals."

"Sometimes you just have to toss ideas about," the commissario replied, without rising to the bait. "In fact, it occurred to me to look on the staircase precisely because I was thinking of a story by Edgar Allan Poe. People go searching everywhere except in the most obvious places."

"Oh, I do beg your pardon. There are two exits here, the principal one and the emergency exit. Where could he have escaped from?"

"Yes, but they believed he'd got clean away, whereas he'd only taken a couple of steps."

Malusardi came over to them. "If you'd like a bite to eat, I'll ask the kitchen to prepare you something."

Soneri and Nanetti exchanged glances and declined the offer. It was better to go hungry than face a hospital meal. In the meantime, the magistrates had turned up and tension was rising once again.

The director did not insist. "If there's anything we can do, just ask."

"If it's the way I think it is, I'll be off quite soon. You'll have to deal with the prosecution office," Soneri said.

The director's expression turned more serious. "I was the first to be misled and let down," he stammered.

"I'm getting the impression that things were not quite as they should have been. The door was not alarmed, there were no lights on the stairs. It's just as well I inspected only the emergency staircase."

Malusardi gave a rancorous smirk. He might not have been accustomed to inspections, or perhaps he was skilled at lessening their scope. "If you are insinuating that we're not properly equipped, let me tell you that we have the most modern security system of any public hospital."

"Exactly," Soneri said.

"What do you mean by that?"

"I mean that nowadays we entrust security to technology as a way of shirking responsibility. We care less and less about how we ourselves behave."

Malusardi made a gesture signifying indifference. "If the alarm on the door had sounded, the nurses would have seen the old man going out and would have been able to stop him. The responsibility lies with the person who unplugged the system. There was no fault on the hospital's part."

"At the end of the day, it's always a question of individual error, but it's too easy to dismiss everything in that manner."

The director gave the impression of not following this line of reasoning, and the commissario became aware that the discussion had carried him beyond his own remit. He said no more and turned away. Later, as they were leaving the hospital and heading out into the mist which by that time in the evening had settled in, Nanetti returned to the subject.

"That guy's in the shit," he said, referring to Malusardi.

"He'll get away with it. He's been pulling in enough money to be able to retain the best lawyers."

"It's a nasty business. An old man suffering from dementia walks out of the hospital and no-one even notices – or thinks of going to look for him on the stairs."

"It's always somebody else's fault. He'll duck out of it and the weakest party will end up carrying the can. The usual false justice. It's a disaster when you stop saying 'us' and say only 'me, me, me'."

"Don't make it too complicated, eh? I told you I'm not an intellectual."

"Do you want me to tell you how I see it at this point?"

"Before you get started, let's go to Alceste's and have something to eat. I've left a tab open."

The commissario nodded and went on speaking. "On the walkway, I saw some cigarette butts. Somebody was going out there for a smoke, and to make it easier for himself he switched the alarm off. On the evening when the old man got out, perhaps he forgot to turn it on again, or maybe he left it switched off every night. After all, who's going to run away? I think the nurses knew all about it, but took it for granted that nothing could happen. The problem is that sometimes the most improbable things do occur."

The *Milord* was still open when they arrived, although the last diners were finishing up. Considering the late hour, they ordered a plate of *salumi misti* and a bottle of Gutturnio.

"Nurses have no imagination, but it's hardly their fault," Soneri said.

"Nurses are supposed to know how to take blood samples and give injections, not to allow their imaginations to roam," Nanetti replied.

"That's not enough. Just think how helpful it is in our line of work to imagine an alternative reality, and then think what a limitation it is to take everything for granted."

"You're off on your flights of philosophy again."

"You don't think it's relevant? Our life has been taken over by automatic mechanisms, and this allows us to avoid all responsibility and duty of care for what we're doing. Most of the time we don't bother about anything, but skip merrily along on a tightrope without a safety net."

"It's all a question of trust. Even now while we're eating, who can tell whether there are any forbidden substances in this *culatello*, and yet to me it seems genuine and irresistible. Who was the guy who used to speak about clear and distinct ideas?"

"Descartes."

"Well, the fact is that even clear and distinct ideas can let us down."

"What counts nowadays is appearance. Innocence and truth have been lost."

"Don't kid yourself! We never had either the one or the other."

"The real pains in the arse are people like us who go around stirring things up."

"And for what? They refuse to believe what's in front of their noses. It's more comfortable to take things at face value."

"Quite true. Take our mayor, for example," Soneri said with a snigger. "A man of straw – rises like puff pastry and has the same substance."

"You can't deny that if you were meeting him for the first time he'd cut a fine figure, what with all the time he spends working out, lying under sun lamps, or at the barber's. But are you really surprised if he pushes off to the ski slopes while half of Parma is in the shit because of him?"

"I shouldn't be surprised in the slightest, but it's stronger than me," the commissario said. "Juvara tells me I'm a moralist, but I don't take it as an insult. I'm proud of it."

"Steady on. When you're on your high horse, you're a right Job's comforter."

"At least when I'm in one of those moods I keep myself to myself."

"And you can be cured with a good meal."

"Ah well, it's a great consolation."

"There might be one other."

The two men had the place to themselves, and the Gutturnio induced a mellow mood in them both. There was nothing which helped Soneri to calm down like wine and good food. On misty evenings, the heat of a *trattoria* seemed to him like the maternal womb. The calm of winter darkness, that pacifying sense of closure which is the deepest meaning of night, soothed every anxiety and delivered him into the realm of the imagination. He felt the need to get out, to walk through the deserted city, avoiding the hubbub of the alcoholic circuits where gangs of consumers displayed their non-conformism by sitting at outside tables, even in the depths of winter. He walked through the backstreets, where isolated figures, dragged close to the walls by their dogs, were making their way home along Via Saffi, Piazza Duomo, Via Manzini and the Ponte di Mezzo, the very fringes of a city that had seen terrible and glorious moments. The wind carried the whistle of trains in the northern districts, on the far side of the Palazzo Ducale and the Palazzo della Pilotta. Soneri himself was heading south, to the spot where he had gazed at the bright peaks of the Apennines that afternoon. He walked through the mist until his mobile rang. He raised it to his ear and heard Adelaide's voice.

"It's started again."

He made no reply but walked more quickly. It was then he realised that he was already going in the direction of the ringing mobile, and that his mysterious nocturnal wandering had a precise objective.

He arrived at the Palazzo delle Poste, which in the darkness looked like a hostile, rocky fortress. He walked around it and clambered over the embankment wall to the path on the other side. The dark riverbank seemed to conceal a cliff-edge, while the lights of the district opposite struggled to cut through the mist. Having caught sight of the last lamp-post and, a little further on, the outline of the road which led out of the city, he looked for Adelaide's doorway. He did not ring the bell but stood waiting. In the distance, he could make out the splash of tyres on the wet road. Just then the bell in some nearby village rang out announcing midnight.

The dampness and the chilly vapour from the river made the place bleak, but the deep silence and the climate of expectation reminded him of a hunting trip and made him linger on the embankment. He did not notice the time pass on that spot which was no longer city but not yet countryside, and so could be anywhere. Quite suddenly he heard it, seemingly far off, an arresting *trill-trill*, like the sound made by telephones when he was still a boy. He tried to work out where the noise was coming from and ran along the path until he heard the ring, coming from a point somewhere below him, in an area of the slope much further down. He descended with care, his feet squelching deep into the mud through a layer of snow and dry grass. Bushes struck him on the face as he attempted to pull them apart or grab hold of them. The further down he went, the closer the sound seemed to be, but when he had almost reached the bottom, the silence and the darkness gathered round him. He had the impression of being in a gully, tangled up, wet and trapped. There was nothing he could do but wait for the next ring from a device that had been ringing in vain for three days.

Something did ring a few moments later, but it was his own mobile. "Not coming home tonight?" Angela asked. "Should I be getting jealous?"

"Yes, you should. I am surrounded by fierce nutrias."

"And you've got the brass neck to tell me?"

"What are you talking about? This is quite a different matter. Are you a rodent? Anyway, it's your fault for pushing me into their clutches."

"It does you no good to go drinking with that drunken guzzler Nanetti."

"I'm being serious. I'm near the house of your friend Adelaide, and I'm crawling about in search of a mobile, so I'm not exactly in the most comfortable of positions."

"I think you're drunk."

"You're wrong. I am the living metaphor of modern man, at the service of the devices he has himself created."

"If you're not drunk, you must be running a temperature. There's a nasty strain of influenza going around."

"Listen. I'm on the bank of the river Parma, up to my ankles in snow, in a place which even a wild boar would find hellish, waiting for a signal from some bloody mobile which has ended up down here."

"Franco, should I be getting worried, or is this just one of your little jokes?" Angela asked.

"No, don't worry. I'm a country boy and I'm not afraid of riverbanks, nor of the night."

"Do you want me to call Adelaide and tell her to prepare something hot?"

"Don't bother. These nutrias are nice, gentle creatures."

Angela did not have time to reply because the commissario heard something ringing out close by and shut off communication. He moved down another stretch of the embankment and had reached a level piece of ground of land when he saw it. The screen was turned face down but gave off a feeble light, like a firefly. He picked up the mobile and just managed to read UNKNOWN NUMBER when the caller hung up. He wrapped the device in a handkerchief and put it in his pocket. He started to climb up the embankment, but stopped and stood quite still for a moment in a darkness which had something primordial about it. It was then that he became aware of something moving about ten metres behind him. He imagined that it was one of the nutrias he had just mentioned, but the noise seemed to come from a bigger animal. He had the impression it was moving in little jumps, accelerating as it came forward. He heard it starting to run and for a few seconds thought with terror that it was charging in his direction, but in fact it was moving in the direction of the city. Shortly afterwards the sound died away, as though the creature was running along the open, sandy space next to the water.

He scrambled back up, clutching at bushes, but was exhausted and wet through when he got to the path. From the darkness, he heard someone calling out. The commissario peered into the solid wall of darkness until he made out the figure of a man holding a dog on a lead.

"I heard a voice down there and the dog started to pull me along," the stranger explained. He moved forward, making it easier to see him in profile. He seemed to be in his sixties, upright and tall, a well-trimmed goatee beard and a neat moustache giving him the commanding air of a commodore.

"I have to admit this must seem a somewhat odd situation," Soneri said.

"No, not necessarily," came the unexpected reply.

"I'm a police officer and I'm here conducting an inquiry."

"I understand. I'm out taking him for a walk," he said, indicating the dog, a sad-eyed hound.

The conversation at that time, in that place, was verging on the surreal, and there seemed to be more than one level of ambiguity to the situation. "I live by night. No-one knows the night like me," the man said.

The commissario was about to reply when the dog began to emit a kind of subdued howl. "He's had enough walking for one evening. He is getting on in years and suffers the cold like all dogs of his type. If you would like, I could offer you a cup of tea."

"Don't trouble yourself. It's very late," Soneri said, embarrassed but also a little curious.

"No trouble at all. As I said, I live by night. I can't stand the dawn. As soon as the sky begins to brighten, I take to my bed."

The commissario discovered that he lived a few houses along from Adelaide and on the nameplate he read: TAN-CREDI VALMARINI. Dark colours were predominant in the house and the windows were screened by heavy curtains. The upper floor, where the two men sat down, had an enormous window which the stranger revealed by pressing a remote control to draw back the curtains.

"Behold the night," he announced. "I have a fraternal feeling for it when it's so close." The darkness, with the density of thick mist, did somehow give the impression it was snuggling up close. "I get the feeling that it isn't displeasing to you either."

"No, it's not, but this evening I wasn't walking for pleasure."

"That's clear, but that's not the most important thing."

"What is important then? Everyone has their own motives for relishing the night and perhaps yours is different from mine."

"The night is pleasing because it leaves us free to release our imaginations. Everything is possible under the cover of darkness."

"As with mist."

"So, you too find the world unbearable?"

"I do all I can to make it acceptable, but I don't always succeed."

The man smiled. "I never succeed, and that's why I try never to see it, or else I construct a world of my own."

"Not everyone is capable of invention. It depends on the profession you practise."

"What we call reality is just a provisional truth, and therefore suspect. Your work, for instance, rests on transitory conventions. Everything is provisional, and so nothing is more than illusion and idolatry."

"There's nothing more useful and more terrible than idolatry, don't you agree?" Soneri said.

Valmarini became more serious. "I do agree, but anyone who is aware of it can also make play of that fact."

"I am in no position to make play of it."

Valmarini served the tea while the dog stretched out on the

rug at the foot of the table. It seemed, in its own way, to be complaining about something.

"There's a great coming and going of animals along the riverbank. Who knows how many scents he can follow?" Soneri said, pointing to the hound.

"He certainly does pick up many scents, but he's too old to follow them. I think he's a little bit like us. He imagines some prey lying among the bushes."

"Over the last couple of nights, have you heard a mobile ringing?"

"One hears so many noises. It's like a motorway down there."

"Are there many people moving about?"

"I think so, although I've never come face to face with any-one. I hear footsteps among the trees, and sometimes make out shadows which quickly disappear. They seem to be on some urgent business they're not keen to share with anyone. Once I went right down, almost as far as the river bed, and I noted several tracks, as though each individual had his own."

"So you do go out during the day?"

"Only at dusk, to encourage the day's end."

The bay window in the room was sharply angled and resembled the prow of a ship. The mist which rubbed up against it gave the impression of cautious navigation. Soneri noticed an easel on which he imagined a helm being placed.

"You paint?"

Valmarini laughed. "Let's say that I reproduce."

The commissario took a sip of his tea. He was beginning to feel exasperated. "And what do you reproduce?"

"Does it matter? Reproduction is the essence of painting. There are some who reproduce landscapes, faces, scenes from life, or else nightmares of their own which assume a material shape on canvas. For my part, I reproduce reproductions. I imitate other people."

"In other words, you do forgeries?" Soneri asked hesitantly.

"Don't be afraid of saying it openly. I am a forger."

"That's illegal."

"Here we go again with conventions and laws. It's not illegal if one is open about it. My clients are well aware of what I'm doing, and out of vanity, to give themselves an air of refinement, they're delighted to have in their homes works of art which lend their rooms a certain nobility. I sell a history rather than a painting. There's a painting, certainly, but there's also the life of the person who made it. I mean the original – the artistic mode and the circumstances in which the masterpiece was conceived. They know next to nothing about what they're hanging on their walls, and they're happy to take in any gibberish. They learn the same way as you do when you read the instruction manual for a new television, and they preen themselves as they deliver a simplistic ten-minute lecture on art history to their guests, every one as ignorant as they are. There's no deceit. Everything is above board. If anything, it's them who cheat their dinner guests by showing off their small, utterly fraudulent museum."

"If I were in your shoes, I wouldn't feel at ease with myself," the commissario said.

"That's because you're a man of the old school."

"I've been told that more than once before."

"Please don't take offence. I'm of the same mind as you, but perhaps I have a greater awareness of what we've allowed ourselves to become, and I can afford myself the luxury of jeering at so-called modernity. So nowadays you want only appearance? Alright then, I will provide you with the sequins. That's all there is to it."

"And your clients are quite happy?"

"They're absolutely delighted! If you could only see those Neanderthals in all their finery! They foam at the mouth at the chance of showing off a forged Guercino or a copy of a Guido Reni, and for half an hour they can hold forth over the squeals of the ladies. They have no idea what to talk about apart from their scams. By the end of these wearisome dinners, the least false things on display are my paintings."

"You must be grateful to these people. You've built a career on their backs."

"Have you any idea how satisfying it is to get them to pay through the nose *and* make a fool of them? For the most part, we're talking about people who got rich by theft, and that's why there's now a culture of anxiety, even if it's a bit late. The fear of being exposed, of being shown to be as vulgar as the rest, means they want to whitewash their past. They're ashamed of what they used to be: of the normality of the tower blocks in the outskirts from which they came, of their bicycles, of their mass-produced clothes, of the stinking offices in which they took the first steps in their careers. They're desperate to give themselves airs and graces, they aspire to the status of nobility. In exchange for the money they give me, I create the ridiculous liturgy with which they celebrate their own success."

"It doesn't seem so different from the role of the court painters," Soneri said.

"Don't be too hard on them. Many of them left us master-pieces," Valmarini said, surrendering none of his equanimity. "But there is some truth in what you say. For my clients, art is no more than a symbol of power and ostentation. It doesn't matter whether it's genuine or forged, because it has the same function as the brightly coloured feathers on a peacock."

"Then it's a bit like the night, which for most people is nothing but darkness," Soneri said.

3

THE MOBILE WAS an expensive model and Juvara would have been happy to spend time explaining its workings, but Soneri soon lost patience and cut him off in mid flow. His interest was not in the device itself but in its memory, the calls made and received, and the contacts list. The inspector was baffled. "All this effort for a mobile!" he protested.

"I don't care what it takes if it helps us trace the owner." Juvara looked askance at him.

"Have you checked for reports of theft?" Soneri asked.

"Anyone who steals an object like this is hardly likely to throw it away."

"You don't always steal something to keep it. Sometimes it's only for use on the spot, as with cars or credit cards."

Juvara nodded submissively, then abruptly changed the subject. "Commissario, something strange happened last night."

"Something else?"

"There was an incident at Villa Clelia. Two undertakers got into a fight."

"What? They wanted to conduct each other's funeral?"

"Not quite. It seems they were quarrelling over a dead body."

"What do you mean? They both claimed it?"

"Exactly. They both said they'd been given the commission

and neither wanted to give way. They ended up coming to blows."

"How did you get to hear about it?"

"Somebody called the police and a car was sent over."

"Did they want to report the matter?"

"No, neither of them wanted to take any further action, but one had been beaten about quite a bit, so the duty officer filed his own report."

"Do you know who these people are?"

"One is a well established undertaker in the city, Pighetti, and the other the representative of a new firm set up three years ago, L'Eterna. It seems that this second lot are branching out, and recently took over management of the Marore cemetery."

"Any idea who's behind them?"

"None at all. So far we've never had to launch any investigations into dead bodies," Juvara said.

"On the contrary, that's our business."

"I didn't mean people who've been murdered. These two were fighting over that poor soul Romagnoli, who froze to death."

Soneri stopped in his tracks. "Don't rush to conclusions. In his own way, he too was murdered."

He opened the office door and went out. A few moments later, the inspector saw him striding through the rows of police cars in the courtyard. Whenever he could not get to grips with what was going on, or felt taunted by some mystery, the commissario became a different person. To calm himself down, Soneri got into a car and headed out of the city. He had in his pocket an address in San Vitale, the town where the only person with whom Romagnoli had had any kind of relationship in recent years lived. Soneri was fond of the village – he used to go there frequently with Angela. He took the road flanking the river Baganza, the salami workshops on either side giving off a stench of lard. He passed through hillsides planted with vines before coming in sight of the sharp peaks of the first foothills where the Apennines emerge suddenly from the plain. The old peasant houses were now the gilded homes of the wealthy. Soneri imagined Valmarini's forgeries hanging on their walls.

The man's name was Luciano Zunarelli, and he must have been about sixty. He lived in a building which had been constructed at minimum expense, with a workspace for the boning of ham shanks on the ground floor. Soneri found him at work, dressed in a long apron down to his ankles and boots up to his knees.

"I'm badly behind with my work and I can't even take a half-day off," he said.

"I'm conducting inquiries into the death of Romagnoli. My name's Soneri and I'm from the police."

"Do you know what happened? Would he have been alright if they'd found him in time?"

"Perhaps. When we get the results of the autopsy, we'll know for sure," the commissario said, glancing at the knives scattered on the wooden block next to some hams which looked like chopped-up corpses.

"His mind was shot to pieces. In the last days, he didn't even recognise me. Do you know when the funeral will take place?" Zunarelli asked.

"We'll have to wait for authorisation from the magistrate."

"I'm told that'll take about a week," Zunarelli said, shaking his head.

"It seems the undertaker has already been chosen. Do you know anything about that?"

"I had a call this morning from the Council social workers who are taking care of arrangements. I told them it was nothing to do with me. I was only a friend. They told me they knew, but still wanted my opinion."

"And what did you tell them?"

Zunarelli was obviously embarrassed by the question and waved his hands in the air. "I said that as far as I was concerned it was alright. I know there's another firm which has offered to arrange the funeral for next to nothing. It goes without saying that, if need be, I'll play my part."

"You know there was a bit of a scuffle?"

"So I was told. It's got so bad they're even arguing over corpses. First of all they leave him to die in the cold, then they fight over his body because somebody dangles a chequebook in front of them."

"Who made the final choice?"

"The City Council. Alfio had no relatives. The social workers spoke to me about the magistrate and the time it might take. Initially they'd left everything to Pighetti."

"Then L'Eterna came onto the scene. Did they tell you if they'd brought any pressure to bear?"

Zunarelli seemed tense and was struggling a bit. He turned one way and then the other, like a restless cat. "There was no need, because their price was much better than Pighetti's. If the officials had turned it down, they'd have been in trouble."

"Do you know how much better?"

"No, but like I said, L'Eterna were willing to do it for next to nothing."

"Don't you find that strange?"

"I've learned that nowadays nobody does anything out of the goodness of their heart, and my first impression was that there was something underhand going on, but when all's said and done what could I do? Maybe they wanted the publicity because they're newcomers, or maybe they want to ingratiate themselves with the Council."

"And Pighetti didn't take it too well, I imagine," the commissario said.

"Obviously. His is an old undertaker's firm and he knows nothing about advertising. All they have is a sign outside their door to say who they are."

"Have you ever had occasion to fight for a public contract?" Soneri asked.

"Absolutely not," Zunarelli replied, surprised by the question.

"Now do you see why I've come to question you?"

"That man Pighetti, I know he got beaten up quite badly," Zunarelli mumbled.

"His doctors say he'll need to spend about a month in hospital. He's lucky it's not his funeral we're arranging."

Zunarelli was plainly uncomfortable, and his manner gave the impression he was holding something back. There was something not quite right about the story he was telling.

"Generosity in business matters leaves me unmoved as well. In fact, it makes me suspicious," the commissario said.

"I've already said I thought there was some dirty work afoot. No-one can rest easy in this crisis. It's the same in my line of work. New companies are springing up all the time, offering rock-bottom prices and sweeping the rest of us aside."

"Maybe L'Eterna is doing the same."

"Maybe so."

"Perhaps you understand better than me what's been going on."

"There are no rules any longer, everything is permitted. Underhand tricks, lies, threats . . ."

"Is that the free market?"

"Not a day goes by but someone tries to do you down, so there's nothing for it but to defend yourself as best you can. When you're up to your neck in trouble, you take any chance that comes your way."

"The Council has a duty to proceed with greater caution."

Zunarelli nodded his head but was obviously unconvinced. "There are certain things only people with money can get away with. First, they draw in customers with bargains at less than cost-price, and once they've swept all the competition aside, they can set any price they like. But you need a lot of capital before you can afford the luxury of working for years at a loss. The little man like me just can't cope."

"That too is the market. The strongest party wins out," Soneri said.

The stench of lard and grease was overwhelming, and the sight of bleeding carcasses, knives, hooks and animal bones in all their fully exposed obscenity was increasingly hard to bear. Soneri stepped out into the whiteness of the snow-covered valley, which narrowed here as the plain gave way to the hills. The dazzling reflection of the sun off the frozen crust of the snow restored his peace of mind. The benign indifference of the countryside, whose beauty lingered like a timid animal in the wild, brought him back into harmony with the world. He continued up to the church in the old town and looked back over the valley. The outrage of the cabins by the river was not sufficient to cancel the enchantment of the ridge, at times softened by rows of vines, at others made treacherous by sudden dips. He walked along a narrow street still covered with snow in the shade. He remembered being there with Angela years before and finding an *osteria* where they had eaten wonderful *tortelli di patate* with mushrooms, but his recollection of that day was displaced by the more recent image of the dialogue with Zunarelli which flashed back into his mind. He tried to identify a motive for that confrontation between the undertakers, but failed. Nagging doubts, as insurmountable as the lowered shutters he suddenly found as he turned a corner, accompanied him on his walk. The *osteria* survived only in his memory. He looked around in dismay until a woman came out on the landing above to see who was there.

"Is it closed today?" the commissario asked.

"It's not open at all anymore. It closed down two months ago. Not many people know and they keep coming."

The commissario was about to ask what had happened, but changed his mind. It was better not to know why things disappeared without warning from one day to the next, like so many wood shavings cut away by a plane, leaving our lives more insubstantial and more formless. He turned back in the direction he had come, but now walking with greater urgency. He was in his car when his mobile rang.

"What's the matter, Juvara? Did you find something in that device?"

"No. I'm preparing the paperwork to make a submission to the magistrate for access to the telephone records. He should be able to respond by this afternoon, but I'm not sure what to put in the motivation."

Soneri took a few moments to think the question over. It was only at that moment that it occurred to him that it would not be sufficient to claim that he was likely dealing with a stolen mobile, given that no-one had filed a report.

"Put down that we suspect it may belong to an illegal immigrant who has disappeared," Soneri said at last.

"We'll see if that does the trick," said the inspector, sounding sceptical. "In any case, there's another surprise. There was an assault, this time on the parish priest in Navetta."

"Did he not go skiing with the mayor?"

"If he did, how could he have taken a blow to the head and a few kicks in the back?"

It seemed that a wave of pure madness had swept over the city. The commissario fell back into the blackest of moods. "When did all this happen?"

"This morning at dawn. They took him to the Accident and Emergency department. Maybe Pasquariello can get more information from the police unit at the hospital."

"Any idea who did it?"

"No doubt one of those thugs who've been pilfering from the alms box. Or some addict. We know it was a young man and the police cars are out searching for him."

Soneri hung up again. He had no real idea what to do, but decided to head over to the Accident and Emergency department. He got there too late.

"He's already been sent home," the officer on duty told him.

"So there's no real damage?"

"A lacerated-contused injury at the left occiput with mild concussion, several contusions to the body and a few grazes," the officer recited.

"How come they didn't keep him in?"

"He signed himself out."

"Where to?"

"Home, I imagine."

He went out without saying goodbye and got back in his car. He was so agitated that he would have preferred to have a flashing light and a siren on its roof to get everyone out of his way.

The church in Navetta was a strange cement building, designed by an architect who had attempted to translate his nightmares into geometry. The door of the parish house alongside was locked and barred. Soneri rang the bell and a few seconds later a voice on the intercom asked who was there. He gave his name and in reply heard the lock clicking open. He was astonished to find himself facing a black priest wearing a full-length soutane, which meant that his thin body seemed almost to disappear in all that blackness. He gave a welcoming smile and introduced himself as Jules.

Soneri introduced himself in turn and said, "I'm here about the assault."

The priest's face turned serious and he waited for the commissario to go on. "Can I speak to the parish priest?" Soneri said.

"Don Guido is not here. He's taken a couple of days off."

"Where?"

"At the San Bernardo rest home in Porporano. The sisters there will look after him."

Soneri nodded his head. "Everyone in the city thought he was in the mountains with the mayor."

Don Jules smiled. "He did go to Andalo, but he came back. He only went to accompany the boys."

"I thought he'd have stayed there the whole week."

"You don't know the parish priest. He invariably has a lot of things to do and he would never stay away a whole week."

"Can I speak to him?"

Don Jules shook his head. "There's no point in going to Porporano. The nuns wouldn't let you near him," he said in a tone which brooked no contradiction.

Soneri felt powerless. He could hardly force the priest to meet him. "How bad was it? The assault, I mean."

"Appalling! Absolutely appalling," the priest said, stretching out his hands towards the commissario as though he were trying to keep him at bay. "This morning, at about six o'clock, Don Guido came down to the sacristy to attend to a few things, and opened up the church. A young man came in and attacked him without a word. He ransacked some drawers, but he didn't touch the offertory plate, the only place where there was any money."

"Did he see anything? Does he have any idea who it might have been?"

"He told some parishioners that the man had a helmet over his head."

"Had Don Guido ever been attacked before?"

"No, although there've been some minor thefts. You know what it's like. This is a district with problems, but it's not too bad, at least not for someone from Nigeria, like me."

"How many boys went to Andalo?"

"About twenty, all from the secondary school and all from poor backgrounds. For the majority of them, it was their first holiday in the mountains, in part because many of them are foreigners. They're being put up in a residence which belongs to the diocese, and the Council paid for the coach."

The priest seemed sincere and his smiling face exuded a child-like candour which left Soneri quite disarmed. Before leaving, the commissario went into the church and inspected the naves. It was dark, even darker than the penumbra which gathers over side-altars. A couple of candles were burning in front of the statue of the Madonna, behind which the commissario noted the entrance to Don Guido's office. He tried to get in, but the door was locked. He noticed that the wood on the jamb and the door itself was scratched, perhaps the result of a previous attempt to force an entrance. He left the church and called Pasquariello.

"Have you got the report of the assault on the priest handy?"

"Don Guido Nassi. Is that the one? What do you want to know? He's a front-line priest."

"What do you mean?"

"He's like the bull's-eye on a dartboard, always in the firing line."

"Has he been assaulted before?"

"A lot of thefts and a few threats. I'm sure it's not the first time he's been beaten up, but he's never said anything."

"Is that because it's a dangerous district, or is there more to it?"

"He's a man who always takes the side of people in need,

but as you know, even among poor people there's never any shortage of shits. There was a time when pushers operated inside the church. Once we discovered drugs stashed in the offertory box at the foot of a statue of the Madonna."

"And what happened after that?"

"We got involved and forced them to clear off, but it's like herding cats. What makes it worse is that the Curia doesn't want to get involved any more than it has to. Perhaps it has given up on a parish which is close to collapse. It's nearly all Muslims living there. We advised the priest to open the church only for services, but he won't hear of it. He says it's essential for it always to be open to everyone."

"At least he has principles," Soneri said.

"There's a fine line between integrity and stupidity."

"I'm well aware of that," the commissario said, closing his mobile and thinking of his own case.

When he returned to the police station, Juvara threw a questioning glance in his direction. "Well then?" he said, with a bemused expression.

"Well then nothing. I've now spent two days wandering aimlessly between mysteries and farcical events which turn out to be nonsense – lost telephones which keep on ringing, old men dying of the cold, squabbles over a coffin, assaults on a priest ... What next?"

"Unfortunately, sir, it's impossible to call anything a farce until you've examined it from the inside."

"I get the impression that some detail is escaping us."

"With your experience, that seems hard to believe."

Soneri was always uncomfortable with compliments and he admonished Juvara with a wave of his hand. "That's just the point. It's experience which suggests to me that there's something unresolved here. All these facts have a common factor – a complete absence of logic."

"The improbable does happen."

"That's true enough, but lightning rarely strikes twice."

The radio was issuing peremptory, urgent orders to all police cars from the operations room. A crowd of demonstrators had gathered at the City Hall to protest against the corruption which had led to the arrests a few days earlier.

"The usual mob," Juvara said.

"If it was me, I'd be even more enraged," Soneri said.

"They're causing havoc in the city."

"The city is rotten to the core. The people who are really causing havoc have the blessing of the citizens of Parma who vote for them. And what are we here for? We should be rushing to hand in our resignations."

"It's not our fault, sir. If only they'd let us get on with the job ..."

"Come, Juvara, it's politics through and through. What else? What would they let us do, seeing that our upper echelons are answerable to politicians of the same party as those in jail? Over and above that, two-thirds of us are Fascists, or near enough. They'd squall and fight until they fell exhausted into the grateful arms of the very people who are responsible for the disaster."

The inspector made no reply, and turned to more practical matters. "The magistrate has asked us to take charge of investigations into this scandal. There aren't enough officers in the *Finanza* force, and so he's called in Musumeci."

"They might have told me. I'm still in charge here," Soneri said, his anger showing.

"The prosecutor's office is in a mess. They're undermanned, and now that there's an investigation into Council affairs, they don't know where to turn."

"Tell Musumeci to keep me informed. That way I'll have a foothold in a real inquiry," the commissario muttered, thinking of Romagnoli and the rest.

"I was astonished you weren't directly involved," Juvara said.

"I'm not politically 'correct', and perhaps you're not either, since you're associated with me. Musumeci is alright, but he's much more malleable than you or me. They can always send him off to the passport office if he doesn't toe the line. They'd find it more difficult with me."

"It wouldn't be the first time they sent someone off to the outer darkness."

"You see? And you say we could do something. What exactly?"

4

THE ROMAGNOLI CASE was headline news both in the press and on T.V. Much of the attention was devoted to L'Eterna, whose generosity was commended. Columnists and leader writers deployed their full arsenal of grandiloquent adjectives, while politicians and administrators, in a display of unctuous gratitude, held them up as an example to be followed.

"Who's really behind this firm?" Angela asked in bewilderment.

The commissario was still not clear which line of inquiry to pursue, and so did not know how to reply. "I've never had so much turmoil in my mind. You remember the saying – 'You can't mount two horses at the same time when you've only one arse.'"

"Very true – and make sure yours is in the right place. But I'm still curious. These people do seem to excel at public relations, if nothing else. It's not the easiest thing in the world to market funeral services. What can you say? 'Choose us for peace of mind and tranquillity'?"

"At least that would be a change from the usual gibberish," Soneri said.

Later in the day, he asked Juvara to make inquiries. He tried to track down Musumeci, who had not been seen for two days, but his mobile rang out. Thinking about mobiles made him remember the one found down by the river.

"Did you manage to have a look at that mobile?" he asked the inspector.

"Yes, I took the whole thing apart, but I don't have much to report."

"Don't tell me technology has at last got the better of you?"

Juvara shook his head. "The thing is empty."

"What do you mean, empty?"

"There are no messages, no numbers, there's not one text or one name in the call log. We don't even know the number of this mobile. It seems somebody wiped it clean."

"And yet it was ringing for three days in the undergrowth. Are you telling me it had been tampered with before my arrival?"

"The most recent calls are still there, but they're all from unknown numbers. Covert calls," Juvara explained.

"How are you getting on with the request for authorisation to examine the telephone records?"

"The magistrate got back to say that the motivation was inadequate. His assistant told us that Signor Piccirillo is extremely exacting. In his opinion, it is not permissible to ask a telephone company to violate confidentiality over a lost object when no-one has made an official report."

Soneri was on the point of losing his temper at this new ambiguity which deepened the mystery of the mobile. He smelled something sinister in the whole business. At that moment Musumeci called in.

"Been off on your holidays, have you?" Soneri said.

"No, sir, but I've got a problem. I've been working eighteen hours a day, and I haven't even had time to see my girlfriend."

"Which of the many? Has it slipped your mind that I am your superior officer and should be kept informed of your whereabouts?"

"I thought that Signor Piccirillo would have let you know."

"Not likely. All he's good for is getting on my nerves. He's set himself up as ombudsman. I'll bet he's more accommodating with politicians."

"It's a very delicate investigation. You know yourself that when certain people are involved, you've got to be cautious."

"Listen, I understand you want to get ahead, but as long as I'm in charge, you're answerable to me. It's not the first time you've ignored that fact and gone running off to the magistrate like a lapdog."

"There's been some misunderstanding."

"From now on I want you to keep me updated on your investigations. Bugger Piccirillo and the good words you might want him to put in for you."

"Are you aware we're edging close to the upper tiers? The Council officials we've rounded up are spilling the beans."

"Bribes?"

"What do you think? Money always changes hands in cases like this. Some elected members are in trouble and there are vicious rumours circulating about the mayor."

"Such as?"

"Nothing in particular. Impressions. He's still top of the heap. I haven't seen all the cards the magistrate has in his hand, but it seems this story about going skiing with boys ..."

"Explain yourself, for God's sake!" Soneri burst out.

"I swear I don't know anything. Right now I can't go into detail, but I've picked up some sarcastic remarks, some throwaway comments, vague insinuations ... You see what I'm getting at? It seems there's something nasty emerging. Or maybe it's just the fact that he's gone off skiing while the Council is under investigation."

The commissario muttered something he could not himself decipher. He put down the receiver, but his head was like a geyser, erupting with thoughts. "Juvara, get me the number of the carabinieri in Andalo."

The inspector stared at him for a few moments trying to work out his intentions, but all he received was a peremptory wave of the hand, so he began working his keyboard. "You can find everything on the Internet," he said. He found the number and asked, "Do you want the website and email address as well?" Soneri ignored this query, picked up his telephone and asked to speak to the maresciallo. Juvara heard him ask about the mayor, but the longer the conversation went on, the more impatient the commissario grew. Finally he slammed the receiver down.

"What a cock-up! This guy won't get off his arse until he receives instructions in writing. It seems we have to send him a stack of paper with the appropriate stamps. Following procedures is a great excuse for not doing any work," he said.

"Commissario, you know what rules and regulations are for the carabinieri," Juvara said, in an attempt to offer a justification, but fell silent for fear of having gone too far. Fortunately, Soneri seemed to be calming down.

"I have to admit he did tell me one thing. The mayor is staying at the *Appennino* hotel, in a single room booked for one week. The hotel manager has followed procedure and registered his residence with the Council."

"You could've got that from the Tourist Office," Juvara said.

"At least we know he's there." He got no further because there was a knock at the door and an officer appeared with a file for the inspector. "The report on the Romagnoli post-mortem."

"What does it say?"

Juvara started reading and did not reply at once. After a few minutes, he put the papers down on the desk. His face had a dubious expression. "Nothing particularly illuminating," he said.

The commissario made a gesture with his chin inviting him to go on.

"It says that the old man had ingested benzodiazepine, a sedative, but that death was due to a heart attack brought on by the extreme cold. In short, his arteries clogged up and his heart gave out."

"You think they gave him that garbage to reduce him to the condition of a moron?"

"Doubt it. He was already in his second childhood as it was. Maybe he was agitated and wouldn't stay in bed, so they sedated him."

"Does it say they gave him an overdose?"

"No, it doesn't say that."

Soneri immediately called Nanetti. "Listen, you're the scientist. Have you seen the results of the autopsy?"

"It's your turn to take the Road to Canossa, eh, Mr Philosopher!"

"I want to know about this benzodia— whatever it's called."

"Benzodiazepine. Get your scientific terminology right. What do you want to know?"

"Did they give him the right amount, or did they overdo it?"

"A good question! It depends."

"A fat lot of good your science does. Ask a precise question, get an imprecise reply."

"Give me a break! Is this a quiz? The doses depend on who you're giving them to. You don't treat a rabbit the same way you treat a cow."

"Was the quantity found in Romagnoli's body appropriate for an old man like him, or was it an overdose?"

"You'd have to look at the overall clinical position."

"So we're back to square one!"

"If you want my opinion, that dose was on the high side," Nanetti said.

"At last! You've stuck your head over the scientific parapet. So, in your opinion, could that dose have been lethal?"

"No!" Nanetti's tone was decisive. "It would only make him drowsy, dull his senses, maybe calm any agitation."

"Do you detect anything malicious in all this?"

"I'd rule that out categorically. We could just be dealing with an exasperated nurse who poured out an extra drop or two."

Raised voices, like those of people arguing, exploded from the radio transmitter in the room. Soneri had to hang up since something serious was happening elsewhere. It emerged that some officers were confronting an unauthorised march which was turning nasty, with stones being hurled at banks, and shops being looted. On grounds of public order, the police chief had summoned every member of the force to attend, and Soneri was no exception. He hated taking on the role of street patrolman in a brawl, just as he hated any situation he couldn't reason his way out of or which was liable to descend into a primitive tussle for territory. Besides, he would have been quite happy to join in hurling stones at the banks.

In spite of himself, he ended up in the heart of the melee at the junction of Via Mazzini and Via Cavestro, where students and other protesters had gathered, each exhibiting a grim determination which underlined their readiness for battle. Objects were being thrown and shutters being pulled down, while people rushed about in search of shelter. He could imagine the curses of the shopkeepers, busily protecting designer dresses, gold watches and Limoges porcelain, all the while issuing the standard Fascist litany of calls for flogging, hanging and lengthy sentences. There was a brief stand-off in the narrow streets in the student district around the Court and the Conservatoire, but it all quietened down as speedily as a bout of coughing in the mist. All that remained of that outburst of rage were some broken fragments, freshly painted slogans on the walls and echoes of yells which rang out like rumours of war.

Juvara came rushing up, sweating and panting. "They were throwing stones at us and one officer was struck on the head," he said.

The commissario said nothing as he set off across the battlefield. Around the City Chambers, a concert of banging pots and clanging dustbin lids, accompanied by jeers and menacing threats, was striking up. The city had taken on the appearance of a precinct of pure hatred, centred on the Council buildings.

"Everything's falling apart," Soneri mumbled to Juvara, who was trotting at his side, gripping the transmitter connected to the operations room.

"Did you see them? Did you get a look at their faces?"

"At least they were expressing honest sentiments. The conformists who proudly display meanness of heart and call it moderation are far worse. If there's one category of real shits, it's those moderates, who are anything but. Always bear in mind that the worst things that took place in this country were done with the backing of such people," Soneri said.

"With the help of the priests, let's not forget," Juvara added.

"Is this you getting into politics too?"

A patrol car sped past them, splashing water on both sides as it raced through Piazza Garibaldi.

"What's going on?" Soneri wondered aloud.

"If you want my opinion, they've arrested some bigwig," Juvara said.

Before the words were out, Soneri was on the telephone to Musumeci. "Who did you say? Montagnani? They've arrested Montagnani! He's a councillor. Ah yes, convener of Social Services. I've seen his name a lot in the papers. So you've got to the men at the top."

"Wow!' Juvara said, as the commissario hung up. "So Piccirillo wasn't kidding."

"No, the warrant was issued by Bergossi in the prosecution office. He's the only one with balls."

"What's he charged with?"

"The councillor was taking a cut from equipment for schools. They're even lining their pockets with funds meant for children."

A bout of sheer rage brought the commissario up short, leaving him glowering silently for a few moments at the vaulted ceilings of the Town Hall cloisters, under which the demonstrators were standing bellowing. He was brought back to his senses by Musumeci, who, anxious to give proof of his zeal, had called back immediately. Soneri put his mobile to his ear, still thinking of the deep mortification of the city, of the suspicious faces of the *nouveaux riches* who plied their trade there, of the rowdy and embittered members of the ex-working class now pacified by the tepid ebb and flow of politics, of the indolence of the bureaucrats, of the incense-burning pettiness of Catholics and of the industrialists always on the look-out for the next deal.

"Hello! Hello! You alright, sir?" The inspector's voice sounded worried.

Soneri gave himself a shake. Juvara had moved away, leaving the commissario on his own in Piazza Garibaldi. The clock on the campanile of Palazzo del Governatore struck nine.

"I just don't believe Montagnani was acting on his own," the commissario said, abandoning his previous train of thought and returning to the call as though there had been no interruption.

"Neither does the prosecutor. That's why he's pushing ahead with the investigation. He was probably turned in by his own people," Musumeci said.

"Friendly fire?"

"A power struggle inside the party. Or maybe I should say a business struggle."

"Nowadays party and business are synonymous."

"Exactly. Bergossi is working on the purchase and resale of lands in an industrial area managed by the P.P.I.S., one of the Council's outreach companies. At first sight it looks like a dunghill where various suspicious, intermediary companies have been playing about, and it seems they've reaped their reward. As you well know, it's when they come to divvying up the loot that the gangs begin to squabble with each other."

"And you believe Montagnani's going to keep his mouth shut?"

"We're hoping he's going to sing like the tenor in 'Rigoletto', but I have my doubts. Listen, sir, these villains are all the same. They don't report their rivals to the police. They'd rather square things up among themselves. The important thing is that the show must go on. This guy will be given no more than a couple of years in jail if everything goes his way, and then, if he keeps his nose clean and given that he has no previous record, he won't spend too long inside. After that, he'll be back to his old ways with the same people, and weaving new deals. Not in politics, I hope. With the furore he's caused, who's going to give him another chance?"

"People have short memories. In a couple of years he'll look as good as new," Soneri said. "Anyway, it's a waste of time waiting for an outbreak of indignation if it's got nothing solid to feed on. And don't talk to me about the law. The only ones that care about it nowadays are us and the magistrates."

"Don't be too pessimistic. It's always darkest before dawn. The honest people come out on top in the long run," Musumeci said, in a conciliatory tone.

"And how exactly? They don't have a party, but the dishonest ones do, and very well organised it is too."

"I have to agree with you there. That Ugolini's a repugnant human being."

"Who's he? The secretary?"

"No, that's Bonaldi, Ugolini's lackey. He's a tough one, the sidekick who attends to all the dirty work, like a hired killer. Ugolini's an industrialist. Curing hams is his line. He's one of the biggest traders in the province."

"As far as I know, he doesn't hold any office in the party."

"In fact he's just an ordinary party member, but what does that have to do with anything?"

"You're right. It's nothing more than a business committee."

"I suppose so. He puts in the money and takes charge of everything by placing his men in the key posts. What's left are the speeches, the programmes and the grand proclamations. The usual shit, while everything here is going to the dogs."

"Tell me about the mayor. Heard anything on the grapevine?"

"I've heard some things, but nothing very precise. In any case, the mayor is another of Ugolini's placemen. Over the last couple of years, Corbellini has set up God knows how many service companies, all at the Council's expense, and has packed them with his cronies. That way, he can control the situation and extend his client base. Commissario, I come from the South and I know these systems only too well. The mafia behaves in the same way, with one man of honour in every part of the city. It's all tied up."

"Except that this is supposed to be a political party."

"Is it? What party? It's all marketing. When you get down to it, it's the way I've just told you."

"Let's see if Bergossi can get to the root of things, or if they stop him first," Soneri said.

"Perhaps Bergossi would like to, but he's surrounded by vice-prosecutors who are dead weights, and without good deputies it's going to be tough. They've already submitted some questions in Parliament to intimidate him, but he doesn't seem to care. He retires in a year's time. Let's hope he manages to clean up this city before he goes," Musumeci said.

"The best he'll manage is to reduce the stench. We need something more."

"Meantime, we go around spraying bleach. Montagnani was in a panic when we carted him off to prison. My colleagues reported that some people were spitting at him."

"Don't kid yourself," Soneri said. "They'll be the same people who elected him and who until the day before yesterday were trooping along to beg favours from him."

Musumeci fell silent. When the commissario got into his stride with his rants against the world, it was best to let him get on with it. The inspector regarded himself as a straightforward police officer, and did not have the knowledge of the city Soneri had. The two of them stood with their telephones in their hands, heaving sighs but not speaking. After a few moments, they said goodbye without exchanging another word on the subject, feeling a mixture of embarrassment and disappointment, the one because he was unable to go beyond his role, the other because he felt he was exceeding it. It was the same with Juvara. Later, in the *Milord*, Alceste's restaurant, he spoke about it to Angela, who freed him from the suspicion of madness which preys on all solitary men.

"They're young," Angela said, referring to the two inspectors. "When we were their age, we were revolutionaries. These two just try to make the world they have inherited work better. They want to uphold the law, without asking themselves who promulgates it. We wanted to put the law itself up for discussion."

"Police officers like us are doing a job which is of little use. We bandage the wound, but we don't heal it. My inspectors believe this is enough, but I don't."

"It's not the job of police officers to change the world."

"Especially if you feel you're in a minority. Criminals are more numerous than honest citizens nowadays. I expect that sooner or later they'll bring about their own revolution, and throw us in jail or put us up against a wall."

"It's already happening. Isn't that what the various mafias are doing? In this country, it's more convenient to behave in a different way, undercover, infiltrating everywhere and maintaining an irreproachable image. The boundary between legality and criminality is a very fine one, and I'm saying this as a lawyer. You can be a criminal within the law. All you have to do is interpret the rules. Look at the banks."

"So what can one commissario do? Arrest Montagnani and a few other councillors? He's not the problem. It's the people who voted for him and will keep on voting for him."

"Take it easy! There are plenty of people of good faith."

"I'm less and less convinced. What I believe is that those who support these people recognise themselves in them and approve of their behaviour because it's exactly what they themselves do every day. And that includes theft. When we arrest them, it's we who become unpopular. So what's all this about trusting civil society? Often they're even less civil than the politicians."

Angela turned her head to look at Alceste, who was coming over with two plates of *tortelli d'erbetta* and *ricotta*. "Thank goodness the cure for all dark moods is arriving."

Soneri threw her a foul glance, but then started to eat. The bottle of Gutturnio helped calm him down.

"Do you think our mayor will make himself scarce, now that they've got part of his Council in a cage?" Angela asked.

"He already has. He's away skiing."

"You know perfectly well what I mean."

"You know what I think? That if he doesn't come back

tonight or tomorrow morning, somebody's going to have to go looking for him."

"Who? Us?"

Soneri nodded. "I told Juvara to let me know if he shows up. His deputy has assured us that he'll be here tomorrow."

"But you think that's all nonsense?"

"I've no doubt about it. It takes around three hours to get to Parma from Andalo, so when you're dealing with something like this . . ."

"If that's the problem, it was ridiculous for him to leave in the first place. O.K., these people have an incredible brass neck, but even so."

"Anyway, we could do it. Today's Friday. Fancy a weekend in the mountains?"

"What are you on about? The snow's right down to where we are."

"The mountains are up there, the Paganella. I give you my word, no tramping about in the cold, fresh air only in the warmer hours, and the pair of us well away from this squalid mess!"

"You're not bewitching me, commissario! I know that all you have in that head of yours is the mayor."

"If I bump into him, I'll say hello."

Angela stared at him, shaking her head ironically. "We'll have to make a booking."

"Leave it to me. I already know a comfortable hotel with reasonable rates."

"What's it called?"

"The *Appennino*. It's very central."

5

"AS SOON AS you start climbing, your mood changes,"
Angela said, as the car made its way up the twists and turns of
the Paganella mountain.

"It's because I'm getting away from the swamp which is
our city."

"We don't really love it anymore, do we?"

"We love it too much, but it betrays us day after day."

The *Appennino*, gleaming with fresh wood and paint, stood
not far from the city centre on the road to Pederu. There were
just a few cars in the car park, and a low-season atmosphere
hung over the whole place.

"It doesn't seem they're planning a dance this evening. Does
that disappoint you?" Soneri asked.

"I'll manage without one for a couple of days, but in all this
confusion it's not going to be too easy to find your mayor."

"I already see the way forward, as you will discover," he said,
but he was lying.

It was lunchtime so they went straight down to the dining
room. Just two tables were occupied in a waste of symmetrically
folded napkins that somehow gave it the air of an English garden.

"What a life!" Angela said.

"Does the idea of spending two days alone with me terrify
you?"

"In no time at all, you'll be off on your investigation, and I'll have no-one to talk to apart from the sledge dogs."

They ordered a plate of *canederli mantecati* with melted cheese and roasted kid.

"The mayor must be having his lunch on the ski slopes," the commissario said, looking around.

"A real sportsman. I heard that he goes to the gym every day."

"That'll be just the tonic he needs, considering the slalom waiting for him down in the city."

They were now the sole couple left in the dining room. The hotel was sunk in total silence. Only the clatter of plates from the kitchen gave any sign that there was anyone else around. They ate without exchanging a word.

"Let's try and take advantage of the hour of sunlight left," Angela said, when they had finished eating.

The commissario followed her out, but in the hall he met the girl from the reception desk and stopped. "When does Signor Corbellini normally come back?"

"I don't know. My shift stops at four o'clock and I don't see our guests returning."

"Does he usually eat here?"

"I don't know."

"Could you tell me the number of his room?"

"You'd need to ask the owner," the girl said, clearly embarrassed.

"Could you call her?"

"She won't be back in the hotel before evening. She's in Belluno visiting someone."

Soneri felt a presence behind him and turned around to see Angela, who, not having seen him go out, had come back to look for him. He looked at her long enough to note that her expression was inviting him to drop the subject. He went over to her, took her arm, and they walked out together.

"She was playing the part of the monkey who sees no evil, hears no evil, and speaks no evil," he said.

"Oh, she speaks alright, but she wasn't being straight with you. She had obviously been ordered not to say anything."

In the midwinter afternoon, the town was almost deserted. Coaches dropped foreign tourists off at their hotels and continued on their rounds, as did some of the hikers. The ski-lifts moved slowly up the slopes of the Paganella along a track cleared through the fir wood.

"Would you like to go up on one of those?" Angela asked. "Maybe you'll meet the mayor in a mountain refuge."

"Better to wait for him down there, and have a grappa in the meantime."

"Commissario, you're not allowed to drink while on duty."

"I'm not on duty. I'm away with you."

"You're always on duty."

Soneri put his arm around her waist to pull her closer to him, and she allowed him to do so. The light in the lower valley began to fail all at once, and the shadow of the mountains moved rapidly over the sloping granite roofs. They made the way back holding onto each other, while the streetlights came on and the bitterly cold air from the snow on the ground made the roads freeze over. It was already dark when they came in sight of the hotel. Angela quickened her pace and the commissario detected in her haste a childish fear of the night. That revelation of her frailty made him feel suddenly closer to her.

When they got to the *Appennino*, Soneri went up to the reception, and on this occasion found himself facing a lady of about fifty, whose courtesy had the astringent tone of mountain people.

"Has Signor Corbellini come back yet?"

The woman fixed her gaze on him as though she were studying him. "Not yet. Do you know him?"

The commissario nodded.

"In that case, if you have the patience to wait for him, he'll turn up sooner or later."

"Doesn't he eat in the hotel?"

"Not always."

"I have a document for him," the commissario lied. "If I don't see him at dinner, I'll bring it along later. What's the number of his room?"

The woman gave him an extremely distrustful look, and did not reply right away. She then said coldly, "Give it to me. I'll make sure he gets it as soon as I see him."

"I'd rather do it myself. You know how it is, he is mayor after all . . ."

The woman seemed unsure, and took a few moments to think it over. She looked at Angela, who in the meantime had come up to the commissario and put her arm into his, smiling like a newly-wed on her honeymoon. That was sufficient to convince the receptionist. "Third floor, room 312," she said reluctantly.

"She'd never have told you if I hadn't been there," Angela said afterwards. "With that gesture, I gave her the impression that we were an ordinary couple, perhaps two lovers. I brushed her suspicions aside. If I've got this right, considering the kind of person she seems to be, she thought I was a kept woman, the kind who hangs about with politicians."

"If she'd known the job I do, she'd never have reached that conclusion. There's not much you can squeeze out of a policeman. At the most, a weekend in the mountains."

"I don't understand why you want to stay undercover. Tell them you're a commissario, and you can dispense with all this awkwardness."

"I'd scare the living daylights out of them. They mustn't suspect anything. Everything has to run smoothly. Anyway, it's just a matter of a few more hours."

Angela looked at him without understanding, and made no reply. There were more people around than at lunchtime, and two tables of skiers were making a din. Outside, the frost-covered roads reflected the light from the street lamps, and a few cars passed by in a cloud of smoke. A waitress in the folk costume of the Trento region brought over the *casunzei*. The commissario ordered a bottle of Merlot. Everything was going as sweetly as though it was a holiday. The faces of the diners glowed with the candour of childhood innocence. A temporary suspension of routine was enough to make them at once light-hearted and melancholic.

"Is this not the point of a holiday? I mean, a momentary rediscovery of childhood?" Angela said.

Soneri, however, could never divest himself of his role. Attentive to any possible anomaly which might arouse suspicion, he observed their fellow guests' joyful animation, on the look-out for any discordant note. The babel of voices, each louder than the next, reminded him of afternoons in the yard outside his home, of football matches with the garage door as goal, of the shouts of mothers from the windows and the darkness which fell in early evening in winter, muffling every sound inside its mistiness. It was only a matter of hours now, he felt, hours which held the arcane fascination of promises kept or prophecies fulfilled. The Merlot and the intimacy with Angela in that noisy, vaguely surreal atmosphere overwhelmed him and endowed him with a kind of visionary inebriation. From time to time, he got up from the table and wandered about to reconnoitre, scrutinising the hotel entrance and peering into the semi-obscurity of the lounge where a few elderly people were watching television. There was no-one on reception, but the manager must have been on the alert behind the door. A couple of times he went out onto the courtyard to take a few puffs on his cigar and to check whether a new car had arrived.

Everything seemed frozen in the cold which made the air as clear as glass. At midnight, the elation began to abate. After the euphoria, the wine induced sleepiness. One by one the company broke up, leaving the hardy few to drain the last drops.

The commissario picked up his mobile and called Juvara, who had been ordered to keep the mayor's residence in Parma under surveillance.

"Well then?"

"Nothing to report, sir. No sign of anyone."

"Keep your eyes peeled. Nothing has happened here either."

Angela threw him a questioning look as he switched off his mobile. "A passion-filled weekend," she said ironically. "You want me to go and patrol the car park? The mayor's not bad looking. Maybe he's picked up some German girl on the ski slopes and is having a passionate encounter with her."

Soneri looked at her askance. "It'll all sort itself out tonight."

"It certainly will," she replied with greater sarcasm. "A couple of days at the most. Just as long as this holiday."

"Let's go to bed," he said.

"That sounds like a great idea, but with everything that's buzzing around inside that head of yours . . ."

He did not reply. As they passed reception, he gave Angela a hug, stopping her in her tracks. She was taken aback and accepted this effusive behaviour without responding, but in a couple of seconds she reacted with a quiet chuckle as she saw the door of the porter's lodge open a little and close almost at once.

"You're a shameless scoundrel! Do you think I don't know you were putting on an act to send a signal to that woman?"

"Sometimes duty precedes pleasure," the commissario said, attempting to justify himself.

"Do you want to make your situation worse?" Angela answered, calming down. "I hope that in a short while you'll be able to cast off your sense of duty and give full rein to your feelings. I've no time for gigolos."

"Sometimes my job is worse than any gigolo's."

When they were in their room, Soneri waited about ten minutes while she undressed, then made to go out. "I'll be right back."

"Are you off in search of an affair, like the mayor?"

The commissario said only, "Hang on a moment," and closed the door quietly behind him. He went up to the third floor, dodging the automatic switch which would turn on the light, and hid in an alcove on the corridor from where he could see room 312. Fortunately, almost the whole company of skiers was already in bed. He could hear snoring from some rooms, whispered talk or the flow of a shower from others. He waited half an hour before he heard some soft footsteps on the staircase. The lights came on, hurting his eyes. The footfall on the carpet alerted him to someone coming along the corridor. If it had been a guest arriving late, he would have felt obliged to justify his presence at that hour. He thought he might play a drunk who had forgotten his room number. Perhaps it was the mayor returning from an assignation with someone he had met on the slopes.

As these possibilities ran through his mind, the footsteps halted in front of a room and someone began fumbling with the lock. He leaned out a little and saw it was room 312. He stepped out into the open, catching the hotel owner in the doorway as she was closing the door behind her.

"You look rather worried," the commissario said.

For a moment the woman looked as though she was about to faint, but she pulled herself together. "What are you doing wandering about the hotel at this time of night?" she asked him. "Are you spying?"

"Yes," Soneri said, without losing his composure. "I'm curious about a person who goes into a guest's room at one o'clock in the morning."

The woman stopped a moment to reflect, and then, abandoning her previous menacing tone, said simply, "Come downstairs to my office. We'll wake everybody up if we stay here."

The commissario followed her down the stairs and into the reception area. They sat down in the semi-darkness behind the desk.

"I think we have one or two things to clear up," Soneri said quietly.

"I think so too. I don't like people who go spying in the corridors at night."

"I do it as a matter of duty, but you seem to me to be going well beyond your responsibilities."

The woman stared at him, her eyes glistening in the half-light. She understood at once. "You're a policeman?"

The commissario nodded. Silence fell between them once again. Soneri realised he was going to have to put pressure on her and not give her the time to get her story straight. That was the only way she was going to betray herself, but in that confessional atmosphere he could not find the right words. She escaped from the trap with one speedy manoeuvre.

"I went up to check there were no documents left lying in the room. I had to do it. The mayor called to say he'd had to hurry back to Parma because of some urgent business, and he asked me to have a look in the room because he couldn't find some envelopes."

"When did he call?"

"Just over an hour ago. He'll be on his way by now."

"Did he leave any luggage in his room?"

"Not that I noticed. I was just checking to see that nothing was left on the sideboard or in the drawers."

"Let's go and have a look," Soneri said.

"What you're suggesting is not legal. You can't search somebody's room without a warrant."

"In that case, I'm afraid that what you were doing was not altogether lawful either."

The woman rose to her feet with a resigned expression and headed once again for the stairs. She opened the door of the room, went in, but stood in the doorway like a guard. "Be careful," she said.

The bed had been made and everything seemed neat and tidy. The commissario opened the wardrobe and drawers, looked under the bed and checked the bathroom. Despite the presence of a shirt on the back of a chair, a suitcase with clothes in it, a toothbrush and toothpaste in a glass on the sink, the room did not appear to have been inhabited recently. There was something contrived about the scene, and the commissario was aware of the kind of feeling he got when the forensics squad carried out the reconstruction of a crime scene. At that moment, he thought of Valmarini.

"You see!" the woman said triumphantly.

"When he called you, was he setting off?"

"I heard car doors slamming."

"In that case, we'll soon find out who's telling the truth."

"Why should he be lying?"

"Not the mayor. You."

The woman smiled nervously. "What's it got to do with me? Let's get out of here before we make a mess."

The commissario led her out of the room and the two of them went back down the stairs. He stopped on the second floor and she carried on without turning back or saying goodnight.

Angela was fast asleep. The commissario lay down beside her and tried to embrace her, but she gave a low groan without opening her eyes, so he had to console himself with the deep satisfaction of having confirmed his suspicions, allowing that to ease his sense of guilt towards his partner. He put his mobile on silent, and sent a text to Juvara asking him to let him know at any time if the mayor turned up. He placed the mobile on the bedside cabinet and tried to go to sleep, but as soon as he stretched out he was assailed by thoughts. His head was spinning, hypotheses fell like snowflakes to deepen his suspicions, doubts and shadows. At two o'clock, he sent another text to Juvara saying, *Nothing?* In reply, he received the same word without the question mark.

The same procedure was repeated an hour later, and at four o'clock the commissario, exhausted, gave up. *Go to bed. He's obviously not coming now,* he ordered the inspector. At that moment, he was not fully aware of having written a message that was quite so definitive, but with the lucidity that comes from exhaustion, he had followed his instincts and deepest convictions.

The following day, he awoke alone in bed. He glanced at his watch and saw it was already ten o'clock. He had no idea where Angela had gone. Perhaps, in a state of irritation, she had gone off like the mayor, but shortly afterwards he found her sitting peacefully in the dining room having her breakfast.

"It's a long time since I slept so late. Tiredness . . ." Soneri began.

"If you're exhausted, it's no fault of mine. I've already gone for a walk around the village. I've had my fill of fresh air and I felt hungry, while you . . . The mountains evidently do you no favours, judging by how you look this morning." Angela was speaking in a jokey voice, but the commissario knew there was a touch of bitterness in her irony.

"The mayor has disappeared," Soneri said, in an attempt to change the subject and, appealing to the wider seriousness of the moment, head off Angela's growing anger.

"Are you sure?"

"He's not here, and he's not in Parma in spite of the fact that everything is falling apart in the Council."

"Might he not be in conclave with his men, deciding how to deal with it?"

"It's possible. In any case, he can't be traced."

"You're beginning to get all flustered," Angela said, watching him glance around nervously. "Do you want to go back straightaway, or can I finish my breakfast?"

Soneri did not rise to the bait. "No, it's better to stay here," he said.

She stared at him, her expression half incredulous and half threatening. "Should I hire a ski instructor?"

"I'd like to go and visit the residence where the boys from Navetta are lodged."

"From the outside, it looks like the ugliest building in Andalo."

"We don't have to stay long."

They proceeded on foot along the road leading down into the valley, lined on either side by dark rows of apple trees which stood out against the snow like lines on the page of an exercise book. After a few minutes, they turned into a narrow alleyway with an arrow indicating ALPINE VILLAGE JOHN XXXII. At the entrance, the commissario asked about the young people from Parma, and a silent nun went to find one of the adults who had accompanied them.

A young woman with a nametag pinned onto her jacket came out to meet them. She was called Rosalba Mannino, and spoke with a Sicilian accent.

"The boys are preparing their suitcases. Are you parents?"

At that question, the commissario felt his past treacherously hauled back before him. He thought again of his dead wife and his unborn son. The soothing balm of time had been spread over the scars, but here he was bleeding once again. With a mixture of curiosity and amazement, Rosalba watched him waver on his feet.

"No, we're not parents," Angela replied for him. "We wanted to meet up with the mayor. They told us he'd come along to greet the children."

"I've no idea. Nobody told me anything," the young woman said.

"Have you ever seen him here?" Soneri asked, coming back to himself, like someone who had fallen overboard.

"Well, yes, the day we arrived," Rosalba said, her cheeks turning red.

"But not since then?"

"Maybe he came when I was away. We're not always together. We divide up the tasks. A couple of the boys took ill and I had to look after them."

"Will someone from the Curia be here to pick them up? Don Guido, for example?"

The girl shrugged to indicate that she knew nothing about it, while behind her a man of about forty, who must have been watching the scene from the veranda on the ground floor, approached them.

"Are you looking for someone?" he asked, while Rosalba took the opportunity to slip away.

"Yes, the mayor," Soneri said.

"So who are you?" the man said, evidently distrustful.

"We know him," Angela said, with her most captivating smile. "We thought we might find him here and wanted to say hello."

The man seemed to relax. "I'm afraid he won't be here today. He had to return to Parma early," he said, stepping back, as though about to flee.

They stood looking at him as he went back into the house.

The commissario took his partner's arm and led her away. "We're never going to get anything out of these people."

"The girl seemed about to speak, but then that guy turned up," Angela said.

"Around here nobody speaks, and when they do, they just prattle."

Towards midday, the sun came out and everything started to sparkle. Instead of heading for the hotel, Soneri turned off along a road up the mountain between villas locked up during the off-season. A few moments later, they arrived in front of the carabinieri office.

"What are you up to? Are you asking the competition for help?" Angela asked.

"The Chief always tells us that the forces of law and order must collaborate with each other."

They introduced themselves to Maresciallo Boldrin, a typical ruddy-faced man of the mountains, who would have been more comfortable in corduroy trousers than in uniform.

"I'm Commissario Soneri, Parma police. We spoke on the telephone. Do you remember me?"

Boldrin was surprised to see him accompanied by a woman. "We're here on holiday," Soneri said, when he had introduced Angela. "We've come across something which has serious implications for the city."

"Yes, I remember you asked me for information about the mayor."

"That's right. I wanted to let you know that they'll probably ask you to look more deeply into the case."

"Why? What's happened?"

"He's disappeared."

The maresciallo slumped back against the chair. "Here?"

"This is the last place he was seen, as you confirmed to me on the telephone."

"But no-one has made any report."

"Not yet, but it's on the way. I'm going to make it myself."

"It ought to be some member of his family, or someone close to him."

"Apart from some of his party colleagues, they all think he's up here skiing, and at least until this evening they'll have no reason to worry. Those who are in the know have no interest in letting the news out."

"Why not?"

"I don't know the reason, but there's certainly something sinister going on."

The maresciallo slipped into dialect. "I don't understand a thing. Tell me what you want me to do."

"For the moment, I'm just asking for information. You know everybody up here. Can I suggest we talk off the record, at least for the moment?"

"Why don't we invite the maresciallo to lunch so we can talk more freely?" Angela said, throwing Boldrin another of her irresistible smiles. Being shy, like many men of the mountains, Boldrin put up no resistance. In addition, judging by his bulk, he was a man who enjoyed his food.

The maresciallo drove them a few kilometres out of town, stopping in front of a little restaurant with stuffed animal heads on the walls. Angela looked at those trophies in disgust, while Boldrin greeted everyone by name, in dialect.

"Here you'll find the authentic cuisine of the Trentino," the maresciallo said. His speech betrayed his difficulty in translating his thoughts into Italian.

Soneri immediately appreciated the dishes on offer, starting with the cheeses. The maresciallo muttered that some of them did not exactly respect the regulations regarding production methods. "But who cares? They've been produced that way for centuries and no-one has ever died. Who knows better, the cheese-makers or the health inspectors?"

The commissario refused the choice of salami, to the disappointment of his colleague. In that respect, he was a rigorous traditionalist.

When they reached the *canederli*, they got down to business. "So then? What do you want to know?" Boldrin asked.

"Some information about the owner of the *Appennino*, and on the time the mayor spent here in Andalo."

"Signora Compagnoni's pretty smart, isn't she? She's well connected."

"What kind of connections?"

"Political. She's in the same party as your mayor, and she's a candidate for the local council."

"I got the impression she's covering something up."

"They'll have told her to play the game."

"What game?"

"Listen, when you called me the first time, I started asking questions. It doesn't take long to find out what's going on around here. The fact is, no-one has ever seen this mayor."

"Maybe they wouldn't have recognised him among all these tourists."

Boldrin was unconvinced and shook his head. "We can easily check. I'll call my friend Schiavon, the administrator of the chair-lift. We'll establish if he took out a ski-pass and how many times he went up and down."

The commissario approved. "Since he came here to ski . . . unless he's been up to something else."

Angela, who until that moment had remained silent, butted in to say, "That's what I've always suspected."

The maresciallo looked at her as though he resented her interruption, but she put him down with a piercing glance. Boldrin took up his mobile, moved aside and started speaking in dialect to Schiavon. Soneri could follow only snatches of the conversation but grasped that the maresciallo was enquiring if anyone had taken out a pass in the name of Corbellini. When he hung up, he looked uncertain.

"He did take out a weekly ticket, but there's something very odd about all this," he said.

"Very odd," the commissario agreed.

"The first day, Monday, it seems there were four journeys up the mountain. Not very many, but O.K. But on Tuesday and Wednesday, he only made one return journey."

"Do you know at what times?"

"He went up in the morning and came down with the second last ride."

"And the following days?"

"He was up and down a lot. He really went for it."

"Until when?"

"Right up until closing time yesterday evening."

"Do you have a C.C.T.V. camera at the ski-lift?"

"More than one. You're not convinced the mayor was really on the slopes?"

The commissario shook his head.

"Neither am I," Boldrin agreed. "I'll let you know. It won't take me long to find out."

6

THEY WERE ENVELOPED in mist on the *autostrada* to Reggiolo. "We're almost home!" Angela said.

Although it was only five o'clock, they had been driving in the dark for some time. A column of cars ahead blocked their way, bringing them to a complete standstill. "The same old logjam," Soneri moaned.

After a few moments, his mobile rang. "Commissario, the prosecutor's office wants to call the mayor as witness in relation to the Montagnani arrest," Musumeci said. "He's summoned him for Tuesday."

"He's wasting his time summoning him. He won't be there."

"Why not?"

"He's disappeared."

"What do you mean, disappeared? He's supposed to be back this evening and there's a Council meeting tomorrow."

"It seems he set off from Andalo yesterday evening. He should have arrived already, but Juvara's told me there's been no sign of him at his house."

"Excuse me, sir, but that doesn't mean he's disappeared. He might have stopped off with friends, or he could be with some woman."

"Trust me. He won't turn up. He's made off."

"Are you sure?"

"Not absolutely sure. It might even be that . . . But I am sure he's disappeared."

"What are we going to do?"

"You're asking me? I'm not involved in this investigation. Think of me as one of your informers whispering something in your ear."

"I'll let the prosecutor know. He'll tell me what to do. In fact, it's entirely up to Bergossi to decide how to proceed."

"Exactly. Leave it all to Bergossi. He's not getting a salary three times higher than ours for nothing."

As the traffic began to move, Angela began thinking out loud. "I wonder where we went wrong."

"I was wondering that too, and I've arrived at the conclusion there was nothing more we could have done."

"A mayor who goes on the run while councillors are being arrested left, right and centre . . . Would we have imagined that a fortnight ago?"

"No. Nor would we have imagined that the courtiers, the lackeys and the whores would have won. The world is theirs."

"My question is, where have our lot ended up? They should have sent someone like Corbellini packing with a boot up the arse."

"They've remained where they've always been. The difference is that they've grown old and their rage has evaporated into disappointment. They no longer need God or the party. Or maybe they do, but they've no idea where to find them."

Angela made no reply, but rested her head against the side window and listened in silence to the car engine as they proceeded slowly through the mist.

Soneri took her home and gave her a kiss, detecting in her attitude a residue of rancour as he prepared to set off again. The exchange of a few glances was sufficient to confirm that they would be sleeping apart that night. The commissario had no inclination to go to bed just yet. He parked the car and began wandering about in the dull atmosphere of a Sunday evening. He crossed Piazza Boito, came out on the Lungoparma, passed the Caprazucca and the Italia bridges at a brisk pace and saw the Monastery of the Xaverian Missionaries come into view. The clock of the Banca Commerciale stood in the middle distance, hanging like an enlarged moon over the rooftops. He felt a need to re-establish that exclusive, dream-like relationship with the city which he experienced in the mysterious silence of the night, when Parma presented herself naked, silent and ready to welcome him back.

He made his way towards Adelaide's house, to that spot between the road, the river and the countryside which seemed to him as ambiguous and mysterious as a hermaphrodite. He continued walking until he saw the slim figure of Valmarini in the light cast by a street-lamp.

"You like this place," Valmarini said.

"Here you can feel the scent of the earth and the water, and sometimes in summer the song of the cicadas."

"We need simple things to be able to feel at ease, but these are also the first things we forget."

Quite suddenly, the dog began to howl and became agitated, pricking up his ears.

"Is he still tired?" the commissario asked.

Valmarini appeared not to be listening, but engaged in an attempt to decipher something strange. He replied only after a few moments had passed. "He's heard something. It could be an animal he'd like to chase."

"A stray dog?"

"I've already said there've been many strange comings and goings along the riverside. And strange people."

"What kind of strange people?"

"Hard to say. Last night there was a racket until about

three in the morning. Someone had lost a dog and was running about trying to find it. There were four of them and they patrolled the area for hours."

"If you were to lose yours ... What's he called?"

"Dondolo."

"If you were to lose him, you'd go and look for him, wouldn't you? People feel greater attachment to pets than to people."

"Nobody trusts their neighbours any longer. Pets are all that's left to us. They don't cheat us."

"Exactly. And if we lose them, we lose our heads."

"The people who were searching yesterday evening didn't seem to be the usual dog owners. I know everybody around here and I've never seen them before. I don't think they were even Italian."

"Maybe some frisky male had run off after getting the scent of a bitch on heat. They can run for kilometres in these cases."

Valmarini shook his head. "We're talking about four dishevelled young men of more or less the same age."

"You mean hooligans?"

"No, not that type at all. And in any case their dogs never run away."

"Did they catch it in the end?"

"Perhaps. They shut up after a while. They must have been very keen to find it, although they seemed to me more angry than worried."

Valmarini invited Soneri up to his house. In the living room with the window that seemed to mark the boundary between the city and the night, he saw on an easel a work which was as yet only roughly sketched out, and alongside it a high-definition print of the original.

"It's a Guido Reni – a great painter, one of the greatest of our seventeenth century," Valmarini said.

The commissario studied it carefully. The man was working

section by section with the aid of a strong lens. "You're not doing him a great service."

"Oh yes I am. No-one understands art as well as someone who reproduces it. These days we're not capable of working with our hands, and that will be the end of us. Not even artists know how to go about it. From Duchamp onwards, the idea, not the manufactured object, is all that's mattered. Do you know that there are some who have never even touched the thing they display? They have them made by the few craftsmen who have survived."

"You have the hands, not the idea," Soneri said.

"All too often, not even those whose names appear in books had ideas. Do you know how many Madonnas Guido Reni copied from his masters, the Carracci brothers? There are thousands of canvases in circulation signed by the great masters but executed by disciples in their studios. There is nothing less trustworthy than art."

"So then, what is it? Nothing other than testimony?"

"For those who know how to look, it's many things, but there are very few such people. In the seventeenth century, they still painted Madonnas but now that we're no longer Christians, all that remains is the mystery to which we are incapable of giving form."

"Just like that movement during the night," the commissario said, returning to more concrete topics.

"Exactly. Seeing as there's snow on the ground, you'll be able to examine the footprints on the path. It looks as though a procession had passed by."

"Do you have politicians among your clients?"

"They're among the most conceited of the lot, and they behave like parvenu industrialists. They've managed to create a world where ignorance is a virtue, but they're still a bit ashamed of it. Having a forged Pinturicchio in their house makes them feel like statesmen. As you know, the citizens of Parma are fond of show."

"Have you done any paintings for the mayor?"

"No, never. Too young, another generation. These people have long since given up on books – outdated, boring, fit only for lecturers and university professors. They prefer to prattle on their electronic devices informing each other about what they've had to eat, or how many times they've farted. Profound thoughts, all rigorously limited to four hundred characters. My clients are more venerable. They still drag in their wake a sprinkling of the twentieth century, and an anxiety about heritage."

"From the Right or the Left?"

"The Right. On the Left, they've no money. They're pathetic individuals, bereft of all courage, continually squabbling like folk on the same landing. They're never going to win because Italy and the whole world is on the Right. That's the way human nature is. The majority think only of themselves and invariably follow the strongest in the pack. There are some stray dogs like me and you who can allow themselves the luxury of laughing at this spectacle."

"We always come back to dogs," Soneri said, his eyes on Dondolo, who was snoozing on the rug. "Is Ugolini another of your clients? You know who I mean – deals in prosciutto and pulls the strings for the Right?"

"I can see you understand my type of man. I'm setting up an art gallery in his villa in San Vitale. Can you believe he has even insured my works and bought authentic frames? Don't you find that grotesque? He's worried about having authentic frames! A perfectly packaged forgery."

"Like advertising."

"That's the cipher of our life now. What distinguishes me is that my work requires the care of a craftsman. This alone is authentic. What I have in common with surgeons is that knowledge is not enough; you also need hands."

They drank their tea in silence, contemplating the darkness, which now seemed solid outside the window.

"The night is the one thing which dies with the appearance of the world," Valmarini said. "This aporia confers on it value and mystery, don't you think?"

Soneri nodded. Dondolo was still breathing heavily, and this brought back to the commissario's mind the search for the dog which they had been discussing earlier.

"In your opinion, the people who were searching yesterday evening were not the dog's masters?"

"Not in my opinion. You can tell from how a person goes about the quest. Some people search to find the dog, others to capture it, you see what I mean? A dog owner wants more than anything else to find his dog again, but those people behaved as though they were on a search mission."

The commissario's eye fell once again on Dondolo, who seemed the very antithesis of all ideas of escape. He said goodnight quietly and went out into the dark.

The following morning, he arrived at the police station a little later than usual. Juvara was already there and had news for him. "I've made the inquiries you asked me to. L'Eterna's legal representative is Avvocato Righetti, whose chambers are in Via Cavour."

"He's involved with funeral undertakers?" Soneri's tone was incredulous, causing the inspector to pause as he stared at him. "He's a very well-known lawyer," Soneri added.

Hearing this, Juvara too became incredulous. "What's he doing getting mixed up with a firm which would seem to be in the orbit of certain families from Castellammare? Alright, at the moment we haven't found anything. In that sense, if you follow."

"Yes, yes, I get it. The camorra."

"The staff is entirely local. Many are ex-employees of Pighetti's."

"What about the mobile? Did Piccirillo give you authorisation at last?"

"No, but I've found a way round it. I got in touch with a friend who often helps us when we have problems with mobiles."

Soneri gave him a sign to carry on, implicitly approving what he had done.

"Unfortunately, I didn't get any information from him either."

"Why not?"

"The S.I.M. card isn't Italian. It's Ukrainian."

The commissario brought his hand down on the desk. He had seemed on the point of clearing things up, and now once again everything was slipping from his grasp.

"Perhaps you were right in seeing something underhand in this story of the mobile," Juvara said.

"Not just there."

"I also wanted to tell you that word has got out – about the mayor, I mean."

Soneri nodded. The city was full of chatter and the most ridiculous theories were circulating. Midway through the morning, Angela called to tell him they were talking about nothing else in the courts. The various conjectures were at first confined to the H.Q.s of the political parties, but because they had been indiscreetly aired, they were coming to the surface like froth and spreading throughout the whole city.

Soneri was the only one who knew more about it, but he could not shake off his state of lethargy. He had no confidence in the investigation. If politicians were involved, it would not go beyond the arrest of a few fringe figures. He hid himself away in his own office, reluctant to answer the telephone for fear it might be Bergossi or, even worse, Piccirillo with his exasperating caution.

He was relieved when he heard Maresciallo Boldrin's voice. "Your mayor went away before Saturday," he said.

"Did you examine the C.C.T.V. footage?"

"It almost blinded me! I said he went away earlier than Saturday, but that's just a suspicion. What's certain is that in the second half of the week he didn't take the chair-lift at all."

"Is there any other way of making the ascent?"

"You could always go by foot." Boldrin chuckled. "We've matched the occasions when the ski-pass was produced at the access points, both for ascent and descent, with the camera images."

"And he's nowhere to be seen?"

"On the first days he was, but not after that."

"So who was going up and down?"

"The same guy always comes up, but I don't know who he is. We downloaded a photo of the mayor from the Internet, and it's not him."

"Send me the image you have via email. It might be useful."

"You always did say there was something not right in this business!" Boldrin said.

"It's a strange story," the commissario said, embarrassed at the compliment.

A few moments later, Juvara printed the image of the man who had appeared at the chair-lift with the mayor's ski-pass round his neck. As soon as he had the photograph in front of him, Soneri gave a snigger.

"Know him?" the inspector asked.

"Yes, I do. He must be a Council official. He was one of those who were accompanying the children from Navetta to the mountains. One of Corbellini's poodles."

"What's his name?"

"I only saw him fleetingly up at Andalo."

"Wouldn't it be better to inform Bergossi, sir? Maybe it's time for you to get directly involved in this business."

"Not likely! I'll tell Musumeci what I know."

Shortly afterwards, Nanetti made his appearance. "While you were having fun in the mountains, I completed the investigation on Romagnoli."

"Any surprises?"

"I did all that the magistrate asked me to do. Routine work."

"So the case is closed?"

"I guess the prosecutor's office will pass it off as an accident and concentrate on the hospital's negligence, but I have to say that there's something that doesn't quite square up."

"Don't tell me you're letting your imagination carry you away, like those of us who always have our heads in the clouds! And you a scientist!"

"Didn't you know that scientists are attracted by anomalies?"

"And what anomalies might they be?"

"I took some fingerprints from the handle which opens the emergency exit Romagnoli used to go outside, and I found something funny. At the point you would normally push to exit, there are dozens of fingerprints, but at the opposite edge of the door, where the hinges are, there was one set on its own. I compared it with the prints on the glass beside his bed and discovered they coincide."

"You mean to say that there could be another person involved? Or could they be the fingerprints of a member of staff?"

"I can't answer that question. The nurses almost always wear gloves, but visitors don't. Besides, I believe the fingerprints belong to someone who was not familiar with the exit and pushed the wrong side. That was what made me suspicious."

"So there probably was someone else with Romagnoli," the commissario said.

"If the prints had been just on the handle, I would think nothing of it. A relative who leaned on the door or who got confused as he was going out. But the same fingerprints are on the glass."

"Have you informed the prosecutor's office?"

"Of course, but he didn't seem very convinced. He asked for further tests to establish when the fingerprints were made. He says that the glass could have been there for days and that even the prints on the handle could be old ones. What do you think?"

"It's a complete cock-up. And you're quite right to pursue these anomalies."

"Alright, but we've no idea where they're going to take us."

"One step at a time. Isn't that what you scientists say? So far we have established that Romagnoli wasn't on his own in his last days, as first appeared."

"Unless the fingerprints belong to a member of the nursing or cleaning staff," Nanetti objected.

"All you have to do is compare them."

"I don't know if Piccirillo will permit an extension of the inquiry. He's in a terrible rush to get it over and done with."

"Well, if he doesn't give you permission, I might have half an idea, but right now it's no more than a feeling."

"Try putting it into words."

"First I've got to sleep on it. By tomorrow, it might seem worthless."

7

ANGELA WATCHED HIM set off with a pair of wellington boots in his hand. "Going fishing?"

"Yes, but with no line and no bait."

"Is there another mobile ringing somewhere?"

"It's already been ringing, and I had the impression it was me they were looking for."

She looked him up and down, feeling that the distance between them had grown wider in recent days. Everything dated from that outing to Andalo, where she had felt unexpectedly isolated, even though she knew that it was always like that when the commissario was engrossed by some mystery.

Soneri put a packet of Parmesan shavings and a couple of rolls in his pocket, and climbed into his car. He did not go very far, and a quarter of an hour later he parked near Adelaide's house, opened the boot, put on his wellingtons and made for the path by the river. The thick mist almost entirely obscured the embankment. He crouched down as he slid forward on the snow which covered the ground as far as the eye could see. He could hear the river in the near distance, murmuring as if it were troubled. As he came close to the riverside, he noticed the footprints – more than one set, all pointing in the direction of the city. The tracks seemed close together, but at the same time they were sufficiently far apart to indicate people who did not know each other all that well. The paw marks of the dogs criss-crossed each another with no clear direction. The city itself was still out of sight, and with the mist and the snow muffling all noise, the scene allowed Soneri to imagine himself on the floor of a valley in the Apennines, or in a wood of young poplar trees alongside an embankment in the Lower Po valley. He followed the footprints into the swirling mist, and as he came near the water it seemed that the river itself was evaporating, concealing a strip of land which looked like a little urban jungle, but which the people of Parma, incredulous and intimidated, could observe from behind their parapets.

He strode on until he sensed the dark shadow of the Dattaro bridge. The footprints stopped here, where the embankment on the right-hand side narrowed, forcing him down to the ford. The water would not come over his boots if he stood on the rocks, and a little further on the river levelled out and became shallower, allowing little rocks to protrude like blades. On the far side, he picked up the footprints and criss-crossing tracks, interlocked like a tangled hairpiece. The rumble of the city, like an enormous aeroplane overhead, was getting closer. He heard a flutter of wings, followed immediately by the frightened cry of a pheasant, its colours illuminating the mist ahead of him like fireworks.

He reached the point where the two rivers embraced each other. The Baganza, with its unquiet waters, flowed into the Parma in front of the park on Via Varese, just beyond the Ponte Nuovo. As he stood looking at the marriage of the rivers, he paused to delight in their union and to savour his Parmesan. He then continued on his way along the path beside the Baganza, following the footprints. Above him, the sun announced itself in the opalescence of the skies, piercing through the mist. Coming to the narrow Ponte Navetta, he glanced up at the cement hood over the church where Don Guido preached, and continued parallel to Via Montanara, where he had played as a boy. The waters of the Baganza were more lively than those of the Parma, which turned bourgeois in the plain some fifteen kilometres from the city. When in full spate, tumbling down from a narrow, steep valley, the floods were devastating, gushing like an overflow from the eaves of a house, but by June the floods died young in the gravel.

Soneri walked on towards a horizon softened by the snow. As he gradually made his way into the mountains, he felt curiosity and suspicion grow inside him, relieving his fatigue, while the brightening sky seemed to offer hope of a revelation. He walked past Antognano, Gaione and San Ruffino, and when he saw another bridge, hazily, as in a dance of veils, he realised he was at Sala. The valley, stretching between hills spaced as regularly as rows of poplars, welcomed him. As he marched along, the light grew brighter until the sun's glare was so strong that he had to shade his eyes. He turned a corner: the Apennines shone before him with uniform brightness, and San Vitale emerged to his right. It seemed to him that there was nothing so beautiful, clear and bright as the sun in winter. He pressed on, following the tracks of the men and dogs until he saw them swerve in the direction of the road up to Marzolara, and then disappear into a little copse of elm trees. He walked through it and came out at a clearing between the road and the river. He searched the surrounding area but saw no further signs of passage. The trail finished there, in a senseless, inexplicable place. He sat down in disappointment on a rock warmed by the sun and ate the remainder of his bread and cheese. Every so often a car passed by with a gust of wind and swept on into the soft darkness of the mist a few kilometres further ahead.

He remained there a while, thinking things over until he saw the early afternoon light begin to fade and the shadow of the hills stretch out from the west. He got to his feet and resumed his walk towards the village by the roadside. In a few minutes, he was walking among the houses, and could make out Ugolini's huge ham-curing factory, with Zunarelli's workshop a little further on. The close proximity of the two brought vague associations to his mind, but he could not attribute any logic to them. He lost himself in what seemed to him reflections as randomly assorted as a hand of different suits in a game of cards. As the sun began to go down behind the ridge, he called Juvara.

"Get into a car and come and pick me up in San Vitale Baganza. I'll wait for you in the village bar," he said.

"But how did you ...?" Juvara began, but Soneri had already hung up.

Soneri instinctively felt himself disoriented. He had the impression of having wasted a day, wandering about as he used to do when he played truant as a boy. And when Juvara arrived to find him wearing the kind of boots cheese-makers wear, the inspector managed to complete the sentence which had been truncated an hour before. "How did you end up here?"

Soneri was not sure how to reply. After a few moments' silence, he said vaguely, "I followed a trail."

"On foot?"

"How else would you get along a riverbank?"

The inspector was puzzled but said nothing more. The mist which greeted them not long afterwards meant that the question was left hanging.

"Any news about Corbellini?" Soneri said after a while.

"No, sir, it's just as you said. He's disappeared, so it's not ... that?" he said, pointing over his shoulder and indicating San Vitale.

The commissario shook his head. "I wasn't looking for him. Can I just say that I was following a hunch?"

Juvara drove on in silence, more confused than ever, until Soneri resumed the conversation. "Have you ever had the experience of seeing something which could be either absolute nonsense or a great discovery? It's the worst thing that can happen to anyone. Either a stroke of genius or a debacle. More likely a bloody debacle."

"A woman came looking for you this afternoon," Juvara said.

"Who was she?"

"Middle-aged. Seemed to be Romanian. She left me her number."

"What did she want?"

"To tell you something about Romagnoli. She told me she was there at Villa Clelia when you turned up, but she couldn't speak then because there were too many people around."

"A carer?"

"Perhaps."

It was already dark by the time they reached the city. Juvara drove the commissario to his own car and handed him a note on which was written FLORA and a telephone number.

"Keep L'Eterna under observation. I want to know who its real owners are. And don't forget that mobile," Soneri said, as he closed the car door. He was very tired.

Angela called the moment he sat down in his car. "Catch any fish?"

"I couldn't decide which ones to keep."

"That's not much good, commissario. Where have you been?"

"At San Vitale. Remember that *trattoria*?"

"I certainly do. It might be worth another visit."

"Impossible. It's closed."

"And it took you a whole day to find that out?"

"No. More than one day."

"So?"

"I followed footsteps in the snow from the Parma riverbank to the district of Mariano. They led me all the way up to San Vitale."

"And who goes from Parma to San Vitale along the riverbank?"

"Quite a lot of people. Or else it's the same people going that way several times with their dogs."

"I doubt there are mushrooms or truffles along that path. And hunting is forbidden there. You must have some solution in mind."

"Not at all. I've got to the same point you've just arrived at."

"Why would anyone walk fifteen kilometres along a river?"

"That's a question I can't answer."

"And above all, who would want to do so on a day like this?"

"People who are compelled to. Compulsion is one of the prerequisites of criminal life."

"That's not good enough for me. It has to be someone who's fit. Somebody accustomed to hard work, someone poorer than us," Angela said. She had no fondness for long walks.

"I went from Mariano to San Vitale."

"You're different. You were brought up in the mountains."

"The only ones I see marching along on foot nowadays are foreigners. They walk kilometre after kilometre." This thought reminded him of the card Juvara had given him.

"Am I going to see you this evening?" Angela asked, in a tone which implied more than an invitation.

"Certainly, I could do with a good dinner."

"Alright then," she said, a note of disappointment in her voice.

Immediately afterwards, he dialled Flora's number. Her reply was hesitant, and in the background laughter and chatter could clearly be heard.

"I live with colleagues," she said. She had apparently taken refuge in the bathroom. "Are you from the police?"

"I am Commissario Soneri."

"Are you the officer who came to Villa Clelia when that old man died?"

"Yes, I am."

"They didn't tell you everything."

"What did they not tell me?"

"For example, that there was no alarm on the night exit. The nurses used to come and go all the time. After dinner, all sorts of things used to happen. They want carers there, to allow the staff to go to sleep. We have to pay to be able to work there. If you don't pay up, they won't give your name to the relatives of the patients."

The commissario listened with some disappointment to a litany of trade-union complaints. "Did Romagnoli have a personal carer?"

"No, he was alright. He slept. It was only in the last week that he began to act up. He would shout and get out of bed. I heard from the doctors that his dementia had deteriorated. He would keep on saying the same things. It was unbearable."

"What did he shout?"

"He used to rant about dogs. He kept on saying that he had to go and set them free. *The poor beasts! Poor beasts!*"

"Did he say anything else?"

"All of a sudden, he would start howling that they were butchering them – *Butchering them! They're cutting them up!* He was in such a state of despair that he seemed to be actually seeing them."

"In your opinion, who was he talking about? Who was doing the butchering?"

"I don't know. I thought he was talking about dogs, but who butchers dogs?"

"Do you have any colleagues who might know more about it?"

"I don't think so. They're all afraid of Malusardi. He's a horrible man. He once threw me out because I spoke back to a nurse. He wants us all to be silent and obedient, but I speak out, as you can see."

Soneri ended the conversation and sat in silence in his car, deep in thought. After a little, he began to feel cold, and since he could not extract even a half-intelligent idea from his own thoughts, he switched on the engine and set off. He found the police station in an uproar. The mayor's disappearance was now official. Corbellini had deserted the City Council, and no-one had managed to get in touch with him. The city seemed suspended over the emptiness of that disturbing absence. Teams of journalists and television crews had arrived in the Piazza and were virtually picketing the municipal offices, intercepting anyone who went in or came out. No sooner had he sat down in his office than the telephone rang. He was assaulted by Bergossi's baritone voice.

"I imagine you can guess why I'm looking for you, can't you?"

"I've got a vague idea."

"It's impossible to imagine a worse fiasco. You'll have to take over."

"The *Finanza* force is already on the job, and my office has lent them one of our best officers."

"That's not good enough. Suspend all other inquiries. The politicians are already exerting pressure, and at the Ministry . . ."

Soneri would have liked to tell him he was already involved, and had been the first to know about the disappearance, but he was overcome by a strange jealousy and preferred to remain silent. He would accept the assignment, but not just yet.

"I need you to authorise me to request the telephone records of a foreign S.I.M. card," the commissario said.

"Does this have anything to do with Corbellini's disappearance?"

"It might have. Right now we cannot ignore anything. Piccirillo turned down the request, but we're going to have to go down many avenues, don't you agree?"

Bergossi mumbled something indistinct, perhaps in disapproval of his deputy. "You'll get it right away."

As Soneri was ringing off and about to leave the office, the prosecutor added, "Please, I need your experience."

"You have to promise me that the politicians won't kick us in the arse if things turn nasty."

"When did that ever happen?" Bergossi said, in apparent amazement, before adding, "Do you really think there's a political angle to this case?"

"I don't know, but I'm afraid it's likely, seeing that the mayor is involved. You know how these things go, don't you?"

Bergossi was mumbling again as Soneri hung up. Immediately afterwards he called Don Jules. "Has the parish priest come back yet?"

"No, he's still at Villa San Bernardo. He's not been well, and he told me to tell you he has already reported everything he knows. He has no idea what he could add."

The commissario slammed the receiver down in annoyance. Juvara, who had heard everything, said, "I have to tell you, sir, that the Curia is now involved in this business. The Vicar General spoke to Piccirillo requesting that Don Guido be left in peace."

"That's all we need! The first spokes in the wheel."

Juvara did not understand and remained silent with an expression of amazement on his face. By the time he had made up his mind to ask for an explanation, the commissario was already dialling another number.

There was no preamble. "I've been thinking about those

fingerprints. They could be Zunarelli's. What do you say? He was the only friend he had."

"Oh well done, commissario!" Nanetti said. "Do you think that hadn't occurred to anyone else?"

"You're turning into my tracker dog."

"Never! I'm not up to that! I carry out orders."

"Get to the point. Have you or have you not made a comparison of the fingerprints?"

"Certainly have. I sent one of my men along to San Vitale. Piccirillo had a flash of inspiration."

"When?"

"This afternoon."

"I was there too."

"And you didn't bump into each other in the mist? The fact is you've had the same idea as Piccirillo. I'd be worried if I were you. I fear you're drifting to the Right."

Soneri had once again the unpleasant sensation of floating about in a vacuum. Nanetti came to his aid. "Anyway – the fingerprints *are* Zunarelli's."

The commissario felt as though he had been robbed.

8

AS THE TIME of the evening meal approached, the city spoke in hushed tones in bars, in doorways, in shop entrances, in dark alleys and on the far side of windows which opened onto pavements, while knots of people on the streets provided a descant which merged into a single, whispering chorus. At the same time, in political circles, dismay was the dominant note. The Town Hall looked more mysterious than any tomb. The crowd gathering outside it exchanged muttered conjectures while awaiting a clear signal. More television crews and their vans arrived to transform Piazza Garibaldi into a campsite. Soneri too felt the excitement, and for a few minutes walked up and down observing the spectacle, forgetting that Angela was waiting for him at home. He remembered her only when he heard the bells of the Palazzo del Governatore strike nine. He called her at once.

"Will I take you out to dinner? What do you say?"

"Are you seeking forgiveness for something or other?"

"There's always something that needs forgiving, but you've really got to get the feel of this evening. It seems like the citizens of Parma have stuck their fingers into an electric socket."

"The T.V. news has been saying there's a revolution under way."

The commissario burst out laughing. "And all this time we didn't notice a thing!"

"Well, some sort of revolution. The king has fled, is that it?"

"We can always pretend. Certainly, that's the climate. We'll make do with it."

A quarter of an hour later, Angela joined him in the *Milord*. She found Soneri on his feet chewing a cigar with an almost radiant air.

"A magnificent re-awakening!' she said when they found a seat.

"If only we knew how it's all going to end."

"In the early stages, no revolution ever knows where it's going to end."

"This isn't a revolution, just an outbreak of mischievousness. It's a tantrum thrown by a bigoted city that grows indignant when its own eternal vices become public. For a revolution, people have to join in, but Parmigiani are such weaklings that they could never manage anything of the sort. At best, they might organise a bit of a tumult."

"Come on! Did we not once choose to play at revolutions?"

The commissario burst out laughing. "O.K., let's play a game – but to get into the swing of things, you need a good meal and a bottle of Bonarda."

In the *Milord* as elsewhere, the talk was of the mayor's disappearance, and snatches of conversation floated over to Soneri's table. They both ordered *tortelli di zucca*, over which Angela liberally sprinkled Parmesan. "Who knows what the mayor is eating at this moment?" she said.

"As he's far away from his gym, he might be on a diet."

"I think he might be in that resort in Tunisia where what's-his-name took refuge."

"Bettino Craxi."

"That's the one. They all go there."

At that moment his mobile rang, causing the commissario some irritation until he heard Boldrin's jovial voice. "I've got a piece of news which might interest you," he said without any preliminary greeting.

"The way I feel right now, everything interests me."

"My colleagues in Val Badia believe they recognised your mayor."

"When?"

"During that week when he was up here skiing. If I've got it right, it was Wednesday."

"Did they stop him?"

"Yes. He was in a car they stopped for a routine check on the road along the valley. The documents indicated that the driver was a politician, a right-wing regional councillor from Emilia. He was breathalysed, but the results were negative. The other two with him looked drunk, or at least under the influence. One in particular was practically catatonic, and my colleagues later identified him from the electronic photos of missing persons: it was your mayor."

"What was the name of the guy who was driving?"

"Somebody called Piero Bonaldi."

"Huh! Another one from Parma. He's the regional secretary of the party," Soneri said, turning to Angela.

"Bernetti, the Undersecretary for Industry, was there too. You know, the one that's always on television?"

"Him too!"

"He was tipsy, and started arguing with my colleagues, making out that it was just a bit of fun. He turned arrogant and boasted about having acquaintances among the carabinieri in Rome. The result was that the station chief got annoyed and made some inquiries. It may interest you to know that the car went back to Parma that night, and exited at the Fornovo toll-booth on the A15, near La Spezia."

The commissario sat stock-still with his mobile in one hand and a fork in the other. Boldrin had to say "Hello? . . . Hello?" a couple of times to be sure he had not lost the connection.

"Fornovo," Soneri repeated in a whisper, as though he were sleepwalking, but his thoughts were racing off in all directions.

"I hope I've made you a welcome present," Boldrin said, unsure how to interpret the commissario's reaction.

"Fornovo," he said again, as though reciting a mantra without being able to associate it with anything.

"He'll be holed up in some villa around there," Angela said. "Who could ever find him out there? They could hide a kidnap victim in those parts."

For a few moments, Soneri turned over in his mind the idea that he really might have been kidnapped. What the carabinieri from Val Badia had seen in the car would seem to indicate that, but if that were the case, and considering the people with him, the party was involved as well.

Angela poured him another drink. "The Bonarda will help you reason more clearly."

Rather than reasoning, the commissario was lost in a fantasy land. He was trying to imagine why that car would have left the *autostrada* at the sliproad for Val di Taro. Was it perhaps making for the Apennines, hoping to disappear in the network of side roads?

"Maybe it continued on the Cisa road? How could we tell? Doesn't the mayor go to Forte dei Marmi in summer?" Angela asked.

"There's no point. It could be anything. They might even have dropped him off before Fornovo."

Meanwhile, the city's frenzy was rising to the surface like

the body of a drowned man, swollen up with its own voices, which were now quite out of control. Some said that Corbellini had been found dead in his own study, but that the news had not been released because they had to deal with certain compromising matters. Others believed he was in a private clinic undergoing detox treatment, others again that he had already left the country with a briefcase full of stolen cash, or possibly had run off with a woman, or even, in another account, with a man. Soneri could take no more of these rumours.

"Come on. Let's go down to the Piazza and enjoy the revolution," Angela said. "Maybe the mayor will emerge like the Pope to offer reassurance."

"No, not the Piazza. If my colleagues see me walking about with you among all these desperately curious people, who knows what they'd think?"

"You're not at work now."

"A policeman's work is never done."

"Exactly. It'd be easier to find clues in the Piazza than among those slobs in the Council offices.

They were both quite light-headed. In the chill of the evening, the mist swirled about the houses, making them vanish and reappear as though by magic. Angela and Soneri walked about hugging each other. They went along Via Cavestro, passed the University, turned in the direction of the Courts and the Collegio dei Nobili, crossed Via Farini into the narrow streets of Borgo Giacomo Tommasini and Via Repubblica, went down Via Saffi and ended up in Borgo delle Colonne, before stopping in front of the one-time prison of San Francesco. Theirs was a venture into a Parma which was more imaginary than real, and everywhere they came across excited people and encountered that continual buzz of conspiracy which seemed to be the order of the day. When they stopped to catch their breath in front of the former prison, they realised how exhilarated they were. They embraced, and for a few moments Soneri experienced genuine happiness.

"Could this be the revolution?" he chuckled, with his partner in his arms. She drew back a little, looked at him with a smile which was at once sad and tender, and shook her head. "No, it's a moment of recklessness, normal enough at twenty, but to be treasured at our age."

"Let's hold on to this image as long as we can," he said, feeling its ripeness fade. They moved from Borgo del Parmigianino back towards the centre, came out on Via Cavour and continued on their way between the Cathedral and the Baptistry. They sat down on the marble seat in front of the Episcopal Palace, their arms around each other like teenagers. The enchantment of that sublime architectural hybrid, an amalgam of the earthy solidity of the Romanesque and the heavenly yearning of Gothic spires, preserved their moment of ecstasy, until his mobile rang out like an alarm clock dragging the sleeper out of a dream.

"They didn't find it." He heard a familiar voice he could not identify. The speaker launched straight into a conversation left suspended a few moments before. "I forgot to tell you before," he said. Only then did Soneri realise that the voice belonged to Valmarini.

"What did they not find?" the commissario asked.

"The dog," Valmarini replied as though it were obvious. "The one they'd lost somewhere nearby."

At last Soneri was able to grasp what was going on, remembering the path along the river and the trail he had followed to San Vitale.

"Did they come back?"

"Yes, several times. They brought along a bitch on heat which attracted all the dogs in the city. Dondolo went crazy and tugged at the lead until he fell over in exhaustion.

"So it was a male?"

"That's what I deduce. They're not giving up. Drop by some evening. You'll find me down at the embankment."

Soneri ended the call. The euphoria of a few moments earlier had evaporated. He stared wordlessly at the Cathedral, as did Angela. The surrounding mist gave the impression that the Cathedral walls were floating inside a cloud. The city was drifting away from him, slipping beyond his gaze, hiding itself in shame, inhabited by too many mysteries.

"Who was that?" Angela asked.

"A painter who does forgeries and lives near your friend Adelaide."

"What did he want?"

"To tell me about a dog which has gone missing near where he lives, and which someone is searching for."

"What's that got to do with you?"

"I don't know, but dogs keep turning up in this story."

They were both feeling the cold by now and stood up. The warmth from the food and wine had worn off. Everything was returning to normal. They walked back to Piazza Garibaldi and learned that Party Secretary Bonaldi was now coming to grips with something everyone else had known and for which he may have been among those responsible: the disappearance of Corbellini. It was now official, and the Council was on the verge of collapse.

"There's no-one in charge of the city!' Soneri said.

"Nothing new there. There never was anyone worthwhile in charge," Angela said sarcastically.

The following morning, Soneri was immediately on the alert. He set off for his office and as soon as he arrived, he called a friend named Cattani who did voluntary work at the municipal kennels.

"Have you picked up any stray or lost dogs recently?" the commissario asked.

"We do that every day, and many of them are in a bad way."

"Half starved?"

"Not only that. Quite sick, I'd say."

"How many have you rounded up this week?"

"About six, I think."

"Can I see them?"

"Come along whenever you like."

"I'll drop by before this evening."

"Are you really looking to take a dog from the compound?" Juvara asked, after overhearing the telephone call.

"What do you take me for, some old queen?" Soneri replied in a tone which cowed the inspector. "Any news about the mobile? I received authorisation from Bergossi."

"Nothing yet. The S.I.M. card probably belongs to one of those call centres where foreigners go to call home. They keep several of them, and hire them out to seasonal workers."

"If you're right, we'll never manage to get to the mobile's owner."

"Not necessarily," the inspector said with a certain optimism, before changing the subject. "I've made inquiries into L'Eterna, and some things are beginning to emerge."

"For example?"

"That it's not clear where it gets the money for the investments it's making."

"What did you expect? We're talking about the camorra here, recycling their money into clean activities."

"But sir, you know better than me that we need proof, and in the case of Petrillo, the company president, we've only got suspicions."

"You're quite right. No-one can deal in mere hunches, least of all us."

"The firm is clean. It has a respectable legal representative. Even if we're convinced you're right, that doesn't mean we can go chasing shadows."

"That's the problem. We've got the enemy in our sights, but we're powerless and we even have to smile at them when they appear to be generous, as in the case of Romagnoli's funeral."

"You always say some of the most vicious villains act within the law."

"Have you any idea how many of them there are? Did you get anything from the company records?"

"It's a tangled web. We already know about the legal representative and the president, and behind them there's another company which is in turn controlled by other companies with women's names, like Samantha, Deborah, Lory and Gioia. It's like a game of Russian dolls, one inside the other till you get to the heart, which in this case is called Posillipo, whose sole chief executive is one Carmelo Lopinto."

"And who might he be?"

"Probably just a proxy. Colleagues in Naples tell me he used to be a janitor in a primary school and now seems to be unemployed. You get the picture?"

Soneri nodded. He understood only too well. He picked up his telephone and dialled Musumeci, while an officer brought in that morning's papers. "Go over to the Town Hall and make inquiries about the official who accompanied the children from Navetta on that skiing trip to Andalo. I think he's called Giovetti or something like that. In the last couple of days, he had the ski-pass which the mayor had been using. Twist his arm a bit."

"Really, there are other things I should be doing today. Bergossi—"

"Bergossi has got me involved in the inquiry, so from this point on I am directing the traffic."

He did not wait for a reply and hung up, then turned back to Juvara. "You go over to Via Navetta and talk to the boys who went on the trip. Question their parents as well to get some idea of how this whole business started."

He picked up the newspapers, which seemed to exude anxiety even when they were still bundled up unopened. They all led with the disappearance of the mayor. He glanced over them for a few minutes until his eye fell on a framed square with the photograph of a dog and above it in capitals the words: REWARD OFFERED. He stared for some time at the face of what looked like a bloodhound and read the description of the lost animal. The caption spoke vaguely about the park on Via Bizzozero, the area where Valmarini lived. It added that the dog was male.

The commissario got up and was about to go out when his attention was attracted by an uproar in the courtyard below. He saw a group of journalists surge towards him, but before they could catch him he made a rapid getaway by the secondary exit onto Borgo della Posta. He asked one of the drivers to take him to the municipal dog pound. Cattani was waiting for him in a state of apparent anxiety. He pointed to the new arrivals, which were making a deafening din in the cages.

"They're almost all female," he said. "They get rid of them because they get pregnant and they don't know what to do with the pups."

"No males among them?"

"Yes, one. He was brought in yesterday evening, and he's in a sorry state." Cattani pointed to a hound huddled miserably in the corner of a cage. "We were told about him by a woman who had seen him near the walls of the Cittadella, and we went along with the local police to pick him up. He's not well and he turns aggressive if anyone goes near him."

"What do you think's wrong with him?"

"Who knows? We've no idea where he comes from or whether he belongs to anyone. No collar and no microchip."

"You get many dogs like that?"

"No, it's unusual at his age, but that's not the only strange thing. Just an hour ago someone turned up to claim him, and very insistent he was too. Fortunately, there were four of us here so he couldn't push it too far, but I got the impression he would have taken him away by force."

"Did he say who he was?"

"No, but judging by his accent he seemed to be foreign, perhaps Slavonic. He said he wanted the dog, that he adored bloodhounds, but we can't just hand over an animal which has no chip and is not vaccinated. I told them that in a couple of days we'd be able to let him have it, provided he was prepared to go through the adoption procedures."

"It doesn't look well," the commissario said.

"He's quite poorly. We're going to take him to the Vet School later today. He doesn't eat. All the other dogs devour their meals because they're famished, but this one won't even sniff the bowl."

The animal was staring at them suspiciously. He didn't seem to have a high opinion of people.

"Why don't we take him there right now? That way, if the other guy comes back you can hand him over as good as new," Soneri said.

"Strange behaviour. Normally they do everything they can to leave the dogs with us, not to take them off our hands."

Soneri nodded. He felt the way he had done the previous day when he was vainly following the footprints along the riverside, as if facing a blinding light or on the point of understanding. The dog had no desire to move and growled at them. They had to put him on a rigid lead and hold him down until they could muzzle him. Once he could no longer use his teeth, he allowed himself to be transported in the van. They took him to the vet, who started by X-raying him. While waiting, the commissario and Cattani went out to buy a panino from a shop opposite the School.

"What makes you so passionate about this particular dog?" Cattani said.

"I'm passionate about everything that defies the ordinary ways of logic. Yesterday I followed a trail along the side of the Parma and the Baganza and I wondered why anyone would wish to make that journey on foot. Today I'm wondering why a foreigner should be so desperate to reclaim an animal which doesn't even have the indispensable chip. And then there was an advertisement in today's paper about a bloodhound."

"I saw it, but all bloodhounds are very similar and it was a terrible photograph. Besides, it only showed the dog's face. But all this seems very strange to me as well."

"Once you abandon ordinary logic, it's more than likely that there's some alternative logic we're not aware of."

"Very probably."

"Maybe the dog will be able to tell us something," the commissario joked.

"Animals tell us a great many things we can't or don't want to understand. We say they're just animals, but they behave better than we do."

"Is that why you're so dedicated to them?"

"Maybe it's because I no longer trust human beings. Take politics. This city, the whole country, looks like one gigantic swindle – everybody cheating everybody else. Animals don't do that. They are what they are. Fierce, perhaps, but sincere."

"The rise in the number of cats and dogs goes hand in hand with a growing distrust in our neighbours. You could take the number of pets in any city as an index of social unease."

"Very true, but having a pet is like getting married: it's a commitment. Too many people think they're just cuddly toys, and so the first time they pee on the carpet they throw them out. Then it's left to us to look after them."

"That's what happens in marriages too."

Cattani looked troubled as he nodded, and only then did the commissario realise that he had hit a raw nerve and remember that his friend was not long separated. "Shall we go and see how things are?" he said.

They got up and went back to the Veterinary School.

"He had a very serious intestinal blockage," the vet said, "and needed to be operated on urgently. My colleagues are already attending to him."

"What was that due to?" Cattani asked.

"Couldn't say with any certainty, but in his intestines there are several foreign bodies too large to be expelled naturally. The dog would have died within a day or two."

"What kind of foreign bodies?" Soneri asked.

"I don't know yet. They're roundish items, evidently immune to the animal's gastric juices. It's well known that hounds are greedy beasts and not at all choosy. They eat everything that's put in front of them. Over and above that, this specimen is still young."

"Could you let me see the X-rays?"

The vet looked at him in slightly piqued surprise. "Do you know anything about it?"

"About X-rays, no, but I've seen more than one foreign body."

The vet picked up the negatives, switched on the illuminator and held the first X-ray in front of it. The dog's belly came up, its intestines as twisted as an Alpine pass, and inside them were a dozen capsules, each about the size of a table-tennis ball.

"If there had been fewer, perhaps he would have passed

them but there were so many it paralysed the intestinal peristalsis," the vet said.

Soneri was no longer listening to him but was focused on the X-ray. It contained an image he had seen before, not in the belly of a dog but in that of a drugs courier who disembarked at an airport and went home to shit out the capsules. Travellers with no baggage but a fortune in their stomachs, people of no value to those who enlisted them, wretched individuals taken from the *favela*s and stuffed like cream cakes, simple containers of cocaine to be loaded and unloaded.

"This dog's belly is filled with drugs," Soneri said, his head now filled with a plausible explanation of the tracks by the riverside, of the path taken by the animals and the obsessiveness of the search for that lost beast. Cattani was perplexed, and his eyes interrogated the commissario.

"You see, there's nearly always some logic to abnormal behaviour."

9

THEY USED THE English word "Full" to name the dog. From its innards, they pulled out twelve spherical containers with four hundred grammes of pure cocaine. The dog was carrying between twenty-five and thirty thousand euros, so it was not hard to see why they were searching for it. New scenarios and new questions now presented themselves. From where and by what means did animals come stuffed like this? Who oversaw this traffic? Soneri now understood the reasons for the tracks along the rivers. It was a no-man's-land, the most secure way, the only one with no customs posts, but he did not understand why the final stretch to San Vitale ended in the desolation of a litter-strewn clearing opposite an oak wood.

When he came into the office, Juvara interrupted his train of thought. "I've been over to Navetta," he said.

"And?" the commissario asked.

"If you like, we can speak later."

"No, no," Soneri said, but his mind was plainly elsewhere.

"It's a simple marketing operation," Juvara said, with a touch of contempt in his voice. "He used those people to make maximum impact on public opinion. The meanest form of charity."

"I've never heard you express yourself so forcefully, but it's high time you started to give voice to your indignation."

"Many of those boys had never been in the mountains

before, and didn't even know what a pair of skis looked like. Now they're living proof of Corbellini's magnanimity, showing that the Right takes heed of the needs of the weakest."

"That way, he'll ensure his legacy."

"Do you really think so?"

"No, I just don't know. People like Corbellini have taught us that nothing is predictable. Have you ever before seen a mayor build great, useless bridges just to make his mark?" Soneri asked, thinking of some of the vainglorious public works erected around Parma.

"Anyway, the parish priest in Navetta district had his paw in it. It was he who selected the group that went to Andalo. He went so far as to let it be known that others would get their chance in the future, just to build up their hopes."

"What do you expect of priests? Did they at least teach the boys how to ski?"

"What you think? All they did was march them about in their snowshoes."

"And did they see the mayor?"

"They did on the first day, then he disappeared. This whole show was planned at the last moment," Juvara said. "Some of the parents told me that they heard about the trip just a couple of days in advance. The children didn't even have suitable clothing."

"Who cares? They weren't there to enjoy themselves, but for a walk-on part in the great show."

"The local newspapers and T.V. stations went along to interview them and their mothers."

"You see the kind of legacy he's keen to leave? The high priests of Finance behave in exactly the same way: shady deals on the quiet all year and then some spectacular work of charity trumpeted far and wide by the media to fool the people. That's how you go about re-yoking the oxen."

Juvara listened to the commissario with a touch of deference. He had to admit that sometimes his superior's rants were instructive, and at least Soneri helped him to see the world in a new perspective. They exchanged understanding glances, and then each picked up a telephone.

The commissario called Musumeci. "Did you get in touch with Giovetti?"

"A nasty individual."

"What did he have to say?"

"Nothing much, and what he did say was not particularly convincing. He says the mayor gave him the ski-pass because he preferred to go out with a guide."

"Do you really see him tramping over the mountains?" The question was addressed to Juvara as well.

"I don't think so. I believe he preferred indoor activities," came Musumeci's ironic reply. "And it was winter time. Giovetti was not all that forthcoming. He kept changing the subject, repeating that he didn't know or didn't remember."

"I'll bet he didn't! Did you ask him what Corbellini was doing in Val Badia with the big chiefs of the Parma Right?"

"He believes they came to meet him to talk about the party. They dined in a restaurant in Corvara and then went back to Parma."

"With him?"

"He denies that. He swears they took him back to his hotel in Andalo."

"You believe him?"

"No, but it's plausible and I can't prove otherwise."

Soneri had to admit the truth of this, but he was disappointed as he hung up. He remembered his appointment with Bergossi. The Courts were not far off, so he went by foot. The previous evening's agitation had calmed down somewhat.

Parma was a volatile city, which, under the impulse of some novelty, got briefly excited but then calmed itself just as quickly, at least until the next time. The flow of time was broken into a series of impermeable moments without past or future. Soneri thought that in many ways Parma resembled Romagnoli. It suffered from the same dementia, mixed up events which had occurred at different times, and remembered and forgot without rhyme or reason.

Bergossi had a high opinion of Soneri but considered him a loose cannon who had to be handled with caution. He always gave him a list of recommendations when he entrusted him with some task. In this case too, Soneri did nothing to reassure or calm him.

"We're going to have to upset the politicians," the commissario said.

The prosecutor looked at him with some concern. "Considering we're dealing with the mayor, that's going to happen sooner or later, but I would have preferred it later when we might have greater support."

"Corbellini was stopped in Val Badia in a car with the regional secretary, Bonaldi, and the Undersecretary for Industry, Bernetti. It seems that Bernetti and Corbellini were drunk or at least tipsy. The car then went back to Parma, but it's not clear who was still inside."

Bergossi scratched the back of his neck. "It's going to be tough with men like this. I see trouble ahead."

"At this point, we can afford to leave them in peace and carry on digging around them. There's cocaine circulating, and it employs a means of transport which is, to say the least, highly unusual."

"What's that got to do with the mayor?"

"Perhaps nothing, even if in those circles cocaine ... Perhaps it does have something to do with the death of Romagnoli."

"Not at this stage, it doesn't."

"You don't always find the things you're looking for, but chances are you'll turn up things you'd been looking for at other times."

"Hand the whole thing over to the narcotics squad and don't waste any more time. You know the kind of government we have, don't you? Our objective is to find the mayor, and I won't conceal the pressure we're coming under."

"I get the impression that the Right would rather put up with the disappearance of a mayor than push us too hard to find him."

"You think so? I'd be more prudent, considering we have nothing in hand," Bergossi said, looking at the commissario with the same concern as before.

Soneri had to agree that Bergossi was right. "I've got a certain feeling, nothing more," he said.

"Tell me about it. Sometimes feelings are important."

"It's been such an odd business from the outset: from the excursion with the boys from Navetta – which already had a whiff of self-serving charity – to the sudden passion for skiing, to the outing with the party leaders who just happened to be visiting the valleys, to the hotel room he may never have slept in, and then the sudden departure, which also has something fishy about it."

"I know. It's all highly unusual, but precisely because we're dealing with politicians, I urge you to proceed with caution. These are people who don't hesitate to invent facts when they have something to justify."

Soneri nodded. "I'd like to continue investigating Romagnoli's death."

Bergossi sighed. "Why are you so pig-headed? The most important line of inquiry concerns the mayor's disappearance. Everybody's going to be talking about it. Why do you care about an old man suffering from dementia who let himself freeze to death?"

"I only need a couple of days."

The prosecutor gave in. "Do what you like, if you really want to work a fourteen-hour day."

As usual, Soneri had not said everything. The inquiry into Romagnoli's death was headed by Piccirillo, who appeared to be on the point of closing the file, something which would throw all the commissario's plans up in the air. In Soneri's mind, a network of connections was taking shape, as flimsy as a spider's web, but perhaps capable of being arranged into a single overarching pattern.

As he left the prosecutor's office and went down the staircase, he saw Angela in the distance in the atrium of the court building. She was walking purposefully, holding a leather handbag. He stopped to look at her, but felt a little voyeuristic. It was always a surprise to him to come across her immersed in a part of her life to which he had no access, and on each occasion it was like discovering another person. It excited him, because in his imagination it was like conquering a new woman. Her slightly haughty carriage conveyed an air of inaccessibility and heightened the exhilaration of profanation. Soneri was conscious that there was something unhealthy in all this, but he steered clear of looking too deeply into it, preferring to savour the moment's dark charm. Enquiring would signify approaching something ungraspable, a well-guarded nucleus of truth.

In the Romagnoli affair, too, there was still a mass of dark motives which might never come to the surface. The thought of the old man made him remember that he ought to interview Zunarelli. As the roads began to freeze over and the afternoon light faded, he got into his Alfa and set off for San Vitale. Night fell as he continued on his way. The village looked like a phosphorescent tunnel inside an enormous tangle of mist. He had some difficulty finding the gate leading to Zunarelli's courtyard. He got out of the car and went in through the glass door to the workshop. Everything there stood out clearly in the uniform, stable light which looked almost solid.

Zunarelli looked at him for a few moments in obvious annoyance, then turned away with resignation. He said hello, but kept his eyes down. The usual row of knives lay on the bench in front of him. Zunarelli put down the one he was using and wiped his hands on his apron.

"There must be a serious problem if you've come all this way in this mist. Are you here again about the funeral?" he said.

The commissario shook his head. "It's about you this time."

Zunarelli looked surprised and pointed his finger at himself. "Me?"

Soneri gave the slightest nod of the head. "You'll have to tell me the whole story."

"What whole story?"

"Your relationship with Romagnoli. Did you go and visit him every evening?"

"No, why? I've already told you . . ."

"Your fingerprints were on the glass on his bedside table. They are also on the handle of the emergency exit. What conclusion would you draw?"

Zunarelli seemed taken aback. He became agitated and began to tremble slightly. "I did go and see him. I thought I'd said that."

The commissario shook his head. He went over to the man and, putting one hand on his shoulder, looked him straight in the eye. He spoke with deceptive gentleness. "Talk to me. Or would you prefer to have a magistrate ask the questions?"

After a few moments, Zunarelli gave way. "Yes, I went to see him the night before he disappeared," he said.

"Was it you who administered the sedative?"

"No, that was the nurses' job, and if you want to know, they gave him an extra dose because he'd been a bit unruly towards the end."

"How do you explain the fingerprints on the glass?"

"I helped him take a drink."

"And then what? You didn't go all the way from San Vitale just to give him a drink? Did you get him to take a breath of fresh air?"

"Yes, we went outside. The alarm at the emergency exit was switched off at a certain time, and the nurses didn't seem keen on taking their turn at looking after Romagnoli. Then we went back inside. The cold calmed him down better than any tranquilliser."

"Did you do that often?"

Zunarelli shrugged his shoulders. "A few times, to keep him happy. Lately he was obsessed with the idea of going back home, so if he didn't get out every so often, he became impossible."

"Were you the only one who took him out?"

"I don't know about anyone else. He didn't *have* anyone else. Besides, he trusted me. He was like a child. You even had to remind him to put on a coat and shoes. Most times, we stopped on the balcony to look at the trees in the garden. He liked them a lot, and I explained to him the different species of plant. Once we went as far as the courtyard, but then he began to get cold and we turned back. When he got really worked up about going home, I'd remind him about the cold and tell him to wait for the good weather. If you spoke to him calmly, he would calm down as well and do what you said."

"Why didn't you tell me all this at the beginning?" Soneri said, with a hint of menace in his voice.

"Is it so important?"

"Let me be the judge of that. Have you ever had a dog?"

"A dog?" He repeated the question more than once, in a tone of astonishment. The commissario sensed he was trying to buy time.

"Yes, a dog. With all the pigskins that pass through your hands, you could easily feed a dozen of them."

"I don't like them. It's not true that they're faithful. Sooner or later they bite you – or worse."

"Romagnoli was fond of them."

"He was crazy, even in his younger days."

"What would be crazy would be you refusing to come clean with me. But it wouldn't be the first time, would it?"

"If there are things I didn't tell you, it's because they didn't occur to me at the time," Zunarelli said, in self-justification.

Soneri paused for a moment to consider whether the man was a fool or was faking it. As he left him, he was more convinced than ever of the second hypothesis. He turned back at the door to say, "You understand you're going to be summoned by the magistrate to give evidence? You'll have to tell him what you've just said to me."

Zunarelli made no reply but seemed troubled. The commissario caught sight of a car approaching the gate. When the driver saw another car in the courtyard, he kept the engine running and reversed away, but Soneri moved quickly enough to be able to read the number plate before the car sped off. Experience made him suspicious. He took out his mobile and called Pasquariello.

"Check up on this registration number, will you?" he said, reading out the letters and numbers.

He heard his colleague clicking the keyboard. "It belongs to the Laudadio Pasquale company. There's nothing pending against them."

"Where is this company based?"

"It's registered with the Parma Chamber of Commerce, but the owner is a native of Castellamare di Stabia, in Campania."

"What's its line of business?"

"How do you expect me to know? The terminal is hardly going to tell me that," Pasquariello said, growing impatient.

Soneri got his reply from Juvara, who had an unbounded faith in the Internet and insisted that everything could be found there. "Here we are!" he announced with evident satisfaction. "Laudadio Pasquale Ltd, waste-food management, authorisation..."

Now Soneri understood where Zunarelli's pigskins ended up. Since no part of the pig should ever be thrown away, as an old Emilian proverb had it, fodder and fertiliser were produced from the skin and bones. In practice, pigs were fattened by eating each other. It occurred to the commissario that, in a more indirect way, the same was true of human beings. He took out his mobile and this time called Piccirillo. "I've uncovered something else."

He was answered by a low, asthmatic whisper from the other end. "In regard to what?"

"Romagnoli."

"Still harping on about that story?" the prosecutor grunted in annoyance.

"Zunarelli's fingerprints are on both the victim's tumbler and the handle of the emergency exit."

"I know. I sent the forensics squad to do tests."

"There's something suspicious about the whole business."

"And when, in your opinion, would he have left these fingerprints?

"He says the night before Romagnoli's death, but who can say if he's telling the truth? The man does not seem to me trustworthy."

"The deeper we go into it, the darker everything gets," the prosecutor said.

"The darker, yes, and that's not all."

"What else have you found?" Piccirillo said in a tired voice, exhausted by all these unexpected developments.

"A very original method of cocaine trafficking."

"I understand. The usual capsules in the stomach."

"In the stomach, yes, but the stomach of a dog."

The commissario heard an aghast intake of breath and remembered that Piccirillo had a French poodle which was always packaged like an Easter egg. The first reaction was followed by a wail of indignation. "What were they doing to those poor animals?"

"They stuffed them so full as to clog them up. With so much matter in their stomachs, they ended up with an intestinal blockage."

Another intake of breath. It seemed that only dogs were able to shake him out of his customary apathy. "How did you discover this?"

"I followed tracks along the Parma and Baganza rivers as far as San Vitale. Then I discovered that in the dog compound there was a much sought-after bloodhound which was in a bad way. At the veterinary clinic, it seemed about to go into labour."

"So you saved the dog?"

"Yes, I think it'll pull through. They sewed it back together."

Piccirillo sighed again, but this time he seemed satisfied. "If no-one else wants it, I'll take it."

"Its name is Full."

"Well, that's the right name for it! We need to get to the bottom of this. I want to know all about it: where the dogs come from, who's using them and how." Piccirillo interrupted himself, struck by a sudden doubt. "But do you think that . . .

if that dog hadn't ended up in the pound . . . I mean . . .
if they hadn't cleaned it out . . . it would have ended up . . .
dead?"

Soneri was pleased to have found the key to arousing the
prosecutor's attention, and so raised the stakes to keep him in
a state of alarm. "I do fear these animals will all come to a bad
end. I can't see a drug dealer caring too much about the life of
a dog."

"I doubt it!'

"If you give me authorisation, I'll continue with these inquiries," the commissario said without hesitating, already certain of
the reply. "I'll request warrants, if it becomes necessary."

"Any time. Keep me informed," Piccirillo said, almost in a
rage.

Soneri felt the cold as soon as he ended the conversation.
Inside the car, motionless in the dark, he seemed to disappear
into the mist. In that hiding place, he saw another car which
he thought he recognised pass by. It was Zunarelli's. He made
an attempt to follow it, but after a while it turned off up a
narrow road which perhaps led to a village or a farm. At that
point, so as not to arouse suspicion, Soneri gave up. He noted
his approximate location, intending to return and investigate
further.

The mist had the power to cancel memory and experience. The
road he was driving along, however familiar, seemed as new to
him as the one Zunarelli had taken. He was doubtful at every
junction, and had to trust to intuition, feeling that a mistake
would send him on the wrong track. When he arrived at Via
Montanara, he was glad to make out the milky halo of the city
at the end of a journey which seemed to him both metaphor
and embodiment of the investigation.

Later, at home, he was not sure how to reply to Angela when she asked him how things were going. "I understand," she cut him off. "If that's the way it is, it's better to leave you to rise in peace, like a loaf of bread in the oven."

IO

SONERI NEEDED TIME to think, and so after dinner he went out for a walk. He had been talking to Angela about the secretiveness of politicians, which seemed to him even more entrenched than that of criminals.

"Criminals defy the law, while politicians believe they dominate it," she said.

The night set the commissario's mind racing. As he walked, he wondered about the servile cronies who orbited the mayor and his party, like that Giovetti who had shown himself willing to take a part in weaving a screen of plausible circumstances to cover Corbellini's flight. The whole city seemed to Soneri to be repressed, too cowardly to express its indignation. Parma had buried its rebellious past and was now incapable of rising above petty rancour. It had moved from riots in the Piazza to anonymous letters or futile squabbles on the Internet, as reported to him by Juvara, where people traded insults from behind a mask of anonymity without ever looking each other in the face.

These thoughts brought him once again to the Montebello district. The frozen snow made the embankment dyke look like a sparkling turret. Surrounded by the darkness, which gave him the impression of travelling in mid-air, he carried on walking in the cold, searching for Valmarini in the circles of light under the lamp posts. He decided to ring the doorbell, and, just as he was about to turn away, he heard the door click open. "Come up," was all the painter said on the intercom, as though it could be no-one but Soneri.

All this reinforced the sense of mystery which took hold of him each time he approached Valmarini and that house of his, which seemed to be inhabited only by night. The door had been left ajar. Soneri pushed it open and went in, greeted by a darkness which seemed more dense than the darkness of the riverbank. He heard the voices of people in conversation and allowed himself to be guided by them into the drawing room with the bay window, where a pair of lamps spread a warm light the colour of Malvasia wine. He picked out a man staring at him from a sofa in the corner, a somewhat squat figure, with ruddy cheeks, a swollen stomach but no neck, like a frog.

"Welcome," Valmarini said. He turned to the stranger and said, "Here's another noctambulant."

Without rising or uncrossing his legs, the man stretched out his hand. "Ugolini. I'm another of this company of owls."

The commissario turned to the painter. "We've adopted this name because we like the dark," Valmarini said with a smile.

Ugolini remained serious, and it was only then that Soneri realised he was facing the industrialist who was leader of the city's Right. He was gripped by a certain unease, which Valmarini noted immediately. "Take a seat. The great thing about these nightly occasions is the element of surprise. You might happen to spend night after night on your own, or else several guests will arrive with no prior notice. This evening, I've been lucky."

From the sofa, the industrialist kept his eyes on him, causing the commissario some embarrassment. Dondolo's head, with his watery, imploring eyes, peeped out from under the table.

Ugolini raised his glass to toast Valmarini's health. "To the artist!"

"To the forger," he replied, warding off the compliment.

"No, to the artist," Ugolini insisted. "True or false, that's an old question. We've left that world behind us," he added, with a theatrical flourish.

"You're flattering me, but I keep my feet on the ground. I was born in the last century. I attended the Academy, and I know what real art is."

"Nonsense! Reality is manufactured, and it imposes itself by convincing and dominating public opinion. Everything else is piffle. Listen to people when they talk. In most cases, they express opinions that have no basis whatsoever, but that doesn't change the fact that everyone is persuaded of what they say. Are your paintings forgeries? Who says so? The people who have seen them are certain they're authentic and that's all that matters. No-one will ever be able to change the opinion of my guests once I've got them on my side. I've even had to endure a couple of burglaries, so even thieves believe I have a treasure in my house."

"It's clear your guests have never been to a museum with any of the original works on display," Soneri said.

"A museum! Who goes to museums nowadays? Museums, theatres, galleries, libraries, these are all things that are kept going because the State throws money at them, but no-one actually goes there anymore, and those few who do are all ancient. Within twenty years the whole caravanserai will grind to a halt. Everything will be online. Who cares if some decrepit old critic accuses me of having a forgery in my house? I can line up ten thousand people who think differently. Is it not the same when we go to the supermarket? Every time we buy something, we're certain it's the best there is. It's not true, but the important thing is to believe it."

Soneri began to feel hot under the collar, but at the same time Ugolini's polemic aroused his curiosity, because it went well beyond the limits of his own imagination. It struck him as new and disconcerting, like some adolescent transgression.

"Don't forget the reality principle," Valmarini interrupted him with a laugh. "After all, you *are* a businessman."

"That's exactly the point. You do business by keeping your emotions in check. A piece of merchandise is a talisman, and possession of it is a desire appeased, not an economic transaction. Tastes impose themselves, like opinions. It's slow, patient work, and success is obtained by flattery."

"Flattery?" Valmarini questioned.

"Of course. There's no need for sacrifice. Quite the contrary, the trick is to make everything seem easy, to enhance pleasures, to appeal to laziness and the infantile sloth which nestles in each one of us. Adam and Eve were chased out of Eden, weren't they? We all have inside us this damnable wish to get back."

Soneri listened in silence, thinking again of Bergossi's words about the capacity of politicians to invent facts, and felt lost and naive.

"This has nothing to do with true or false," Valmarini objected.

"You're wrong there. Truth, assuming the word still has any meaning, requires research and effort and, let me add, futile effort." These words were addressed to the commissario, who merely shrugged. "The Apostles themselves say the same thing: truth is unattainable. It's hard to understand why everyone keeps searching for this chimera."

"There are demonstrable truths. It'd be easy to prove that my paintings are forgeries."

"If you say so! You know perfectly well that nowadays a good fifty per cent of critics would confuse your work and the original. Truth is provisional."

"You're a sophist," Valmarini said.

"I am unconstrained by preconceptions, and that makes me a free man. I'm not hobbled the way you are. What's the good of intellectuals and their lofty reflections? Industrial processes impose quantity as the dominant parameter. If I succeed in convincing thousands of individuals, I couldn't care less if the opinion I impose is false. The so-called guardians of truth will have to face up to the fact of quantity. Here democracy is a great advantage. Assuming for a moment that true and false exist, a vote for what is true counts as much as a vote for something false."

"That's an unquestionable truth, as shown by the election of Corbellini," Valmarini sneered, giving every impression of enjoying himself.

"Corbellini is a good actor who knows how to play his part. He's got looks, youth and glamour on his side. Nowadays there's no getting away from image."

"And where has he ended up?" Soneri asked.

"That's a question I should be putting to you. I make my contribution to the party, but I have no control over private lives. Do you have any idea what's become of him?"

"No. And if I had, I wouldn't tell you."

It was Ugolini's turn to shrug his shoulders. "In any case, it would only be one more opinion."

"Unlike you, I have the duty to provide proof."

"Are you standing on your dignity? At the end of the day, all your work ends up being debated in court – that's to say, in a play which establishes who has the best lawyer."

"True enough. Very few of the rich and powerful end up in prison," Valmarini said.

"Anyway, I like you. I am fond of combative individuals," Ugolini said, his demeanour taking an unexpectedly good-humoured turn. "If you were a businessman, you'd be a success."

The commissario glowered at him. Ugolini's conciliatory tone betrayed the overbearing self-confidence of a man who considered himself untouchable. Soneri changed tack. "Does Zunarelli work for you?"

"I throw him bits and pieces that need boning."

"You keep him going?"

"Like all of us contractors, but we also fight among ourselves."

"Being in politics helps. It gives you greater protection," Soneri said.

"I'm less hypocritical than those who pay the parties. You're better off on the inside. What's the point of politics now? Are there any ideas to curb self-interest? If not, why not let the splendid, putrid swamp that is the market triumph? There, law is suspended, and at the end the strongest, the most intelligent or the most cunning come out on top."

"Why don't you just say 'the biggest bastards'?" Soneri said sarcastically.

"Don't be such a moralist. Like it or not, these are the dominant values of today. The West has stopped making war, but it has not forgotten cynicism and callousness. All it has done is disseminate them on the streets of our cities, between the buildings, even on the landings and in the bedrooms. I've no time for those prissy little souls who pretend not to have noticed."

"There are some who have noticed and who do stand up against all this," the commissario said.

"And in the name of what? Equality? Justice? Throughout history, anyone who upheld those ideas had to impose them in opposition to human nature, and in the process transformed himself into a tyrant. No, it just doesn't work! Men wish to tear each other apart, and when those fine souls burdened with ideals realise they're in a minority, there's nothing left for them but to defend equality and liberty with a gun. What a strange destiny, don't you think? To achieve equality, you've got to make yourself superior to your neighbour, to transform yourself into a tyrant, in other words, to dominate by reneging on your principles. And in that case, isn't this mercantile bordello better, because here each and every individual has at least the illusion of rising to power one day in pursuit of his own chimera? Isn't that what they call the American dream?"

"I dream of being a great painter," Valmarini said, attempting to take some of the heat out of the debate.

"And you are," Ugolini said, raising his glass in a triumphant salute, giving Soneri the impression that he was a bit tipsy. He was displaying a level of exhilaration that went beyond the natural limits of exuberance.

"I don't deny that I've made the effort," Valmarini said.

"No statement is ever true or false. The difference lies in the conviction with which it is delivered. The U.S.A. made war on Iraq after telling the world that it had weapons of mass destruction. It was not true, but what does that matter? A majority of parliamentarians in Italy swore against all the evidence that a Moroccan girl was the niece of the President of Egypt. So what? Will history reverse it? The only certainty is that those who stated things which were not true spoke with greater force and conviction than those who opposed them in the name of truth. But what is truth if it is denied? Nothing at all!"

"That means I have strong convictions when I try to bring out the truth," Soneri said, becoming increasingly irritated.

"We'll see if that's enough for you, but if you're so keen to carry on your noble struggle, let me say that I respect you."

"I don't get the impression that your party is making much of an effort to search for Corbellini."

"The party will deal with the emerging political problem, but takes no interest in private life."

"You think this is a purely private issue?"

"And do you think that if someone decides to disappear it's an exlusively political issue?"

Soneri said nothing, and at that moment Dondolo started whimpering as though he was tired. "He's troubled. He hears something that we can't," Valmarini said. The dog had got up and was looking out of the window at the darkness with the eyes of a blind man.

"He feels a call and would like to launch himself into that great unknown," Ugolini said, indicating the night outside. "We do the same. We follow our instincts and believe in them as we believe in our faith. We don't care about all the rest."

He took a sip of his wine and refilled his glass. It was now clear that the alcohol had gone to his head. "Painter! I want a painting for next month. I don't care who you imitate. My guests always need a new topic for discussion, and a painting will serve that purpose for a whole evening."

The commissario got to his feet. "Don't go yet," Valmarini begged him.

"Aren't you enjoying yourself? We were just getting warmed up," the industrialist said.

"I'm only a half-nocturnal animal. I live only part of the night. I'll leave the rest to you."

Valmarini escorted him to the door. "Does he disgust you?" he asked.

"Does he not disgust you?"

"When he's been drinking, he goes a bit too far – although even when he's sober he's every bit as cynical. However, he's my best customer and he pays very well."

"If he pays you so well ..."the commissario said with a shrug.

"Don't be too severe. I agree with you. He doesn't convince me at all. He admires my hand, which he knows will provide him with objects to cultivate his vanity."

"As long as he's useful to you," Soneri said as he went out into the freezing cold. Once outside, he heaved a sigh of relief and suddenly found the trees, the houses and the streets extremely reassuring. He felt as though he had inhaled a lungful of opium, but he now had a clearer idea of the political world which surrounded Corbellini. He had lacked sufficient imagination to grasp it fully before. Something useful had emerged from Ugolini's alcoholic haze. Zunarelli did work for him and the commissario had the impression that he was not merely a supplier. He had the idea that Ugolini had him in the palm of his hand.

He walked home in the silence of the night. The conversation had left him in a state of unusual insecurity, wavering inside himself in the same way as he slid about on the frozen pavement. When he got home, he went to bed filled with regret at not being with Angela. He would have embraced her like a drunk hugging a pillar.

All that night, he was tormented by a gnawing curiosity. Where had Zunarelli been heading that evening when he had drawn level with him without being aware of his presence? The moment he awoke, he had a quick breakfast and got into his car. So as not to be disturbed he did not switch on his mobile, even though he knew this would send the magistrate and Capuozzo, the Chief of Police, into a rage. After driving for about ten minutes alongside the Baganza embankment, he emerged into the countryside at its most elegant, like a bride in a white lace dress. To get on the right road, he drove through the village and turned back as he had done the previous night. Light changed the world: no place was ever the same by day as by night. When he found his road, a drive of no more than few hundred metres led to a huddle of houses with no name.

There was a van parked outside one house, and a sign on the gate which read: LAUDADIO S.R.L.

The commissario could never understand what led him to have suspicions before he had reasoned the matter out. It was almost involuntary, like blinking – or perhaps it was an amalgam of acts of reasoning which had remained inert, waiting for the right agent to unleash the necessary chemical reaction. The fact was that everything now appeared totally clear to him. He took out his mobile and dialled Piccirillo's number.

"I may have discovered where the dogs end up," he said, trying to strike the magistrate at his weakest point.

"Where? Where?" The magistrate sounded anxious.

"I think it's a slaughterhouse."

"My God! What beasts!"

"Of the two-legged variety, yes indeed," he said, sensing that Piccirillo was now drained of every residue of prudence. "You ought to issue search warrants now."

"If you think so."

"We've got to stop them at all costs, or else the massacre will continue. This is big business," Soneri said, indulging in a touch of showmanship.

The magistrate gave way. "Alright. You'll have everything you need by this evening."

Soneri set off back to the police station, and as soon as he got to his office he called Isernia, the head of the narcotics squad. "Make preparations. One of these nights, we're going to spring a surprise."

"Whose party are we going to?"

"Someone who's probably disembowelling dogs as we speak."

"Good Lord! My dogs will tear him limb from limb."

"Serve him right. I'll let you know when the time comes."

Nanetti showed up at that moment. "I thought I'd bring

you the final results of the tests on the fingerprints in person, and seeing as it's nearly one o'clock ..."

"Good of you to remind me – I'm starving," Soneri said, picking up his briefcase. He turned to Juvara: "I want to know everything about this Laudadio firm: where they go, what they transport, where they deliver to and the places where they take the waste food."

"Everything's on the Internet," the inspector said.

Soneri looked at him doubtfully. "It isn't, but it will have to do." He went out, followed by Nanetti. "Well then? What can you tell me about those fingerprints?"

"There's not much to add, except that they're fairly recent."

"What do you mean? How recent?"

"A week, ten days at the most."

Soneri digested this new fact, trying to work out if this information should modify the ideas he already had in his mind, but could not decide one way or the other. As he turned his thoughts to Zunarelli and the raft of suspicions he evoked, his colleague suggested they eat in the *Milord*.

"Better go to Bruno's. It's quicker and I've a lot to do."

"I anticipate some sort of scene. Should I alert the media?"

"I don't know," Soneri said with a shrug. "I'm not quite convinced myself."

"If you're talking about Zunarelli, I too am of the mind that he's mixed up in the whole business in some way or other."

"I agree, but the only way is to be daring. I think we can only make progress with some surprise manoeuvre."

"It depends how daring you want to be."

"Zunarelli's been lying from the outset and I think he's covering up for someone else. There was something ambiguous about his closeness to Romagnoli, which might seem like an act of charity if he wasn't such a vile individual and so obviously self-serving."

"In any case, Romagnoli died of exposure. Of that, there's no possible doubt."

The commissario nodded. "That still leaves the question of the dogs."

"The dogs?"

"Someone's been marching up and down along the riverbank of the Parma and the Baganza with dogs, and the footprints go as far as San Vitale. A couple of days ago, one of the animals got lost in the Montebello district. It was brought to the local authority compound where it was found to be stuffed full of cocaine."

"And you think that . . ."

"An ingenious system of transport, wouldn't you say? Until now, this stuff was swallowed by human beings who then shat it out in a toilet with a bidet, but when that game was exposed, they tried the same thing with dogs. In all probability, they're brought in from abroad as hunting dogs. They're perfect. If they're sniffed at by other dogs trained in anti-drug operations, nobody would pay any heed because dogs sniff other dogs. I think they're nothing more than throw-away containers."

Without even taking an order, Bruno knew what to prepare. A wave of his hand was sufficient to make a plate of *culatello*, *coppa* and *spalla* together with some chunks of Parmesan and a bottle of Fortana del Taro appear on the table. They began eating, and with slices of salami pinched between his fingers, Nanetti performed liturgical gestures which looked like a kind of thanksgiving to the pig.

"So the drugs end up in San Vitale?" he asked.

"And that's the risky part. I think that's the terminal, but it's possible they load the dogs onto a van and take them somewhere else, to some cottage nearby. But then you'd need a lot of equipment – to slit open their bellies, I mean."

Nanetti shuddered. "Well, with all the carving knives going about, you could do worse."

"There's just one piece missing to complete the jigsaw puzzle. If Juvara is able to confirm . . ."

"You'll be able to checkmate Zunarelli? What are you looking for there? The cocaine? They can make that disappear in a flash."

"No, some side-effect," Soneri said vaguely.

Nanetti turned up his nose. "Hold on. It's better to wait than take a false step. You know what our environment is like. They've just about put up with you so far, but you tread on shit and they'll crucify you."

"I met Ugolini last night. You know who I'm talking about?"

"Who doesn't! He got into politics to avoid bankruptcy and keep his business afloat."

"He's convinced that the important thing is to believe in what you say and do, without caring about whether it has any basis in fact."

"In the borderland he inhabits between politics and business, maybe that's the way it is."

"There is some truth in what he says, and I've convinced myself that some daring is necessary to unblock certain situations."

"So you're going to push on?"

"I'm waiting for confirmation from Juvara."

"You might be right, but I'd hold off, not least because I don't see what all of this has to do with the Corbellini case."

"I don't either, but I've got the impression that it's all one big family business, with Ugolini manipulating everything in the party, Corbellini dealing with things in the City Council, and Zunarelli held by the throat by Ugolini. Business and politics, the same old story."

"If you fish about there, you'll always find something, but you know those waters are mined."

"That's exactly why you've got to avoid a frontal attack. It's essential to catch them at their dirty work, and fortunately there's plenty of it. I'm going to keep away from all the grubby games they play in politics."

"We're going to be enemies of the people. The citizens of Parma have cheered this lot on."

"And we're going to break their balls. People like me who believe in the rule of law feel more and more isolated. How can a policeman live in a world of thieves and their accomplices? I feel like throwing it all in and taking up surfing the web, like everybody else."

"Forget it. In no time at all you'd end up in the mouth of some shark."

They consoled themselves with the *culatello* and the Fortana, and said no more until Soneri's telephone rang.

"I've made those inquiries, sir."

"And?" the commissario said.

"The Laudadio company belongs to one Carmelo Giacalone, who comes from Castellammare di Stabia, and whose business is waste food disposal."

"We knew that already, but what kind of waste?"

"A bit of everything, from refectories to supermarkets, but he works principally for the salami-curing factories in the area around San Vitale, Sala Baganza and Felino."

"In other words, what does he take away?"

"Entrails, pigskins, animal fat and bones from hams."

"Where does he deliver them?"

"I'm not entirely clear about this. A lot of the discards go to the Carosel cattle-fodder plant on Via Emilia just beyond San Pancrazio, but I'm not too sure about the rest."

Soneri thanked the inspector and dialled Isernia's number.

"Get ready. We're going to pay a visit this evening. Maybe two."

"When you're involved, it's normally something major."

"I'm not totally sure, but it might well be."

"You've made up your mind?" Nanetti said, when the commissario ended the call.

"If it all goes belly-up I'll have wasted my time, but I couldn't give a damn about what my colleagues think."

II

HE SWITCHED OFF his engine in the piazza in front of the
trattoria Il Fiore. The sky looked like a Venetian stucco ceiling, and among the woods which darkened the hilltops, bright
strips of clay stood out like the first signs of baldness. Soneri rolled down the window and lit his cigar. Before he had
inhaled twice, the darkness drew in on the undulating horizon.
The commissario turned to look at the road which swept down
from Val Baganza and noticed that the mist had pursued him,
enveloping everything, but he saw Isernia's vehicle approach
through it. The head of the narcotics squad had brought along
his deputy Pilotti, a tall, swarthy, imperturbable man.

"How do we go about this?" Isernia asked.

"We'll pay a visit to the boning outfit first," Soneri said.

They proceeded with caution. The commissario set off down
the road for Parma, then turned into the courtyard he already
knew, braked and got out. His colleagues jumped out with their
dogs. Soneri saw the men struggle to hold back the animals as
they pulled and tugged at their leads, sniffing the ground in a
state of great agitation. They marched into the building, taking
Zunarelli by surprise. He turned sharply, dropping his knife
on the block in front of him.

"What the hell . . . ?" he stammered. The commissario paid
no heed as he strode past him with the officers and dogs into

the back premises, which were divided into a number of rooms. The dogs, in growing excitement, looked around in every direction as though they were in a cage full of birds. They stopped in front of a locked door, where Zunarelli joined them.

"What do you think you're playing at?" he barked.

"Open up," Soneri said.

The man obeyed, muttering as he did so that they had no right to do this and that he would be taking appropriate steps.

The decisive steps were taken by Isernia and Pilotti, who burst into a kind of laboratory with a large table in the centre, surrounded by half-empty shelves that gave the impression of an unfurnished shop. They were not fully in charge, since while they were waiting for Soneri to make his move, the dogs dragged them forward, yelping as though stung by a tarantula. The two officers did their best to restrain them, but the dogs were barking and baring their teeth as though they could sense invisible threats all around them. Pilotti, with his heavy bulk, managed to keep his dog under control, but Isernia found himself dragged across a floor reeking of animal fat.

"They're terrified. There's something in here which has really got to them," Pilotti said, without losing any of his composure.

It took some time to calm the dogs down, and even then their eyes continued to express alarm. With meticulous care, Soneri examined the shelves, some holding hams waiting to be boned, others pieces of equipment. He opened a small cupboard and pulled out a pair of dog leads. On a hook, he found a muzzle and some collars.

"I thought you said you didn't like dogs," he said to Zunarelli.

"I didn't say that. I had one for a couple of years."

"Maybe he was as foxy as you. This is the third time you've lied to me, and I think you're still hiding the best part."

"I'm not hiding anything. It's all here. You can search as long as you like."

"Why do you keep these things in your house?" the commissario said, holding up the leads.

"I've already told you. It was a long time ago."

Meantime, Isernia went through the laboratory, pulled along by his dog who was following a scent. There were some areas where the dogs were especially tenacious, sniffing wildly. Once, they scraped at a shelf, but did not come up with anything.

"Take a good look, look all you like," Zunarelli said, as though issuing a challenge. "I've no idea what you're after, but go ahead. Just don't let the dogs pee on the hams."

For half an hour, they continued searching high and low, but the more time went by, the more insolent Zunarelli grew. "You want to look over the house as well?"

After a while, Soneri was forced to tell him to shut up, since he was making such a nuisance of himself. "For God's sake, cut it out!" he said, raising his voice, but he had to admit to himself that the risk of executing the search warrant had not paid off. He realised, as he thought back to Nanetti's warnings, that he had started on the wrong foot, and saw defeat on the faces of the two officers from narcotics as they came back to him, despondent.

They made their way out, past Zunarelli's sneering face. Only Pilotti, famous for never losing his composure, managed to say goodbye civilly, as though addressing a next-door neighbour.

"All too often, that's the way it is. The dogs get a scent in their nostrils, but the goods are not to be found," Isernia said.

"You think they really smelled something?"

"Definitely. I know them. And that's not all. They sensed something else and were terrified by it."

"What could it have been?"

"In my opinion, it was the smell of the blood of other dogs."

"Yes, I too am certain this is the place where they were slaughtered," Soneri said.

"There certainly was something, and maybe there still is. I think we were just unlucky. Several times, I've felt certain I was in the right place and the dogs have confirmed it for me, but unfortunately their evidence is not admissible."

"How many things we're sure of but just can't prove. Anyway, we haven't finished our work yet," the commissario said.

They got into their cars with Zunarelli looking on, shaken but triumphant. As he drove out of that courtyard where so many mysteries remained, Soneri looked back at him standing in the glow of the light from the house.

It was a struggle to find the road again, but he got there at last and made his way between the parallel ditches on either side. An illuminated globe marked the gate to the Laudadio residence. He yelled over the intercom: "Police! Open up!" As he made his entrance, followed by the narcotics squad car, lights went on automatically to frame the mist rising from the valley. A woman watched him from a window on the ground floor, while a man in slippers came out and strode towards him.

Soneri held out the warrant. "Pasquale Laudadio?"

"In person," Laudadio said, in a tone of aggressive astonishment.

"Giacalone is the owner of this company and you're the manager, right?"

The man laughed. "Giacalone was the previous owner. I've replaced him, but the changeover has not yet been registered in the Chamber of Commerce. They're always a bit behind."

"We're here to carry out a search of your property," the commissario announced, indicating his colleagues with the dogs.

"Yes, I guessed as much. Go right ahead," Laudadio said, seemingly compliant, as though he'd been expecting something of the sort. In the doorway, his wife was staring at them with undisguised hostility.

Isernia and Pilotti went into a warehouse filled with large metal containers, each containing waste materials whose stench hung in the enclosed, stagnant air.

"You don't get a lot of work," the commissario said, noticing that the containers were all but empty.

"This sort of stuff goes off quickly, so I can hardly keep it at home. I've got to make a trip in the lorry even for a couple of quintals," the man whined, keeping his distance.

Soneri made a sign to him to be quiet. His colleagues had disappeared among the partitions in the warehouse. "Is there anything in the lorry?"

Laudadio nodded. "Thirty quintals of pig bones to be dumped tomorrow morning."

"We're going to have to rummage about in them," Soneri said.

"For God's sake! There's a mountain of the stuff. What are you looking for?"

"Corpses. What else would you find among bones?"

The man stretched out his arms and then let them fall to his sides, giving every sign of nervousness. Isernia and Pilotti came back out. The commanding officer shook his head and the dogs seemed exceptionally quiet.

"Empty the contents out," Soneri ordered Laudadio.

"They're on metal pallets.

"Empty out the lot. We've got to check it."

Laudadio, livid with hatred, climbed into the cabin, cursing under his breath the commissario, the police and even the dogs. Seconds later he switched on the engine, clambered onto the back of the lorry and began to manoeuvre the small crane behind the driver's seat. As soon as the contents of the first skip tumbled out, the two dogs began sniffing about, but seemed more interested in the bones and fragments of meat than in possible traces of drugs. They appeared to be torn between the instinct to lick or bite and the task for which they had been trained. Fifteen containers later, the courtyard was a mountain of bones that gave off an unbearable stench of decomposition. Isernia asked him to let down one side of the lorry and climbed aboard. In a corner on its own there was a pile of various types of waste. As Pilotti began digging among them with a spade, one of the dogs jumped in front of the officer, stuck his nose in and began scratching away. Suddenly, he emitted a wail and clambered into the opening he had made. A paw appeared followed by a tail and finally the whole body. It was the carcass of a medium-sized dog, perhaps a breed of hunting dog. Pilotti pulled it out and showed it to Isernia. The body was rigid and desiccated.

"So, there was a carcass there after all," Soneri said to Laudadio.

"That? The Council landed that one on me. You do know that dead animals are a special category of refuse?"

"What's the Council got to do with it?"

"Some public-spirited citizen found this dead dog and reported it to the police. They brought it round to me and ordered me to dispose of it as special organic refuse. I'll be doing this at my own expense, seeing how that lot pay!"

"We'll take care of it," Soneri said. He was already seeing reality dissolve as had already happened too often in the course of this inquiry. There was always an alternative explanation of the facts to overturn his conclusions. He was not yet old enough to escape the trap of optimism.

They wrapped the carcass in a big rubbish bag, but as they were about to put it in the van the dogs began to howl loudly and seemed on the point of mutiny. In the silence of the night, their laments were so pathetic as to be unbearable.

"Give it to me," the commissario said. He opened the boot of his Alfa Romeo and put the carcass inside. On his way back, he called Cattani.

"I'm going to have to trouble your friendly vets once again," he said.

"Another stuffed dog?"

"This one, rather than being stuffed, seems to have been emptied out. This time we'll need an autopsy."

"You didn't make it in time?"

"Far too late, if my hypothesis is right, although I have to say that all week my hypotheses have been off the mark."

"Bring it round when you get here. I'll wake my vets up early tomorrow morning. Where did you find it?"

"On the back of a lorry belonging to a man who disposes of organic refuse. He claims the police in Sala Baganza delivered it to him. It was dead when it was found by somebody or other."

"Is that likely?"

"He seemed sure of what he was saying, but it's my duty to be suspicious."

"Well, it could be. There's no shortage of dogs run over by cars or poisoned."

"The first thing is to ascertain if it's got some chip on it, and what kind of trauma it had suffered. Are your vets capable of establishing that?"

"Of course! What are you getting at? They're on top of their game."

"So much the better. You know how it is. I don't know if there's such a thing as an animal anatomist."

"There is, there is, and he'll probably be more use to you than your colleagues in forensics."

Meantime, he had arrived back at the police station. He said goodbye to Cattani, telling him to expect the arrival of the carcass within half an hour. He called a squad car and handed over the bag to the officers, who turned up their noses in disgust: "Commissario, this thing is rotten."

He called Musumeci. "I've got a delicate piece of work for you."

The inspector mumbled something incomprehensible, knowing that a premise like that invariably signified trouble ahead.

"I want you to check on the movements of a lorry," Soneri said, dictating the number plate. "A white Iveco Turbo. The name of the company, *Laudadio*, is written on the door."

"When you put it like that, it seems I'll be tailing it for days!"

"No, listen. Do a tour of the dumps and the producers of cattle fodder from food waste. Juvara will give you a list in two minutes," the commissario assured him, exchanging a conspiratorial glance with the inspector standing in front of him. "It'll take you no time at all."

After hanging up, he assured himself that the dog's carcass had already been delivered, then told Juvara to find the addresses Musumeci required. He prepared to go out and was almost at the door when the telephone rang.

"Commissario, where are we with this story of the dogs?" Piccirillo enquired apprehensively.

"I found one, but it was already dead."

"The bastards!" the prosecutor swore.

"However, I don't yet know if things are the way you and I imagine them to be. This animal was found in the countryside and handed over to the police. We'll know more tomorrow. I've had it taken to the vets."

"Good," Piccirillo said.

"I'll continue working along the same lines," Soneri said, secure in the knowledge that he had got on the right side of the magistrate.

"Certainly, certainly, keep me informed."

At last he managed to get away, pushing past groups of colleagues in the corridors. He couldn't stand being in the police station for more than a few hours, with all those quasi-Fascists drooling over women and motorbikes, calling freakishly attired left-wing students "apes". And anyway, Angela was expecting him. With her, he could rediscover his true self; with her he would be lost and disorientated among the multiple roles he was required to play: so many costumes without a body. He could speak to Angela in dialect, share their past experiences, recall places and circumstances in which they had been happy together. Once, all these things could have been taken for granted, but with time he had moved away from the people he would have shared them with, and now only Angela was left. This was the most upsetting sign of middle age: the dimming of one's own world, fading like a fresco discoloured day by day by the lime.

12

STRETCHED OUT ON a sofa after dinner with Angela, ignoring the television droning away in the background, Soneri turned the conversation to cuisine. She had purchased everything in a delicatessen and Soneri expressed the view that the women who prepared these take-away dishes were the final repositories of tradition. "They're the only ones who know how things should be done. When they die out, we'll be left with nothing but American rubbish."

"I still know how to cook," Angela said.

"But you don't have the time. Our drive for efficiency cheats us of the best things in life, and impoverishes us by allowing us just a single role. If you tried to make gnocchi, you'd make a complete hash of it."

"You underestimate me, and anyway my mashed potatoes are a real treat."

"I'm speaking for myself as well. I wouldn't be able to change a flat tyre."

"Nothing is ever really lost. There's always someone who takes advantage of an opportunity, and the fact that someone like me doesn't stand over a hot stove anymore has given many other women an opening in life. It's the same with undertakers. Nobody nowadays has the humility to do that kind of work, but those who have taken it up get rich."

"What have undertakers got to do with it? There's no faster way to spoil a good meal."

"It's just an example. Did you know that L'Eterna has won the contract for the management of about fifteen Council cemeteries to the east of the mountain?"

"I didn't know anything about it."

"Neither did I, until some guy turned up in my office wanting to raise an action against the company because it had failed to respect a contract for the maintenance of the family tomb."

"Quite right too, but what's that got to do with anything?"

"It's got everything to do with it, because now L'Eterna has a monopoly. They don't give a damn about anybody and they can charge what they like. If you want to die, you'll have to pay a higher price, otherwise you've no choice but to get cremated."

"A lovely example, but if you don't mind I'd rather pay a high price for a plate of *tortelli di zucca* than for a burial plot."

"I always told you to keep an eye on those people. I don't like that Petrillo one bit."

"I will keep an eye on him. Juvara says they're tied up with the camorra, but we haven't been able to prove it."

"Very often things that are clear to see can't be called by their name. It should be enough to ask how this Petrillo manages to invest so much. He's bought five hearses in one year and has a huge number of employees on his payroll – with a high turnover."

"Why would he want to invest in a sector like that?"

"Perhaps because he's certain it's recession-proof. Our mountain is full of old folk. If I were employed by some rating agency, I'd give him a favourable assessment."

"Alright, but it's on the sidelines."

"This is something you're going to have to try to understand. Why are they so keen on coffins? You say you're attracted by anomalies!"

"When it comes to hard cash, anomalies don't exist, and if they do there's a reason for it."

"That's another good reason for investigating what's behind the facade."

The commissario nodded, deep in thought. "Did that client of yours have any other complaints?" he asked.

"He says that no-one at L'Eterna answers the telephone, they make promises they never keep, they use the cemetery like their private property, they come and go and get on with their own deals."

"Which cemetery is it?"

"The one at Lagrimone, but as far as he knows they behave that way everywhere. He told me there's been a lot of activity around the graves and the burial slots in the cemetery walls. They move bodies about as if it's a work yard."

"They need permission from the family members."

"Of course, but nowadays that's often not the way of it, because many of the dead have been forgotten or have relatives who've moved away and no longer care."

Soneri muttered something indistinct and stared distractedly at nothing in particular until he was disturbed by the sound of his mobile. He recognised Piccirillo's number and instinctively looked at his watch. It was a quarter to midnight.

"Listen, something terrible has happened," the magistrate said in a shaky voice. He must have been aroused from his sleep. "The carabinieri in Sala Baganza have just informed me that they've found the body of that man who does the ham boning – Zunarelli."

"Murdered?"

"No, it seems he hanged himself."

"Seems?"

"He was found in his workshop hanging from a hook for sides of pork."

Soneri was struck by an overwhelming sense of guilt. He suspected that the search had disturbed the man's mental equilibrium and that his arrogant behaviour had been a front for some deep fear. He called Nanetti, and as he was informing him about what had happened, he realised he was reaching out not for a fellow policeman but a friend, perhaps in an effort to lift a burden from his own shoulders. He went out reluctantly and stood on the pavement waiting for his colleague to arrive. At night, the city lost its charm for people who had urgent business to attend to or who were moving across it with a definite purpose. The essence of those silent hours lay in the sleeping mystery of the city walls and the bell towers, and in not having any precise task in hand. In the company of Nanetti, who was irritated by the sudden emergency and was driving too fast, everything appeared normal and indifferent. At those moments, he discovered that the world was inside and not outside him, that the outside world was a pretext for awakening something inside.

"Who knows what was on his mind," Nanetti said.

"Whatever it was, I believe it was prompted by us," the commissario replied.

They spoke without meeting each other's eyes, their words sounding like isolated thoughts, or private considerations with coincidental connections.

"Is this getting to you?"

The commissario nodded in the darkness of the car, and his colleague picked up his meaning without taking his eyes off the road ahead and the oncoming headlights.

"It's nothing to do with us. Each person builds their own life, including their own end."

"Up to a point," the commissario said. "We are all victims and executioners – sometimes we aren't aware of it, but that doesn't lessen the seriousness."

They parked the car in the courtyard which by now Soneri knew very well. Piccirillo had not yet arrived and so the body was still where it had been discovered. Nanetti went in first, followed by Soneri. The maresciallo and another officer were on the door.

"When did it happen?"

"We don't know precisely when. We were informed at eleven o'clock," Maresciallo Pasqualuzzo replied.

"How did you find out?"

"An anonymous telephone call. The caller said that someone had hanged himself in the workshop next to the Ugolini salami factory, and then hung up."

"Male or female?"

"A man."

"Did you record the call?"

"Certainly, but no number came up. I think it came from a public place, maybe a phone box. One of the few left in this area is in the village."

"I imagine you already know if there's C.C.T.V. in the vicinity."

"There's one on the bank, but I'll need to check if the visual field takes in the phone box. Assuming that's where the call was made."

"Let's try them all," Soneri said.

He made his way into the workshop, disturbed by an unknown fear which he attempted to conceal by assuming a professional air, but faced with Zunarelli hanging there like a maturing ham, he had the impression that the firm ground which he was accustomed to walk on was giving way. The man's face was violet-coloured, his tongue protruded slightly between his lips, the thin rope had already cut into his skin and was covered with blood. The suspended arms seemed to belong to a sleeping body. He was barefoot, as though he had wished to leave the world without making any noise. Nanetti was already at work with cold professionalism, but Soneri preferred to go back outside. He turned to look one last time at the corpse so obscenely exposed, and imagined all the ups and downs of life which had, day after day, tied that noose round Zunarelli's neck. It seemed to him that no-one was free of his fate, and that perhaps there was a rope ready to choke him too.

He met Piccirillo at the exit. They exchanged no more than a glance as the magistrate went in. Soneri made a sign to indicate that he would be waiting for him outside. In the courtyard, a few people who did not dare go too close had gathered. The mortuary hearse pulled up, waiting for Piccirillo to come out.

"There doesn't seem to be any room for doubt," Piccirillo said.

"We'll see what the forensics squad say, but it seems quite clear to me as well."

"Did you expect this?" the magistrate asked.

The commissario shook his head. "No-one had charged him with anything yet."

"It's one of the risks of our profession. We always play the same notes, but for those who hear them they can be either insignificant or unbearable."

Soneri shook his head once again. "He was either a very sensitive man, or else he was deeply compromised."

"Or both. But the slaughterhouse . . ." The magistrate accompanied his words with a circular motion of his hand.

"I'm virtually certain it was here, but I don't have proof. Tomorrow morning I hope to be more precise."

"In any case, I've blocked off access to the house and workshop. We'll search the premises again."

The police doctor came out. He had established the time of death as being between 10.15 and 10.30. The rope had not broken the man's neck, so he had died of suffocation, the worst of all possible deaths. Half an hour later, Nanetti emerged, and at the same time the stretcher-bearers carried out Zunarelli in an aluminium coffin.

"What a terrible way to go. It seems to me out of all proportion," Nanetti said.

"Totally."

"In any case, there's no doubt. He took his own life."

"And seemingly there was no need. That's what I don't understand."

"Maybe we don't know enough about it. When people are not really criminals, it doesn't take much to shatter their nerves," Nanetti said.

Perhaps that was the truth. Soneri thought long and hard about it as the car swayed from left to right as it made its way slowly through the night. He had had no sleep, and was made uneasy by some ill-defined malaise. He sent Angela a text saying that, so as not to awaken her, he would not be returning to her house that night, and was dropped off by his colleague in Viale Rustici on the Lungoparma. He needed to walk around a bit to calm down. He went as far as Ponte Dattaro, turning into Via Montebello before going in the direction of the riverbank, where, he thought, he might bump into Valmarini. He placed his feet gingerly on the snow, passing through the freezing mist, his breath gathering around him like condensation from a warm sandwich. He stopped in front of the painter's door and went in. Dondolo shook himself when he saw him arrive, but did not bark. Valmarini was bent over the canvas he was working on.

"On your own this evening?" the commissario asked.

"It's not easy to find true night walkers. You're not really one."

"I wish I had your job."

"I'd never manage to do yours. Alarm clock set at dawn, the

obscene light brightening up a world of puppets all ready to start jumping up and down, running here and there, getting worked up into a frenzy to make sure their card is stamped on time."

"You've got to stamp yours as well," Soneri said, pointing to the canvas.

"He's got it into his head that he wants a Goya!" Valmarini said, referring to Ugolini. "I've told him that he's too famous an artist, that they could easily expose him, but he won't listen. Every day, he becomes a little bit more arrogant and ambitious."

"Just say no."

"I would deprive myself of a privileged point of view on the world," the artist sniggered.

"You mean Ugolini?" It was Soneri's turn to laugh.

"Don't undervalue him. He's a member of the ruling class."

"There's no chance of me undervaluing him! He's a very interesting specimen."

"Anyone who's retained a minimum of culture is liable to undervalue him. Perhaps it's unconscious, but they do it all the same. If we can't get beyond snobbery, we're going to end up humiliated. People like Ugolini have been so successful in vulgarising the world that we're left looking ridiculous."

"I feel ridiculous upholding a law which no-one respects anymore, but I'm not giving in. I'm in a minority, but sometimes minorities can carry the day. You, on the other hand, have opted for a subservient role."

"Don't start preaching at me! I'm on your side, but it's the side of the wicked stepmother, who out of cowardice prefers to do a deal with the enemy. If no-one is prepared to gather together those of us who are in opposition, each of us will have to set about saving himself. I think I live well, in a state of self-sufficiency in this house, in the dark and in silence, shutting out the noisy, senseless world of daytime. And if living well means I've got to please a cretin like Ugolini, so be it."

"Meanwhile, he establishes the line you've got to follow. The proclamation of victory read out in the face of the vanquished," Soneri said with a bitter laugh.

"Judging by the mess they're making of the world, in no time we'll all be vanquished. I won't be around to see it – and it's one spectacle I'll be glad to miss," the painter said, raising his eyes from the canvas and turning to face the commissario. "Ugolini is the most powerful man in the city. He's got it all in the palm of his hand, both politics and the economy."

"There's no such thing as politics anymore – just business."

"Let's say that he's involved in politics for the benefit of his business. It helps if you're into wheeling and dealing."

"I know. The Right is under his control. If all that's left is the market, it's as if we're being governed directly by businessmen."

"And that's much more the case in a city like Parma. Not that the rest of the world is all that different."

"In my opinion, he knows the truth about the disappearance of Corbellini."

"Very probably, but he's smart and he isn't going to let even half a word slip out. He's so used to keeping his cards close to his chest that he hides the truth even when he's drunk."

Valmarini carried on speaking as he worked on the canvas under a strong light that looked like the sun in May.

"You're not telling me the truth either. They've bought your silence," the commissario said.

The painter turned round sharply, and this time stared aghast at the commissario. "I'm being discreet, nothing more. I choose not to talk about Ugolini's business to you, and about your business to Ugolini."

"I understand you perfectly. If I were in your shoes, I'd do the same when dealing with unscrupulous people."

"I know what you're getting at. Most of the city bows and scrapes before him for convenience, and I'm one of them. That allows Ugolini and his ilk to stay in command, even if they're held in contempt."

"The contempt remains private, while their command is public. The effects are different. And anyway, contempt is the most common of feelings even among people like Ugolini. You must despise your partner so as not to see him as a danger. The only thing that matters is the chain of command."

"As far as that goes, Ugolini is on top and the rest below."

"Did you ever meet Corbellini in person?" Soneri asked.

"Yes, he came around here a few times with Ugolini."

"What kind of man is he? I mean, what kind of character?"

"He seemed insecure to me. If it's the case that painting always represents the transfiguration of time, Corbellini sums up the years we live in: pure image. As we empty ourselves, all that remains is the crust, and that has to at least be presentable. We'll never have politics again, only the spectacle of politics. No more politicians, only actors. It started with Reagan in America, remember? An actor. You need an actor capable of playing his part well. That way, everything becomes pure sales talk. Do you understand now why I live by night, well away from reality?"

"And he's convinced of the part he plays?"

"Who can say? He seemed quite content, that's all I can say. Better to be a mayor than a P.R. man in a discotheque."

"To be mayor, you need a thick skin."

"That might be the problem. You'd have to see the script written for him by people like Ugolini. Have you seen the character he plays? Pitiless, don't you agree?"

"Repulsive."

"There are worse. Murderers."

"There's not much difference."

"There is for me. It's much worse to kill someone than to get up to dirty tricks in politics."

"People like Ugolini kill as well, but in an indirect, underhand way, so that no-one notices."

"You know something? In spite of the vile things they get up to in this city, I can't manage to feel any resentment towards Corbellini himself."

"Why not? You think he's just a puppet?"

"He's a child of our times. Everyone wants to be famous. When they don't have the steel for it, they put their lives in other people's hands. It might be a T.V. producer, a politician, a godfather of some sort. Anything is acceptable as long as it gets you recognised on the streets, mentioned in the newspapers, interviewed as an expert on anything at all. Corbellini is a man of that ilk – a human facade, a mere mask."

"In that case, why has he disappeared? If his house is a stage, with the footlights full on, then why?" The commissario was putting the question to himself as much as to Valmarini.

"Perhaps he realised they'd dumped him. Maybe he had no other part to play, or it was the pressure of the debts accumulated by the Council . . . Who can say? The fact is that in politics, and in the parties today, one person is in charge and the rest aren't worth a fart. We've gone back to the feudal model and underneath, believe me, there's a putrid desire for a dictatorship emerging."

"That's an atavistic longing in this country, nostalgia for the severe father figure that we can all bow down to. We haven't grown up," Soneri said.

"Where have you got to with the inquiry? Do you understand what's going on?" the painter asked.

"No, not really. I'm busy with too many things, and I'm afraid I'm not getting anywhere. You know what it's like when there are politicians mixed up in it."

"The worst thing that can happen. Ugolini seemed to me very worried about this affair. Normally nothing affects him, but it's different this time."

"What makes you say that?"

"Whenever he has a drink, he keeps coming back to the subject."

"And what does he say?"

"Not a great deal, but it's significant that he's always banging on about it. Apart from women, he has no one fixed interest."

"Does he articulate even the slightest regret?"

"I don't believe so. The affair might be causing him some problems, but he's the sort of man who's always tied up in himself. He has such a huge ego that it prevents him from considering other people, unless they are useful or a threat."

"Corbellini couldn't be any use to him now that he's disappeared – from which I deduce that he sees him as a threat."

"That's the most probable hypothesis, but tread carefully. Ugolini is diabolical. It could be quite the opposite – that the mayor is more use to him now that he has disappeared. You know something? He's started to sell the works I paint as though they were authentic. He cheats people who are as ignorant as him."

"That could be a threat to you."

"No, I take precautions. I make him sign a contract where it's written that I'm providing him with forgeries. The responsibility for passing them on to someone else is his alone. He doesn't give a damn about it. He believes he's above the law. Meantime, he has a great time at his little parties – with all his whores."

"Now you're playing the moralist," Soneri said with a smile.

"I'm no moralist. But I still find them loathsome."

"Look, three-quarters of the population of Parma admires Ugolini and would love to be in his place. And they did vote for Corbellini!"

"I didn't," Valmarini said.

"What are we supposed to make of your private rebellion if you then pin sequins on his jacket?"

"I do my work, commissario, in the same way that you do yours, defending people like Ugolini," Valmarini replied acidly. "Don't you enforce the law they wrote for their own use and benefit?"

"That's as may be, but I can entangle them with a rope of their own making. That's already happened to one councillor."

"A scapegoat. People like Ugolini never go to jail. If they do fall into disgrace, they put a pistol in their mouth. That's the way they're made."

"Sooner or later they too end up in the dust," Soneri said, with a dose of fatalism.

"They never think of it. They want to win, by any means, and such is their conviction that they almost always succeed."

13

IT WAS LATE when he woke up. He decided not to go to headquarters that morning, but set off instead for the Veterinary School. He was so absorbed in his thoughts that he almost skidded on the ice in a badly lit street. The fright he got shook him to the marrow, but it was not fatigue which had distracted him so much as the thought of how the dog had died. He was haunted by the suspicion that he might have got it all wrong. If it turned out that the dog had indeed been run over by a car, he would be a laughing stock for years to come among his colleagues. Even Nanetti had warned him off with the jocular remark "You'll go down in history as the man who ordered an autopsy on a dog". However, it was no laughing matter, and he had asked everyone involved not to talk about it. He trusted Cattani but not the staff in the clinic. He could just see them gathered round the operating table sniggering and sneering over the shrivelled body of an insignificant animal.

The grim expression on his friend's face as he greeted him removed all his doubts. "Butchery! Carnage!" he said.

What was horrifying to Cattani was good news for the commissario, even if he was a little ashamed of himself when his colleague the vet explained what he had found.

"He'd been cut open along his belly, and his innards, as far as I could see, had been torn apart at multiple points. Part of the intestines is missing. Quite apart from the incisions, it looks as though he'd been attacked by a pack of hyenas which were chased off halfway through their meal."

"I hope that at the very least . . ." the commissario said.

"I hope so too. His skull was smashed by a blunt instrument," the vet said, implying that he would not bet on the compassion of the slaughtermen.

"They could at least have stunned him," Cattani said.

"The person who did this didn't even have the competence of a butcher. The cut is amateurish, exaggerated, and the animal seems to have been disembowelled haphazardly, probably in a rush," the vet said.

Soneri got up, thanked the vet and went out with Cattani.

"It looks quite clear to me. They used the dogs to bring drugs into the city. I've never seen anything like it," Cattani said.

"They're nothing if not inventive," Soneri said.

When he was in his car, chewing an unlit cigar, he made his report to Piccirillo and put his own thoughts in order. The magistrate listened in horror to the commissario's perhaps unnecessarily graphic account.

"I've no idea how they got them into Italy, perhaps quite simply by car," he said, attempting to reply to Piccirillo's compassionate curiosity. "They're made to swallow the stuff before setting off – most likely abroad, we don't know where yet. We don't even know where they cross the border, but they take advantage of open pathways, like the river bed, to get through the city. Once they reach their destination, the drugs are no doubt divided up into smaller packages and distributed through the usual channels."

"And the slaughterhouse was that workshop where the hams were boned?"

"I think so. Who would ever have imagined that cocaine was being extracted from dogs' bellies in a place like that?"

Piccirillo gave a low moan, uttering incomprehensible phrases of condemnation. If it were up to him, the people responsible would be facing nothing less than life imprisonment. "What we've got to do now is build up a strong case and catch every one of them," he said, in a vindictive tone. Just as the commissario was about to end the conversation, Piccirillo spoke up again. "Do you think Zunarelli took his life because he knew he'd been found out?"

"Probably," Soneri said, without having given the matter much thought.

A few minutes later, behind the wheel of his car, it occurred to him that Zunarelli was indeed the biggest mystery of all, and that his death confused things even further. He was at the heart of everything. He was involved with Romagnoli's death, with the drugs trade and even, through his relationship with Ugolini, with the world of politics, the same world which seemed to have swallowed up Corbellini. However, Soneri knew that all these thoughts were nothing more than conjectures, and that he would need a lot more to convince Bergossi.

"I've already told you that the problem is the mayor," Bergossi told him peremptorily on the telephone. "You've no idea what pressure I'm under from the Ministry. The Prefect and Capuozzo are going off their heads. For God's sake, they want news, anything that will make it seem that we're following a specific lead, that we're on the job!"

"I can just imagine," Soneri said, bottling up his anger inside himself. He hated all hierarchies because they exercised control from behind little desks and showed no interest in people like him who had to deal with the complexities of real life. "These shits, why don't they move their arses?" he bawled out as he drove on after ending the conversation. Some of those bigwigs at H.Q. or in the Prefecture had actually done the same job as him, but now from the safety of their offices, under the shelter of the national flag, with framed diplomas and the portrait of the President of the Republic on their walls, they derived pleasure from sending people scurrying all over the place. All too typical of the Italian mindset, he thought. "All you have to do is give a beret, a uniform or some stripes to an Italian and he'll instantly turn into an arrogant bully," Angela used to say, based on her experience of moving in a court system unchanged since the age of the Napoleon.

As he reached San Vitale, his mobile began ringing. It was Juvara. "I've got some news, sir. That mobile that used to ring during the night, you remember?"

"How could I not remember?"

"Of course. I just wanted to tell you I've identified the person it was stolen from. From the registry—"

"Who is it?" Soneri interrupted brusquely.

He heard pages being turned. "His name is Pontiroli, Raffaele Pontiroli."

"Damnation!" the commissario exclaimed. "He's president of the Laboriosa cooperative – the biggest in the Red employers' association."

"No, sir, it's not called that any longer. Its name is now 'New Job'. They changed it a year ago when it swallowed up the old Cooperativa Birocciai. They merged."

"Ah! 'New Job'! What a fantastic name!" Soneri said with ironic contempt. "English names are a sign of modernity."

"Anyway, someone pinched this state-of-the-art mobile from Pontiroli. I wonder when they'll grab the Rolex from his wrist."

"He's as rich as they come now. He drives about in a Porsche Cayenne and he's a member of the *Cavalieri di Malta*, one of the most exclusive clubs in the city. Ugolini and the mayor are often seen there as well," Juvara said.

"How the mighty communists have fallen! But how come you're so well informed about the most chic circles in Parma society?"

"There's nothing to it. All you have to do is consult Twitter. You do know you can find everything on the Internet, don't you?"

Soneri said nothing. He had clearly lost the first round, and as he was trying to get back on his feet, Juvara went on: "Some blogs say that the most important decisions for the city are taken at that club."

"And then they have the celebrations in the Council Chambers, just like a wedding."

"That's not all."

"What else? Women?"

"That's quite normal. Where there's cash ..."

"That's where you fall short," the commissario said, getting his own back.

"Could be. They're talking about cocaine."

"That's normal as well. No doubt they extracted it from the bellies of dogs."

"You think so?"

"I don't know, but the coincidence is suspicious. Parma isn't Milan, where they need a supply pipeline as wide as the one for gas!"

"We've got some good noses here as well."

"That's true enough. And they're sprouting like Pinocchio's."

He had arrived at the Town Hall in Sala Baganza, the local authority which took in San Vitale. The chief of the local police was a man with a drinker's belly and a ruddy complexion. He knew the story of the dog, and took Soneri into his office in the heart of the Rocca Sanvitale. He drew out a file and explained that someone had found the animal in the gutter near his house after he became aware of the stench. The police took over and delivered the carcass to the Laudadio company, who disposed of organic waste. The incident had been filed under "unsolved car accident".

By recounting this story, the officer had implicitly provided Laudadio with a cast-iron alibi, even if the report from the vets demonstrated that the animal had not been run over but slaughtered, perhaps with a club. Even if the fracture to the cranium was compatible with being run over by a car, that did not explain the disembowelment. As he left the office, Soneri realised that once again he had ended up in a cul de sac, but Pasqualuzzo got him out of it ten minutes later.

"You remember the C.C.T.V.?" he barked down the telephone.

"Of course I do!"

"It's captured a motorcycle at around 11:45 p.m., and the manoeuvre it was doing suggests it was setting off from the phone box. It comes into the field of vision from one side, do you understand? If it was simply going along the street, it would have followed a more rectilinear trajectory."

"You're sure?"

"Commissario, we're carabinieri, not amateurs! We've even tested our hypothesis with Officer Vincenzi's motorbike."

"But can you make anything out?"

"That's the point," came the maresciallo's slightly disappointed reply. "We can only read the first two letters and one number."

"That's something. Nowadays even scooters have to be registered."

"I'll be back in touch," Pasqualuzzo said.

The maresciallo had rescued him as surely as if he had

plucked him out of the sea. The motorbike might still turn out to be of no relevance, but at least it was a lead. Another was provided by Musumeci shortly afterwards.

"We've found the bones," he announced, breathless.

"Where?"

"In a factory in Viarolo."

"Are you certain?"

"A vet has confirmed it. The bones of a medium-sized dog."

"Were they delivered by Laudadio?"

"In person. I've reconstructed his routine rounds, almost always the same. A few hours ago I followed him, and he went in the direction of the Lower Po valley. After a bit, he turned into the yard of a company which doesn't feature on the normal circuit, the Rigenera Mangimi. I went round the back and climbed over the fence. It was early and there was no-one around apart from the guard. Laudadio unloaded several containers and went on his way. At that point I began rummaging about. I shone my torch on containers which had been there for a couple of days and I found some quite slender bones. The ones extracted from hams are all the same, so it was easy to distinguish them."

"Were there many of them?"

"Couldn't really say! I didn't go through them all."

"You're sure they were from a dog?"

"As I just said, the vet has no doubt."

"You're making real progress. You're as enterprising in these investigations as you are with women."

"I'll take that as a compliment, with your experience – of investigations, I mean," he added hurriedly.

"It's not that you're being more cautious, now that you're getting on in life? You've found someone who can keep you in check?"

"Commissario, nobody can ever keep me in check."

"Alright, alright, come on! Draw up your report and we'll explain everything to the magistrate."

He made his way back to the city and parked his car in front of the courts. He called Angela but her mobile was switched off, so he left the car and went in, pretending to be looking for something in the prosecutor's office or in the chancellery, avoiding known faces. He recognised lawyers who had defended characters from the criminal world, judges he had appeared before, as well as some of the more elderly clerks from the archive offices, but all that busyness from people with the obligatory tie, leather briefcase, bundles of papers and anxious demeanour repelled him. He wondered how Angela managed to survive in that world which he found as phoney as the gossip magazines.

"We dirty our hands on the dunghill of criminality, and yet we seize some slivers of life's dismal truth, which you then scatter wastefully with your rhetoric," he used say to her in reproach. Angela would get angry, but agreed that many of her colleagues saw life from an upper window and never had to descend to street level. "Mine is a profession which is handed down from one generation to the next, and some of those who inherit it have no idea of what it means to struggle. They just can't understand poverty or need."

When his partner appeared in the hallway, Soneri observed her from a distance, as he enjoyed doing. He loved the way she spoke to her colleagues, displaying an insouciance which had an element of haughtiness to it. He, a proletarian, felt he had none of that. Being born poor leaves a precariousness which excludes self-confidence. When put under pressure, he was liable to become churlish and even dismissive, but he knew this was a mechanism for warding off fear. His ancestors had been crushed, generation after generation. He was the first to be able to raise his head, so some incredulous vertigo was quite normal. If his son had not died, perhaps he would have acquired Angela's ease of manner.

When he saw her make her way towards the exit, he hid. He did not like being seen around the courts with her. Everyone knew, but it was better not to feed malice by flaunting their relationship. He followed her for a short distance without being seen, and then ambushed her under the colonnade of Via Mazzini.

"So that's where you'd disappeared to! Down a manhole," she said, looking at him severely.

"I was searching for Corbellini."

"Well, he's reappeared."

"High time. We've been looking for him for days."

"Seriously. He's written a letter. The news appeared a few moments ago on the websites of some newspapers. It was addressed to them."

"Are you kidding me?"

Angela took her tablet out of its case and switched it on. She turned to the news page and showed him the few lines of the communiqué.

Dear Fellow-Citizens,
  Serious health issues have compelled me to go abroad for treatment. I apologise for my absence, but as soon as I recover, I will be back at my post.

The commissario remained silent for a while, then shrugged.

"You're not convinced?"

"Not in the slightest."

"No matter, but there's a storm brewing," Angela said, manoeuvring her tablet and showing him a range of political reactions. "For better or worse, you're going to have to deal with this."

"These devices provoke collective hysteria," he said, pointing to the tablet. "It's like putting a match to a haystack." He was annoyed, because this was the second time in a few hours that he felt himself diminished by the trappings of modernity, which was inducing in him a growing sense of inadequacy. He took Angela by the arm and led her to the *Milord*. "Let's keep our feet on the ground, or better still, under the table."

"So he's turned up?" Alceste asked.

The news had gone viral. "Do you believe it?"

Alceste shook his head and the couple at the next table laughed out loud. Nobody believed in the letter, but everyone was talking about it. Valmarini was right to wager on falsehood, the new cipher of life.

Bergossi was no more convinced, but as he said on the telephone, "We've no choice but to follow it up." Once, Soneri would have examined the stamp, the paper, the date and place of postage, but what could he do now?

"If the message really did come from abroad, it's not going to be easy for any police force to trace it back. Our first job is to ask why they sent such a bizarre missive," Bergossi said.

Soneri agreed. "Yes, what's the point of it? It could be a message aimed at one person in particular."

"Quite likely, but this makes things even more complicated. The Ministry will be on my back again."

"So, neither of you has any idea?" Angela said, when Soneri hung up.

"Some ideas, but they don't lead to Corbellini. Drugs."

"In this city, there's more cocaine than talcum powder."

"It comes from abroad, packed into the bellies of hunting dogs to dodge border checks. To keep them out of sight, the dogs are walked along the riverbank to San Vitale and there cut open to extract the stuff. From that point, getting it into the city is child's play. The paths on the hills are hardly kept under observation."

Alceste served the steaming *anolini*, and poured the Gutturnio.

"Do you know who's my opposite number in the case my client has raised against L'Eterna?" Angela said, "Righetti, lawyer to the Parma aristocracy."

"There's no-one left who's not soiled in some way. Parma itself stinks – with the stench coming first from the head, as with fish."

They were interrupted by his mobile once more, causing Angela to make a gesture of impatience.

"Sir, I found out the name of the person who rented the S.I.M. card for the mobile stolen from Pontiroli."

"Go on, tell me."

"It comes from an Internet centre at 36 Via Bixio. The owner is Polish, name of Wiesniski."

"I'll pay him a visit later on." He broke off the conversation so as not to irritate Angela any further.

"We've discovered who owns the mobile which was ringing near Adelaide's house."

"The one responsible for the humiliation of a highly regarded officer like you!"

"It belongs to Pontiroli – the Red Czar."

"Red! Him? Hand in glove with the most right-wing of industrialists! How could he have ended up like that? You've plenty of anomalies to look into."

"Parma is one big anomaly – rotting away while it stares at itself in the mirror, convinced that it's the most beautiful place in the world."

"What's this? Rebellion against the father?" Angela said with a smile.

"For years they've been harping on about the glory of our

illustrious forebears without bothering to look to the future, and the people have been willing to follow the first pied piper who promises new grandeur for our little Paris! And in this age of sequins and spangles, a foetid mould has emerged and covered the Teatro Regio and the Pilotta. We've got a new caste of administrators garlanded by our fellow citizens, like primitives dazed by the sight of a collection of trinkets."

"And the Left is on its knees before big business – when it's not actually complicit, that is," Angela added.

"Parma suffers from the same anxieties as a girl from the backwoods, who'd go along with anyone who promised her stardom and celebrity."

"You're behaving with the rage of a jilted lover."

"If they'd at least behave like big-time criminals, but even when it comes to theft, they can't avoid being petty and provincial," Soneri said, still unable to repress his anger. He turned his attention to his *anolini*, but was interrupted again by his mobile.

"What is it?" he said.

"I'll be very brief," Juvara said, realising that his timing was bad. "I just wanted to say that Laudadio's son has a Facebook page filled with photographs. You might find something interesting there."

"For God's sake, Juvara! You still believe that these little toys are any good for serious investigations? You're really getting on my nerves with this Internet stuff," he said, clicking his mobile shut.

"If you want my opinion, you're making a mistake," Angela said.

"Not you too!"

"Try to be reasonable. If a person hasn't understood that nowadays a great part of available information goes through these channels, he's either obtuse, elderly or arrogant."

"And which am I? Or am I all three?"

"You suffer from intellectual arrogance, a disease affecting people who're good at what they do, but if you carry on this way you'll end up exhibiting all the obtuseness of the elderly."

"Me? Arrogant?" Soneri was cut to the quick.

"You're perfectly aware that there are many kinds of arrogance. Yours takes the form of the belief that you're happily self-sufficient, even in your investigations."

"You'll have to admit that up till now I haven't made many mistakes."

"You see! This is pig-headedness."

"No, it's a matter of statistics. If a method works ..."

"It's worked till now, but the world is changing and there's no saying it'll always work. Flexibility and adaptability are the best antidotes against being viewed as decrepit."

"There we are! The triad is complete. Arrogant, just a little obtuse and now decrepit as well."

"That's not what I said. You know that prevention is better than cure, and anyway, stop making out you've got flies up your arse," Angela said, using a saying once common in Parma, and which served to lower the tension.

"Are you telling me to create a profile on Facebook and start using Twitter?"

"In your line of business, best not to, but you could use a pseudonym or a generic icon and that would let me write to you freely, and maybe even make virtual love to you." She gave him a wink, but followed it with a reproachful look.

"You're asking too much. An old fellow like me prefers direct contact."

14

EARLY IN THE afternoon, Soneri decided to pay Wiesniski a visit. He walked over the Ponte di Mezzo, past the statue of Filippo Corridoni, who seemed somewhat troubled even in the immobility of bronze, and turned into Via Bixio. The shop was little more than a stall, with one telephone cabin and three computers standing on shelves. There was a Russian woman inside the cabin braying in a language with abundant vowels, and a man seated in front of a computer screen tapping on the keyboard with an air of stoic boredom.

Soneri introduced himself and explained why he was there. He pulled out the data on the S.I.M. card. Wiesniski examined it with professional thoroughness and at last gave a nod. "It's one of mine. I had given it up for lost."

"Can you tell me who you rented it out to the last time?"

Wiesniski took out a large exercise book and began flicking through the pages. Soneri was comforted by the fact that he still used pen and paper to record the rentals.

"Yuri Belankov, a Ukrainian."

"Did he give you any I.D.?"

"Certainly," Wiesniski replied, taking out a file from underneath the counter. He opened it at the letter B and handed a photocopy of a driving licence with a photograph to the commissario.

"When did he take the card?"

Wiesniski turned over some more pages and said, "The sixteenth of October. It was for two months, so it's overdue. I told you I'd given it up for lost, but I'm used to that sort of thing. I take a deposit to cover it."

"Do you know where I can find this Belankov?"

"Anyone's guess. This is like a seaport. I've never seen anyone come here for more than three months at a time."

Soneri nodded. Wiesniski asked timidly, "Can I have the card back, please?"

"It's not possible at the moment. There's a police inquiry under way. Keep the card active for a while yet," he said. The shopkeeper nodded, disappointed.

Soneri went out and started walking towards the police station. In January dusk fell quickly, so it was possible to enter a place in daylight and come out in darkness a quarter of an hour later. The mist had grown thicker, softly embracing the buildings in the centre. Under the City Chambers, a small crowd could be heard protesting, drumming on pots and pans, the soundtrack of shame.

Juvara welcomed him with a simple nod and Soneri understood he was still upset by the rebuff at lunchtime. "I'm very sorry, but this inquiry is really getting to me," the commissario said. The inspector indicated with another sign, this time with his hand, that the matter was closed.

"Suppose we take a look at those photos on Face— what's it called?"

"Facebook. If you like. Even criminals are betrayed by the mania to go public. There's always a friend or family member who puts something useful for us online."

"Everyone wants to be part of the show," the commissario agreed.

He drew up his chair next to Juvara's, and they began to

examine the profile. The younger Laudadio was seventeen years old and had 520 photographs on his site taken on his mobile. Soneri was full of admiration for the inspector's ability to operate the computer. Dozens of images showed the young man with his friends in the usual, supposedly original poses: tongues out, glowering expressions, faces pressed together, backs turned as they pretended to pee collectively. There were some of domestic pets, a cat and a dog, and some with his girlfriend, amorous selfies, birthday with cake: the imitation was obvious even in souvenir photographs. After a while, the commissario snorted. "See? The more the means of communication expand, the more the content diminishes. Gestures with no message."

"We've got to look out for what's in the background. A photograph can tell us a great deal without meaning to," Juvara said.

"If you say so."

They got to the three hundredth photograph and were on the point of falling asleep. Quite suddenly images of the yard Soneri knew well came up. There was his father's lorry with the boy in the driving seat, in the back of the lorry, holding the steering wheel, and in various other poses. A motorcycle stood out clearly in the background.

"Can you enlarge that image?" he asked Juvara.

"All you have to do is zoom in."

The commissario stared at his colleague for a moment in bewilderment, but then turned his eyes back to the detail. The enlargement of the scene permitted him to read the letters and numbers on the number plate, and he wrote them down on a piece of paper. Juvara was delighted to have demonstrated the value of new technology.

"Will we look at them all?" he asked.

"Maybe later," Soneri replied distractedly, as he reached for the telephone.

"Can I speak to Maresciallo Pasqualuzzo, please?" he asked the receptionist.

"At your service, commissario."

"No need for all this formality. This isn't a meeting at the Prefecture."

"I'm honoured! Any developments?"

"Have you the number plate on that motor . . . ?"

"Certainly have."

"How much of it can you read?"

"Two letters and one number: A, X and a 5."

"And it looked to you like a motor scooter?"

"My colleague Vincenzi, who knows about these things, says it looked like a Honda SH50."

"In that case, it's very likely that it belongs to Laudadio's son."

"You're saying it was him . . ."

"I don't think it was the boy himself."

At the other end of the line, he could hear the maresciallo speaking to Vincenzi. "Did it seem to you like a boy's voice?"

"No, Vincenzi says it was a man's voice."

"Yes, that would be right. The father used the motor scooter."

"Probably," Pasqualuzzo agreed, "but what was Laudadio doing at Zunarelli's workshop?"

"Who knows? Perhaps he was playing the angel of the Annunciation, but announcing death. Or perhaps he went over to talk and found the body."

"What a mess!" the maresciallo said.

Soneri rang off and dialled another number. "Isernia, listen," he began without any preliminaries. "You'll have to go back to Zunarelli's place in San Vitale and do a search of the house. It's been cordoned off."

"You think he kept some cocaine on the shelves with the washing-up liquid?"

"Why not?" the commissario said, his mind already on the next move. He was gripped by a sense of urgency bordering on frenzy. He put down the telephone and jumped to his feet. "Juvara, you've convinced me. This new world of technology is a great resource, and you're right that the tracks on the web are indelible. It even gives us the illusion of immortality."

The inspector, flushed with triumphant pride, was happy to confirm this. "In theory, that's true. A website or a profile on social media is permanent – at least until someone cancels them."

"So, we have little personal mausoleums, but they recount more than was intended. For example, the number plate on young Laudadio's motor scooter."

"As I've already said, a photograph can be a mine of information, every bit as much as the C.C.T.V. at the bank that you looked at. However, everything has a flip side. Technology obeys its master, and if he's a criminal, it's on his side."

"You've just convinced me that your devices are worthwhile, and now you're trying to disillusion me, is that it?"

Juvara was not given the time to offer reassurance because the commissario was already out the door. As he was driving towards San Vitale, it occurred to him that the impetus to keep busy was merely a diversion from the anxiety caused by this impenetrable investigation. The gleam of light which shone each time he was given a fresh piece of information was deceptive, and he knew he had to face up to the chameleon-like adaptability of the clues. He was convinced they were there to be found, but could not yet manage to pick them out.

Half an hour later, he arrived at the Laudadio house. His wife appeared in the doorway like a ghost in a cloud of vapour framed by the light. She seemed terrified and did no more than point him in the right direction. Laudadio had a little glass-walled office in a corner of the workplace. Soneri made his way into the box.

"I'm here to talk about Zunarelli, he said without any preamble.

"I thought I'd already explained—"

Soneri did not let him finish. "It was you who found the body and tipped off the carabinieri."

Laudadio's lip trembled slightly and the commissario thought he had before him a man not up to the demands of his part in the drama.

"Why did you go and visit Zunarelli after dinner? What did you have to tell him? Did you announce they were going to have his balls on a platter after we'd discovered about the trafficking?"

"What trafficking?"

"You know perfectly well. You didn't really believe I'd swallowed that tale about the dog in the ditch, did you? When you all realised we were onto it, you prepared an alibi in case we found a carcass."

Laudadio shook his head but said nothing.

"Well then, explain to me your nocturnal visit to the workshop."

"We set things up for the following morning. I had to load up the bones and the waste material."

"When we searched the premises after the discovery of the carcass, there was no sign that there were bones to be disposed of. Maybe you were talking about the most recent consignment of cocaine, is that it? Zunarelli was done for, and you had to clear everything up. It must have seemed to him like a death sentence."

"I guessed what was going on in that workshop of his, but I had nothing to do with it. My job was waste disposal, nothing else. The remains of those dogs ended up among the refuse. The bones, once they'd been scraped clean, were thrown in with those of the pigs, while their flesh was mixed in with the leftovers of the salami and hams which had gone bad. Zunarelli told me to keep one eye shut, and I was just doing my job. I wasn't in any way responsible for what they put into their containers."

"Don't play the fool!" the commissario snapped. "You knew exactly what was going on, and you went to tell your partner that he'd need to take full responsibility, and to warn him not to open his mouth. At that point, Zunarelli was facing either jail or, if he spoke, death. He had to decide, and in fact he decided to pre-empt your threats."

"What a load of shit!"

"It's been established from the telephone company's records that you called Zunarelli at ten fifty-three and, not receiving any reply, took your son's scooter to go over to the workshop. Wearing a helmet, in that mist, wrapped up in a heavy jacket, you could have been mistaken for the young man himself. Having discovered the suicide, you stopped off at the village telephone box and called the carabinieri. It was better if they found the body right away, because that would divert attention from the rest of the inquiries."

"Think what you like. I called to make arrangements for the following day, but he didn't reply, so I went over to his place."

"So why the anonymous call? Were you so sure he was dead that you didn't call the emergency services? That should surely have been your first thought."

"What was the point? He wasn't moving, his face was purple, and the rope had cut into his skin."

"And you heaved a sigh of relief."

"There's no obligation to show your real feelings to a policeman," Laudadio hissed with real venom.

"Ah yes, there you're quite right, not least because it'd be extremely compromising for you."

Laudadio made an effort to remain impassive but his lip started trembling once again.

"The magistrate will decide on your position, but I don't believe you're going to get off scot-free, because your story just doesn't stand up."

Not long afterwards Soneri joined Isernia and Pilotti, who were finishing up as he arrived. Zunarelli's apartment was a sorry sight, a reflection of his life. Everything seemed shabby and dull. The furniture was nothing more than functional, an assortment of badly chosen, mass-produced objects purchased in a warehouse. Isernia showed him a greasy ledger book and a strange bundle. "These are the most interesting things," he said.

The commissario flicked through the ledger, with its yellowing, curled-up pages, and then turned to the other things: a plastic ball composed of two half-spheres held together by a ribbon to stop it opening in the stomach or intestine of a dog. "How do you explain this?" he asked Isernia.

"No doubt Zunarelli squirrelled some away for himself, or else it might have been his pay for the work he was doing."

The commissario made no reply, not knowing what to say. The deeper he delved into this inquiry, the more the mysteries multiplied. It was like walking in the woods on his own Apennines, already well-trodden by people searching for mushrooms or truffles, the paths criss-crossing like a maze. He picked up the ledger, wrapped it in a bag and put it in his pocket. He concluded that that place had nothing else to reveal. He said goodbye to his colleagues, got into the car and drove off.

Angela had been waiting to have dinner with him. Both felt a desire to be on their own, free of any other concerns, and focused exclusively on each other, like children at play. They made love after a period of abstinence that had lasted for some weeks.

Angela sat up in bed and spoke in dreamy tones. "We're giving up on life and throwing away the best part of our time, me in the courts and you running after good-for-nothings. How stupid!"

"Ever since we were chased out of the earthly paradise . . ." he began, in an attempt to laugh off what she had said, but Angela did not seem to find it amusing. She sat staring into the middle distance, in the grip of some vague regret.

"The paradox is that to live, you have to sell your time to someone, so you renounce living," he said.

"Time is the most precious thing we have, and at our age you come to realise that it no longer seems infinite. And then, for a woman, the years leave even deeper marks."

"You're young in your career! I came spying on you in the courts, did you know that? You were like a Fury."

Angela's expression did not change. "Yesterday a good friend of mine confessed she was menopausal. She's the same age as me."

"It's not a disease."

"No, but I was afraid. I had a terrible feeling of emptiness. I thought I had deprived myself of something better."

"What?"

"Of being a mother. I'll never know what it is to have children. And I'm not one of those women who can take a cat or a dog to compensate."

Soneri said nothing. He clasped his hands behind his neck and tried not to think of his unborn son. That was the day when both love and youth were snatched away from him. Angela noticed that she had wounded him, and gave him an affectionate kiss. "We're both miserable, but we can cure each other," she said.

The commissario nodded and for a time both remained in silence, before getting up and going to the table. No more than a vague trace of resignation remained from what had passed between them a few moments earlier. He gave her a hug, awkward but sincere, like a baby. "Are you still sad?" he asked her.

"I have moments of happiness, but the overall context weighs heavily on me."

"It's better not to think about it."

"It's not possible, and you know that. It's a combination of forces pressing down on you, and you seem to be at the very heart of them."

"And they could crush you, as happened to Romagnoli and Zunarelli."

Angela turned her attention to what he was saying and invited him to go on. The commissario saw this as a means of talking about what was troubling her, but from a safe distance and with other people as the protagonists.

"Until now, I've only met induced death, no direct violence, except for the slaughter of the dogs, and that's why I say the context can kill you. They allowed Romagnoli to believe he'd be going home, stuffed him full of sedatives, and left him to wait on the service stairs in the care home until he froze to death. They gave his executioner Zunarelli the role of scape-goat in the cocaine trade, and if he'd talked, he'd have been signing his own death warrant. If you're up a blind alley, the only way to escape is to disappear."

"Killing himself makes it look as though he wanted to save his jailers," Angela objected.

"In these cases, it's fear that decides. What's more terrible, the death you inflict on yourself or the death that's inflicted on you?"

"He could have decided not to speak and accept his guilt."

"He'd have gone to jail, and at his age that was the end of everything."

"It's going to be hard for you to get to the end of this chain if some of the links are missing."

"And when exactly do we ever get to the end? In minor matters, perhaps, but when politicians are mixed up in it, it's a different story. If only there had been someone there to pull the trigger! As I said, the real assassin is the context, and the context doesn't have just one weapon. It's got thousands. It's like a fakir's bed on which you sink slowly, with the nails piercing the body millimetre by millimetre."

"Or like a fly-catcher."

"Politicians don't tolerate intrusions. They flaunt their mandate from the people, and so consider themselves above the law. *If that's what people want*, they say, *take us as we are. It doesn't matter if we're criminals*."

"And you think that politicians are tied up with this business?"

"Zunarelli was kept on his feet by Ugolini, who gave him work. And don't forget that we're investigating the disappearance of a mayor."

"Another fine mess!"

"As you say, a fine mess. And did you know that Pontiroli has changed the name of his cooperative? It's no longer called Laboriosa, but New Job."

"If the name's not in English, it's for also-rans."

"Wait till you see the logo."

15

FROM THE VERY moment he opened his eyes, Soneri was thinking about the next step. He wasted no time in getting to the police station to look over Zunarelli's diary. His death was like a bridge which had collapsed across the path of their investigations, and the only possible way forward was that notebook that had been worn away by being kept in too many pockets and touched by too many fingers. Most of the entries were to do with suppliers, curers, craftsmen and professionals who had been in and out of the workshop, but he also found the number of Ugolini's mobile and that of the hospital where Romagnoli had been a patient. This number was a quite recent entry, but the commissario's attention was drawn to another number he thought he had seen before. It ended with the sequence 7-4-7, like the aeroplane he had travelled on with Angela when she had once persuaded him to travel to Mexico: Boeing 747. He compared it to the telephone card rented from Wiesniski's, and saw it was the same. Zunarelli had not put a name beside the number; an ingenuous precaution. So he had had some relationship with Belanov, assuming the card had not been passed on.

He picked up the telephone and called Pasquariello. "Be good enough to send out an order to all cars to search for a Ukrainian named Yuri Belanov."

"Is he, as far as you know, an illegal immigrant? Have you already checked?"

"His residence permit is still valid, but it's not certain he's still in Parma, or even in Italy."

"Should we be widening the search?"

"I've already seen to that, but I don't want to neglect keeping a lookout for him here. Isn't there already a community of Ukrainians in Parma?"

"There is. A lot of them hang out in a bar in Via Venezia. We did a raid there a couple of months ago after a fight broke out."

"Let's try there. You never know."

The commissario was once again sunk in uncertainty. It was as though he were leaping across a river from one stone to the next, keeping his balance but in danger of getting soaked.

"Zunarelli was not quite so ignorant of technology as he led us to believe," Soneri said to Juvara. "If it was him who made the last calls to that mobile found near the river, he knew how to encrypt the number."

"It's quite easy really. In any case, Belanov's S.I.M. card had been modified to receive only incoming calls."

It occurred to the commissario that he would have had no idea of how to do that, but he refrained from saying so.

"Zunarelli's bank transactions are more interesting," Juvara said.

"Tell me. Money talks louder than words."

"Serious money, but some of the payments are none too transparent."

"He was a good worker in a particular field, who charged high prices, mostly likely cash in hand."

"Probably, but there are commissions for bits of boning work where the cost is higher than the market price."

"For Ugolini?"

"For various companies. It's impossible to establish exactly who's behind them, but according to our consultant they can likely be traced back to Ugolini."

The commissario mumbled something to himself. "There's a lot that needs clearing up," Juvara said. As he was speaking, an officer appeared at the door. "There's a woman who wants to talk to you, sir." Soneri got instantly to his feet, without understanding what made him jump up in that manner. Perhaps it was the surprise of having someone looking for him when he spent so much time searching for other people.

He saw the woman sitting somewhat uncomfortably in the waiting room among the suffering, somewhat boorish specimens of humanity who populate police stations. She introduced herself as Aurora Guatelli. Soneri took her into his office and offered her a seat. Judging by her face, she was still under forty and had obviously looked after herself. She had a physique formed by diets and sessions in the gym. The commissario sat down in front of her and with a gesture of both hands invited her to speak. "I'm a friend of Giancarlo, the mayor," she said.

He made the same gesture as before. "I'm worried," she said, while seeming to be searching under the desk. "Worried because of his character. Giancarlo is an insecure lad." She raised her eyes suddenly as she spoke.

"You're speaking about him as though he's a teenager. He's mayor of a city of two hundred thousand inhabitants!"

"Exactly. All those responsibilities, problems ..."

"The day he was elected, he seemed to be euphoric, even arrogant."

"Yes, yes, that's a typical vice of shy people, but afterwards I think it caused him a lot of pain."

"Such a role would have that effect on anybody, but I don't understand where you come in."

The woman squirmed uncomfortably so that her bracelets clink against each other. "It was to help you understand. Nowadays politics is conducted by some real sharks. That's just it, Giancarlo wasn't like that. I wanted you to know that."

The commissario sat in silence. He was struggling to grasp what she wanted to communicate to him. There was a subtle thread of ambiguity twisted around her words. "The Council is corrupt. I find it hard to believe that the stench has not in some way attached itself to him," Soneri said.

"I believe he was ashamed and perhaps that's why . . . Please believe me, Giancarlo had to perform in a context which compelled him to do things he didn't want to."

The word "context" almost made the commissario leap out of his chair. What was this if not a tidal wave, a collective contagion or the same sound passed around by inertia, starting off slowly, picking up pace due to lack of resistance, and finally dragging everyone in its wake by mass force?

"The context? He was the symbol of it. I remember posters with his face and the words *Parma: a Model of Life*."

"You already know that symbols become so in spite of themselves."

The commissario was beginning to lose patience, but he tried to restrain himself. The discussion was drifting onto questions which were scarcely police matters. His irritation got the better of him, and he cut the woman short: "Have you anything to tell me which might be of use to our inquiries?"

"I hoped to let you see what kind of man Giancarlo is. The newspapers are full of so many insinuations."

"Journalists have that luxury, but I don't, and that's why I'm asking you whether or not you can help me. Are you in a relationship with the mayor?"

The woman stared at him in bewilderment. "No. As I was saying, we've been friends since schooldays."

"And afterwards? Were you members of the same party?"

"No, but for a couple of years we did the same kind of work, P.R. in discotheques. We were also both reps in holiday camps, but Giancarlo wasn't really cut out for that kind of work. Too introverted."

"So that's why he went into politics?"

"In the *Baretto* in Via Farini he got to know some people in right-wing circles in Parma. I think he made a good impression on them because he has real presence. He's quite diplomatic but he has the knack of getting right to the heart of things."

"Do you mean he was obedient?"

The woman leaned her head to one side, as though she were making an effort to think things through. "I would say that if he makes a promise, he will always keep it."

"It's easy to see that you've been involved in public relations, but you're still not giving me any worthwhile information."

She looked disappointed. "I thought ..."

"What did you think? You came here with some fear, and you're taking a wide berth round the explanation you still haven't given me, or don't want to give me."

"My fear is that he's fallen into the wrong hands," Aurora said.

"If that's what you're afraid of, it wasn't a recent event."

"They might make him do things – things he'll regret." She was becoming more agitated by the moment.

"We're doing our best to find him," the commissario said, increasingly irritated by her whining tone. "However, I think these regrettable things have already been done. By the time the police get involved, that's normally the way it is."

Aurora once again looked down, and said nothing. After a few moments, she got up, shook his hand and said goodbye, leaving a scent of perfume in her wake.

After she had gone, Juvara said, "You were very hard on her, sir."

"I've no time for people who bask in the sunlight when the times are good and then start moaning when they turn bad. They were having a ball until a couple of months ago."

"If you want to know what I think, that woman will be back. You made an impression on her."

"What are you on about now?"

"She's one of those women who like their men a bit rough. In that respect, she's like everybody else in this city. They have to be cosseted, but also knocked about a bit. It's not enough to play the flute. You've also got to bang the drum."

"Are you turning philosopher on me?"

"No, I'm just someone who listens while you speak."

"Women are much less gregarious than men. Think of what Zunarelli got himself into."

"Into a noose."

"Exactly."

"What do you think she really wanted to tell you?"

"That the mayor might have put his head in a noose as well."

"Do you think . . . ?"

"No, I don't think anything. You can expect just about anything from politicians. Corbellini, wherever he is, is not in a good way. Perhaps he's studying how to get out."

"Out of what?"

"What do you mean, for God's sake? Don't you see they're putting half the Council in jail? That woman was talking about the context. O.K., this is the context that's got him trapped."

"You're right that the prosecutor does seem intent on getting to the very bottom of things," Juvara said.

"That depends on finding out where the very bottom actually is. Do you honestly think that the politicians aren't working to fend off the next blow? Have you read about the volley of questions that the Right in Parliament are submitting down about Bergossi? They're trying to save what can be saved, and to decide who to sacrifice. At the end of the day, there'll be some unfortunate who'll act as a lightning conductor, a bit like what they attempted by inducing Zunarelli to do away with himself."

Juvara nodded. "But what does the traffic in cocaine have to do with Corbellini's disappearance? I don't see the connection."

"Nor do I, but Parma is a small place and everything overlaps in the end. Do you think there is no overlap between cocaine and the politicians?"

The conversation was interrupted when the telephone rang. It was Pasquariello, plainly delighted with himself. "We've traced Belanov. It was easier than we thought. He was in the bar in Via Venezia with some other Ukrainians."

"And where is he now?"

"He's still here. He's not going anywhere. He's afraid, and this is the place he feels safest."

"I'm on my way," Soneri said. As he was leaving he turned to Juvara. "Who do we have as our financial consultant?"

"Signor Pacchioni."

"Excellent. Sit down with him and go through all Laudadio's business affairs, his companies and those of his colleague, Petrillo. Do an X-ray of him."

He got into his car and drove to Via Venezia. The bar was halfway up the street, in the north of the city, where the mist hung immobile among the remains of abandoned factories, those final vestiges of what had once been an industrial city. Soneri made his way through the group waiting for his arrival and went in. A young girl with all the customary accoutrements – miniskirt, high heels, heavy make-up, gaudy, low-cut dress – was serving at the bar. The intrusion of uniformed officers had left a feeling of tension that was evident from the expressions of the clients. When he enquired about Belanov, he set off murmurs in the soft language he now recognised. The girl, who spoke Italian and who had a somewhat brazen attitude, came forward. She took him through a backroom to a door, and knocked. A voice could be heard inside, and she opened it, standing back to let Soneri through. Bathed in a neon light which gave them all a lunar whiteness, three faces turned towards the commissario.

"Belanov?" he said to the man standing before him.

"*Da*," he said, before switching into his fumbling Italian. Soneri introduced himself, and the other two men went out, leaving them alone. "Know why you here," Belanov began.

"Are you afraid?"

The Ukrainian nodded. "You, in my place, no?"

The commissario nodded in his turn, showing that he understood.

"I, away," the man began again after a short pause. "Leave Italy, go home. Here no place for me."

"You've got into bad company."

"Me driver, only driver."

Soneri encouraged him. "Explain everything more clearly to me. Where did you pick up the dogs?"

Belanov shook his head energetically. "If I tell you, then ..." His voice tailed off as he pulled his index finger across his throat.

"The alternative is an interrogation in the police station where you'll face a charge of trafficking in illegal drugs."

"I tell you. Only driver, and take dogs along river."

"This does not change anything, and certainly not the charge. Once you're in the police station, you could be taken to jail, and there you might bump into someone from the gang who might wish to shut your mouth. Or, if the judge puts you under house arrest, it could be even worse for you. I imagine they'll know where to find you."

"If I not speak, they nothing, let me go and nothing."

"In that case, you wouldn't be able to leave the country and the price of your silence might be seven or eight years' imprisonment. How does that sound?" Soneri said, overstating the possible charges facing Belanov to increase the pressure on him. Belanov remained silent, the first sign he was weakening.

"Let's do a deal," the commissario suggested. "You tell me everything and I'll pretend we've never met. You can leave tonight and head back home. You have the afternoon to get organised. I can see you're not short of friends."

The Ukrainian's eyes lit up with venom. "A deal?" he repeated, as though hearing the word for the first time, but he said it with a cynical smile which only served to remind the commissario that he had crossed a line. They both stood silent for a time, long enough to allow Soneri to acquit himself for this transgression of the law, conscious he was dealing with a low-level criminal, an operative whose arrest would mean nothing except an extra place in some cell. Didn't colleagues who boasted of having informants in the criminal underworld close at least one eye? A nod from Belanov confirmed his willingness to talk.

"Right then. Where did you pick up the dogs?"

"Romania. They eat there," he said with a wink, meaning that they were forced to swallow the capsules. "Then drive, very quick. Dogs can die in three, four days."

"No customs check?"

Belanov gave a shrug. "Car, me, bags, all regular. Dogs nobody look, pass and away."

"How many trips did you do? One, two, three a month?"

"Depend on orders. Sometimes four or more. Not only me, not always same car. Travel with two people, man and woman, like family, with cases from Romania and Ukraine to Italy and back. Important things in animal stomachs."

"Did you come directly to Parma?"

"To farm in Mariano, where was house of our friends. Then river to pass city. City always difficult, many police, many eyes."

"And where did the drugs end up?"

"Not know. Zunarelli killed dogs, took stuff, then other people come, but I not know them."

"How come you had a stolen mobile?"

Belanov began to appear nervous. Perhaps he had not expected the discovery of the telephone. "I not steal, I buy."

"From whom?"

"Tunisian friend. Maybe he steal."

"A pusher? One of the 'mules' who carry the cocaine around?"

Belanov nodded.

"So why did you throw it away on the riverbank? Did you realise it was too hot?"

"Knew it belong important person. Afraid."

"If you'd taken it back to Ukraine, they'd never have found it."

"Tunisian spoke to my bosses. But I said no, not true, no mobile."

"They were very keen to get it back. Was the owner one of their clients?"

Once again Belanov nodded. "Tunisian work at *Cavalieri di Malta*. Lot of stuff sold there."

"Who are your bosses?"

"Not know all."

"Who do you know?"

"Heard name Petrillo, but not real boss. Others higher, but I not know. Other bosses in Romania, but not come here in Italy."

"There's an agreement over supply?"

"I think yes."

Soneri imagined Parma enveloped in a criminal web which grew more tangled by the day, while an indifferent, foolish population swarmed about on the streets, cheerfully surrendering to its new lords and masters.

"And are these the people you are afraid of? Petrillo, who's also an undertaker."

"They search for me. I safe here. My Ukrainians faithful."

"Are they looking for you because it was you who lost the dog in the Montebello area? When you realised you weren't going to find it, you threw away the mobile near the river and made your escape. You knew they would never forgive you for the loss of almost half a kilo of cocaine. They probably suspected you'd kept it for yourself, as it seems Zunarelli did."

"That dog evil. Broke lead then ran away. I search hours and hours, but nothing. What to do?"

"The problem was that when you didn't turn up, Zunarelli started calling the mobile, and perhaps he wasn't the only one. Eventually, someone heard it ringing and ringing, and raised the alarm."

As he reconstructed the events, it occurred to Soneri that everything was the result of pure chance, or of a pre-ordained plan if it was read *a posteriori*. The information from Adelaide, the encounter with Valmarini and his revelations, the discovery of the footprints on the riverbank, Zunarelli's links to Romagnoli's death, the powder showering down on the city more copiously than snow, the *crème de la crème* of Parma using it in their exclusive clubs, and the criminal underworld getting rich by controlling the space between the Duomo and the Pilotta.

"What to do?" Belanov repeated.

"You know what to do," the commissario said with a wink. "And do it tonight."

He cast his eye over Belanov before getting up, and came

close to envying him, since he could escape from the stench of decomposition which was now polluting the city. He had merely identified the worms who were devouring it.

16

IN THE AFTERNOON, Nanetti arrived with the results of the toxicology tests on Romagnoli, and news of another surprise. The old man had taken a dose of anti-inflammatory tablets before swallowing the benzodiazepine.

"Do you know the side-effects of anti-inflammatories?" Nanetti asked.

"Am I supposed to be a pharmacist?"

"Somnolence. Romagnoli must have been dropping off to sleep as he started going down the service stairs."

"Were those medicines prescribed by the doctors?"

"Yes. He was suffering from pains in his joints but the combined effect . . ."

"Are you telling me that Zunarelli knew all about this?"

"No. In my opinion he just did what someone else told him to do."

"Someone who knew the treatment Romagnoli was receiving."

"All he'd have had to do was ask a nurse."

"That's clear enough, but unfortunately it doesn't get us anywhere. The person who was responsible isn't around anymore, and a charge against the care home wouldn't stand up. It was perfectly legitimate to administer both the anti-inflammatories and the benzodiazepine. Romagnoli would have slept the whole night, which is what they wanted."

"So everything was above board and the dirty work was left to Zunarelli, who took all the blame. Hypocrisy is a wonderful cleanser of consciences," Nanetti said.

"And what can we do except wait for someone to make a wrong move?"

In his report to Piccirillo, Soneri explained how the cocaine arrived in Parma. He deliberately spent some time on the butchery of the dogs, how they had been treated as disposable containers, beaten unconscious and then cut open while still alive. He attributed everything he had been told by Belanov to unspecified "confidential sources", and concluded by indicating the two lines of inquiry to be followed: the supplies from abroad and the distribution network in the city. In connection with this latter point, he mentioned the name of Petrillo.

By the time he completed drafting the report, he was ready for dinner. Angela had been invited to a colleague's birthday party, leaving the commissario on his own for the evening. Juvara had left half an hour earlier so the only people still in the building were a few officers from the motorised division on evening shift. He switched off the lights as he went out, and in the falling semi-darkness he had a flashback. He was once again a university student on one of those dark winter mornings when he left home to run for a train, filled with the anxiety which precedes an examination. Everything had then seemed to him so crisp and important that it aroused in him some nostalgia even for that anxiety. It lasted just a few moments, the time it took him to go out onto the pavement of Via Repubblica and to notice that the weather had suddenly changed. The air was no longer so biting and the snow was slowly melting. Only the mist seemed unchanged, though perhaps it was now more moist and heavy. Groups of young protesters bedecked in the styles – anoraks and Palestinian scarves – their parents had donned in 1977 were stationed outside the Town Hall. Not only had imagination not seized power, but it was clearly dead and buried under a subculture of dissent, itself now a part of the system, celebrated in the ditties of unkempt singer-songwriters. The protesters gathered in a specified area, where, like prisoners during their exercise hour, they were at liberty to express all their wild fury.

He went to Alceste's restaurant to find something authentic. He chose not to go into the dining room itself but to linger in the kitchen where the official language was dialect and the aromas provided solid anchorage for an identity which outside he saw dissolving and melting in rivers of cash, cocaine and alcohol. The *tortelli d'erbetta*, which he ate standing up listening to the proprietor's chat as he came in and out between serving one client or another, calmed him down. Alceste's common sense brought back to him those few things which really count. With a sprinkling of witticisms, he spoke of his family, his health and his friends in a casual way which made everything else seem worthless.

Soneri went away in a better frame of mind, and walked about for half an hour among the deserted lanes until, having crossed Piazza Boito and climbed the slope of Strada del Conservatorio, he found himself once again on the Lungoparma. Proceeding to the Montebello district, he turned along the riverbank, searching in the darkness for Valmarini. When he got to the painter's house, he rang the bell and, as was now customary, heard in reply the click of the lock.

"Do you always open it this way in the dark?" Soneri asked.

"At this hour, I know who's ringing. No-one else comes."

Dondolo rose lazily and stretched, first forwards and then backwards. It seemed a familiar gesture among members of the household. In the centre of the room which Soneri now knew well there was yet another canvas in preparation.

"I don't want to disturb you," he said.

Valmarini dismissed these words with a wave of his hand. "I have all the time I want, and anyway, making clients wait establishes your importance."

"Have you a lot of work in hand?"

"Yes, and I find that distressing. The only consolation is money. Have you any idea what a relief it is to be aware that from now on I could live without ever picking up a brush?"

"I wish I could say that."

"Money gives an enormous sense of liberty to dreamers like us. All the others are its captives. Take Ugolini ..."

"He is the freest man there is. He believes he's omnipotent."

"Don't delude yourself. He's his own slave. Pardon the apparent contradiction, but liberty lies in having limits. He does not set limits and is in pursuit of some self-satisfaction which is purely momentary. There's always someone richer and more powerful, and this creates endless frustration for him. Ugolini is an unquiet soul. Here he can unburden himself by drinking until he reaches an artificial state of exultation which dulls the torment he carries inside himself. Sometimes I feel sorry for him, even if he is the most powerful man in the city."

"Does he snort cocaine here as well?"

"I think so, but he does it in private. Some nights he goes into the toilet and comes back out with a certain look in his eyes. Dondolo barks at him because he can read in his face the demon inside him, the same demon which makes him insatiable in his quest for everything, and which is simultaneously devouring him. He must feed it, or else he'll end up its victim."

"Have you ever been to the *Cavalieri di Malta*?"

Valmarini nodded. "A centre of power."

"Yes, indeed. For business. But I'm interested in the environment."

"You're still a commissario even when you're here."

"Who better than a painter to describe the club?"

"Anyone who wants to understand the destiny of the city should go there. In the Council, Corbellini was its executor, and in the stage play of committee politics there was even room for the supposed opposition of the Left."

"Ah yes, the Left!" Soneri said. "Dazzled by the market, neophyte of the profit motive, piously on its knees on the velvet of the confessional!'

"At long last, a show of passion! Have you decided to divest yourself of the uniform?"

The commissario made a gesture to him to drop the subject, but Valmarini went on, "You can do it here. Here they all stand naked. The night relieves suffering. It's truth incarnate and makes us all more authentic."

"Authentic! You of all people speak of authenticity?"

"I who openly declare that I produce forgeries am much more authentic than those who swear they are telling the truth."

Soneri shook his head with a laugh.

"Yesterday one of my works was attributed to a painter of the sixteenth-century Sienese school by a critic who signed the report. Clients sell on my works as originals, so now it's hard to identify the ones which really are such. They've even started corrupting art historians, if that's necessary, and have made a profitable market out of it. They exploit me by selling on at twice the price they paid me. Some of them even reproduce phoney attribution reports by experts from auction houses."

"They're just doing their job."

"Cheap labour," Valmarini said, with contempt in his voice. "They're on the same level as the printers of Monopoly money, but I'm an amanuensis. If I'm not an artist, at least I'm a craftsman, and I do everything transparently."

"You can hardly deny you're the progenitor of the forgery."

"The whole world rests on forgery, as we have already said. Mendacity is the cipher of our times. By lying, they sell everything to us – goods, information, life projects and expectations of happiness. There have never been so many instruments for deception as there are today. They actually embody deception. Galileo's telescope was more sincere than the computer."

"In fact, I'm of the old school – I go and have a look personally. Sooner or later I'll find Corbellini, and you'll not tell me it's only appearance," Soneri said.

"Corbellini walked for years on a veneer of appearance until at last he fell through."

"Or as long as they kept supporting him?"

"It was in their interests to do so. He was the facade, don't you agree? A mayor with real presence, good looks and athletic appearance. One of a kind, a super-accessory who, however, was guided by others."

"Like certain young ladies on the catwalk."

"Don't exaggerate! It's like advertising. The products they present you with have the face of the people who do the publicity. In the same way, Corbellini sold the Parmigiani things thought up by others."

"The odd thing about this episode is that the outcome contradicts the premise," Soneri said, thinking aloud. "According to what you're saying, the mayor had no reason to disappear."

"It might be that at a certain point the actor got fed up with his role. There are many more people who disappear than we think, and all of them want to free themselves of responsibilities. That includes you, and don't you deny it. The people who come along here are motivated by the desire to vanish. I can read it in the way the night attracts them. Night is the complicit mother who conceals us in the darkness of her garments, and spares us punishment."

"Corbellini is an ambitious man, too ambitious to throw it all away. He's escorted glamorous women, dealt with the powerful and attended first nights at the Teatro Regio on black-tie evenings. It's not likely he'd want to give all this up, and for what? A gilded residence in some South American hole with a false name on his passport?"

"You give me the impression of not being aware of the abyss of callousness and cynicism which animates the powerful in this city. Forgive me if I accuse you of naivety. I realise it's almost an offence to you in the part you play, but believe me, in my eyes it enhances your value as a human being."

The commissario invited him to go on. He was not offended. "Naivety can be an admirable quality in a policeman. It permits him to be surprised and to take nothing for granted."

"I know power in all its psychotic degeneration as well as any analyst. There is nothing human in Ugolini. When he drinks and snorts cocaine, he lowers the bulwarks of his mind, and then a tide of venom floods over me. I know no deeper fear than when I listen to him in his state of delirium, for this is the humus which fertilises his conscious universe. For him, the world is something to be used. He's prey to an obsessive narcissism which leaves him insatiable. It's like infantile regression, a two-thousand-year leap backwards towards the Emperor, the divine incarnation and sole custodian of human fate. Do you understand the danger now? We're marching towards this terminus. The democratic rituals of elected assemblies are so bereft of sense as to appear like witchcraft or prophecy," Valmarini said.

"It's true that someone has already swept Parliament aside and reduced it to a bivouac, but I don't believe that Corbellini has vanished because of remorse. He doesn't seem to me to have the balls to rebel, nor the depths to be aware of evil."

"I don't believe it either, and anyway the price would be

very high. We're talking about pitiless people who recognise no limits. Political power is entrusted to men of straw. They make laws at home and the judges corrupt themselves. Who can stand up to people like that? The opposition? Pontiroli, the man from the cooperatives who manages businesses similar to Ugolini's, is in charge there."

"If you don't like what's happening, help me."

"Am I not helping you? Let me explain the context," Valmarini said, causing the commissario to register yet another use of that word which returned obsessively in every conversation. "What do you intend to do? Don't be imprudent, commissario. Limit yourself to adjusting things without looking too deeply into them. I am aware this is cowardly advice, but you're an honest man and will remain so even if you don't immolate yourself. What good would it do? It wouldn't change a thing, except in your own life, and then for the worse, much worse."

"No need to exaggerate. At most, they'd send me to the passport office. That's not martyrdom."

"They won't take away your salary, but they'll dig a ditch around you. Theirs is not a dialectical, but a binary world. It's either black or white. Everyone is either friend or foe, and you're a foe. Everything is based on obedience and loyalty. Are you fully aware of how far advanced the programme for the destruction of democracy is? Ugolini is the people's elect, unchecked by any law."

"This city has never loved despots," Soneri said, but he did not sound convinced.

"Oh, it has digested several. The people of Parma have allowed themselves to be lulled by flattery, though they're not the only ones. We are an infantile people, a child as treacherous as an old man but still ingenuous enough as to believe in fairy tales. Today these are called marketing, image-building or some such nonsense, and they have the advantage of making a petty-minded majority feel part of something grand."

"It's over now. There's not much that's presentable left," Soneri said.

"They'll fight to the last man, and they won't give in easily. They can count on flocks of clients who will keep them going because their destiny is intertwined with that of the Council. How did you interpret that strange message from the mayor on Twitter?"

"A means of forging ahead, of dragging things out."

Valmarini approved. "You see? They're doing their best to keep the Administration alive while waiting for something to happen, or else to find a solution. In the meantime, if the mayor lets it be known he's still around and expects to make a return, everything will proceed as before with his deputy in charge."

"I think they'll need to re-shuffle the deck, or patch things up to make our work more difficult," Soneri said.

"You'll not get very far. They'll only allow you to scratch the surface."

For a moment the commissario made no reply, because that was his fear as well. "Anyway, for once they won't be able to decide on their own. We'll have a say as well."

"You want to delegitimise those who have been elected by the people?" Valmarini sniggered.

"You ought to hope they're going to persevere," the commissario said.

"I've already explained what I think of them," the painter replied sharply.

Soneri bowed his head. "It's not enough to get indignant. I'm putting my reputation on the line. I'm taking risks, and the prosecutor even more so. Do you know how many politicians have come out against him?"

"I do understand, but I'm not a herd animal. I go my own way in the world, like a cat. I've no ambition to construct anything, just to find myself a corner where I can live well without obeying anyone. You, on the other hand, must obey."

"I don't know how aware you are of having just touched on the disease which afflicts us all."

"What does that mean?"

"This thought of saving yourself, by yourself. The rupture of every relationship of trust, the renunciation of every kind of solidarity. Without a relationship, no-one will save him- or herself and you too will be crushed along with the world you have rejected."

"That's not going to happen in the time left to me, and thereafter I don't care."

"An artist has no right to talk in those terms. Someone who deals every day with beauty, painting and the harmony of form . . ."

"You're right. Every so often I'm overwhelmed by vulgar thoughts. Forgive me, but I've suffered too many disappointments. All that's left to me is Dondolo, and I don't know for how much longer."

Soneri nodded and got to his feet, disillusioned. As he moved towards the door, the dog peered at him gravely, and the painter followed a couple of steps behind. At the doorway, the commissario turned around and saw that Valmarini was anxious to speak but could not find the words. They stood in that position for a few moments until they exchanged glances of mutual understanding, the equivalent of the unspoken stipulation of a pact. The commissario, not wishing to disturb the equilibrium of that perfect communication, went out without saying another word and disappeared into the darkness.

17

THEY STARTED CIRCLING around Bergossi after a succession of Parliamentary Questions led to an inspection of the prosecution office. At the same time, Capuozzo was advocating a dishonourable retreat in the face of the many honourable Members of Parliament who were launching attacks on the investigation itself.

"With the stance they're adopting and the reassuring messages on Twitter, they're trying to divert attention from the thieves on the Council," the prosecutor fumed, as Soneri gave him an account of developments. "We're isolated, do you understand? The Left babbles away, because it's complicit and is afraid that one of its members, Pontiroli for instance, might get his fingers burned. We're an easy target."

"Is it possible there's not even one member of the Council prepared to come out in the open?" the commissario wondered.

"We'll do our best to find him. It might be someone who couldn't get his snout in the trough. When politicians are on the offensive, the best thing is to carry the war into their ranks. The way to win respect is to be daring," the prosecutor said.

"At last we've found a magistrate with balls," Juvara said later in the office.

"We'll need to be careful not to let him down. He's an endangered species," Soneri said.

"You!? Let down a magistrate!?"

Soneri signalled to him to stop. "Do you know the councillors? Is there one of them who's got so much accumulated resentment that he'd want to reveal where the bodies are buried?"

"Musumeci knows more about this. He was with the team that arrested Montagnani."

"Do you know if that crook has spoken out?"

"He did say something, prompted by his lawyer. He says he sold himself for a few coins and a computer."

"You believe that's all there is to it?"

"No, but he won't go any further."

The commissario picked up the telephone and called Musumeci. "Where are you? I need to talk to you in person."

They met at the Barriera Repubblica. It was mid-afternoon and the mist had lifted a little, making it possible to enjoy the view along Via Emilia, which sliced the city centre in two and passed in front of the Town Hall and the pastel facades of the twin rows of patrician palaces. Parma was a city of semi-tints, like its bourgeoisie, which never deviated, neither from cowardice nor convenience, from an anodyne median point.

"Have you put the screws on Montagnani?" Soneri asked.

"A waste of effort."

"I guess he's trying to cover up for the others."

"Yes, he's taking the blame for everything."

"And who's going to believe a word of it? A prick like him!"

"No-one does believe a word of it, sir, but we need evidence before we can go any further. The way he's behaving is common enough among criminals. How often have we run up against that sort of attitude?"

"These people are not criminals. They haven't got the balls to be real criminals! Perhaps Montagnani will think better of it after a week in prison."

"The magistrate has already put him under house arrest," Musumeci said.

"We need to keep the pressure on. One of them will crack sooner or later. We'll let them all kick their heels for a bit, time to get the wind up."

"Yes, but I'd like to understand ..."

"What?"

"Who should I listen to? Capuozzo, who takes us aside and invites us to slow down, or Bergossi, who's driven by all the furies of hell?"

"Am I or am I not your superior officer? Well then, pay heed to me."

"But you, in turn, have Capuozzo on your back, and if he takes it into his head, he could bugger us all good and proper," the inspector said, making a circular motion with his hands.

"Bergossi is in overall charge of the investigation, isn't he? But feel free to heap the blame on me. You can say you were just carrying out orders, like the Nazi war criminals," Soneri said, with a chuckle.

"No, I'll behave like Montagnani. I'll sacrifice myself."

The commissario made as though to aim a punch at him. "Is there someone inside or outside the Council who could help us with the next move?"

"There's Sgarzi, a madman who's been banging on for years about what he calls 'the regime', without anyone giving a toss. He was elected as part of a protest movement which is in the general opposition area. Our colleagues in the D.I.G.O.S. know him well because every so often he picks up a soapbox and goes into the Piazza to harangue passers-by."

"Where can I find him?" Soneri said, remembering an

individual who would periodically bawl at people through a megaphone. He had never stopped to listen, because he had no patience with people who made a display of themselves.

"I believe he has an office in Vicolo Santa Maria, near the University and the public library."

"Have either the D.I.G.O.S. or the prosecutors ever seriously considered what he's been denouncing?"

"I don't think so, but I couldn't say why not. Perhaps his accusations have no basis. He's quite eccentric and is generally viewed as a nutcase. When he talks in the street, people stare at him and laugh."

"Under a dictatorial regime, all opponents are dismissed as crazy," Soneri said. As he made his way towards the Ponte di Mezzo, beyond which the Torri dei Paolotti in Via d'Azeglio stood out, he inexplicably felt the solitude of Councillor Sgarzi descend on him. He experienced it as something familiar, almost fraternal.

Vicolo Santa Maria was a narrow lane situated between the old city hospital, a historic building which the brutalist, entrepreneurial spirit of the day hoped to convert into a flashy hotel, and the green oasis of the park, designed by a duchess in the days when the cult of beauty was still alive. Access to the office, which consisted of one room piled high with documents, was through a wooden door corroded by humidity and giving onto a narrow, dark staircase. The moment he saw him, the councillor peered at him suspiciously, while the commissario's attention was caught by a megaphone leaning against a pile of books, a souvenir of demonstrations past.

Sgarzi gave him no more than a peremptory greeting with a movement of his chin, and did not speak.

"I'm Commissario Soneri, from the police."

"I guessed as much. I can always recognise a police officer."

Without waiting to be invited, the commissario sat down on the only chair free of documents. Inside the office, a little electric heater was fighting a losing battle against the cold. The councillor was dressed in a heavy military jacket and fingerless gloves.

"So, what do you want?" Sgarzi asked with deliberate rudeness.

"I'm developing an interest in politics."

"You really believe there's still such a thing as politics? It's dead!" he said, raising his voice. "The Council is nothing more than a business centre."

"Alright then, let's talk about business."

"I've been talking about that for ages, and if you people in the police had taken any interest in what I've been saying instead of trying to shut me up and dragging me off to the cells . . . but around here, if a dog barks at robbers, you beat the dog because it's woken you up."

"Well, here I am with my club. The dog barking has put me on the alert."

"What do you want me to say? Look around, consult, read," Sgarzi said, picking up files and folders. "For years I've been drawing up reports only to be dismissed as a lunatic with a grudge. We're now so comprehensively fucked that we've forgotten even the minimum of decency. Anyone with a glimmer of honesty is shouted down as crazy, not so much by the puppeteers as by the judgment of ordinary people, those apathetic souls who make up what's called 'public opinion'. They've succeeded in transforming criminality into routine. Stealing is part of day-to-day life. It's normal. The context is rotten through and through."

"The context," Soneri repeated, hearing that word yet again. "How does Corbellini figure in this context?"

Sgarzi shrugged his shoulders. "A man of straw. He was useful for dirty operations, especially regarding the 'areas'."

"The P.P.I.S. industrial area?"

"They bought agricultural land for eighty euros a square metre when the market price was thirty. This over-estimate allowed them to request loans from the banks on the basis of an inflated value."

"And the banks accepted that?"

"Of course! In any case, the loans were underwritten by the Council. Who's behind Raig, a secretive company which in a single day can purchase land from private individuals and sell it on to the Council, realising a surplus value of fifty euros per square metre? That's what you've got to uncover. When there's not a single euro left in the Town Hall, even the one bank in the city under political control will founder, or be sold off at a knockdown price. The bill will be met by the people of Parma."

The councillor's eyes shone between the tufts of hair which hung over his forehead and the beard which encroached on his cheekbones. He pushed towards the commissario a file extracted from a stack. "Read this. It's all laid out here, including the questions I put to the mayor and his inner committee."

"Did you receive any support from the Left? What did the ex-communists do?"

Sgarzi tapped his finger on the side of his nose. "They remained silent because there are takings for them as well. The cooperatives do business with the city bosses, and together they're devouring Parma. Their jaws are chomping all the time. There's already a tacit agreement to put Ugolini forward as mayor."

"If they're in charge of business matters, it seems to me quite logical that it'll go that way," Soneri heard himself saying.

"You're beginning to understand. Parma, like the whole world, is now a business concern ripe for the plucking. Until now, there was an administrator delegated by the bosses, but in future the boss himself will be our representative. And these people accuse me of wanting to blow up the world! Are these gentlemen actually defending democratic institutions? They do what they like. They spend the citizens' money to obtain the consent of the self-same citizens, and to multiply their clientele with boards, agencies and commissions."

Sgarzi spoke on and on, blitzing the commissario with words. From his tone, it was clear he was repeating speeches made in vain before contemptuous listeners in Piazza Garibaldi. His outburst caused a film of spittle to form on his lips and dribble onto his black beard. "And I'm the one who's supposed to be the destroyer! What about them? They ignore questions of rights and law, even of the law of the market they claim to believe in. To remain part of this world, they'd make a pact with the Devil."

"The Devil? And who is this devil?"

"It's you who should be telling me! Don't you see how this city is changing? The various mafias, together with their allies in the banks and the business world, are devouring the Duomo and the Pilotta. Some cretinous prefects deny what's happening, because they're imbued with petty bourgeois disdain and behave like certain fashionable ladies who hide away a drug-addicted child because he might ruin the family's reputation."

Soneri had no idea how to reply. These were the very questions which, in moments of bitterness, he had been asking himself or putting to Juvara. Now that Sgarzi was tossing them in his face with maximum effrontery, he was wounded by them.

Sgarzi noticed his reaction, and decided to be more conciliatory. "I know, I know. Above you, there's a hierarchy nominated and controlled by the politicians who break bread with the different mafias. Favours in exchange for votes. But more and more frequently the criminals collect the votes directly and elect mafiosi to Parliament. Some magistrates uncovered this, but were silenced by dynamite ..."

"I know about Laudadio, Lopinto, Petrillo, the *avvocato* Righetti ..." Soneri started before being interrupted again.

"Laudadio is a poor wretch, Lopinto a rank-and-file mafioso, and Petrillo a trusty. The man who's in charge here is Carmine Santurro, and he's affiliated with the camorra gang from Castellammare di Stabia. Through a series of frontmen like Righetti, he controls local nightclubs, bars, pizzerias and even some companies. If you want to find him, go to *Boing*, a disco in Strada Argini, or you could go around one o'clock to the *Fritto di Paranza*, where he has a table reserved and a parking space set aside for his Mercedes."

The commissario wondered why he was unaware of a large part of what Sgarzi was telling him. A sense of disillusion, accompanied by a feeling of impotence, overcame him, making him suspect that he too had been affected by the desire to avert his gaze, a trend dominant in the city now that it was faced with a shameful reality far removed from the happy island it wished to be.

"The local division of the anti-mafia agency is responsible for these matters, and doesn't bother informing us. The magistrates in charge are in Bologna. Only occasionally have they asked for our collaboration, mainly when dealing with people under curfew," Soneri said.

"Hardly surprising! Here the camorra has infiltrated quietly, without any great fuss. All it had to do was exploit the weakness of the scions of the great local business families. In the third or fourth generation, they don't care about the family company anymore. They throw themselves into the *dolce vita*: fast cars, women, cocaine, nights on the town in places like Forte dei Marmi, and at that point the sharks make their entrance. They offer bundles of money and take over the business, or else they strangle it with usury. Anyone who doesn't give way will find an unscrupulous rival set up alongside him, and sooner or later he's going to find it more convenient to do a deal. Better to be friends than enemies with people of that sort, and so the mafia takes its seat at the tables in the grand palaces. Money makes them equal to the others, and they have more money than anyone else. Do you believe that Ugolini hasn't done a deal with them? One of his closest colleagues is related to Santurro, and did twenty years in prison for murder."

Soneri sighed and raised his eyes to the walls where photos of Guido Picelli, leader of the anti-Fascist barricades of 1922, and of Giacomo Ferrari, partisan leader and first post-war mayor, were fading into a sepia-coloured oblivion.

"The fact that I'm believed to be crazy has saved me from their reprisals. No-one pays any attention to me so I'm considered harmless, but among bandits, it's a mark of honour to be an outlaw. You, I and all those who are still bound by ethics, whatever those ethics are, we're outlaws."

"You mean we'll be the leaders of the revolution," Soneri said, with a strained laugh.

For the first time, a smile, even if a bitter one, appeared on Sgarzi's face. "Once people in power had you run through with a bayonet, or left you to starve, but now they reduce you to an infantile state, which is even worse."

"Is L'Eterna one of the many branches of the Santurro empire?" Soneri asked, returning to the investigation.

"Read this," the councillor said handing over another file. "It's a perfect example of infiltration, a case study. You identify a company in trouble, you recycle loads of money in the form of investments, you sell at less than the going rate to undermine your rivals and when you're big enough, you initiate real marketing operations but present yourself as a philanthropist. The image is the final stamp of approval and the guarantee of entrance into the charity business. With ready cash, you can buy anything. They even took over the project to build a big hospice to put all the elderly in one place, and the idea was favourably received in a city of exhibitionists where everybody goes about wearing designer clothes, suntanned, showing off how fit they are, driving big cars with sexy models beside them. Elderly folk don't fit in with this image. They're out of place. Corbellini, handsome and well coiffured, was the embodiment of this type. Montagnani worked out every day and spent time under the sun lamps. They called him Cicciobello."

Soneri studied Sgarzi, and in his battered features he detected the irreparable damage which rejection had done to him. His pockmarked skin, his shabby appearance, his hunched profile and those dark tufts of hair which wrapped themselves over his head gave the impression of poverty and distress. At that moment he saw Sgarzi's eyes glistening, but just for a moment. The councillor looked away to shield himself. "Sometimes when I think of Corbellini, I understand him a little," he said, starting up again. There was no longer any anger in his voice, but a pained inflection. "If you had met him in a bar without knowing who he was, he might even have seemed a sensitive and fragile human being, but someone like that should never have donned the straitjacket of such a role."

"You think he wasn't up to it?"

"Few people really know themselves, and the flattery of fame can be a terrible burden."

"Unless you're sufficiently cynical, but you need a talent even for that."

"More often it's indifference. The cynic is someone who reasons and realises where good and evil are, and chooses whichever is more advantageous. Indifference is another matter.

There's a generation of politicians who are as imperturbable as reptiles, free of all passion and cool in the face of either applause or condemnation. These are the ones who are most appreciated, and perhaps Corbellini passed himself off as one of them without being like that under the surface."

Soneri rose to his feet in silence. At that point, the councillor stared at him with an intensity which might almost have passed for gratitude, and, in his usual ungracious way, he handed him a couple of folders. "Take these and read them. It doesn't matter whether you believe them or not. It's likely you'll never lay your hands on the proof of what I'm telling you, but I believe this is the way things stand. With the means at its disposal, the State could expose everything, but the State will never go against itself and lay bare its connivances and complicities. The context is what it is, complicated, contorted and irremediably compromised."

"But you still believe?" the commissario asked, realising as he spoke that he was asking the question out of personal curiosity.

"In what? In justice?"

"No, in the revolution, not the socialist revolution but a more modest one. A law-abiding revolution, for example. Even legality has become revolutionary, don't you agree?"

"Certainly I believe in it. It shows I'm completely mad," Sgarzi said, almost roaring as he closed the door in the commissario's face.

18

"YOU'RE BEHAVING STRANGELY. This inquiry has forced you to rake over vast quantities of paperwork, and you're as unsure of yourself as a student cramming for exams," Angela said, watching him work through Sgarzi's files.

"I'm glad I'm not doing your job. You're on intimate terms with paperwork," he replied.

"Not at all. I'm a woman of action. You should have seen me in court this morning. I was a wild beast facing a thug who'd been beating his wife."

"I can well believe it. I am well acquainted with the wild beast in question."

She came up to him, her fingernails stretched out like claws. "Would you like to be torn apart?"

"I'd be the executioner's willing victim."

Angela let out a roar and gave him a gentle bite, but then drew back.

"Don't you like me?" he asked.

"I'm hungry."

"Exactly."

"Later. First let's attend to your taste buds. I've bought some *tortelli di zucca* and some tripe."

"First attend to the senses, in every sense."

"Life must be enjoyed, but you didn't give me an answer."

"To what? To the fact that you think I'm behaving strangely? This investigation is different from all the others."

"Different in what way?"

"There are no common criminals among the protagonists, only people normally considered respectable. Respectable criminals."

"You mean politicians?"

"Politicians, industrialists, professionals, lawyers like you, civil society!" Soneri intoned sarcastically.

"That doesn't leave much else. What's going on? Is this an inquiry into the world?"

"No, it's an inquiry into power in this city, which in its own small way is a mirror of power in general. I'm going through the dossiers Sgarzi gave me."

"Who? That madman?"

"So you think he's mad too? What he says is so plausible as to be beyond belief."

"I stopped a couple of times to listen to him. He has the courage to say out loud what everyone else says in a whisper."

"But you still call him 'mad'. Is that because anyone with the courage to denounce the authorities in public must be off his head?"

"It's because the powers that be drive their opponents crazy."

"That's down to our conformism, cowardice and intellectual laziness."

"It's not enough to say the right things. There are so many of them chattering away, all over the place. To be listened to, you've got to be authoritative."

"And who is authoritative?"

"People who are popular on television and whose success is measured in the number of 'likes' on websites and blogs. That's the screen that matters. The considered word of an unknown genius is worth less than the brainless word of a popular idiot. Sgarzi looks like a clown with that megaphone of his."

"Yes, I know. It's out of date, makes him look like a loser."

"Do you remember what we learned at university? The medium is the message. But standing up in public . . . exposing himself to the respectable provincialism of a city which is such a slave of fashion . . . in their eyes, Sgarzi is playing a dud hand. He dresses badly, he uses an old-fashioned instrument, he stands up on a kind of stool and lacks the aura of people who're never off the television screens, the poor sod."

"And they throw stones at him, as they do at poor sods."

"It's only with hindsight that you realise who was right. Conviction arrives late, like happiness. At the time, we just don't notice."

"But that's not true of *tortelli*," Soneri said, turning his attention to the dish his partner had put on the table. "There's something which makes you instantly happy. If heroin addicts could savour its taste, they'd take it up instead of the other stuff. We should be sending them to a good restaurant instead of locking them up."

"Politicians are aware of this, which is why they spend half our money dining out."

"Have you been reading the dossiers?"

"No need. I can imagine. Politicians have a special talent for enjoying the pleasures of life," Angela said.

"If what Sgarzi says is true, this city is rotten through and through. The word I've heard most often in the course of this investigation is 'context'. There's not just one guilty party or even a circle of guilty people, but a collection of individual guilt complexes working in unison. That's why I feel so uneasy. In this case, it won't be sufficient to go after them, to mount a raid, to keep watch, to gather fingerprints. We're going to have to consult papers, balance sheets and financial operations. I'm a policeman from the backwoods, trained to pad about in the mist. I'm not an accountant."

"Stop feeling sorry for yourself! I can't stand it," Angela said. "Police stations are overrun with consultants. Pacchioni is excellent, and you know the city very well."

"No, that's not true. I've discovered a city that I didn't know, or perhaps that I prefer not to know. I've been as guilty as the rest of the Parmigiani for averting my eyes and pretending we're different, but it's more serious in my case."

"I know. It's a silent disease, but perhaps it's not incurable."

"Sgarzi writes that a quarter of our economy is under the control of criminals, and that a large part of the rest is infected because it does business with them. There are cooperatives which permit mafia-controlled companies to tender in the north of Italy in exchange for business in the south. Private firms accept capital from mafia sources, thereby becoming partners with the bosses. However, since it's easier to do business when you're in power, you end up with businessmen in collusion with the city administration."

"Are you talking about Ugolini?"

"Him, and others at lower levels."

"It's hard to stay clear of it."

"Most of our fellow citizens believe they're in the clear. That's the real problem."

"What else does Sgarzi have to say?"

"A lot. There are two principal lines: the P.P.I.S. areas and the boards, which under Corbellini have multiplied ridiculously. There are boards for mobility, for urban embellishment, for tourism and, would you believe it, they've even set up one for public decorum! According to the dossiers I've been reading, with all these useless boards the mayor and committee chairpersons have been creaming off money. Thanks to a cycle of inflated invoices, the cash ends up in private accounts which finance election campaigns worthy of a satrap. The traffic in vacant sites, where the Raig outfit acts as intermediary, is even bigger. The company headquarters are in the office of an accountant linked to the party of Ugolini and Corbellini. In the course of a few hours, some sites were snapped up by private companies and sold to the Council at eye-watering prices, sometimes with the help of the one entirely Parma-owned bank left in the field. It has given out loans in line with overvalued property. Here too the Right had its own man in place."

"Do you believe these allegations are well founded?" Angela asked.

"Maybe not all of them, but in large part they are. I asked Juvara to check if those lightning sales at inflated prices had really taken place, and he's confirmed that they have. Now Pacchioni is trying to work out who's hiding behind the Raig company."

Angela shook her head and laughed nervously.

"It's astonishing that an official could do things like that and that a banker could ratify them without anyone reacting. This collective passivity is terrifying," Soneri said.

"We'll have to get involved. I wish we'd listened to Sgarzi and the few others on the Council who raised objections."

Soneri pushed his plate away, leaving the tripe half eaten.

"Come on, we mustn't poison our own lives. What's done is done, but we'll respond in future," Angela said.

"The many people who did know must have said the same, but they let everything carry on so as not to poison their lives. The others kept us distracted and we failed to look at the evidence. A moribund city which doesn't even want to be told it's sick."

The commissario was now in a thoroughly bad mood. Angela took away his plate and put it in the fridge. She sat down beside him and put an arm round his shoulders.

"Did you ever imagine we'd end up like this?" Soneri said, realising a couple of seconds later that he had asked the same question a couple of days earlier.

"Nobody could ever have thought it, but the bulwarks against disgust weaken little by little. The first time we see a little section give way, we think to ourselves that it's nothing, the structure's solid, couldn't collapse, could never crumble. We never notice the sly, patient, silent work of the waters which gnaw away at it."

"We've taken too much for granted. That's the guilt of our generation. We thought the conquests we'd made were for ever, while they needed to be consolidated and defended. We failed in the maintenance of our ideas. We left them to rust."

"Alright, now get to work on the restoration," Angela said.

"There are only remnants."

"Remnants are very useful. Just a couple of days ago, I made an application for the exhumation of a person who's thirty years dead. There was a dispute over the inheritance," Angela said.

"You've had a lot of business with corpses and graveyards lately."

"More than the average policeman. In reality, it's a banal question of finance, a woman who had no hesitation over publicising the love affairs of her dead mother so she can have a share of the cash."

"Typical! But who is she?"

"The Montanari family, the ones who run the arts centre at the foundry. Costante, the owner, died without heirs and left everything to the Church, but a female cousin has made a declaration that her mother, who was married to Costante's father's brother, had an affair with her brother-in-law which produced her. In other words, this cousin claims to be Costante's half-sister, and on that basis is claiming her part of the company. So we've got to do an analysis of the D.N.A. of a pile of bones."

"Reminds me of the old saying about selling your mother."

"Not so fast with your judgments. Two million euros might make a hermit change his mind. Perhaps that's why the judge has authorised the exhumation."

"And where will this spectacle take place?"

"In the Lagrimone cemetery, in the town of Tizzano, one of those managed by L'Eterna. Does that tell you anything?"

"They've got the monopoly now."

"So they have. I checked up and all the graveyards in the mountains belong to them. They offer advantageous terms to the councils, and these days . . ."

"Do you know when they're going to open the grave?"

"I'll know in a matter of days. A decision is imminent. Why? Does it interest you?"

"You told me to keep an eye on L'Eterna."

"You know the reason better than me. Anyway, it'll be no more than a week."

"That's not the only reason."

"If there's something else, I'd like to know. It might help me with the case."

"That's where they buried Romagnoli."

Angela was about to reply when Soneri's mobile rang.

"Forgive me for phoning at this hour, but there are some funny goings-on over at the Council offices," Musumeci said.

"What's happening?"

"People coming and going with black bin bags."

"Any idea what's in them?"

"They seem very heavy. Might be papers."

"Where are they taking them?"

"No idea. They're being loaded into the boots of cars, which then drive away."

"Follow them. Try to find out where they're headed. I'll come and take over at the Council building."

Once he was out on the street, he found it was raining, fine drops which stuck to his raincoat like frost. As he crossed through the centre to Piazza Garibaldi, he noticed that many of the lights in the Council building were still on, but he could not see anyone under the Portici del Grano. He continued along Via Repubblica and turned into the adjacent lane, passing in front of the statue of Hercules and Antaeus locked in a struggle, a statue called in dialect *I du brassé*, "The Embracing Couple". He stopped at a point from which he could observe the courtyard of the Town Hall and the side that was in shadow. The fountain at the foot of the statue was gurgling in the darkness. He waited about ten minutes during which he tried in vain to contact Musumeci, then saw a man appear stumbling under the weight of a large bag. He waited for him to come close enough to allow him to recognise him as the man who had used the mayor's ski-pass.

"It's not easy to find someone who works as hard as you," the commissario said, stepping out to block his way. "I imagine you must have found it less of an effort to go up and down the Paganella," he added, pointing to the bag.

"The company was better."

Soneri did not react. "Tidying up?" he said, in the same tone as before.

"It's got to be done every so often," the man said, walking past him as though he were a beggar.

The commissario obeyed an impulse which surprised even him. With a lightning move, he grabbed the bag from the man's hand. When he was about to react, Soneri pushed him away with his left hand.

"What are you doing?" the man asked.

"I've always enjoyed rummaging about in rubbish."

He undid the ties but when he pulled back the sides of the bag he was mortified by what he saw: a quantity of narrow strips of paper, bundled together like dry, inert worms. He stuck his hand in, moved it about and then closed the bag, disappointed.

"See? What did you expect?" the man said triumphantly.

"Is this the last one?" Soneri asked, feeling powerless.

"That's the lot for this evening," the man replied, with irritating calm.

"Let me give you a hand," the commissario said between clenched teeth, taking hold of the bag once again. "I'll take care of this."

"As you wish." The man let him do what he wanted, but this time a touch of suspicion and even of fear was evident. He turned back towards the Town Hall and disappeared under the dark colonnade.

Shortly afterwards, Musumeci called.

"Come and join me in the Council building. I've taken possession of some material," Soneri said.

The inspector turned up a quarter of an hour later. "The car I followed had two bags in the boot. One was thrown into a bin in Piazza Lubiana and the other ended up in Via Savani."

"Did you take a look inside?"

"Yes, but they contained nothing but shredded paper."

"The same as this," the commissario said, pointing to the bag at his feet.

"Well, it seems clear enough. I see now why they were trying to gain time by putting phoney messages on Twitter," Musumeci said.

"We got this wrong. We should have moved at once to get hold of this material, and to search the mayor's office."

"If the magistrate won't give us authorisation ..." Musumeci concluded with a shrug.

"Bergossi has the majority in Parliament pursuing him, and he has no desire to play the martyr. In any case, I don't believe that if we'd got a warrant earlier it would have made any difference. They've had almost a week to get rid of everything. Corbellini was officially on holiday, but no doubt they knew that wasn't the case."

"And here's the outcome," Musumeci said.

19

DON JULES CALLED just as Soneri was entering his office. "The parish priest has come back and would be happy to talk to you," he said.

"So we've changed our minds now, have we?" the commissario asked, somewhat testily. He had forgotten all about the priest.

"Don Guido has something important to tell you about Corbellini."

"Why else did he think I was looking for him a couple of days ago?"

"At that time, he was still badly shaken after the assault, but he's recovered now."

This reply irritated Soneri, who had no patience with hypocrisy.

"Don't mess me about. You can tell Don Guido that as soon as I've got a free moment, I'll call in."

Juvara came in.

"Where have you been?" the commissario asked.

"I've been with our accountant, Pacchioni. We're examining the patchwork of enterprises and businesses involving Laudadio, Petrillo and Lopinto's holding company, Posillipo Ltd. It's a much bigger network than we thought, with dozens of pizzerias, bars, nightclubs, shops rented out to Pakistanis, wholesale operations at the Interporto, lorries, hotels and even pharmacies."

"Evil transforms itself very easily. And what can you tell me about Santurro?"

"There we're struggling a bit, sir."

"What do you mean?"

"It's another level, and we can only make vague guesses. We can get as far as Lopinto, but Santurro is in a higher category. As a businessman, he's affiliated to the association of industrialists, he's a friend of many bankers, and he's on the Council of the Chamber of Commerce. In other words, he's clean, and for the moment, at least formally, he's untouchable. These people send their children to the Bocconi University in Milan, and then to the U.S.A. to do a Masters. They speak English the way their parents spoke dialect. In ten years they can make what it took other people two generations to acquire."

"Money – they've got more of it than anybody else," the commissario said.

"Enough to buy up reputable companies, as Santurro has. They've already gained power in political institutions, and with that they have access to people in government."

"They can influence law-making. They're able to build a ring-fence around themselves."

"We're here to prevent that," Juvara said.

"If only it depended on me, on you and these other men here. Have you ever asked yourself why the mafias have been around so long?"

The inspector made as if to reply, but the commissario carried on before he could open his mouth. "It's because they're the manifestation of what we are. Isn't Corbellini really a mafia man, setting up worthless boards to create his own clique, complete with a circle of dependants and semi-criminal henchmen? Isn't the corruption practised by Montagnani textbook mafia? And what about the links between the banks and politicians to overvalue the P.P.I.S. lands and cheat the tax man?"

Soneri was working himself into a fine frenzy, as had been happening more and more frequently. He noticed that Juvara was staring at him agog, so he fell silent and attempted to calm himself down. "Alright," he said more tranquilly, "for the moment we can't get to Santurro, but what about the others?"

"Laudadio is under investigation, and we're tapping Petrillo's telephone in an attempt to work out the links with the upper level. I mean with Posillipo Ltd."

"Where has Lopinto ended up?"

"As soon as he discovered the way the wind was blowing, he must have scuttled off back to Campania. They're white-collar operatives and they don't want any trouble. As soon as they feel the heat, they're off, leaving the rank and file to be picked up by us."

"I know, I know. So what are we going to do with somebody like Petrillo?"

"He'll never talk, if that's what you mean, but he's the secret manipulator of the whole business of the drugs in the dogs' bellies. We've intercepted more than one conversation between him and his 'mules', and the narcotics squad are just waiting for the right moment. You know better than me the damage that can be done by prematurely cutting off a promising line of inquiry."

The commissario appeared cheered up by this conversation. Every so often, when he felt it was his duty to redeem the world, the immensity of the task which opened out before him extinguished every light inside him, but then a single glimmer, like the one just indicated by Juvara, was sufficient to rekindle hope.

The telephone rang and the inspector picked it up. "It's for you, sir. Aurora Guatelli."

"Can we meet?" she began.

"Do you have any news?"

"Not really, but my suspicions have grown stronger."

"If that's all there is to it, we can talk on the telephone."

"No, I want to meet you. I'm not the only one who's afraid."

"Who else?"

"Don Guido. He's afraid that ..."

"Alright then. We'll meet at Don Guido's. I was due to go there anyway."

He got into the car and set off for Navetta. Parma seemed to him a brooding place, as if sketched in pencil, and the air felt like breath exhaled from the pavement and stagnating among the houses in the back streets. The damp wind was causing the snow to melt slowly, and the dank slush on the roads created an aura of decay that might corrode the walls, swallowing up the bell towers and the palaces inside which the city pondered its days.

In the outskirts, among the crumbling buildings in the housing estates, that oppressive sense of decomposition hung even more heavily. And then the church: a swirl of cement devoid of all finesse, sombre in its indecipherability. Don Guido had a bandage prominently displayed over one side of his forehead, and this gave him a convalescent appearance. Don Jules was buzzing around him with an anxious expression. Aurora must have arrived early and was already smoking a cigarette in the half-opened bay window.

The parish priest gestured to Soneri to take the seat opposite him, and exchanged a couple of glances with Aurora. She was the first to speak. "Just now we're very worried about Giancarlo."

"What has changed since we last met?"

"Two more days have passed, for one thing."

"I got the impression you didn't believe he'd fled. If he hasn't, what do you think has happened?"

Don Guido intervened. "The commissario is quite right. We immediately had an instinctive feeling about what was behind his disappearance. In the early stages we were afraid, but now we're certain, me more than anyone else."

"Why did you cover it up?" Soneri asked.

"Because I was warned off."

"Who by?"

"Commissario, power has many faces. The person who assaulted me was not the one who wanted me to stay silent."

"But he did order you not to say anything."

"That's a detail. He was rank and file."

"The rank and file have masters."

"There's no doubt that someone sent that man."

"And that was enough to make you keep your mouth shut."

"No. If I didn't speak out, it wasn't because of the threats, but because I had no support. It may seem strange to you, but even we priests can feel isolated, especially if you're on the front line, like me. Have you had a look around this district?"

Soneri nodded. "Do you mean to say that the Church wasn't at your side?"

Don Guido stayed silent. Aurora spoke for him. "Not only was it not at his side, but it even compelled him to shut himself away in that home at Porporano for the chronically ill. It's almost a prison."

"I never had any doubt which side the Church was on," the commissario said.

Don Guido reacted angrily to this statement. "Not the whole Church. There are priests like me who have been denouncing corruption and immorality for ages, but what can one individual do on his own? Do you see what this city has become? You can get angry, but you can't make war by yourself. You might get into a rage and perhaps take it out on your neighbour, but he might be equally enraged, perhaps for the same reasons. The fact is that all this anger hasn't found anyone to organise and represent it. The parties have been posted missing, and there's no shared horizon in politics!"

"You priests have gone missing as well. Today the Church's vineyards . . ."

"I admit that what you say is true, but no-one listens to priests who work on the streets, like us. You've seen how they treated me. Christ is not in fashion. Christ is a dangerous revolutionary whom they crucify anew each day."

"Perhaps, but you've made deals with the Antichrist. You gave Corbellini enough rope. You covered up for his disappearance."

"What do you mean, Antichrist? If anything, he was a poor wretch. He played the game, that's all."

"The killer is just as guilty as the man who orders the murder."

"Yes, yes, I know. Giancarlo was weak. He was carried away by ambition. He was foolish enough to believe he could change politics, interpret it in his own way. He was deluded."

"Did he really believe those powerful interests would defer to a nightclub P.R. man?"

"What does ambition drive us to?" the priest answered. "Be that as it may, I repeat, he was fundamentally a good person."

"Was? Are you sure he's dead?"

Aurora butted in. "No, we're not sure, but otherwise what do you think has happened to him? Even if he's not dead, he won't be seen again. I hope for his sake that wherever he is, he's happy."

"Wherever he is, I doubt he'll be happy," Don Guido said.

The commissario lost his temper. "What are you trying to tell me? I've always believed he was dead as well, but I can't manage to see through the politicians' smokescreens, the attempts to intimidate the magistrates and the *omertà* of those who won't stand up to the authorities in this city. If they have killed him and you know something about it, speak up, otherwise we're all wasting our time."

This tantrum produced a moment of embarrassment, broken when the priest started talking in the same calm voice as before. "We can tell you we're virtually certain he's dead, but unfortunately that's just an opinion based on our knowledge of Giancarlo. If we've invited you here, it's because the mandarins of the Right want people to believe he's still alive. For them, it doesn't matter in the slightest if he's dead or alive. The important thing is that all the various rackets are kept under wraps. Meantime, they'll be thinking up some way to get out of this mess."

Soneri calmed down and continued speaking. "This city is a theatre, and some illusionists skilled in the art of turning the impossible into reality are standing before the footlights. This is the new shamelessness of power."

"The worst thing is that many people are taken in by it," the priest said.

The commissario got to his feet. Aurora accompanied him but signalled to Don Jules, who was about to go over to them, to stay where he was. She opened the door and as she stood back to let the commissario pass, she put her hand on his shoulder. "Don Guido is sincere when he says that Giancarlo is a good man."

"I'm convinced of that too, but the context in which he was a pawn placed him on the side of the corrupt."

Only when he was out on the street did Soneri realise that he had once again employed that word which was recurring so frequently as to become a refrain.

He got into his car and set off, still unsettled by the conversation. The figure of Corbellini floated into his mind, as unfocused as a faded painting. The image remained with him for the rest of the journey. He kept going back to the scene described by Maresciallo Boldrin when the carabinieri from Val di Badia stopped the car and found inside the regional secretary Bonaldi, the undersecretary Bernetti and the mayor himself. Perhaps everything happened that night after they passed the tollbooth at Fornovo. He made up his mind to send someone to interview Bonaldi once again.

When he walked into his office he found Juvara in a state of high excitement. "Another message has come in on Twitter," he told him.

"From the mayor? What does it say?"

"This time he's given a definite date. He informs the city that he'll be back within a month, give or take a day."

"It's all turned into a farce."

"And that's not all, sir. The right-wing lot have mobilised their followers to express their support for this Council. They're appealing to their better feelings, saying that the people who are clamouring for it to stand down show no respect for a sick man. They say the critics are a pack of jackals."

"Indeed! And what about Montagnani?"

"A bad apple," the inspector intoned ironically.

The commissario walked over to the window and stood there for some time staring out. The darkness falling on Parma seemed to him more metaphorical than real. "Is there any way to work out who's sending these messages? If only they'd leave some clue!"

"We've tried, but whoever is sending them must be an expert. He's careful to conceal where they're coming from. The Internet is like that. You can throw stones and hide away."

"It's all false! Your web is a phoney world, the perfect image of these times. The equivalence of lies and truth has found its technical legitimisation, and I'm not just talking about the mayor's messages."

"I've warned you about the virtual world," Juvara said.

"You? But you're its apostle!" Soneri said, staring at him in astonishment.

"That's why I know its vices."

They were interrupted by excited voices coming from the police radio. The situation in the city was reaching boiling point once again. There were scuffles in Via Farini, in the university district and on Viale Mariotti. Soneri grabbed his overcoat and went out.

The shouts of the protest marchers could already be heard in Via Repubblica, where there was the customary frantic rushing about, but when the commissario arrived at Piazza Garibaldi he was surprised to see it half deserted. The noise from under the Portici del Grano sounded like an aria bawled out from an open window. "The usual three hundred refugees from the torpor of the Left," he said bitterly to himself.

A bored-looking colleague from the D.I.G.O.S. division came up to him. "It's the usual suspects," he started, but stopped when he saw the commissario turn his back on him, plainly disgusted.

A gust of wind carrying the acrid smell of some burning chemical substance swept across the Piazza, presumably coming from a refinery. Soneri followed the smell along Via Mazzini. The smoke, the same colour as the darkness of night, could not be made out easily by the eye, but could be felt as a heavy, dense sensation in the throat. In Viale Mariotti, dozens of bins were blazing like carnival bonfires, changing the colour of the facades of the houses in the Oltretorrente district, and making it appear as though blood were flowing down the walls. Other bins had been tossed onto the area where once the popular Ghiaia market had stood, before it was transformed from a symbol of the city into an insignificant row of useless boutiques.

Yet another sterile demonstration of some malaise, the

commissario thought to himself as he watched the flames leap angrily upwards. People passed by, had a look and then walked on, alarmed and disconcerted. Only a small circle of curious elderly folk stopped to stare. After a while the firefighters arrived, accustomed to flames which seemed to spring out of nowhere. Soneri remembered the words spoken by Don Guido some hours previously. It was indeed a world of angry people, each looking out for themselves, distrustful of his neighbours, individualists even in their rage.

When they sat down together at table, Angela said to Soneri, "The first person who can interpret this rage will attract general consent, provided he's famous enough and able to hold the stage. For instance, it might be someone who's recently appeared in a television series, someone who can give the dignity of policy to the visceral reasoning of this enraged population. He might say something like 'Politicians are all the same, Left and Right. They're all thieves'..."

"He'd be partly right," the commissario interrupted.

"What matters is to have one enemy clearly in view: politicians – all politicians. And a clear division of the world, on the one hand the corrupt, on the other the honest folk – but that's not the way it is. The honest folk can become corrupt, good people can turn wicked, altruists degenerate into egoists. Very few people have consistency written into their being. Take the case I'm dealing with just now ..."

"The one about the inheritance?"

"Money unleashes the most unbridled avarice imaginable. Extreme cases always demonstrate the depths of the human mind, and scrape away the normal facade of decency from people's conduct. To access a particle of wealth, wills have appeared in every drawer. Women swear they were the lovers of the dead man, cousins turn up from distant parts attracted by the scent of cash, and that's before we get on to the so-called friends and even the doctor who was attending him. Each one of them has a sheet of paper duly stamped by a notary, ready to fall on the executor like a pack of hyenas."

"And the exhumation? Do you know when it'll take place?"

"In a matter of days, but the magistrate doesn't want to set a date just yet because the newspapers have got hold of the story. The Curia doesn't want too much outcry. And of course, when sex comes into the story..."

"Is the court still convinced by the story of an affair? It reeks of opportunism to me."

"There's no way of knowing until it's all been verified, but if it is a hoax, it'd be even worse. This cousin would have branded her mother a whore, and all for nothing," Angela said.

"Anything that can be used to arrive at a deal will be. It might even be that this threat will induce the Curia to divide part of the inheritance with the relatives. Supposing for a moment that this female cousin really is the product of adultery, they'd lose much more. Priests are good at doing the sums," Soneri said.

"I'll be at the exhumation. I'll tell you all about it."

"You must. Don't forget that Romagnoli is buried in Lagrimone too."

"Where does Romagnoli fit into all this?"

"I've no idea, but the cemetery is managed by L'Eterna, and Petrillo is about to be hauled in. We've got to tread warily with these undertakers."

Angela nodded, but did not seem convinced. She could not see the connection, but nor could the commissario, as he admitted to himself when he left after dinner. By then he could not even locate the reasons for his suspicion.

*

Bergossi called on the mobile, and changed the commissario's evening. "We have sufficient proof to arrest Petrillo," he announced with no preamble, a sign that he was in a bad mood. Only then did Soneri remember that this was the day of the ministerial inspection. "If you've nothing against it, I should leave everything to the narcotics squad. The charge is drugs trafficking."

"That's all?"

"For the moment, yes. We can look at it again later. We know what's going on, and it will all come out. It wasn't just trafficking for its own sake."

"What about Lopinto?"

"Can't be found. He must be in hiding."

"In hiding? Has a warrant been issued for his arrest as well?"

"No, sorry. Nothing yet. I was just putting my hopes into words. I'm convinced he's the managing director of this whole criminal enterprise, and I wouldn't be surprised if it was he who ordered the covering fire they're aiming at us in the guise of Parliamentary Questions."

"Lopinto controls both business affairs and a sizeable number of votes in Campania, Rome and Parma. It's not hard for him to set a couple of servile honourable members on us."

"Commissario, we're on our own." The prosecutor raised his voice a fraction, with an undertone of resignation. "In the state it's in, the Left couldn't put even a thousand people on the street against a corrupt administration."

"They spend their time knifing each other in the back," Soneri said. "Ever since they gave up on having joined-up ideas, they're left with nothing more than the worship of power. They fight mercilessly among themselves. Instead of carrying the struggle to the Right, they trip each other up. They're desperate to lord it over everything and everyone, and they've got the hide of an elephant! The cooperatives rival the bosses to see who's more productive, efficient and competitive, and the workers can kiss their arses."

Bergossi sighed. "I see you're even more bitter than me. Tomorrow, after thirty years of service as a man of the law, I will be put on trial by the inspectors from the Ministry. You and I are the accused."

"That's what you must expect in a country of outlaws," Soneri said. The only reply from the other end was the sound of a receiver being put down.

20

HE REALLY WAS alone. In a city suddenly aflame, in a climate produced by lies believed by too many courtiers, Soneri felt an outsider. It was too late to go to Alceste's and sink himself into the purifying waters of dialect speech, spoken as though it was the language of another, not impossible city. He walked on and on, roaming about without any specific destination among the deserted backstreets where the cold and the fear of rioting had imposed their own curfew. As often happened to him, it was in those moments of silence and stillness, among those houses reduced to an amiable backdrop, that he rediscovered his relationship with Parma's pallid grace and mysterious, modest shadows. He strolled for half an hour along streets named after Resistance fighters, feeling reinvigorated every time he thought of their fate: torture and the firing squad. However badly things went for him, he would suffer nothing worse than a comfortable exile in the passport office.

Half dreaming, he found himself in the amber-coloured light of Via Melloni, crossed the lawn in Piazzale della Pace, and was welcomed by the vaults of the Pilotta. There was not a living soul in sight, not even on the staircase of the Biblioteca Palatina – normally peopled by tramps. As he was listening to the subdued crackle of the lamp-posts on the street leading to the Parco Ducale, his mobile began to ring. The mocking acoustics of the vaults made the sound appear mysterious and arcane, like an offstage voice.

"Are you coming along this evening?" Valmarini asked.

"I wasn't aware I was expected."

"Nothing was pre-arranged. Opportunities and desires arise without warning."

"Precisely because everything is so random, we've always left our meetings to occur as and when they do."

"Sometimes events require a midwife."

"Are you playing the man of mystery?"

"You love mysteries. Unpicking them is your profession."

The commissario, troubled and a little irritated, switched off his mobile. Still not quite sure of what he was doing, he turned along the Lungoparma in the direction of the Montebello district. As he did so, he became aware that his conflicting feelings were caused by Valmarini's seductive reticence, although he had no wish to admit he was being taken in. He made his way in the mist, which rose in swirls from the river, getting lost as a shadow among shadows. He rang the doorbell and heard the click of the automatic lock.

He almost tripped over Dondolo, who was lying stretched out in the dark entrance hall. The dog emitted a little yelp which sounded to Soneri like a warning. Valmarini, standing beside his easel, turned only when he heard his footsteps.

"Welcome!" he said, inviting him with a wave of his hand to take a seat. The commissario cast his eyes around the small sitting room and noticed Ugolini curled up in an armchair, almost fading into its upholstery.

"Here he is at last!" he said, in the tone of voice of someone who has been waiting impatiently for a latecomer. His eyes darted about, and his head turned with the jerky movements of a parrot. He must have consumed a lot of cocaine, and had a bottle of grappa at his side.

"It should have been me who said that."

"Birds of a feather seek each other out, and sooner or later find each other."

"Birds of a feather?" Soneri said doubtfully.

Ugolini gave a high-pitched laugh. "I know what you think but, like it or not, we resemble each other. We're flesh of the same flesh."

"I really don't think so, no matter how hard I try."

"It's true all the same," Ugolini insisted, growing more excited by the moment. "We're two combatants."

"For different causes."

"What does that matter? What distinguishes us is that we have beliefs. There's something burning inside us."

"Fired by different fuels."

"That's not what counts. What matters is the flame. Most people have none. We are locomotives, the others are carriages."

"But we're going in different directions."

"At the end of the day, we'll meet. The locomotives are movement and action, while the carriages stand in a line, linked one to the other, passive, waiting to be shunted."

Soneri began to grow impatient with all these metaphors. The cocaine seemed to have made Ugolini over-excited. His hand trembled as he reached out for his glass.

"Rather than meet, I think we'll collide. We're running on the same track."

"That'll depend on you," Ugolini said. "Together we'd be an irresistible force, but pitted one against the other we'd be wasted energy, and only one could emerge as victor."

"You and I can never work together."

"Pity," Ugolini said, shrugging his shoulders. "I almost admire you for your courage."

"Considering the people you do business with . . ."

"And just who do I do business with? In the eyes of the law, I am an honest entrepreneur. You'll never be able to pin anything illegal on me."

"If the image were all that's needed . . ."

"Why? What else is there? Appearance is an unsurmountable bulwark, or a frontier post to be defended. A person is what he appears to be. Nothing else matters."

"We're not addressing a court of law, so I've no need to produce proof. What I know about you is quite enough, and there is an inquiry under way."

"You'll not find a thing against me. To be quite frank, I couldn't care less what you think. I am no different from those business people your conformism makes you regard as respectable. Go and search the history of the various grand dynasties, and you'll find that today's respectability is born of yesterday's villainy: fraud, theft, acts of cowardice, political convenience, marriages of mutual self-interest, exploitation, murder, workers killed by disease or crushed by machinery. Shit, all shit! The ancestors of the great families with heraldic titles were assassins, whoremongers and bloodstained executioners. Even the saints! At the time of the Crusades, it was sufficient to slay a hundred Moors to receive God's grace. To gain a shining halo, you could show up with a collection of bleeding, disembowelled, lacerated, decapitated or flayed corpses. Well, I've never committed such acts of depravity. My employees are well treated. I continue to provide work. I've never sacked anyone. Go and tell that to your damn communists in the trade unions!"

Dondolo had taken up his usual position on the rug and stared at Ugolini with instinctive distrust.

"What's the matter? Are you suffering for want of a coat of arms? Will they not let you into the salons of the commercial nobility?" the commissario asked ironically.

"I'm not going to be hanging about in the corridors of power for two or three generations, that much is certain. With my money and my power, I'll force my way in, and I'll piss on their titles."

"Some things can't be bought. You can purchase phoney paintings because you can't acquire the real thing. Culture takes time."

"I don't give a damn about culture!" Ugolini roared. "A new breed has emerged who'll smash such old notions. Business and I.T. are the new culture, and nobody, but nobody, is going to call me an ignoramus!" He spoke in a crescendo of hysterical delight, before casting a glance of real hatred in Valmarini's direction. "And I'll burn your paintings! The day will come when they're no use to anyone."

"You can burn them right now if you wish," Valmarini said disdainfully.

"Take it easy," Ugolini said, calming down. "For the moment, they still serve a purpose. There are lots of people I still want to confound."

"The bosses and paymasters of the camorra?" Soneri said acidly.

Ugolini did not lose his composure. Either he had the thick skin of a crocodile, or else the cocaine had given him an overbearing self-confidence. A contemptuous smile spread over his face. "I thought you were sharper than that, but I now see you haven't understood a thing."

"There are many things I don't understand."

"You're an old man," Ugolini said, tapping his forehead. "The days are gone when an ideological or cultural cabaret was sufficient to interpret what's happening. Now reality emerges in all its naked brutality and beauty. Religions, monarchies, philosophies and fear of the Divine, they've all been swept away, and what's left are solitary figures like you and me, burning with the desire to live and to assert themselves by any means available. And today there is only one means to do so – money. This is the age of absolute individuality, of men in sole command. I know, I know what you're going to say," he said, heading off the objection he saw being formulated on the commissario's lips. "We live in a democracy. That's part of the image or the illusion which serves to fill the minds of the majority, but you must remember that they're just carriages, and being all linked up one to the other, they can be shunted off in any direction."

Soneri turned to Valmarini, who was standing listening silently as he worked at the reproduction of one of Tintoretto's lesser works. "You're the real prophet," he said to him, "the man who makes what is false authentic, a fount of new truth, like Corbellini's Twitter messages."

"What a bore it all is!" Ugolini said, changing the subject. "The camorra, of whom you accuse me of being a partner, is the new militia of a free-enterprise community which is struggling to assert itself. This is the initial phase I was talking about, the bestial phase when you have to dirty your hands with blood and trickery. It's the moment when you risk your life, and where ferocity is the one sure way to get ahead, but it's followed by the moment of command when you can order other people to do the killing and swindling. Then, with the same ferocity as before, the real entrepreneurial career begins. It involves in part the purchase of recyclable activities, in part strangulation by usury and in part the formation of alliances. I'm talking about the north of Italy, where it's easier to do well for yourself. If all goes to plan, you pass to the third stage, where you send your children to study at the most prestigious institutions, create a dynasty, feature in glossy magazines and get into politics to influence legislation. At this point, you can be a criminal inside the law, as happens with bankers and financiers who choke the world in a perfectly legal way, hiding behind the smokescreen of an impeccable public image and occasional acts of charity."

Soneri was obliged to admit to himself that Ugolini was right regarding bankers and financiers, but he raised the objection. "Your partners in Castellammare have not yet been legalised."

"They're no partners of mine. You've no right to say that."

"Oh yes they are."

"I could sue you if you said that in public, and the whole city would spit in your face. I am a well-known and highly regarded businessman. People stop me in the street to congratulate me. I have received countless public honours. Soon they'll want to make me a saint."

"That's as may be, but you know I'm right."

"Suppose you are? Who cares? Nothing beyond the public arena, nothing behind the veil of the collective image counts for a thing, any more than what you tell me you believe."

"The screen might fall away, like this notion that the mayor is receiving medical treatment somewhere or other."

"What's one mayor worth? If he doesn't come back, we'll find another. No-one's losing sleep over Corbellini."

"What has actually become of him?" Soneri asked abruptly.

"How should I know?" Ugolini replied in annoyance, pouring himself another glass of grappa. "The higher the stakes, the greater the tension. Roles judge people. They take their measure. If you haven't got what's required ..."

"You all put Corbellini where he was. And Montagnani too."

"Montagnani sold himself for a trifle."

"Inadequate people."

"Anyone can make a mistake. Loyalty is rewarded, but often it's the virtue of fools."

They heard Valmarini lay down his brushes. He had turned his back on them and was looking out the window, where the night resembled a wall of obsidian. On the canvas, colours similar to those of a genuine Tintoretto were beginning to appear.

"Is my new jewel ready?" Ugolini asked brusquely. Valmarini paid no heed and shook his head without turning round.

"It must be ready in two weeks. I want to put it on display at the reception for the thirtieth anniversary of the company." The painter remained unruffled and did not speak a word. Dondolo moved over and sat beside his master.

"You'll be there too, artist." Ugolini pronounced this last word almost in falsetto, with a sardonic sneer. "You will comment on the entire collection. I'm not up to that and I have no wish to learn such a demanding line of chatter. I struggle already with a single canvas."

"No!" Valmarini said, his back still turned on the others.

"You must come and speak about your works," Ugolini said, in the same imperious tone as before.

"They're not mine. I reproduce them. That's all there is to it."

"Of course they're yours. You made them!"

"There's nothing here that's mine."

"What is there that's not yours in that painting?" Ugolini said, pointing to the forged Tintoretto.

"The very idea!" Valmarini said, in a near scream. "If you don't have an idea you're not an artist. You're nothing – a camera, a mirror, a piece of carbon paper!" he continued, addressing the night with an anguished voice, searching for the inspiration which had never come to him.

"Nonsense! What the hell do you care? I've made you rich with all these paintings. Is that not enough for you?"

Valmarini made no answer, seemingly petrified in his position, facing the silent darkness.

"If you're in a party, you'll have some ideas, will you not?" Soneri asked.

Ugolini burst out laughing. "Of course I will. I believe in myself and in the balance sheet. The two things reinforce each other."

A silence pregnant with embarrassment fell over them all. Ugolini seemed once again in the grip of one of his mood swings and flopped back in the armchair as though asleep. Valmarini moved slowly, followed by Dondolo. He turned the painting to the wall and then went over to Soneri. In silence, without making any sign, the commissario got up to go. Valmarini stopped him in the hall. "This evening you witnessed one of his moments of delirium."

"Are you saying he was actually raving?"

"Unfortunately not. If anything, he's too sincere at these moments. It's frightening, don't you agree?"

"He's capable of anything. He's not in control of his complexes, but he's right on one point. You and I are old, while he is of the present."

"I hope to be able to free myself of him soon, and to be able to think only of art."

"Your freedom comes at a very high price."

"Ugolini would say it's a valuable asset for which demand is high and supply low, and so the price goes up."

The commissario shook his head. "Unfortunately, I don't believe there is much demand."

Valmarini was still on his mind the following morning when Bergossi told him about the arrest of Petrillo. Soneri already knew because of the clamour on the early-morning radio and television news bulletins. It seemed odd that funeral undertakers should be at the centre of drugs trafficking. "Like a manufacturing line. First they kill them, then they bury them," was the prosecutor's sarcastic comment.

"We know that's not all they're doing," the commissario said.

The prosecutor nodded gravely. "Just take a look at that network of investments. Everything's there – property, commercial activities, finance, gold purchasing, and at this point the inquiry widens out. Since the centre of the operation is Posillipo Ltd, I've devolved part of the investigation to Castellammare."

Soneri shook his head sceptically.

"I know, I know, but what could I do?" Bergossi said. "Our resources are limited, and with three deputies, of whom one . . ." He did not complete the sentence, but the conspiratorial glance at Soneri made it clear he was referring to Piccirillo.

"What about the anti-mafia squad?"

"I've kept them informed, but you know the state they're in. Two men and a dog here in Emilia, facing a criminal underworld growing exponentially."

"Knife to a gunfight."

The prosecutor stretched out his arms. "Have you ever wondered why?"

"If I did, I fear we'd all have to resign, starting with you and me."

"The mafia are useful. There's no getting away from it. They provide backing and are a boon for dozens of politicians. They're in the government, and that's not a recent phenomenon. Do you really believe that a bunch of cattle-herders could checkmate the State if they weren't present at the top levels? The disease is now widespread. It infects an entrepreneurial class debilitated by prosperity and fosters the ambitions of unscrupulous bastards like Ugolini."

"Ugolini is the most dangerous," Soneri agreed. "He controls the Right, he has the Council under his thumb, he has a big following in the city and does business with Petrillo's camorra."

"If only we could say that openly, but I doubt it'll ever be possible."

"Just look at the people he has around him."

"Brazenness is the mark of this new caste of businessman, and the overturning of reality is the consequence. However, our enemy is not Ugolini. He's nothing more than a symptom of the disease."

Soneri remained silent for a few moments. "My fear is that our enemy can't be pursued by judicial means."

The prosecutor half closed his eyes and assented. "I think you've understood."

"Investigating someone with the backing he has, with the underworld defending him . . . The law has always lost out in battles with power, and we're on the side of the law," Soneri said.

"The law lost out when there was no-one, or just a bunch of semi-complicit nonentities, left to uphold it."

"Like now?"

"We'll see. On the local level, political power is the weak link, so that's where we must attack."

"Political power now acts on the same my-lips-are-sealed principle as criminals. In covering up for his accomplices, Montagnani is demonstrating this point."

"Divide and rule. We'll set the one against the other. Politicians don't risk their necks if they speak, and they don't have the same balls as the camorristi."

"We'll need to put the screws on them," the commissario said.

"Right now, they're the ones putting the screws on the prosecution office. We just need an opening, something to make them understand that each and every one of them is facing judgment, that our investigation is under way, and that no-one in the majority party can consider himself safe. In other words, it's a general danger and as such it's even more insidious because there's no knowing where it will strike, like lightning in a storm. That's it – we need to get some black clouds over their heads and intimidate them with thunder."

"I might have an idea," Soneri said.

"What would that be?"

"Do you know Councillor Sgarzi?"

"The one who rants in the Piazza? I've never listened to him. The D.I.G.O.S. officers say he's insane."

"So you've fallen for it too."

"Fallen for what? Is it not true?"

"It could be that Sgarzi goes a bit over the top, but in his own way he makes us face up to the collective deformity we're all victims of, you and I included."

Bergossi shook his head. "What do you mean?"

"Right-wingers have used their influence with the press and T.V. to create a widespread state of mind which makes truth seem implausible. It's as though we've been staring so long at a powerful light that we're incapable of seeing other colours. Sgarzi was standing up in the Piazza denouncing mis-deeds, but no-one believed him. He's mad, they said, but his words were a challenge to that blinding force, the puppet show we'd been told was reality."

Bergossi looked away and seemed to be deep in thought. "So what are you proposing? We can't just take Sgarzi's word as gospel. How can you be sure he's telling the truth?"

"That's not the point. It would be in our interests to use the media in the same way as the Right has, and get the press to believe we're even considering the denunciations made by the madman Sgarzi. When all's said and done, he does hold public office."

"That's true. He was elected to the City Council."

"All we have to do is leak the news that we're examining what he's been saying, and we don't rule out the possibility that it might be useful to our inquiries."

"You want to declare psychological warfare."

"The entire political class must feel itself under pressure, including those on the Left. We must establish an atmosphere of chaos and suspicion, and in their desperation to save themselves, they'll end up betraying each other. After the *Divide et Regna* of the Romans, there always follows the *Mors tua, vita mea*, your death, my life," Soneri said.

"How do you intend to proceed?"

"I'll release confidential information to individual journalists – three or four, no more. I have an inspector who's extremely able in this field," he said, thinking of Musumeci. "If the information can be dropped by someone in the investigation team, it'll have twice the value. Off-the-record briefings, if well prepared, carry greater weight than official communiqués."

"I didn't know you were such a strategist," said the prosecutor, a little surprised. "I have to admit that, seeing how things stand, this approach could be useful, especially since the route of the traditional investigation is blocked to us. We're in a swamp."

"I wish it were a swamp! The problem is the stench!"

2I

MUSUMECI'S BRIEFINGS WERE so convincing that the news caused an outcry almost immediately. The newspapers first, and the television stations later, seemed to have found an inexhaustible source of conjectures, hypotheses, reconstructions and behind-the-scene manoeuvres. The political parties went into a state of fibrillation. Some politicians could not resist taking advantage of the situation to attack their opponents, and once the chain reaction had been triggered, there was no stopping it. Sgarzi continued to deliver his invectives in Piazza Garibaldi to an ever-increasing audience, which, once he was off the platform, he disgustedly branded as hypocritical. "I said the same things a week ago and was treated with contempt, but now I'm greeted with applause."

Soneri waited, like a hunter in a hide, for the verbal guerrilla war to unsettle the political world and encourage some politician, anxious to protect himself from the blitz of accusations, to come forward. To his surprise, the first to speak was Petrillo, an anomaly which put the commissario on his guard. He distrusted accounts provided by camorristi on questions of public contracts, corruption and bribes. Besides, Petrillo's precision was suspicious. Pontiroli, the "Red" manager of the cooperatives and the bridge between the two political factions, emerged from this version as one of the most active in oiling the machinery that awarded contracts for building work.

"Your strategy has borne fruit," Bergossi commented with satisfaction, "but you don't seem very convinced. Have you repented just when we seem to be getting somewhere?"

"I don't understand why a small-time boss has started spilling the beans like the resident gossip on the landing in a block of flats."

"What does it matter? The main thing is that he's helping us. As to his reasons, I think I understand."

"One thing is certain. He's not doing us a favour, and nor should we assume he's helping us."

"He's sending a message to the politicians. This is not so much a plea to his accomplices as an act of intimidation. He's not telling us everything, only that part which doesn't affect his own interests.

"That much is clear."

"He's putting them on notice. Watch out you don't stitch me up, or there'll be hell to pay. He's trying to restrict the inquiry to the lower echelons, like Montagnani. It's a warning: keep your mouths shut in Parma, but talk to whom it may concern in Rome and make sure the knife doesn't cut too deep."

The commissario thought this over for a bit before replying. "We'll have to decode his words every time."

"We'll verify everything he says. So far he seems to have been reliable, not least on Pontiroli."

"I'd like him to talk about the mayor."

"Let's take it day by day, one step at a time."

"The way things are, it's Petrillo who's in charge of this investigation. An impeccable director," Soneri said ironically.

"There's always some chance event which disrupts the most impeccable productions, and that's the way it'll be this time too. Just wait for the lead actor to trip up on stage. I have an almost unlimited faith in chance. It's often spared us huge embarrassment, and I've always wondered if that happens by accident or because we went searching."

"Just like mushroom-picking: a bit of luck and a bit of rooting about."

Chance and mushrooms continued to dominate the commissario's thinking, even after he had left the prosecutor's office and turned into the narrow Vicolo San Tiburzio where the sun never shone and where it would not have taken much for mushrooms to start growing on the thick walls. Wandering through the woods, groping about in the same mist which now hung over Parma, was the exercise which most resembled an investigation. It was a perfect metaphor for life, if life is an endless quest. No matter how much planning had been done, the result never corresponded to the premise. It was a continual refutation of the presuppositions or, on the contrary, a sudden and unexpected revelation. The plot of the play taunted its characters, who ended up mocked and disillusioned, like Rigoletto.

He had often spoken over lunch about "Rigoletto" with Nanetti, a frequent attender at the Teatro Regio. In keeping with his thoughts, the commissario chose *tagliatelle ai porcini*, a pasta dish with his favourite mushrooms. It was not one of Alceste's specialities, but in that uncertain winter climate of snow and mist, the host had decided to vary his menu. Soneri found in that woodland flavour memories of willow mats, of attics with the scent of dust, mildew, hanging salamis and drying fruit, and of sideboards packed with childhood souvenirs.

"Hello there, commissario!' Nanetti, noticing his vacant expression, gave him a shake. "You look like someone who's been blown off course. It wouldn't be that little assistant of Bergossi's?"

For a moment, Soneri's thoughts turned to the young woman who was currently enlivening the erotic imagination of the police station. "Not in the slightest! I was thinking about mushrooms."

"Nowadays you only get worked up at table. A bad sign."

"Going mushroom-picking has many meanings. If you think about it, you can deduce from it how important it is to surrender to instinct and reduce planning to the minimum, not least because plans always go awry."

"Are you trying to revive the old argument between scientists and humanists, forcing me to defend scientific method and you to construct hypotheses and theories on the inscrutability of existence? Look, you're right on one point. Making plans doesn't get you very far. Look at Lo Giudice, the guy who used to work in the operating theatre. He'd prepared great schemes for his retirement: children settled, return to Puglia, wife arranging a transfer for herself, and then he suffered a heart attack last night. End of story."

"You see? We delude ourselves and then ..."

"Bloody hell, Soneri, I'd no idea you were entertaining thoughts of destiny! Any day now I'll find you've become a pious believer."

"In the case you've just described ..."

"There's always an explanation if we have the will to search for it, but if we choose the easier path of attributing everything to fate, this absolves us *en masse*. In the case in question, Lo Giudice ate and drank as if there was no tomorrow. He smoked, and took his car even when he was going to the toilet."

"Not everything can be explained. As Bergossi says, when it comes to events like this investigation – where our hands are tied – we've no choice but to confide in the imponderable, as when lightning puts to flight an overwhelming enemy force."

Nanetti gave a scowl of amused horror as he confronted the commissario's farcical grandiloquence. "It certainly is a fine mess. Landmines planted, and the prosecutor's office under scrutiny."

"Meanwhile the camorrista Petrillo, with his carefully timed confessions, is doing his best to push the inquiries in the direction he wants."

"Do you know something? I can't detect clear links between all the various elements that are occupying our attention: Romagnoli's death, drugs in the bellies of dogs, Corbellini's disappearance, the infiltration of organised crime, bribery on the Council and so on. Perhaps there is no link. Perhaps these are the autonomous products of a putrid city."

Once again the word "context" sprang into the commissario's mind. It had indeed become a refrain. "The only link seems to be the deadly embrace of the camorra in its attempts to throttle Parma."

"And I fear that Parma is a consenting partner."

"Not entirely, fortunately. Parma is like a good-looking woman who's offered a lot of money to sell herself. The temptation is strong."

"I think she'll concede, and she's just teasing to raise the price."

"In fact, once you've lost your identity, the risk is that nothing matters except profit. Ugolini and his gang have, with the consent of the majority, made a whore of this city. We'll see if there's a minority capable of another revolution."

"Uhh! Revolutions presuppose an assault mob of starving people and a circle of intellectuals to guide them. I don't see either the one or the other."

"The starving mob, perhaps not . . . but the intellectuals . . .

in any case, nobody pays the slightest heed to them. A shop selling mobiles attracts more customers in one day than the numbers who read a philosopher in twenty years," the commissario said.

Nanetti, his fork in mid-air, stopped to reflect. "Coming back to the investigation, the anomaly, the thing which is most out of line, is Romagnoli's death. The other matters we can deal with. The mobile stolen from Pontiroli and then thrown away by the Ukrainian near the river, opening the way to the discovery of the drugs business; the cocaine trafficking with the dogs which caused Zunarelli's suicide and got Laudadio into trouble, leading to the revelation of camorra interests; the network of criminal affairs, from the cemeteries to the finance houses, from involvement in companies to their eventual purchase; the flow of dirty money threatening the city but tempting a lot of the people who might well be the first to go under in the next crisis . . . What did Romagnoli have to do with all this?"

"There's one other thing which it's not easy to link in, but it's the one which started off the inquiry: the disappearance of the mayor," Soneri said.

"My impression is that the context we've just outlined contains the explanation of that event as well."

"Context! The very word. Everything can be explained in this way. Let's not forget that Zunarelli, the suicide victim, might have been the shadowy figure who killed Romagnoli."

"Perhaps, but we don't have a motive."

"No, we don't. Perhaps Romagnoli had heard about the sacrifice of the dogs and, in his state of dementia in his final weeks, was unintentionally reporting what was happening in the workshops in San Vitale."

"Who would take seriously the howls of a dementia patient?"

The two sat in silence, pondering the inexplicable. Soneri had not yet reflected sufficiently on the possibility that Romagnoli's death did not fit into the overall chain of events, but when he thought of Petrillo's company, L'Eterna, taking possession of the corpse and exploiting it for advertising purposes, his suspicions grew. Even if he was not able to prove anything, he followed his nose and concluded there must be some link.

Relishing the last of the mushrooms, he recalled his walks in the woods, roaming about on his own and coming across beds of mushrooms, spread out like a munificent display of gifts for anyone who had the patience and humility to wait. Time was not on his side in these investigations. The political uproar, initially provoked by the leaks to the press, was centred for the moment on Petrillo's revelations. The right-wing factions under accusation charged the magistrates with having violated the secrecy of legal proceedings and of giving undue credit to the words of a known criminal. The Left, paralysed as usual, issued plaintive declarations of confidence in the magistracy and called for the suspension of judgment. They locked themselves in total silence even when faced with a bombardment from their opponents, who attributed to them a project of "judicial aggression". DELUGE OF ACCUSATIONS OVER THE CITY ran the headline in one newspaper, causing Soneri to smile when he thought that a little mist prevented people from seeing clearly. Considering that the mist had been long stagnant, the garden gate had been for some time the farthest horizon.

He walked towards his office, savouring on his tongue the delights of the meal he had just enjoyed. Parma seemed to him unsettling in its afternoon tranquillity, as though he could detect an underground tremor. When he got to his office, he sat down and looked over at Juvara, who returned his gaze without speaking.

"What's the matter?"

"Bergossi's in the shit," the inspector replied.

"Another torpedo fired at him? What are they objecting to now? Anything serious?"

"No, it's a question of form. If I've got it right, it's something to with stamps, validations, delivery deadlines, things he doesn't even attend to personally. Absolute nonsense, but that doesn't matter. The afternoon news on T.V. came out with guns blazing, and the politicians on the Right charged forward as one man to allege that the magistrates were prejudiced. They brought up the old story about the supposed left-wing sympathies of the magistracy. A complete shambles!"

"What did I tell you?" Soneri said angrily. "Sooner or later the political world was bound to come out in favour of the criminals."

"Nothing has changed. Today the Guardia di Finanza arrested another two councillors and three Council officials, and there's a rumour that a warrant is about to be issued for Corbellini's arrest. Maybe that's why he's lying low."

The commissario shook his head. "Anything could happen now." He grabbed the telephone and dialled Bergossi's number, but his secretary's sensual voice came on the line. "I'm sorry, Signor Bergossi is out and didn't leave word when he would be back."

Soneri hung up, disappointed, and tried to imagine the prosecutor's state of mind at that moment. His mobile rang and Angela's number appeared on the display. "It's complete chaos here," she began. Shouts and general hubbub could be heard in the background. "The Right has called for a demonstration and blocked Piazza del Tribunale."

"What's stopping them clearing them off?" Soneri said.

"That's your job! The police have been alerted and there are two cars and a group of carabinieri here, but they're just hanging about watching."

"Capuozzo is a fool," the commissario burst out, forgetting that he was just two floors beneath his superior's office.

"No, it's simply that his sympathies are with the Right."

"How many of them are there?"

"Less than a hundred, and half of them are councillors, secretaries and party workers who've been conscripted."

"The tribe defending its hunting grounds."

"You mean the raiding party," Angela said. "Anyway, your colleagues are ignoring everything. If these were young people from the University, they'd have already charged and dispersed them."

"They always show greater deference to the bosses. Have you heard what they're accusing Bergossi of?"

"Nothing of any substance – formal mistakes committed by clerical staff, but you know that Italian justice is more concerned with official stamps than with serious crime. They've let some killers out of prison because of the lack of some scribble or other."

"What do you think's going to happen now?"

"They could declare some acts invalid and delay the investigation considerably. The most damaging factor is the intimidation of Bergossi and the prosecution office. They might be tempted to slow down so as not to be beaten over the head any further."

The evening T.V. news devoted a lot of attention to the story of the irregularities in the prosecution office and to the protests. The ongoing story of bribery and corruption had disappeared from the opening headlines. The Centre Right had succeeded in diverting attention.

"The thieves have put the judges on trial," Soneri said, tossing one of his files onto his desk. He got up, but once he was on his feet he had no idea what to do. He felt like throwing in the towel and going to meet Angela. For a moment the temptation to surrender, to climb out of the trench waving a white flag, passed through his mind, and felt like an act of liberation. He already had his coat on and was about to leave when he bumped into Juvara coming into his office. "It's for you," he said, handing over a letter.

It was from the prosecution office, one of those grey envelopes which Bergossi used for official communications. It contained a search warrant for the mayor's private apartment and for the office he used for his work as an accountant.

"The prosecutor is not giving up." Juvara had recognised the envelope and forms.

"The man has balls alright!" Soneri confirmed, feeling his determination return as he spoke. A few seconds before he had put on his coat without knowing where to go, but now he had a precise idea.

He called Musumeci and Nanetti. He asked the former to get hold of the keys to the apartment or to bring a master key, and the latter to make himself available for a search. He set off on foot. His first port of call was Corbellini's house in Borgo del Parmigianino, where he found the inspector in the company of an elderly woman with a worried, afflicted air. She identified herself as the mayor's aunt, and opened the door silently, as though she was the maid. The apartment was tidy but did not have any kind of lived-in feel to it. Steel was the most common element in the furnishings, and the flat itself looked somehow like a surgery. The living room had two enormous sofas, a large, ultra-fine plasma television set, a stereo unit linked to a home entertainment system, a modest bookcase lined almost entirely with catalogues and photography books – probably a collection of works presented to him – and a stylish round table. There was a room fitted out as a gym, while the study contained a desk with a large computer. The bedroom had a bed with rounded sides and several mirrors, including one fitted on the ceiling. There was a large collection of jackets in the wardrobe, and shirts, ties, jumpers and underwear in the chest of drawers. In the bathroom, Soneri found a bath equipped for hydro-massage and a three-shelf cabinet with various cosmetics, including skin cream, aftershave, slimming potions, shampoos, deodorants and hair conditioners. Under the sink there was a compartment with dozens of tubes and little bottles. He held one or two up to the light to examine them, and discovered that they were mainly psychoactive drugs, sleeping pills, anxiolytics, antidepressants and tablets for mood dysregulation disorder. An entire pharmacy of brain-enhancing drugs.

"He was not in the best of health," said Nanetti, who was curious about the range of drugs available.

"From the gym and the equipment in it, you could draw quite the opposite conclusion."

"Muscles are almost invariably a surrogate for a weak personality." Nanetti was known for his detestation of sport. "Some people drink, some snort cocaine to strengthen their self-confidence, and some build up their physique, but the problem is always the same."

Soneri looked around in silence. The apartment seemed to be communicating something he could not quite decipher. He went back into the living room, where he found the mayor's aunt still seated, an expression of resignation on her face. He looked into the small kitchen, and on opening the fridge found nothing but a bottle of water. The only contents of the cupboards and drawers were two boxes of biscuits, piles of plates, cutlery and a colander. Everything appeared neat and tidy as though on display.

"Is it you who cleans up here?" the commissario asked the mayor's aunt.

"There's a woman who comes in twice a week," she replied, shaking her head.

"Do you come here often?"

"Only occasionally. I live nearby and Giancarlo asked me to keep an eye on the flat when he had to be away."

"Did your nephew have a woman, a girlfriend? Did you ever see him with someone else in the house?"

"I know he was much courted," she said, warding off the question with a smile, "but I . . . his affairs . . . I never saw anyone here, but I was never here in the evening."

Nanetti signalled to him from the bathroom door. "Found something?" the commissario asked.

"Nothing of great interest on first inspection."

"Did you notice if there's a suitcase?"

"What are you getting at? I don't follow."

"Corbellini did go away, didn't he? We're sure of this?"

"I don't think there's any suitcase here."

"Another thing that's missing."

"There could be so many things missing, but we don't have an inventory."

When the commissario went out into the gathering dark of early afternoon, he thought about that house and analysed his own impressions, starting with what he felt was missing: an unmade bed, plates waiting to be washed, a shattered mirror, clothes lying about in the bathroom, slippers under a radiator.

"It looked like an operating theatre," Nanetti said as they went into Corbellini's office in Borgo Montassu, a few steps away from his house. There too they found everything in place as though it had been recently vacuumed and dusted. "Alright, you can get on with the search. Maybe they've left something behind."

After giving instructions to his men, Nanetti left with Soneri. "You were expecting much more, weren't you?"

"No," Soneri said. "Someone who did a search without a warrant got there before us, but in spite of that it was still useful."

"My squad might come up with something."

"We'll see. Meantime, we found manic order, and in all maniacs for order there's a hidden kernel of chaos."

"Another of your emotive conclusions," Nanetti said.

"Didn't you see what he had in the bathroom? Order, care for the body, a chilling precision in the steel furnishing, and then all that brain chemistry. You yourself said that muscles provide cover for a feeble personality."

"O.K., but these are impressions, rough and ready statistics."

"In any case, it's a good summary of Corbellini's world," the commissario concluded as he made his way back to the police station. In Via Cavour, his mobile came back to life. The first words were sufficient to allow him to recognise Boldrin's voice. "How are things down there?" he asked in a high-pitched tone, giving the impression that he was in a state of some excitement.

"Misty as ever," Soneri said.

"I'm calling you because they've brought in the registers from the hotels in Andalo for the last couple of weeks, and do you know what I've discovered?"

"Several Parmigiani with a passion for the mountains?"

"Several Parmigiani already known to you. Bonaldi and Bernetti were resident there from Monday to Wednesday, the day they were stopped in a car in Val Badia together with your mayor."

"In the same hotel as Corbellini?"

"No, in a four-star. And there too, on the night between Tuesday and Wednesday, there was another man."

"What's his name?"

"Pietro Ugolini, fifty-eight years old . . ."

Boldrin was reading the form filled in by the hotelier when Soneri interrupted him. "I can't thank you enough!"

"For what? There's not much going on up here, except drunks and cars ending up in ditches."

The information was enough to suggest a conspiracy, with

Ugolini bringing in the killers. He grew more agitated as he continued on his way to his office, and as he entered from Borgo della Posta he almost bumped into Musumeci, who was rushing out. The courtyard was abuzz with activity.

"What's going on?" Soneri asked.

"Officers from the *Finanza* have arrested Pontiroli, and Capuozzo has called a press conference."

"Incredible! When they arrest somebody on the Left, it's a sensation."

"Excuse me, sir, the only thing that's left-wing about him is one of the side mirrors on his car!"

"Capuozzo is convinced that communists still exist."

"Anyway, they won't keep him in custody much longer. He's already singing like a tenor."

"Who signed the warrant?"

"Bergossi. A couple of hours ago," Musumeci said.

The commissario went up to his office. Feeling that everything had become more fluid, he sat down to think things over in solitude, until Juvara switched on the television for the news. The order of the stories covered had been inverted once again. The arrest of the head of the cooperatives had galvanised the Right. Even if they had been implicated in the corruption scandal by Pontiroli himself, they managed to crucify the other side, whose activists appeared betrayed and crushed. Soneri was so surprised by the acceleration of events that he did not even notice Nanetti's arrival.

"Bergossi is a genius!" Nanetti said, pointing to the television screen. "Now how can they say that the investigations are one-sided?"

"He's wrong-footed them," the commissario said.

"They'll pull back their troops and give him a free pass," Nanetti went on, while Soneri was still coming to grips with the move.

"Let them party. They're cheering their own downfall," Soneri said.

"Don't get carried away! These people never die."

"You're right. They're up to their necks in it, but they still make it seem it's all about the other lot."

"Look, I came to show you this." Nanetti held out a photograph of the mayor with an elderly gentleman whom Soneri did not immediately recognise. He took another look and turned to stare at his colleague in amazement.

"Romagnoli!"

"This is more unexpected than Pontiroli's arrest."

"Where did you find this?"

"In his study, stuck at the back of a drawer. That's why it's so crumpled."

"They'd never have left it where it was if they'd seen it. Well, now you have the answer to one question. There is a connection between Romagnoli's death and all the rest of it after all."

"We've still got to work out what the link between him and Corbellini was. Looking at the photograph and the way they're smiling, it certainly doesn't look like the souvenir photograph of an admirer."

The commissario picked up the telephone. "Musumeci, get back to the house of that old aunt of Corbellini's and ask if she knew Alfio Romagnoli."

The two men stood in silence while interviews followed one after the other on T.V. Bernetti came on with the elegantly triumphant look of a government man. He attacked the Left and their supposed thirst for justice; for all their moralising they had been caught red-handed. He finished by praising the efficiency of the magistrates.

"Bernetti is speaking in the name of Ugolini, but they've let Bergossi off the hook," Soneri said.

"Do you really think he's done it to get the Right and the inspectors from the Ministry off his back?"

"I don't know. Bergossi keeps his own counsel, and I prefer to think he's followed the natural course of the inquiry. Since mud is being thrown about everywhere in this swamp . . ."

Musumeci's telephone call came through at last.

"Well then? What does the old woman have to say?"

"Nothing. She can't stop crying."

22

EVEN SONERI WAS surprised at how easily he managed to calm the old woman down just by taking her hand. Elderly people, in their insecurity, tended to revert to a childlike state.

"Tell me about Alfio," he asked her, in the gentlest voice he was capable of.

"We were more or less the same age, although he was a bit older," she began, before stopping to stare into the middle distance. Musumeci took advantage of the pause to slip the commissario a card with the words *Delfina Corbellini, Widow of Signor Torreggiani, 78 years old.*

"Did you grow up together?"

"My brother, Giancarlo's father, was an accountant who did the books for several companies. Alfio, who had been left fatherless, was taken on as office boy. He carried the papers and parcels around, picked up the mail and was sent on errands."

"How long was he in your brother's employment?"

"Until the very end. He was like an adopted member of the family. Giancarlo inherited a thriving business, but it wasn't the career for him. He was always a restless young man."

"And Alfio stayed with him?"

"Yes, even after retirement. My nephew was very fond of him, and Alfio was more like an older brother than an employee.

They were very close. And now they're both gone." Delfina's voice trailed off and she broke down once more.

"What did Romagnoli do with himself after Corbellini was elected mayor?"

"Anything that Giancarlo required. He was his faithful servant, but he stayed in the shadows. He kept his distance from the Council and took care almost exclusively of private matters."

"He became unwell – in the head, I mean."

"That all happened in the last months, but it wasn't serious. Sometimes he would ramble and lose track of his memories, but the doctors said that treatment would slow down the progress of the illness. The worst thing he suffered was loneliness, like all old people."

"Did you know Zunarelli? He claimed to be Romagnoli's only friend."

The woman tried to remember. "The man from San Vitale who produced salami?"

"Yes. He boned the pork."

"Well, I don't know about being his only friend. Alfio was passionate about dogs and hunting. Everything started from there, I think."

"In what sense?"

"This Zunarelli was a breeder, and Alfio went to look after the animals."

"Is that all there was to it?"

"How do you expect me to know? I hardly ever leave the house."

"Did you know that Romagnoli was on his own when he died?"

The woman put her face in her hands and leaned forward a little. "When I found out he was in hospital, I went along. Giancarlo had already gone to the mountains, and I took a taxi. The driver took me to the Maggiore hospital, but I walked all over the place asking for information and got nowhere. All they would say was that he was in a private home."

"You and Alfio," the commissario said quietly, putting his two index fingers together to symbolise a relationship.

"No, there was never a hint of what you're implying." The woman sounded indignant. "I loved him very much, partly because he'd had a hard life. My brother and I always tried to protect him."

"What kind of work did Romagnoli do? More recently?"

"I don't know. He went around Parma on his bicycle. Once he came to visit me with an armful of files, and he always had a bag with him. One day he got lost in San Lazzaro and they had to call the police to look for him. It was then that he was taken to hospital."

"Did the police mount a search for him?"

"You should know. Aren't you a policeman?"

"There are quite a lot of us," Soneri said, but already an idea had occurred to him and was taking him elsewhere. Despite that, he asked: "When was this?"

"Three or four months ago. He suffered a sudden, unexpected collapse. He made a good recovery but then he had a relapse, and when your head isn't working properly . . ."

The commissario left, walking a short way along Via Cavour in the direction of Piazza Duomo. The yellowing lights lent their own colour to the mist, which looked like a giant vestment stretched between the Bishop's Palace and the Baptistery. From Borgo Venti Marzo he turned into Via Repubblica where the police station stood. He made straight for Pasquariello's office.

"What's this? A raid?" Pasquariello asked with a laugh, when he saw the commissario stride in at top speed.

"I need to know about something you did three or four months ago, in the district of San Lazzaro."

"That's a bit vague."

"No, hold on. I'm talking about Romagnoli. He went missing and you went looking for him."

Pasquariello looked doubtful. "I don't remember anything of the sort, but four months ago I was on holiday for two weeks." He picked up his telephone and called his deputy, Giarruso.

"What has this poor Romagnoli done that he can't be left in peace even now that he's dead?" Pasquariello asked.

"He was Corbellini's factotum, but he stayed in the wings, so I'm only getting to know about it now."

"And you think that his death . . ."

"Who knows? There are grounds for suspicion but no-one can prove anything. There's no real lead actor in this story, just a chorus. Things happen, and the responsibility never lies with one person alone."

In the meantime, Giarruso arrived, in plain clothes. Pasquariello addressed him directly. "Do you remember going looking for Alfio Romagnoli, a man who'd lost his memory and went missing in the San Lazzaro district, three or four months ago?"

"Yes, I remember we found him sitting under the Arco della Porta in Via Emilia."

"In Strada Elevata," Soneri interjected, using the name by which the spot was known locally.

"Did you call the emergency health services?"

"No, after a short time he seemed to have recovered his memory, so we put him in a car to take him home, but on the way he wasn't able to tell us where he lived, so we went to the Accident and Emergency department."

"Did he have anything with him – a file or some folders?" Soneri asked.

"I think so. He had a small bag. In fact, after a while a man turned up and took it away."

"He didn't say who he was?"

"A relative, or at least that's how he identified himself. He actually sat down next to the old man and began talking to him."

"Did any of you draw up a report and identify this relative?" the commissario asked.

Pasquariello kept his eyes firmly on Giarruso, interrogating him with his stern look.

"To tell the truth, we didn't draw up any report because we received a telephone call asking us to drop it."

"Who made this call?" Pasquariello asked in evident alarm.

"It was a V.I.P., sir."

"Who?" Soneri insisted.

"Undersecretary Bernetti," Giarruso said, speaking as though he was giving away secret information. The commissario, on the other hand, began to see things more clearly.

"It was all a bit confused," Giarruso went on. "However, I couldn't say we went by the book."

"Has the Chief been informed about this call?"

"I think so, seeing as he was the one who authorised us to ignore normal practice."

"What a shambles!" Soneri said. "Did Romagnoli stay in the Accident and Emergency unit?"

"Not as far as I know. A blue car arrived to take him to a private care home."

"Villa Clelia?"

"Yes, as far as I remember."

Soneri and Pasquariello exchanged glances. "What can we do if they've taken over, even in our house?" Soneri murmured.

Pasquariello shook his head. "What do you think he had in his bag? That was what they were after, wasn't it?"

"I don't know. It was only today that I discovered Romagnoli attended to Corbellini's private affairs, although I don't believe it was limited to private business."

"The fact is, they took him to a clinic where they could keep an eye on him more easily. Malusardi, the director of Villa Clelia, was in the mayor's party. But with a man who was so unbalanced . . ."

"He had moments of lucidity and perhaps they were afraid of him even in the state he was in. In any case, in this city the madmen tell the truth. Take Sgarzi, for example," Soneri said.

"The fact is that we – without seeking any verification – handed an insane man over to someone who said he was a relative of his," Pasquariello said. "Have we at least got his name?"

"He was called Giovetti," Giarruso said.

"He's an official in the Council, always at the mayor's side," Soneri explained.

"The Chief gave his permission," Giarruso said, in the face of Pasquariello's severe and puzzled look.

"He wasn't even a relative! Did you at least register Bernetti's telephone call?"

"Of course," Giarruso said, with a complacent smile.

Shortly afterwards, as he was walking home, the commissario called Bergossi. "Surviving?" the commissario asked.

"It's a dreadful time, but I'm thick-skinned. Your friends on the Left didn't exactly go out of their way to defend me, did they?"

"Maybe they sensed it would be their turn next. Look at Pontiroli. Anyway, I have no friends and certainly no party."

"Don't play the fool with me!"

"I have some ideas but they don't fit with today's politics. By the way, in the city they say it's you who's playing the fool, arresting someone from the red cooperatives only after the Right sent inspectors after you."

"Nonsense! I almost wish it was true, but regrettably I've come to the conclusion that the stench has spread everywhere, and that if you have to hold your nose to the Right, you've got to do the same to the Left."

"Has Pontiroli decided to talk?"

The prosecutor emitted a pained groan. "He'll say what suits him, like the rest of them. He'll try to show he was under pressure, but we'll see tomorrow. I'd like you to be there."

"Do you believe he's being threatened?"

"The most serious threat is that the camorra in the south slams the doors on the cooperatives. Pontiroli is just a pawn, and there are hundreds of others like him."

"I'll be there tomorrow," Soneri said.

"And put your trust in Fortune," Bergossi said as he hung up.

Later that evening, the commissario was forced to admit that one of the most agreeable aspects of coming home was finding the table set. As he embraced Angela, creator of this pleasant surprise, he said: "There's all the reassurance we need in seeing the table set – food, unity, a common purpose and the certainty of family."

"Just like wolves," she joked. He made a trip to the bathroom, and when she saw him come out and noticed how dishevelled he looked after the day's work, she went on: "When you've solved this case, we'll take a few days off, and then we'll find the table set every day for lunch and dinner."

"And where would you like to go?"

"We could even go back to Andalo," she said, winking at him. "I've remained keen since the last time."

"Liar! However, I think spring will be here before I untangle this muddle. Today I learned more about Romagnoli. He was in charge of the mayor's private affairs. Don't ask me what kind of affairs, but it's not hard to imagine."

"So the old man was caught up in the game as well?"

"I believe that's why he ended up the way he did."

"But your hands are tied."

"We're powerless. Political and business circles are doing their best to leave us impotent. They can't get rid of us completely, so they prevent us from taking any action by imprisoning us in a slimy web of laws, masonic organisations and criminality. In fact, politics is now turning into a criminal sphere."

"Don't exaggerate! Not all politicians are criminals, and the law provides a guarantee for citizens."

"You see how you're becoming indulgent as well? It's as though you're admitting that a little bit of criminality among politicians is quite normal. Just a short time ago it would have been abnormal to find even one criminal politician. You see how we give way bit by bit? And nowadays laws give no guarantee to honest people. All they do is legitimise swindlers."

"Come on! You're not going to tell me that politicians a decade or so ago weren't corrupt and complicit."

"Perhaps they were, but today they have the impudence to behave like that in public. At least in the past there was someone who raised moral objections." The commissario was becoming heated, and getting into a state of angry ill humour.

Angela went over to him and put her arm round his shoulders. "I was serious when I spoke about Andalo. Look, you and me, couldn't we let ourselves live a little? The mountains would be ideal."

The piping hot minestrone completed the job of restoring his peace of mind. "A lovely caress inside," he sighed, supping his soup in great spoonfuls.

"The most beautiful thing about getting to know someone is being able to make them happy," Angela said.

"Just like tickling a cat's back. You can't go wrong."

"Or like gratifying your palate."

"There are other senses, you know."

She stared at him with a glance of pseudo-malicious reproach. "I know some other things that would fire you up much more than what I'm about to say."

"If it's a vulgar word of appreciation, have no fear. I love them."

"I've always known you were anything but refined, but the subject I want to broach is not in any way stimulating. More deflating, I'd say."

"I was already dreaming of a couple of steamy hours."

She looked at him with ironic uncertainty. "The exhumation at the Lagrimone cemetery is scheduled for tomorrow afternoon."

"At what time?"

"Two o'clock. It gets dark very early in this season."

"I'll be there."

"What do you think you'll find in a pile of bones?"

"I don't know myself. I'm being dragged along by irresistible curiosity, or maybe it's just the desire to see where Romagnoli is buried. In some ways, I feel sorry about his fate."

"Tell me the truth. It's the world of the dead which attracts you, and since in your mind Corbellini is dead, unconsciously you're going to look for him where his most trusted henchman is buried."

"Who can say? Even I can't decipher my own thoughts, but I know by experience that they should be pursued. If the worst comes to the worst, I'll have spent the afternoon with you."

"In a graveyard! If you're really doing this to see me, I'll have to assume it's another of your perversions."

"Perversion is the mental illness of magistrates and policemen who stick their noses into the affairs of politicians," the commissario intoned.

"You're crazy," Angela whispered, putting her lips up to his ear.

He turned round to embrace her and they ended up on the sofa. In those moments, Soneri thought that making love was a simulation of the animal act of feeding off each other. The initial excitement was the same, but the outcome was not pain and torment but the pleasure of contact. Even so, the groans which it produced retained something of the lament and the anguished yell.

"Do you believe in chance?" he asked her, when they were dressed again.

"No," she replied. "It only serves to provide an explanation for things we don't understand."

"Bergossi is a believer in chance. He invokes it as though it were a saint."

"This doesn't raise my opinion of his investigative abilities, but maybe it's just a mild superstition, like carrying an amulet in your pocket. Do you believe in it?"

"Well, it's one of those subjects where the pros and cons are equal. In other words, whether you believe or not, you're placing a wager or committing an act of arrogance."

"As with God," Angela said.

"More or less. It's an act of faith."

"Tomorrow, on the other hand, it will be a formal act and one of the most unpleasant imaginable."

"As for me, tomorrow morning I'll be at another exhumation, a much more painful one."

"Whose?"

"They're interrogating Pontiroli, and that's inevitably going to make the founders of the old cooperatives turn in their graves."

'Just as well they're dead. At least they're spared this disaster."

"I'd rather Bergossi had done it on his own, but he's forced me to take part in the whole buffoonery. I hope this cooperator takes advantage of the right to remain silent."

"That depends on whether he wants to serve time in jail for holding fast, or on how much he risks by talking. You know what I mean, in that company ..."

"He'll do the same as Petrillo. At this stage, both will have realised they're not facing simple politicians, but people just like them, using the same methods," Soneri said.

"You're facing two exhumations: one of the body of a man, and one of the soul of a movement," Angela said.

23

PONTIROLI WAS A small, squat man, who wore rectangular steel spectacles and had the subdued air of a chaplain. Having been hauled brutally out of his own world to pass a sleepless night in the cells, he had a hunted look, glancing around uncertainly, alarmed by every gesture. He was accompanied by his lawyer, Trombini, the most accomplished of the left-leaning advocates.

Bergossi tried to be cordial and to put the accused at ease, but such was the character of the man that he had little chance of succeeding. The magistrate read out the charge sheet, summarised the terms of the inquiry, and then asked if the accused intended to reply to questions. At this point, his lawyer intervened with an infinite series of queries, seemingly preparing for a duel over points of law. Soneri found the whole thing rather boring, but eventually Pontiroli agreed to cooperate.

"We had to pay. There was no other way. That's the way the system worked," he said.

"The officials and the councillors we have spoken to all say there was no coercion, that you offered money for contracts first," Bergossi said.

Pontiroli gave a contemptuous laugh. "What would you have done? Those were the terms. My cooperative has a grass-roots membership of some three thousand, as well as five hundred worker-partners. Was I supposed to send them all home?"

The prosecutor took no notice of the reply. "From what has emerged, it seems there was an upper tier which took the greater part of the contracts for itself and guaranteed a flow of money into the political system. It wasn't your partners who were being sent home, but those with companies excluded from the process."

"Do you think they didn't try to get in on the act? Do you believe the others didn't pay up? Even tradesmen have to pay the administrators of a condominium to guarantee work. Large or small scale, that's the way it is," Pontiroli said, interrupted from time to time by his lawyer, who reformulated his answers in a convoluted style which was almost incomprehensible.

And then Trombini used the word which made the commissario tremble. It was the prevailing "context" which made payments necessary; he pronounced the word as though the prosecutor's questions, which laid bare the whole scenario, were proof of his profound naivety. Even when Bergossi began to raise specific facts, confirmed by the confessions of politicians and Council officials, Pontiroli's attitude did not change. Money changing hands was the prerequisite for work. He referred to these activities as "financing political life", and Trombini commented that financing was not a crime but an infringement punishable by a fine. "We'll pay that as well, but you see how difficult it is to run a company in this country?" the lawyer said, by way of conclusion.

Pontiroli entered a plea on his own behalf. "There was no other way, sir. You either adapt to the system or you die. A man with my responsibilities has his back to the wall."

"You could have reported it. That's what we're here for," Bergossi objected.

"But where was the proof? You don't have any proof either, and this inquiry, with all due respect, will come to nothing."

His lawyer was about to intervene to calm Pontiroli, who was beginning to recover the arrogance of a man accustomed to being in charge, but the prosecutor got in ahead of him. "The proof will emerge in due course," he threatened.

Pontiroli resumed his earlier, humble mien. "Forgive me, but if someone submits a report to the authorities, he's not going to get any more work. And not just in this city but anywhere. Given the system, everyone is open to blackmail."

"That's why the villains are successful," Bergossi said.

"If you don't play along with them you're an exception to the rule. I've often thought about it," he said in a more unctuous tone, "but I've always been afraid of the consequences, not for me personally, but for the company. And then you lawyers ..." He did not complete the sentence, chastened by a fierce look from his own lawyer. He tried to remedy the situation by veering away from the real intention behind his words. "I mean to say, in your position, if you were presented with reports of that sort, you'd be tempted to file them away."

Bergossi kept his eyes on him, showing he had understood. Trombini intervened to assist his client but made no progress because the prosecutor cut him short. "If you're trying to say we're politicised, I deny it immediately. Will you now tell me about the relationship between you and these companies that have been infiltrated by the camorra?"

"I don't know anything about companies infiltrated by the camorra."

The prosecutor cited three with which the New Job cooperative had established temporary links in bidding for contracts.

"They're all clean," Pontiroli assured him.

"More than one member of the management committee of each of them is under investigation, and the anti-mafia squad has listed them among the organisations which collude with organised crime."

"If that can be demonstrated, we'll break all contact with them, but until clear proof emerges ..."

Trombini intervened again. "The certification is completely regular. A company has to base its activities on documentation. You cannot rely on conjecture."

"Certainly not, but some companies you worked with until a year ago have been suspended for mafia-associated activities. In addition, there are the sub-contracts, which make it much easier to elude the checks on organised crime."

"I am not corrupt, sir. I am a businessman who works in the context that has been established, with the aim of creating employment and making sound investments. My partners request that the cooperative should have a positive follow-up in the area we work in, and that it should generate business." He spoke with passion, proudly employing such English terms as "follow-up" and "business", even though his pronunciation was shaky. "It's as though I've got thousands of bayonets at my back – I walk forward to take advantage of all possibilities that arise, because any negligence on my part offers advantages to others. I am a soldier and I must adapt to the rules of engagement."

"Including doing business with people who collude with criminal activity."

Trombini intervened. "I must correct you. My client has never signed agreements with members of the camorra. We assess the people who come to us and I assure you that all signatures on contracts are invariably those of people with no kind of criminal record."

"What do you take me for?" Bergossi said, raising his voice. "Of course you know that the representatives of these companies are clean. They've been selected for just that reason, but in at least three cases, you've worked with firms in Campania that were later closed down for involvement with the camorra. Meanwhile, the same companies which headed bids in the south of the country worked as your subcontractors in the north."

"As soon as we knew they were under investigation, all contact with them was terminated,"Trombini said.

"We lost out. That's the truth. We were never paid by the companies that were closed down,"Pontiroli said.

"But you did pay, and paid a lot, to politicians in Parma," Bergossi said, putting his notes in order and preparing to refer to specific cases. He had a long list.

Trombini rose to his feet once again. "I repeat: these were normal financial transactions. I accept that some were not declared and we are prepared to pay the normal administrative fine."

"But you're part of the cooperative movement. You're not a private company. Your history . . ." Bergossi said, causing Pontiroli and his lawyer to look at each other in incredulous amazement.

"I don't understand,"Trombini said in a near whisper, like a frightened child.

At that point, Soneri rose to his feet and rushed from the room. The inquiry no longer held any interest for him, or perhaps it interested him too much. He was out of his depth, with no role to play. As he was moving across the hall, he felt a hand on his arm. He turned round sharply and saw Angela.

"You have the face of a condemned man, and considering the place we're in . . ." she said.

The commissario made a dismissive gesture with one hand, inviting her not to proceed.

"Remember our appointment at the cemetery? You're in the right frame of mind. You'll find it a romantic place," she said, attempting to make him smile.

"I'll be there, but first I want something to eat. Do you want to come with me?"

"No, I'm going to skip lunch today. I've got things to do here first, but we could go up together."

"Better not. We're on professional duty and you know our roles are not always compatible."

"No, all too often they're not," she said, in a tone of good-humoured reproach. "It does seem a bit hypocritical to me, but let's observe the niceties."

"That's all that counts, even if no-one believes it."

"What's the matter with you? What's put you in such a foul mood?"

"I've just left hearing the Pontiroli case."

"Ah, so that's it!"

"Rarely have I felt so deceived."

"The world of economics is one big lie, but you must know that. Economics is the continuation of war by other means, isn't it? They share the same objective, to destroy other people by any means available."

"But the cooperatives . . . Even a Liberal like Bergossi said it."

"They've agreed to play by other people's rules. In the market, no differences are allowed, neither on the Right nor on the Left. No ideals are permitted to stand in the way of profit. In the same way, there never was any code of honour in war."

Soneri thought of Valmarini, who made no attempt at pretence. He embraced the lie and professed it like a credo. In his own way, he was sincere. A sincere forger: a paradox, a logical somersault, a contradiction in terms. In comparison, Pontiroli was a desolate figure, a mere trafficker, lacking self-awareness and ignorant of the history of the movement which had given birth to his own company. That too was a symbol of the times: the absence of memory, trapped in the present with no sense of the past and no notion of the future, a civilisation slipping into senile dementia.

"See you at Lagrimone," Angela said, as they went their separate ways.

Soneri set off for Bruno's wine bar. He relied on the host's discretion and intuitive ability to understand from Soneri's face that words were superfluous if not actually an annoyance. Sitting in silence in a corner, he consumed a plate of mixed salami, bemused by his own absence of thought and fearful of being ambushed by an acquaintance. He felt an insistent sense of impending closure, the disconcerting awareness of watching the endgame unfold.

He arrived at the police station and got into his Alfa. As he drove through the Val Parma, it occurred to him that a graveyard was the perfect place for someone in his state of mind, but the hills which stood out ever more clearly once he was beyond the village of Pilastro, and the light which grew brighter the higher he ascended, brought him a certain cheer. As he arrived, the sun was still shining and gave some warmth to the afternoon. These days, it was warmer in the mountains than on the plain, where the mist hung heavily. In the graveyard itself, the silence was disturbed only by the song of the robin redbreasts, cold-weather birds.

He was not made all that welcome. Angela gave him a wave from a distance but did not approach. The lawyers on both sides looked at him with evident distrust, while the Council workmen were not in any case unduly pleased with the overtime they had been called out to do. A representative of L'Eterna, recognisable by his distinctive black suit and overcoat, was in attendance, causing the commissario to wonder why policemen and undertakers always stood out. The civil magistrate, named Coscelli, was a corpulent man of solemn gestures. The person whose body was to be exhumed was Cavaliere Costante

Montanari, alleged by a would-be granddaughter to have had an affair with her mother, which had led to her birth. Although the tombstone carried in italics the words *Master Workman, Exemplary Husband and Loving Father*, they were all gathered to judge the truth or otherwise of allegations of his infidelity.

There was no time to be lost, because evening was drawing in and the shadows were lengthening between the tombs. The stonemason set to work to remove the marble and open the burial niche in the graveyard wall. Everything was dispatched in a short time and the coffin, once extracted, was placed on a trolley and loaded onto the mortuary attendants' van.

"Spectacle over and perhaps much time wasted," Soneri murmured, moving alongside Angela. As the small crowd began to disperse, he walked away from her to inspect the graveyard in search of Romagnoli's tomb. No memorial stone was yet in place, and perhaps one never would be. There was nothing more than a recent indentation in the plaster, and a note nailed on with the name and dates. He wandered about for a few moments along the alleys in the graveyard until he realised that the light was fading rapidly. There was still some warmth in the air as he made off on foot for the centre of the village.

He looked up at the snow-capped Monte Fuso and felt an irrepressible desire to take the afternoon off. He went into an *osteria* at the side of Strada Massese, ordered a half-litre of Malvasia and sat observing life in that huddle of houses along the roadside: children getting off the school bus, tractors moving up and down, old folk chatting together, women coming out to close the shutters of shop windows, craftsmen in their overalls and employees from the salami workshops rushing about as their shift was ending. It seemed to him that it was all unbearably trivial and insignificant, but he knew it would not take much to rip apart the subtle fabric of it all. He was thinking about the possibility of the eruption of the unforeseen into that serene current of life, when his mobile rang.

Angela sounded excited. "Where are you?"

"The place you brought me to."

"You should be here. There's been a major development."

"What's happened?"

"Inside the coffin, in addition to the bones of Cavaliere Montanari, there was also another corpse."

"Whose?"

"No idea, but the magistrate says it's recent."

Soneri was already on his feet. "I'll be right there. Meantime, I'll tell Musumeci to come along."

"It's not a pretty sight," Angela said.

"If they identify him, call me right away. Is there anyone from the prosecution office there?"

"Not yet. I don't know who's on duty."

"Better that way." Soneri ended the conversation. He had made his way rapidly to his car while still talking on the telephone.

His head was once again filled with ideas. He imagined that another whirl on the merry-go-round was ahead of him, and that this might only be a new beginning. A corpse in the wrong place meant that other men on the chessboard of his imagination had been tampered with. Racing through the mist at top speed, he was ready to challenge the unknown which lay ahead of him. He arrived at the Forensic Medicine department just as Nanetti, still dressed in his white coat, was coming out. He pulled off his face mask and burst out, "God Almighty! What a stench."

"Has an autopsy been authorised?" the commissario asked.

"No need. It's already been done. He was an old acquaintance and it will come as a great surprise to you, like bumping into a friend you thought was dead," Nanetti said, with his customary macabre humour.

"What the hell are you getting at?"

"It was Romagnoli. So where does that leave us?"

Soneri was taken aback, and as he made an effort to re-order his thoughts, Nanetti continued: "They must have opened the tomb, undone the screws on the coffin, cut through the zinc wrapping and thrown poor Romagnoli on top of Cavaliere Montanari's bones. Montanari was always one for the ladies, but when he was dead they put a man on top of him."

"Any idea how long he'd been there?"

"From about the day of the funeral, or so it would seem. The tear in the zinc was not yet oxidised."

"But if Romagnoli is there, who's in the grave in the wall with his name?"

"They must have shoved someone else in," Nanetti said.

Soneri pulled out his mobile and dialled Musumeci's number, but a few seconds later the inspector turned up at his side with his telephone in his hand. "I've been here for an hour. Did you see me, sir?"

Soneri did not bother replying. "Listen, take the car and go as fast as you can to Lagrimone, and stand guard there. Make sure that no-one touches Romagnoli's tomb."

"You want me to guard a dead man?"

"Take a couple of officers with you, and in the meantime I'll ask Bergossi to authorise cordoning the cemetery off temporarily."

"There's not much risk of anyone escaping," Musumeci grumbled, not exactly thrilled at the prospect of passing the night in a cemetery.

"There might be," Soneri contradicted him.

"Sir, it's a well-known fact that there's not a living soul in a cemetery, apart from the odd Satanist or flower-thief. The only thing in Lagrimone that makes me weep is the village's name," the inspector continued with heavy irony.

As he dialled Bergossi's number, Soneri thought things over and became aware of the fragility of his suspicions. He recalled what he had told Juvara about intuition: that it could lead either to a great breakthrough or to the square root of bugger all. This unusual investigation was forcing him to face the thin line between being showered with honours and jeered at.

The magistrate too was perplexed. "Yes, I understand your suspicion that one body has been substituted for another, but where does that take us?"

"At the very least we must clarify where we are, don't you agree?" From the ensuing silence, Soneri grasped that Bergossi was contemplating this. "A crime has indeed been committed and I could ... pushing things a bit ... Alright," he decided at last. "Put the tape up around the cemetery. Thankfully, we've arrested Pontiroli and that's shut up the Right, otherwise ... Now we can even allow ourselves the luxury of taking a few risks."

"How did it go with Pontiroli?"

"He's aiming to pass it all off as extortion in some cases, and unlawful financing in others."

"The lesser evil."

"He won't get away with it. The system is all linked up. In Emilia, private companies need to help out the New Job outfit because the Left is in control here, but outside the region, where the Right is in power, it's in the interests of the cooperatives to present themselves in partnership with private companies. United in business, understand? This all happens without any scrutiny from Legacoop, the central body for the cooperatives. Nowadays these big enterprises couldn't care less about anything and are happy to go their own way," Bergossi said.

Not long afterwards, Angela called. "See you in the bar on the corner to the right of the Forensic Medicine offices."

By five o'clock it was already dark, and mist was sweeping along the side streets. Soneri looked at the time and calculated how long it would take Musumeci to get to Lagrimone. Everything depended on the timing.

Angela arrived at the bar before the inspector could have reached the mountains. "When was L'Eterna advised about the exhumation?" the commissario asked her.

"Coscelli was very helpful in that respect. He wasn't required to give much notice, so he told the manager just half a day in advance. In any case, the whole job was to be carried out by the Council workmen."

"I see your little paw in all this."

She winked at him. "We've been thinking along the same lines and entertaining the same suspicions. We did talk it over together, remember?"

Soneri nodded. "I've sent Musumeci up with two officers and I've convinced Bergossi to cordon off the graveyard. I got in touch with the inspector a short while ago to tell him not to let anyone touch anything. I only hope he gets there in time."

"Do you think they're already trying to sort things out?"

"What else can they do? Once Romagnoli was found out of place ..."

"Commissario, if I've got this right, this is checkmate. Whether they move or stay still, the outcome is the same."

"Are you sure there have been no leaks? It would be hellish if we'd got it all wrong."

"I don't think so, but they're diabolical, this lot. There's nothing to do but wait."

"I doubt I'm capable of that. I'm heading back up there shortly."

Musumeci called in again. "I'm here in the dark and, as I said, there's not a living soul around."

"Is anyone with you?"

"Two colleagues. Not enough for two sides in a game of cards."

"I'll be there quite soon, and I'll make up the numbers. We'll see what kind of hand we've been dealt."

"Go on, get on your way. You can hardly contain yourself," Angela said, looking at him shrewdly as though she were a doctor.

He was indeed in a state of excitement, and the only way to calm down was to keep active. Within a quarter of an hour, he was driving in the dark and the mist up the valley he had come down just a few hours previously. If he had heeded his instincts, he would have remained up there, waiting in some quiet premises in that village in the Apennines. When he at last got free of the mist on the slopes of the Pastorello, the night's clear skies opened out before him. This seemed to augur well, pointing to a possible solution to the case. Five minutes later his mobile rang. Musumeci sounded concerned.

"Sir, a van has arrived and parked in front of the cemetery entrance. Three men have got out and they're standing talking beside the tape we put up."

"Did they see you?"

"No, we parked behind the trees and can't be seen in the dark."

"I imagine this'll be the team. For the moment, keep an eye on them. See if they try to force an entry despite the notices."

"One is on his mobile, and the other two have got back into the van. It's bloody cold out here."

"I'm on my way, but if they decide to make a move, call me back."

"What about us? If they do try something, what are we supposed to do?"

"Nothing. I believe they'll get on with a job we would have had to do ourselves."

From the silence that followed, Soneri deduced that

Musumeci had not understood a thing. The commissario, however, had grasped everything, and the van which had appeared in the night near the cemetery was confirmation enough. He accelerated, bumping over holes in a road built on the clay of a hunchbacked mountain whose slopes had been loosened by the autumn rain.

Musumeci called again. "They've gone in. They must have received orders."

"Leave them be. You have the two officers with you?"

"Yes, I'm with them."

"Are they wide awake?"

"In what sense?"

"Are you awake, Musumeci?" The commissario, already tense at the thought of what might happen, raised his voice. "I wasn't asking if they were actually asleep, but if they're bright and ready for action."

"Oh, I see," the inspector said. "They're fine, sir. You can rely on them."

Soneri parked his Alfa in the car park and proceeded on foot. Lagrimone was asleep; even the lights in the roadside bar were off. The glare from television sets could be seen through only a few windows. When he was in the vicinity of the cemetery, he sent a text to Musumeci telling him to be prepared, and looked over at the van to make sure there was no-one inside. He approached the nearest cemetery gate, and saw three shadows at work in the colonnade in front of Romagnoli's tomb. Everything was falling into place. He heard a portable circular power-saw bore cautiously into the wall containing the burial niches, and assumed the men were removing the bricks to extract the casket. He stood waiting in the cold of the night, the silence broken only by the strident hoot of an owl disturbed by the lights from the road some metres lower down, and by the rumble of the saw, which eventually died away. The three men, puffing and panting, set to work. The commissario heard the dull sound of something being dragged, and thought he saw the outline of the coffin. The three bent down and raised it onto their shoulders, but at that point Soneri threw open the gate and shouted to them not to move. Musumeci and the two officers rushed over to his side, pistols in their hands. The men let go of the coffin, which fell to the ground with a bang, and rushed off in different directions among the tombs, their overcoats flapping. The inspector and the two policemen ran forward, while Soneri remained where he was, watching the absurd pursuit past flickering lamps and dead souls.

The commissario saw one of the men clamber onto a tombstone and jump onto the top of the wall before disappearing beyond the compound. He had already lost sight of the other two, but from the scrape of shoes on the ground, he deduced they were making for the rear of the cemetery. A few seconds later, he heard an iron gate being slammed shut and a couple of loud oaths echoing under the vaults.

"They gave us the slip," Musumeci moaned, still out of breath from the chase. "They'd left the gate at the rear open and slammed it in our faces. Half a second more was all we needed."

"You've been weakened by all those women. You're not as agile as you used to be," Soneri said.

"But they got away," the inspector said, taken aback by Soneri's good humour.

"Doesn't matter. They were just three labourers, and we've got the van and above all the coffin. Didn't I tell you they were doing us a favour by getting it out for us?"

Musumeci nodded, but he still didn't seem to understand.

24

THE CARABINIERI FROM Langhirano provided a truck to transport the coffin. The van had been impounded and was parked at the police station. One of the three grave robbers was captured in somewhat comic circumstances. Slipping and sliding in the snow while attempting to make his escape, he ended up in a muddy swamp and could not get free. They found him at first light, trapped up to the navel, as upright as a ramrod.

For his part, Soneri was overwhelmed by conjectures and the excitement of expectation. He got home at about four o'clock in the morning, but did not get any sleep, so the following day only adrenaline was keeping him going. As he went into the Forensic Medicine department half an hour before they were due to begin the examination of the remains, the effect of exhaustion on his eyes was clear. The doorman looked at him with a mixture of surprise and alarm, and hesitated before greeting him. Nanetti arrived not long afterwards.

"You're the greatest collector of dead bodies I know," he grumbled.

Soneri stretched out his arms. "Pure chance. Who'd have imagined that an exhumation for an entirely different case ..."

"Bugger all to do with chance! How come you were on the spot waiting for it?"

"Cornelio was the lawyer dealing with a civil case concerning the inheritance of Cavaliere Montanari. In other words, Angela . . ." The commissario stopped in embarrassment.

"And you're involved in all your partner's cases?"

"No, but Romagnoli was buried at Lagrimone, and I went along for no other reason than to pay him a visit."

Nanetti burst out laughing. "You're a complete arsehole! Do you expect me to believe that guff? Come on, you know I don't go around gossiping."

"I swear I only went to Lagrimone for the reason I've already given. It was a hunch, a suggestion, a bit of guesswork. Perhaps the word is 'hope'. All these things come into an investigation, don't they?"

Nanetti shrugged his shoulders. "How should I know? I never go beyond what I can see or experience. What kind of suggestion are you talking about?"

"I was struck by the avarice that drives people to blacken the name of the dead, and maybe even more by what Bergossi was saying about inquiries and people's behaviour in general."

"Money makes the world go round," Nanetti replied, underlining the obviousness of what he was saying. "I'm more interested in Bergossi's reflections."

"He believes it's never possible to predict everything, and that chance always erupts onto the scene. In his opinion, this is an incontrovertible natural law."

"That's true. Not even the most perceptive assassin can foresee every eventuality."

"No, that's too simple. As I said, Bergossi makes an existential law out of it. A theory about the intractability of life. The fact is that things don't depend just on the murderer, but on a multiplicity of other events which can upset his plans without warning. Take this case. How could anyone have imagined that a civil case would lead to the discovery of the secret burial of Romagnoli? Our prosecutor insists that some intervention of the unforeseeable will disrupt even the best-laid plans, and if we don't pick up on it, it's because we let it elude us. It's our fault for not observing attentively enough."

Nanetti looked at him thoughtfully without abandoning his scepticism. "What strange ideas magistrates have! I'd always viewed Bergossi differently." Seeing the door of the post-mortem theatre open, he added: "Anyway, let's go and see what chance has in store for us." They went in. The coffin was already lying open on a table. The metal casing had still to be cut, but this could not be done until the prosecutor arrived.

When he made his solemn entrance a few moments later, Nanetti nudged Soneri: "Here comes the unexpected."

"Not every sight will be a welcome one."

In reply, Nanetti handed him a face mask. "Here, put this on. At least it'll shut you up for a bit."

The assistants cut through the zinc plate. The sides of the coffin became hot as the teeth of the saw cut in, spreading the smells of the foundry in the air. When the casing was cut clean through, an even more unpleasant stench polluted the atmosphere and one of the assistants switched on a fan. In spite of the foetid smell, everyone gathered round to take a look. What they saw no longer possessed any savour of the human. The corpse had lost its form, and under the disintegrating lineaments, the prickly, sinister outline of a skeleton was beginning to emerge. The clothes suggested a male, but no-one could have recognised it as such, at least not until the forensic surgeon began his summary inspection of the body. Pulling aside the jacket which had attached itself to the stomach, he revealed a white shirt, stained here and there by already dried organic fluids, and embroidered with the initials "G. C.". Soneri had no further doubt. Bergossi and all the others exchanged knowing glances over their masks.

A quarter of an hour later, the prosecutor approached the commissario. "It all seems quite clear. At least we've located him," he said.

"At least that . . . Now the fun begins. Meanwhile, let's try to work out how and when he died," he said to Nanetti.

"I'll arrange the autopsy for today or tomorrow," Bergossi said. "I'm in a hurry to bring this to a conclusion."

"Do you think you can really bring a case like this to a conclusion?"

"Our part, at least. The rest's not up to us."

"Will you make an announcement to the city?"

"First and foremost, I want certainty. He's waited so long that one more day won't make any difference," the prosecutor said, turning away.

"There's no chance of keeping this a secret until tomorrow," Nanetti said. "There are crowds of journalists out there. They've smelled something rotten."

"If Capuozzo gets hold of the story, he'll sell it right away. The moment he sees a T.V. camera, he'll have a hard-on."

"The truth is, it does all seem perfectly clear now, doesn't it?" Nanetti said, with a shrug of his shoulders.

"To me it does, but scientists like you always need proof."

"It'll come. All it needs is something he was wearing."

An hour later, Delfina Torreggiani turned up, supported by Musumeci. She was shown some personal objects including a ring, a chain and a metal bracelet. The old woman took them in her hand one by one and put on her spectacles to get a better look. She touched them with all the delicacy her dry, trembling fingers were capable of, put them down on a settee and ran her hand over them. She stood there staring at them for a few seconds before raising her eyes to Soneri, who saw tears, magnified by the lenses, silently well up and flow down her cheeks, filling her wrinkles and forming a transparent mesh like a layer of ice over her face. The sobs came later, and the commissario concluded they made any further verification unnecessary.

The city sensed the death of Corbellini well before being officially informed and stopped to question itself with the incredulity of a lost orphan. CORPSE OF MAYOR FOUND IN CEMETERY AT LAGRIMONE IN TOMB OF MAN FROZEN TO DEATH IN VILLA CLELIA was the headline on the evening television news, and that seemingly paradoxical statement brought Soneri back to the day when everything had started with the equally paradoxical announcement of the week's break on the Paganella.

"We're back to all this nonsense, sir," Juvara said. "I imagine people listening to this won't understand a thing and will wonder why he was there, and why he was found in that mountain graveyard in the very place where his trusted henchman was supposed to be."

"There are things even we don't understand, and that's the problem," the commissario agreed. "Maybe reality as such doesn't make sense."

"We spend our time looking for a logical thread."

"It's that attitude that leads us astray. All too often inquiries are shaped by instinct rather than reason."

"Do you think that's just how people work?"

"I'm certain of it. And anyone who goes sticking his nose into other people's affairs had better face it."

Juvara sank into a reflective silence, giving every appearance of being deeply disturbed. Time and again, Soneri was taken aback by the naivety of the young inspector, a consequence of his belated encounter with the world, but was glad of the silence. Outside, the afternoon was fading in the deepening grey of the silver firs in the courtyard. He felt his body relax as he settled down for an evening of waiting. The first results of the autopsy would not be available until the following day, and the inquiry would take off again from there. There would now be a lull. Weariness overtook him, while the city outside throbbed with clamour and commotion.

He awoke with the unpleasant sensation of having fainted. The office was dark and deserted. A note expressing some concern had been left on the desk by the inspector: *I let you sleep because you obviously needed some rest. See you tomorrow, Juvara. P.S. Aurora Guatelli came looking for you.* He tore the note up and threw the pieces into the wastepaper basket. He got to his feet, racked with pain, looked at the clock and saw it was now eleven o'clock. His mobile had been turned off from early afternoon when he had gone to the Forensic Medicine department, and when he switched it on he found a host of messages waiting for him. He heard a low, rasping sound, and took a few moments to grasp that it was coming from the telephone on his desk. Juvara must have turned the sound down to the minimum so as not to disturb him.

"Where have you been? I was worried!" Angela said, her words tumbling one over the other in her alarm.

"I was beginning to think no-one cared about me," he said.

"Your mobile was switched off and there was no reply from the office."

"Even the toughest of men have their moments of weakness. There's always the chance of dropping off to sleep, as the motorway signs warn you."

"Did you fall asleep?"

"Dead to the world, like a new-born babe after being fed."

"Alright! Now you can shove off to bed in your own house," Angela said, somewhat annoyed at the commissario's tone.

Feeling revived, he got up and stretched his arms in the

semi-darkness of his office. He left without being seen, and made for the outskirts, well away from the commotion in the city. He headed for the Lungoparma and found along the riverbank the silence he had been craving. He knew he would find an explanation of what had been happening only in that silence and darkness, so now he was making for the place – that amphibious, dual world, no longer city and not yet countryside – where he had received the first indication of the whole affair. He walked along a pathway which had been cleared of snow, rang Valmarini's bell and saw the gate spring open in the usual way.

He went into the house, hung with drapes and curtains, which made him think of dark oil slicks at sea every time he saw them. Dondolo greeted him by raising his face and sniffing him from a distance. The artist came to greet him.

"He's through there," he said, anticipating the commissario's question. "He's devastated, but perhaps for that reason he's more cynically lucid."

"You think he didn't know?"

"Perhaps he did, but hoped for a different outcome," Valmarini said, leading Soneri into the other room.

Ugolini had a glass in his hand and did not at first notice the commissario's arrival. When he became aware of him, he spun round and stared intently.

"Congratulations. I'd never have imagined he was where you found him."

"Neither would I."

"It seems he did what he could to end up that way. We're all, to some extent, responsible for what happens to us."

"I don't see how Corbellini could have been even partly responsible ..."

Ugolini continued staring at him, and his was not an attractive stare. "He lacked balls," he said, with a grimace of contempt.

"And if you don't have balls you end up murdered, in someone else's grave?"

"I don't know how it went, but in this world there are those who decide for themselves and those who let others decide for them. In the latter case, you end up where they put you."

"Corbellini was where he was. You had him elected because he enhanced the image."

"He himself wanted to be there. Sometimes ambition is stronger than self-awareness. There are trees that collapse under the weight of their own fruit."

"Wasn't the choice down to you?"

"No-one can ever guess what's inside a melon, but he'd been warned. There are some risky roles in life. You need a thick skin," Ugolini said, almost in a whisper.

"Who killed him?" the commissario asked abruptly.

"I don't know. Do you really think I would know something like that?"

"Your party knew everything, including the fact that he was dead and perhaps where he was buried. You dragged the whole affair out to give yourselves time to fix things up in the Council, conceal the evidence and work out a political solution. If we hadn't found him, you might have struggled through to the end of the electoral cycle. There wasn't long to go."

"An intriguing hypothesis," Ugolini said calmly. "I'm not going to reply, and in any case a denial from me wouldn't make you change your mind. I couldn't care less about Corbellini – he wasn't up to the job. In some ways it was right that he disappeared. He should have known that politics and business enlarge that kernel of primitive savagery which is in all of us."

"Your world, with its glittering designer labels, doesn't seem terribly savage. I had a gentler notion of it."

"Even tigers can look good: beautiful, elegant and sensuous, but solitary and pitiless. We are no different except in the desire we nourish, and that desire is so boundless as to make us even more ferocious. We're engaged in a constant struggle. And I don't like losing," Ugolini said, raising his voice.

"Sooner or later you'll lose too. Defeat is one of the few things which make men equal."

"Don't seek refuge in worlds of which we know nothing. I reason about things I see, and it is struggle alone that selects the fittest. Once cultural barriers are removed, that is the one thing that has always mattered: struggle by every means at our disposal. That includes me professing myself a liberal, or giving myself airs by hanging on my walls daubs of paint that mean nothing to me. I made this gentleman wealthy in this way," Ugolini said, indicating the painter.

"As well as by establishing links with the criminal world," Soneri added with a touch of malice.

"I've already explained to you that criminality is the infancy of entrepreneurship. I can even understand that from your point of view the whole financial world seems criminal, since its ambition is to free itself of every rule which limits its freedom. Let me repeat that I have a sneaking admiration for your stubbornness, but it's a loser's stance. I regret your naivety in not noticing that since we took over the political space, we've been tearing down one after the other the obstacles that used to hold us back. It's now we who decide how the game will be played, and how people like you will play it. Unfortunately, in the case of Corbellini, we made a bad choice, but what is a Corbellini? A soubrette, nothing more, nothing less. We'll find another. Might even be a woman. They're more popular. A good-looking woman who excites imagination when she speaks. Isn't this a lovely world?" he sneered, pouring himself another glass of grappa.

The commissario turned towards Valmarini, who shook his head slightly.

"And that expedition to Andalo with Bernetti and Bonaldi,

was that when you decided on the strategy to avoid scandal?" Soneri asked.

"You were on the point of arresting a councillor, and the whole Council was in crisis. The party could not ignore it," Ugolini replied.

"And what did Corbellini say?"

"Oh, him," Ugolini mumbled, with a dismissive wave of his hand. "He asked for help and advice, but how can you help someone who's landed himself in the shit up to his neck, and who above all doesn't have the balls to sack half the inner cabinet and reshuffle the rest? All you can do is tell him to hold his nose. But if you're mayor, you've also got to know how to avoid being bitten by guard dogs, like you."

"Did your people bring him home? The carabinieri who intercepted you in Val Badia reported that Corbellini seemed semi-conscious and confused."

"What the hell do I know about what he was taking? Tranquillisers, perhaps?"

"Benzodiazepine? The same drug you were administering to his henchman, Romagnoli?"

"Don't try and make accusations against me by implication," Ugolini roared, removing one finger from the glass he was clutching and pointing it accusingly. "You won't find a shred of evidence against me. The men and women who make up my party were elected by the people, so they're employees of the state, like you and the magistrates. You'll never be able to subvert the will of the electorate."

Soneri remained impassive and kept his eyes on Ugolini, who in turn stared back. His expression changed from enraged to sardonic. "Resign yourself," he said in a calmer voice. "I offered you the possibility of an honourable armistice, but you turned that chance down, so you are now definitively numbered among my enemies."

"The prospect does not displease me."

"Remember the responsibilities that go with different roles: it's essential to have the balls to carry them through."

"No, there's less to it than that. It's sufficient to be bright, dishonest and devoid of scruples."

"Do you imagine your words have any effect on me? I've long since freed myself from conscience. Conscience is merely the self-castration one person imposes on the majority to liberate himself of them and dominate them. There's no conscience for winners, and everything will be cancelled. A great criminal will go down in history, but you won't. Hitler, Stalin, Mussolini and the bloodiest of Roman emperors are immortalised by their achievements, but there's no place for the victims. Rather than seeking compensation, the victims bear the burden of upholding the immortality of their butchers."

Ugolini set before the commissario a world of extreme, raw cynicism with such clarity as to make it almost admirable. His intuition told him that behind Ugolini's talk there was, perhaps implicitly rather than consciously, an inner store of resources. He had looked inside himself and had discovered an array of sharp blades with which he was now dissecting reality and creating carnage.

Soneri brushed aside Ugolini's practical reasoning, leaned his head to one side and asked: "What did you want Corbellini to do? You went there to give him instructions, didn't you?"

"Do you know what the popes say? 'There's no descent from the cross.' We reminded him of that several times. We even suggested several exit strategies and he seemed to have understood, but then . . ." Ugolini seemed to be winding down, but then started up again with what almost sounded like a sob. "If he himself had charged the corrupt councillors and removed them from office, like a political street-cleaner, the Council would still have been in office. Half a dozen crooks would have been handed over to you, and Parma would have considered itself purified."

It was Soneri's turn to smile. "Instead, by exiting the scene he's forcing you to hold new elections right after the scandal, with the risk you won't win and someone will go poking his nose into Council affairs. Corbellini didn't have the courage. Perhaps he counted some of the councillors under investigation as personal friends. Or perhaps he had doubts about loyalty to the cause. Perhaps one of them would have spoken out."

"If you're a sentimentalist, being mayor is the wrong job for you. The United States is a great country because once sons and daughters begin handling dollar bills, they're no longer relatives. His job was to push things as far as they could go," he said, swallowing a glass of grappa as though it were prosecco.

"He wasn't quite a big enough bastard."

"Those who aren't disconcert me. I don't understand them. I find them unpredictable, dangerous."

"Dangerous?"

"Yes. Everything must work by intuitive logic and if someone interrupts its workings, nothing at all can go forward. If something is not recognised and identified, the whole scheme falls into disarray. And don't believe for one moment that he was prey to some attack of morality. Quite the contrary. He wanted to be a real bastard, but didn't have the guts."

"I have to confess that your cynicism has a certain fascination, but the world you have in your head just wouldn't work. The expenditure of energy needed to keep it afloat would outweigh any advantage that might be had. The balance sheet is in the red," the commissario said.

"The world you imagine wouldn't function either."

"Oh, I don't believe in a world of angels any more than you do. There's no way to eliminate all the bastards. The best you can do is keep the ratio down."

Ugolini adopted a more confidential tone. "Commissario, don't imagine I was born thinking the way I do now. I became like this because I saw real life in all the obscene nudity with which it presents itself. I was even more of a moralist than you, but when you get to know how people are made, you have to come to terms with your own illusions. At that point, it's better to accept that humanity will always slip towards the most ferocious egoism because that's its natural tendency. Two thousand years of priests have not managed to change all that. In the end the priests genuflected too. Do you think that you, a mere provincial policeman, are going to succeed where they failed? Don't waste your life. Welcome the world as it is and abandon yourself to it. Make the best use of the time afforded us."

Soneri stood in silence for a while in the semi-darkness of the room. Dondolo got up, stretched his legs and then went to sit between him and Ugolini, his eyes turned towards the latter with a look of instinctive distrust.

Ugolini changed tack. "Come to the party for the thirtieth anniversary of my company. The whole city will be there."

"At least the part of it which isn't already in jail," Soneri said sarcastically.

"The people who count have never been there," Ugolini replied in the same tone, and it was clear he was referring above all to himself.

"You know more than anyone else that it's all phoney," the commissario said, glancing at Valmarini. "Isn't it enough for you to make a fool of your colleagues?"

"You've no idea how amusing it is! The Chief of Police is always there, squealing with delight at the masterpieces! He doesn't understand a thing, and yet he's understood everything. He smells power and he reveres it."

Soneri's disquiet changed into rage. Once again, Ugolini

was telling the truth. Capuozzo and a large part of the *nomenklatura* at the Prefecture debased themselves before the upper echelons, whose servants they were. The industrialist was forcing him to face his own limits, and he felt disarmed. He jumped to his feet, surprising Dondolo, who swung round in alarm.

"What's got into you?" Ugolini asked calmly, almost confidentially.

The commissario made no reply. An excess of thought is the equivalent of an empty mind. He shook his head and mumbled a goodbye. As he was going out, accompanied by Valmarini, he heard Ugolini calling out after him: "I prefer an intelligent enemy to a fatuous ally." Perhaps he was expressing admiration, in his own way.

"Did you see how Dondolo was looking at him?" Valmarini asked in the darkness of the courtyard. "Dogs are capable of recognising fear, and Ugolini was rancid with it."

The commissario indicated he had understood, and left without a another word.

25

THE AUTOPSY WAS scheduled for eight o'clock, but Soneri was already in his office by seven. He dispatched Nanetti to oversee proceedings, making him promise to get back to him as soon as he had any results. In the event, he got in touch more quickly than expected.

"It's a good sign if it's over already," Soneri said.

"Sorry to disappoint you. It hasn't even started."

"Someone not turned up?"

"On the contrary, there are too many people."

"What do you mean?"

"Journalists! Never seen so many of them in all my life. They're blocking the entrance and some of our colleagues had to step in to clear the way. Now they've gathered in the court-yard and they're stopping anyone who tries to get through."

"When do you think you'll get started?" The commissario was getting impatient.

"Very soon. The city's in uproar. There are public meetings and demonstrations all over the place, making it impossible to move. Even the police surgeon was held up."

"O.K. When you do get some news, give me a ring."

As Soneri was about to hang up, he heard Nanetti shout down the line: "Listen, I had a look at the body and at first sight there appears to be a complication."

"What you mean, a complication?"

"I'll be able to be more precise later on. I might be wrong, but I've got some experience in this field."

"Explain yourself, for God's sake!"

"As far as I could see, there's no sign of any injury on the corpse. I examined it when it was removed from the coffin and laid out."

"You mean there's no clear evidence of the cause of death we expected?"

"Afraid so. It seems intact, if you see what I mean."

Soneri made no reply and after pausing for a few moments, Nanetti went on: "You can see for yourself that, if that's true, everything becomes more complex, especially with a half-decomposed corpse."

"Who knows how we'll get out of this one," Soneri muttered as he put the telephone down. Meanwhile, as he was wondering how to get out of the office and avoid the journalists he could see wandering about in the courtyard, Juvara came in. "Excuse me, sir, Aurora Guatelli is outside and wants to see you."

It was only then he remembered he had meant to call her. "Show her in." A few moments later, Aurora came in, walking slowly and hesitantly, mumbling a "good morning". The commissario invited her to take a seat and she obeyed. She seemed embarrassed and unsure where to start.

"I'm here on behalf of Don Guido as well," she said, speaking with such genuine contrition as to make her appear almost seductive. "We've decided to tell you everything. You must forgive us if we've been ... It's a bit like going to confession, if you understand me. Don Guido is a priest and his role is sometimes not all that different from yours. You hear confessions too, don't you?"

"Go on," the commissario said.

"That night, Giancarlo called Don Guido."

"Which night?"

"I think you know that on the Wednesday after he'd left for Andalo, he came back with Bernetti and Bonaldi. There had been a meeting that Ugolini attended as well. On their return, they dropped the undersecretary at Fornovo, while they continued to Calestano. Giancarlo had a house just outside the village, and from there, at four o'clock in the morning, he called Don Guido."

"The last telephone call?"

"Yes, I think so, but it wasn't just an ordinary call, more a long-distance confession."

"Was that Don Guido's impression?"

"He had the feeling something irreparable was about to happen, and he did what he could to head it off. By the end, he was convinced that he'd calmed him down."

"What state was he in?"

"His voice was thick, perhaps caused by tranquillisers, and at times he started shouting. He seemed lucid, fully aware of the situation that was pressing down on him."

"Were they threatening him?"

"He kept saying he was in a cul de sac, and couldn't see any way out. The party considered him a nonentity and for that reason demanded blind obedience. His councillors threatened revelations if he betrayed them, and he himself was compromised. None of them had clean hands. They could all be blackmailed, you understand? There could be no partial solution. Either they all kept their mouths shut, or anarchy would break out. The context didn't allow him any other option."

He heard that word, "context", for the umpteenth time, an entity which designated a multitude and yet no-one, definable only by negation, faceless and thus elusive, but at the same time oppressive and destructive.

"Was there anyone with him in Calestano or was he alone?"

"Don Guido got the impression he was alone, but at one point Giancarlo said the party had put Bonaldi on to him to convince him to carry on. He wasn't to give up while the Members of Parliament were bringing pressure to bear on the magistrates. They were engaged in damage-limitation. They didn't care about the half-dozen councillors who were under investigation so long as he remained in post."

"Did he tell the priest he was planning to end it all, or did he have other ideas in mind?" Soneri asked.

"Giancarlo always lived in the realm of appearances, and in this he was the mirror image of the city. Once his image as a man and politician had been shattered, he felt stripped of any sense of belonging. He knew how volatile people can be. Being a symbol requires perfection in every aspect of one's life."

"And so?"

"In his nakedness, deprived of his role, Giancarlo discovered his vital, human self, but at the same moment he realised he'd always betrayed it. He was in a blind alley with no easy way out."

"I need to know what his intentions were, if he had any idea of how to escape from the situation he was in," Soneri said, his impatience growing by the minute.

"After Don Guido managed to calm him down, Giancarlo confided that he was thinking of fleeing, but first he wanted time to reflect. I think he was considering making a new life somewhere far from Italy. After all, even his week's holiday started with the intention of getting away from Parma while the turmoil was raging. Over and above that, Andalo is close to the border."

"Why do you think he didn't carry out this scheme?"

"I believe they prevented him. There's no escape from the party; it's impossible to resign. You know what form power takes nowadays: politics as a fig leaf for the interests of a mafia-style organisation. There's no free will, and once you're on the inside, you don't belong to yourself anymore but to the group which made you a public figure, and which expects you to do as they require."

"Did they block him or did he not believe strongly enough?"

"I simply don't know." Aurora shrugged her shoulders, mildly irritated. "How could I? Don Guido didn't tell me everything. He relayed to me only those things he considered might be useful to you in uncovering the truth. Perhaps he went beyond the seal of the confessional."

Forgetting about Aurora for a moment, the commissario picked up the receiver. He meant to call Musumeci, but twice dialled the wrong number and became annoyed with himself. At last he got it right, and heard the inspector reply in a tired voice.

"What were you doing? Sleeping?"

"After three nights with no sleep, I was just about to drop off."

"You'll have to track down Bonaldi, the regional secretary," he said, showing no interest in Musumeci's condition. "As soon as Bergossi is free, I'll ask him to add his name to the register of suspects under investigation."

"But sir, is it a good idea to start messing in politics once again?"

"There's no choice when politics have become a police matter."

"So you think it was Bonaldi who stopped Giancarlo from making up his own mind?" Aurora asked when the commissario put the telephone down.

"He was the last to see him. And anyway, if I remember correctly, was he not once a wrestler? Putting pressure on a man must be one of his strong points."

"If that's right, it explains a lot," Aurora said, bowing her head.

"It would've been better for them to make him stay in office. Flight would have been too risky, or at least it would have introduced an extra complication," Soneri said.

Aurora got up from her chair. "If there's anything else you want to ask, you know where to find me."

The commissario tried to imagine what must have happened that night, but at that point his mobile rang. It was Bergossi. "Any news on the autopsy? All the mobiles have been switched off."

"No, they're still in there. I'm afraid it's a complex matter."

"What's ever simple?"

"We must question Bonaldi. He was the last man to see the mayor alive. He took him to his house in Calestano."

"Are you sure?"

"Aurora Guatelli was here to tell me about a late-night telephone call between Corbellini and Don Guido Nassi."

"We'll have the whole Centre Right up in arms again."

"Whatever. We must question Bonaldi, even if only as a witness."

"Doesn't make much difference. Have you sent someone to look for him?"

"Yes. Musumeci's already on his trail."

"Let me know about the autopsy if you find out before I do," the prosecutor said, worried about the possible emergence of further problems.

Soneri stood for a moment looking at Juvara, who was attending to the bureaucracy, then decided to leave the office. He went out onto Borgo della Posta, crossed over Via Ventidue Luglio, turned up Via Repubblica and walked through Piazzale del Carbone behind the City Chambers. In the Piazza, the crowd occupying the entire space between the church of San Pietro and the Palazzo del Governatore prevented him from proceeding any further. It was then that he heard someone speaking into a loudspeaker and recognised Sgarzi's voice haranguing the multitude. He realised that Parma was yet again ready to work itself up into a teenage infatuation with the first performer to fire its imagination.

He hurried along Via Cavour, stopping on the grass of Piazzale della Pace to get his breath back. He had not quite managed to sit down on the low wall around the Verdi Monument when his mobile brought him back to the investigation. It was Nanetti. "It's over. Afraid I was right."

"They didn't find anything?" the commissario asked, disappointed.

"There are no wounds on the body to indicate a violent death. At this point the only approach is chemistry."

"What do you mean?"

"Come on, Soneri! Either they poisoned him or he poisoned himself, but to establish the facts we need to do further examinations of the tissues. The forensic medic needs a bit more time."

"With the pharmacy he had in his house, there would have been no shortage of ways for him to poison himself."

"Let's be patient. It won't take too long."

"What do you say to taking a trip up to Calestano? It was there that Corbellini dropped off the radar."

"I'll come only if you invite me to lunch in that *osteria* in Fragno. You know what I'm like when it comes to a plate of truffles."

"Agreed. I'll come and pick you up."

"Just give me time to get rid of the stench of the corpse."

The bright winter morning and the sparkling snow restored their cheery mood. After their close proximity with the dead, they both felt the need to re-establish contact with life and with the cruel, beautiful light of the sun on the horizon, but briefly visible in January and all the more precious for that.

They made their way to Fragno, situated opposite the enormous hunchback of Monte Sporno. Over the *risotto al tartufo*, they asked Mariella, the hostess, about Corbellini's house. It was not in the village, she said, but a short way outside in a district called Chiosetto. They lingered over a dish of wild boar, while the frozen crust of the snow outside projected slender shards of incandescent light onto the windows. When they went out, they paused to preserve that state of delight, until the sun touched the ridge of Monte Sporno and the mountain cast a cold shadow on the valley below.

"Now to work," Nanetti said, and the commissario realised that until that moment they had hardly spoken at all, absorbed as they were in the food and in that brief brightness which glittered like sparks from blazing wood.

They went down to Chiosetto and picked out the mayor's house among the half-dozen which were uninhabited in winter. Soneri pulled out the key which Aurora had given Musumeci to pass on to him. Inside, everything was in complete disorder. The kitchen looked like a boxing ring. Two chairs were lying on their sides, the tablecloth was trailing on the floor leaving sections of the table uncovered, one windowpane had been smashed and fragments of the glass were glistening on the sofa.

Nanetti set to work on his inspection while the commissario examined the upper floor, where there were two bedrooms and a bathroom. He noted that the beds were still made, a sign that no-one had been sleeping there. One drawer in the sideboard was lying open and looked like a shelf in a chemist's shop. Everything gave the impression of agitation and rush. There were little opened medicine bottles and an overturned pillbox. The commissario rummaged among the papers and found some photographs. One was a portrait of Corbellini and Aurora embracing when they were little more than teenagers at what looked like a seaside resort. Others depicted him posing in a gym showing off his muscles. Soneri also came across an image which made him curious: the mayor standing alongside Romagnoli, both holding bloodhounds on a leash. He did not know how it had happened, but the threads of his inquiries were all coming together: animals, drugs, business, camorra, politics. It all joined up. The investigation had originated when he went following tracks left by dogs alongside the river Parma.

"Go and have a look at his pharmacy department," Soneri said as he came downstairs to find Nanetti still busy with his instruments.

"There's nothing much here," Nanetti said. "What I can tell you is that there was a scuffle. There are marks of shoes on the wooden seats as well as on the table legs. I'm almost certain that blows were exchanged."

The commissario made no comment. "I'll go and have a look upstairs," Nanetti said. Soneri sat down on the sofa and looked around the room, trying to imagine what had taken place there. He remained unmoving until Nanetti came back down.

"There were some hairs on a cushion and several fingerprints on the medicine bottles," Nanetti said. "I'll take them to the laboratory and have a closer look."

"They'll help us understand who was last in this house," the commissario replied as he made for the door.

Outside it was almost dark, and the enchantment of the morning had disappeared. They got into the car without exchanging a word and set off. Only when they encountered the mist at the bottom of Val Baganza did Nanetti say, "Well, is it any clearer now?"

The commissario, keeping his eyes fixed on the black wall ahead of him, smiled and nodded. Not long afterwards Musumeci got in touch to say he had tracked Bonaldi down.

"Where will I find him?" Soneri asked.

"In the *Cavalieri di Malta*."

"A right hellhole!"

"They always gather there," Musumeci said.

He parked his Alfa at the police station and said goodnight to his colleague. "I'll keep you posted," Nanetti said, holding up the bag packed with medicines.

Soneri gave him a wave and set off on foot. His path took him through Borgo Riccio, across Via Farini and into Borgo Torrigiani where he found himself facing the deconsecrated church of Sant'Andrea which stood alongside the entrance to the club. Dimmed lighting guaranteed sufficient intimacy in that place where the fate of Parma was decided. He immediately felt uneasy. The clients were almost entirely male, dressed with an elegance that scarcely concealed their innate vulgarity. From somewhere in the semi-darkness a girl, seemingly somewhat tipsy, would not stop laughing. A man at the bar, dressed in a gold-coloured waistcoat, gave the commissario a condescending smile.

"I'm looking for Bonaldi," he said, without any preliminaries. The man, the smile still playing on his lips, pointed vaguely in one direction. "You'll find him at the billiard table."

Soneri walked over, attracting the attention of a group of people seated on low settees. In the flickering light and shadow from some lamps on the floor, their faces wore spectral grins. Bonaldi looked up as he came over, his expression of the kind used to summon a waiter. He folded the newspaper he was reading, removed his glasses and invited the commissario to take a seat.

"Can I offer you something?" he said in a tired voice.

The commissario shook his head. Bonaldi made a sign to the barman, who was obviously familiar with his tastes. "So, you want to ask me about Corbellini?" he said.

"You were the last man to see him alive."

"I wouldn't be so sure."

"I'm not absolutely certain, but that's very probably the truth."

"If you have any suspicions about my involvement, let me tell you that I only tried to help. In any case, with the state he was in, he could have done it all by himself."

"That doesn't explain why he was hidden inside someone else's tomb."

"That's your line of business," Bonaldi said arrogantly.

The commissario looked closely at him. He was a large, well-built man of imposing appearance. His jacket tightened between the shoulders as he bent over to pick up his glass.

"You took the mayor home on the Wednesday following his departure for Andalo. Why this early return?"

"He was not well, but it was also necessary for him to return in view of what was happening. He had responsibilities."

"Were you all afraid he might run off?"

Bonaldi sat in silence for a few moments before replying. "There was also that possibility."

"So you loaded him into a car and perhaps even made him swallow some tranquillisers."

"Out of necessity!"

"What does that mean? He was unwilling? He didn't want any more to do with you and turned rebellious?"

"Commissario, don't you know that Corbellini never stopped inhaling something or other? For him, it was a necessity to enable him to keep going. Some drink, others sniff. At the end of the day, these are venial sins. Show me the man who does not indulge at least occasionally. Viagra for screwing and cocaine for business."

"Did he get his supplies from the same people who buried him? Petrillo's camorristi?"

"Once again, that's your business. I simply don't know. I hear they were obtained for him by that old man who froze to death, but I don't know where he got his supplies. Probably someone above suspicion, someone who wouldn't attract too much attention. Behind every commodity there is an organisation whose power is proportional to the risks of the trade. Some things are known only to a very few people."

"It's my belief that you know those circles very well. Corbellini was not the only one who—"

"How much can a man involved in politics and occupied with the world really know about these things? What can I do? Everything can be bought and sold. If there's demand, nothing can stop the supply. We have to live with the camorra."

"Did you stop off at the mayor's house that evening? Were you keeping an eye on him in case he did something foolish?"

"I tried to put him to bed and get him to sleep, but once he was in the house he threw himself onto the sofa and wouldn't move."

"And what did you do?"

"I waited until he fell asleep, and then I left."

"That's all?"

"What do you suspect? Do you think I killed him? On the contrary. If I had stayed, perhaps none of this would've happened."

"Perhaps what did happen occurred precisely because he was prevented from making his own choice."

Bonaldi shrugged his shoulders. "A man in his position cannot decide for himself. The party which put him there is the guarantor of that."

"Do you think the mayor had other visitors that night?"

"I don't think so, but it could equally be that he did see someone."

"What was in your mind? Did you all go back to look for him the following day?"

"He'd asked us to leave him in peace until Sunday since everyone thought he was away from the city. Up there in Chiosetto no-one would've noticed, because the place is dead in winter."

"But you personally did go back because you weren't sure."

"Yes, I did go back, but I didn't find him and I reported back to the party. We assumed that he'd made his escape because he was afraid he'd be arrested like his councillors."

"That was a possibility," Soneri agreed.

"It certainly was a possibility, but if you've created havoc, you can't just run off and leave others to clean up! The party required him to remain, keep his nerve and find a remedy."

"In other words, cover everything up, lay a false trail."

"It was legitimate to demand that he didn't leave us in the shit. He was on the Council to manage things. Once you're there, it's up to you to make sure everything runs smoothly."

At that moment, the commissario felt his mobile vibrate. He looked at the screen and read BERGOSSI. He signed to Bonaldi to wait while he took the call.

"I've interrogated Petrillo in prison," the prosecutor began. "He must have received orders to drag other people into this and send out warnings, because he's informed us they were the ones who hid Corbellini's body."

"They were managers of the cemetery," Soneri said.

"We can't take anything for granted. In any case, they've saved us the trouble of proving it. But that's not all. Petrillo says that it was Bonaldi who called him to tip him off about the corpse."

"I've got him here," Soneri whispered uneasily into the

telephone, looking over at Bonaldi, who had started reading once again.

"Petrillo says the party was in a panic and had no idea what to do. The simplest solution was to hide the body, so they decided to put it in the one place where no-one would look for it."

"They needed time to keep the Council in office. That would've given them the chance to corrupt the evidence and leave every possibility open, including escape. That would have been – for us – the most awkward outcome."

Bergossi muttered something which sounded like a lament. "Whichever way you look at it, what Petrillo is doing is trying to spread the guilt. He's raising the stakes to keep the politicians on the ropes, and I have to say he holds all the aces."

"These are messages. The camorra gang want to come to an arrangement in Rome. They're demanding that the party chieftains intervene to block or divert the inquiry. You know that mafia and politics—"

"I know, I know. All we can do is hope that the game gets out of hand."

"Let's hope so, but it's hard going. These people are much more powerful than us," Soneri said.

"There's no doubt about that," Bergossi said, and for the first time Soneri heard a note of resignation in his voice. He went back and took a seat facing Bonaldi, who carried on reading.

"Be good enough to put down your newspaper," Soneri told him, with an authoritarian air. Bonaldi looked up and took off his glasses, startled and threatening at the same time.

The commissario began: "I want to speak frankly, and it's in your interests to do the same." Bonaldi looked straight ahead and for a moment seemed disconcerted. "What more do you want to know?"

"About the relationship with Petrillo's camorra gang, whom you asked to make the body disappear."

Bonaldi was momentarily thrown off balance, and the commissario realised he had played the right card. The man's hands trembled slightly and his chest seemed to heave under the pressure of having to reorder his ideas and face up to an act of betrayal.

"It was they who reduced Corbellini to a shadow of himself," he managed to say at last.

"They'd never have managed if he hadn't gone along with them."

"They stuffed him to the gills with cocaine. They covered Parma with powder."

"We know this already."

"They've got bags of money. They can buy everything."

"That's in part because there are too many businessmen in this city who prefer to live on unearned income. And they do business with your party as well."

"Not with the party as such, but with some members."

"With the mayor?"

"Are you joking? You know perfectly well that the supplier has the upper hand over the addict. Perhaps they didn't even need to pay. Blackmail was enough."

"And yet Corbellini was answerable to the party. You said so yourself. All of you facilitated their business."

"It wasn't us who brought in the camorra! It's no fault of the party if they're now part of our business world. They set up front companies, so they're in the clear. In Parma, things are done without any great fuss, with every appearance of legality. It's sufficient to clear the path for business matters and everything goes smoothly. No law-breaking and just a minimum of pressure: a variation in planning on the one hand, an alteration of intended use on the other; the restructuring of

an industrial estate with a much-needed park to win over public opinion, a touch of cronyism ... What are we talking about?
You'll never find anything underhand."

"The occasional bribe?" Soneri suggested.

"If anyone's taken bribes, he'll be answerable for it, but the
party never had any money. We have businessmen who can
provide."

"Ah, yes. Ugolini. He's the man in charge, the one who keeps
things rolling. If you don't obey, he can sack the lot of you."

Bonaldi shrugged his shoulders.

"It would be a good idea for you to tell the truth, or else I'll
get Petrillo to cough up the whole story."

The man glowered at him with an expression of ill-concealed
hatred, but it was clear he had surrendered. "I found him the
following morning. I never left the house," he confessed. "From
the moment he woke up, Corbellini was in a state of deep agitation. He was desperate to leave and run away."

"And you stopped him?"

"Yes. He was in no condition to move, and he would have
been seen if he got out."

"Was that all, or was there more to it?"

"He was in a panic. He said he'd spill the beans, that the
party had abandoned him and that the councillors who were
under arrest would drag him down with them. He seemed to
have lost his head."

"The long and the short of it is you used force to keep him
in Chiosetto."

"What did you expect me to do? He was my responsibility."

"Did you come to blows?"

"No, not at all. You know my past – I'm tough and I know
how to go about it."

"What happened next?"

"Corbellini started yelling and insulting me, and went up

-319-

to his room. I was afraid he had a gun hidden somewhere, so I followed him, but when he got upstairs he threw himself onto the bed without another word. I thought he needed sleep."

"Carry on," Soneri said.

"I lay down in the next room, but then I heard him get up. I watched what he was doing and saw him rummage about in a suitcase. He pulled out a small container of the type used for pills. I asked him what was in it, and he told me he'd forgotten to take an antibiotic. To reassure me, he even specified that he had a urinary tract infection. I couldn't foresee—"

"What? That it wasn't an antibiotic?"

Bonaldi nodded. "A short while later, I heard some bumps and then a crash. I raced in and saw him lying on the ground groaning. I took a hold of him under the armpits and tried to drag him over to the bed, but as I was moving him, I felt him go limp and he didn't seem to be breathing anymore. He died in my arms."

A silence fell between the two of them. Bonaldi seemed to be weighing the impact of his words, while Soneri was attempting to run over all the details of the account to see if it was credible.

"Do you know what was in that container?" he asked.

"No idea. Drugs, I think. I found a fifty-euro note on the window ledge in the bathroom, and it must have been used for snorting, but he'd been doing that for some time and nothing had ever happened."

"We'll check that out," Soneri said, remaining deliberately ambiguous. "Did it not enter your head that it might have been a momentary cardiac arrest? Did you make any attempt to revive him? Did you dial 118?"

Bonaldi stared at him with an expression of indifference and surprise, mumbling tonelessly: "He was dead. It wouldn't have made any difference."

"Seeing how things were, you might even have been relieved, isn't that so? Better a dead man than a hostile witness." Bonaldi continued staring at him with an expression of hatred and shrugged once again.

"Apart from the fact that if it was a poisonous substance, you might have put it there yourself."

"I did not put anything anywhere, and I've never dealt in those substances. I'm one of the few who can say that."

"What did you do when you realised he was dead?"

"I laid him on the bed and informed the provincial secretary and the group leader."

"What about Ugolini?"

Bonaldi looked up with a start. "No, he knew nothing about it," he said.

"Then what? Did they give you any advice, or did you make your own decisions?"

"We were all in agreement that we had to save the Administration."

"By covering up the whole sorry business and getting rid of the evidence."

"We only wanted to conceal the mayor's operations. The important thing was to let people believe he was still alive, that he might return and reshuffle the top jobs."

"But the councillors who were under arrest might have spoken out."

"Without evidence? We could convince them to keep their mouths shut. There are ways of dealing with people like them. They make threats so as to clear their own names. Corbellini was the problem."

"You didn't think he'd go to pieces, did you?" the commissario asked, thinking of what Bergossi had said about the unforeseen.

"Who could have imagined he was so completely gutless?" Bonaldi raised his voice in a state of rage. "Anyone else would have defended himself and the power he held to the last, issued denials, fought back ..."

"They're not all bastards." Soneri smiled sardonically.

Bonaldi looked at him coldly, attempting to show indifference to this insult. Behaving as he was doing must have come so naturally to him that he had no need to ask himself why he did it. "Corbellini was nothing more than a shit and a coward," Bonaldi sneered, now out of control, but knowing he was lost and finished, facing the fate of the scapegoat.

"If you had any courage you'd have told the whole story, but in your turn you're such a coward that you stayed silent out of fear. Reality can be turned on its head, depending on your point of view."

This time, Bonaldi's eyes filled with hatred. "Whatever you say, you'll never get anywhere and I'll walk away a free man."

26

AT DINNER THE previous evening, Soneri had turned to Angela to say that when all was said and done, it was thanks to her that he had discovered Corbellini's body. "When I think of Fortune, I see your face," he said. She looked at him severely, asking if he considered her presence only an occasional event. He rushed to deny this, surprised at the interpretation she had chosen to put on his words, but he understood she was reclaiming a role which the inquiry had taken from her. When they embraced and sank on to the sofa, she warned him never again to compare her to Fortune, however flattering the comparison might seem.

Nanetti had to wake him up the following morning. For the second day in a row, he had not heard the alarm clock. He was paying the price for his accumulated exhaustion.

"What response does science offer?" Soneri asked.

"The response I expected, even if I let on."

"That is?"

"An overdose. He died in a few minutes."

"How could that be? Bonaldi says he'd been on drugs for years. He should've been an expert. Did you know that he was using Romagnoli as a mule? Perhaps that's why they hung him out to dry."

"If he'd been taking what he thought he was ..."

"Wasn't it cocaine?"

"He might have thought so, but it was in fact white heroin."

"What's that?"

"A drug introduced not so long ago, the same as cocaine in appearance but with a much stronger active principle. It's hard to detect the difference, so if someone snorted it, he'd be in trouble. But this makes the whole question more complicated."

"More complicated, yes," Soneri murmured, already wondering what this discovery signified. Nanetti cut in before Soneri could continue. "The point is this: did he take it voluntarily or did someone mix it in deliberately, taking advantage of the resemblance? And if the former is the case, was it just to get high in a different way, or did he know it would be lethal?"

Once again, many new leads opened out in front of the commissario. The inquiry continued to shoot off in different directions, making a mockery of any hope that there would be one single conclusion. "What do you think?" he asked Nanetti.

"What can I say? In these cases anything is possible, but I wonder. If he'd wanted to kill himself, he could have overdosed on sleeping pills. He had plenty of them and it would have been much easier."

"So you think they killed him."

"I can't say. In the last month, there have been two deaths caused by white heroin. I don't believe these people wanted to kill themselves, even if anyone who uses that stuff, in the long run ... It's a drug toxicologists don't know much about, which is why it's so dangerous."

"How come they fail to distinguish it from cocaine?"

"It's not easy. It's got the same colour and the same feel but it's five times more powerful."

"I must ask the narcotics squad where this substance comes from," the commissario promised himself.

"It doesn't take much to guess," Nanetti said.

"I never take anything for granted."

"You know who controls the drug trade in Parma."

"Of course I do, but whoever it is, the best way is to start with the rank and file."

"In the case of the mayor, there could be a direct relationship with the importer via Zunarelli and Romagnoli," Nanetti suggested.

Soneri hung up and got out of bed. He felt somewhat befuddled, perhaps on account of the doubts which Nanetti had planted in his mind. In this state of anxiety, he hurried to his office and called Bergossi. "We must get hold of the records of Bonaldi's mobile," he told him.

"The request has already been made there. I had to add his name to the register of people under investigation."

"Do you know about the autopsy?"

"They've already told me. We're adrift once again."

"If only everything had been clearer . . . a bullet, a stab in the back, a blow to the head, whereas—"

"Whereas it might be anything," Bergossi said, completing Soneri's sentence. "Just as it was at the outset."

The commissario replaced the receiver, already feeling exhausted even though he had just got up. He flicked through his diary looking for Isernia's number. "What can you tell me about white heroin?" he asked, with no preamble.

"That there's an invasion of it under way."

"Is it cheaper?"

"It might be for the producers and the big dealers. If they've decided to produce so much, it means it's in their interests. Addicts are less and less willing to inject, so they snort the stuff. It's much easier that way." He stopped for a moment before adding, "There was some in the belly of that dog. You know the one I mean? The one Piccirillo adopted."

"Now you tell me!"

"You never asked. The prosecutor told me you'd abandoned that line of inquiry. In addition, it was a while before we noticed, and even then it was almost by chance. We examined samples of the contents of its stomach, and the last of the capsules contained a substance which seemed slightly different. When we looked more closely, we saw it was a bit darker, less shiny and with particles which somehow resembled ivory, but we were only certain when we handed it into the laboratory for detailed examination."

"That's enough. I know everything." Soneri cut him off abruptly.

"You see! You never take the time to listen and then you come moaning," he heard Isernia protesting, but Soneri was already hanging up.

He turned to Juvara: "Let me know as soon as you get Bonaldi's telephone records." With these words he left the office, hoping a walk in the fresh air would help him shake off his drowsiness, but the frenzy of the over-excited city unsettled him. Everything seemed excessive, like a strident scream, and this was out of kilter with the torpor he felt. He sought the peace of the backstreets, but the ringing of his mobile dragged him back even from that refuge of mouldy walls now used as urinals.

"I've got the records," Juvara said.

"What do they tell us?"

"Bonaldi made four calls that night, three to the party H.Q. and one to Ugolini."

"They'd stayed awake waiting," Soneri said.

"We've also got the incoming calls, sir."

"Go on."

"Three communications from telephones on the party's account, and two from Laudadio's mobile."

"Laudadio?" Soneri repeated.

"I've checked. The first call was transmitted by the relay station at Sala Baganza, and the other from the station at Fragno, just above Calestano. Our man was obviously moving about, and maybe even got as far as Chiosetto."

"If he was in the vicinity, he must have gone there," Soneri agreed.

Juvara's call had given him the necessary jolt to shake off the soporific state resulting from being awakened so abruptly. He turned back to pick up his Alfa and set off for San Vitale.

He drove alongside the Baganza, whose water, in the dry winter weather, was almost hidden in the gravel. He could make out the clear blue sky above, but a cocoon of mist continued to envelop the road. With each passing kilometre, he hoped to pierce that shell and come out into the light, but this occurred only when he reached the crossroads near Laudadio's house.

He got out and rang the bell but before anyone could answer, he saw a motorbike arrive. It was impossible to make out the face behind the visor, but the bulk of the body told him it was the man he was after. He became certain when the rider took off his helmet. The two men stared at each other, each resigned in his own way. Laudadio seemed to have turned to stone, his face an inexpressive mask of cold surprise. He signalled to Soneri to follow him into the house. They sat down as they had done previously, in the same glass cage with the same stale odour of cigarette smoke.

"What's new?" Laudadio asked, although he seemed to have understood the reason for the visit.

"I didn't think of you as a pusher. I thought you acted at a higher level."

"I'm no pusher."

"No, you don't go selling pills in clubs and discotheques,

if that's what the word means. You deal with V.I.P.s, businessmen."

Laudadio looked him up and down with cordial rancour. From the words spoken, he understood that the commissario knew something, but it was not clear how much he knew, so he was unsure how to marshal his defence.

"You overestimate me. I deal with neither the one nor the other."

"The night the mayor died, you went from here to Calestano. Do you want to tell me what you were doing, or would you prefer to wait for the transcription of the intercepted calls?"

Laudadio banged one hand on the coffee table, muttering something, perhaps an oath, which the commissario did not catch.

"You know how to get revenge if you feel betrayed," the commissario urged. "I'll take care of the rest. All you have to do is talk."

Laudadio gave a furious laugh.

"Are you afraid?"

In reply, Laudadio assumed an expression of scorn, even if for a moment fear had touched him. "Alright, I did go there," he said, as though issuing a challenge.

Soneri, who had expected him to make a full confession, was disappointed. Although it was an admission of sorts, he knew that Laudadio would go no further. He was sacrificing himself to save the others.

"Did you bring drugs?"

"They asked me to, but that doesn't make me a pusher."

"Did you know what you were bringing?"

"How could I? It was delivered to me. Didn't he take cocaine?"

"Who delivered it to you?"

"They sent two foreigners, two Romanians."

"Did you know them?"

"Yes, they worked for the organisation. Your colleagues arrested them after you found that dog."

"Why didn't they bring the stuff directly?"

"They believed they were being watched, and the less they were seen moving about, the better it was for all concerned."

"Are you aware that those drugs caused the death of the mayor?"

"I'd no idea what was in the packet, and I don't believe the two foreigners did either."

"Who supplied them with the stuff?" Soneri said, raising his voice.

"I have no way of knowing anyone more than two grades higher up in the chain of command. The organisation is structured that way, to remove the temptation to blurt things out."

"It goes right up to Petrillo, I imagine."

Laudadio remained impassive, leaving the commissario to wonder if everything was once again slipping through his fingers. The enemy seated in front of him was like a lizard, capable of shuffling off its tail to cheat a predator, and the tail was all he had in his hand. But what was he to do with Laudadio? Without question, Capuozzo would be happy, and would even pass the arrest off as a brilliant operation.

"How did it go that night?" Soneri asked in a tired voice.

"I got a call from Petrillo telling me to take a package to somewhere near Calestano. I met the two foreigners in a bar in the Montanara district of Parma, where they handed over the goods. After that, I came back here and called Bonaldi to say I would be coming to Chiosetto. When I got there, I made another call from Fragno to make sure I wouldn't encounter any surprises. Once I'd made the delivery, I went away again. I swear I didn't know what the package contained."

"I'll verify what you're telling me when I receive the transcription of the telephone calls."

"You do that," Laudadio said, with a shrug.

As he made his way back, Soneri's thoughts turned once again to the lizard strategy. Both criminals and politicians made use of it to safeguard the public, unsuspected aspect of their activities. In that way, Petrillo and Laudadio on the one hand, and Bonaldi, Corbellini and the councillors on the other, were the tail which could be surrendered to anyone pursuing them. Bergossi, whom he called on his return journey, compared the tactic to that employed by resistance cells, where each member knows no more than three others. The outstanding issue now was to establish whether the mayor wanted to kill himself, or whether he had been murdered.

When he got to the office, Juvara had the transcriptions of the calls made by both Laudadio and Bonaldi, and they confirmed what he'd heard from them directly. As he was handing back the file, he heard the rumble of cars in the courtyard. The flickering blue lights coloured the walls of the little Prefecture cloister.

"What's going on?" Soneri asked.

"Today we've got the Minister of Justice and half a dozen undersecretaries," Juvara explained. "There's a meeting with the Prefect, and then they're going to see representatives of the Right in the Hotel Stendhal. As you know, Bergossi has the inspectors from the Ministry on his back."

"What did I tell you? They'll never let us get anywhere. They haven't come to terms with the arrests, nor with the inclusion of the regional secretary in the register of suspects."

"The discovery of the mayor's body has driven them mad."

"They wanted to let the whole business die down. They know people have short memories."

On his desk, he found newspapers screaming about a

counter-offensive by the Right against the prosecution office. The commissario had the sensation that everything was falling apart, a feeling enhanced when he heard shouts coming from the direction of Via Repubblica and Piazza Garibaldi.

Juvara told him, "This is 'Kick-Their-Arse Day', organised by various movements on the occasion of the Minister's visit. I've no idea who they are, but they've got it in for the politicians. They want to get shot of the lot of them."

Once again, Soneri felt he had lost his moorings. He couldn't understand what was happening, except that everything – politics, the investigation and he himself – was going to the dogs.

Juvara noticed his state of mind and said: "It's as well to get rid of them all *en masse*, isn't it? Politicians are all the same. They only know how to cheat and steal. We need new representatives drawn from all walks of life."

These were words he'd heard thousands of times before, but society was made up of individuals like Ugolini, Capuozzo and hundreds of normally indifferent citizens who were now agitating to take maximum advantage of the misfortunes of the people they had voted for year after year. And once again that word, "context", forced itself on him as powerfully as a bout of nausea. The context was putrid. The political mould which covered it was the product of its decomposition.

When Bergossi received him, he told him that in a few months he would be forced into early retirement. He spoke with clarity. "In a world like this, we should jail half the nation, for complicity if nothing else. The criminals have taken over. The major players, along with the banks and high finance, have fashioned laws for their own ends, and so carry on committing crimes without the nuisance of our interference. The minor delinquents have to endure the masquerades we put on to convince people that there is still justice. We too play our part in the comedy, but I'm not enjoying myself anymore. At least we've got nothing to reproach ourselves for – we've given all we can, heart and soul," he concluded, slamming both hands down on the desk. To Soneri, that gesture sounded like the solemn, dramatic finale of a symphony.

They remained in silence for a few moments, the commissario a little shaken, the prosecutor with a bitter smile, like Socrates confronted with the poisoned chalice.

"How can we get out of this?" Soneri said, as though speaking to himself.

"Only with a dictatorship of the honest minority," Bergossi said, with the same half-smile. "That's a rare circumstance which is normally associated with some tragedy. I don't know if I can wish for it. The price would be very high."

They got up at the same time and shook hands. They exchanged a look of understanding, and went their separate ways without another word.

Immediately afterwards, Soneri called Angela. As he waited for her to answer, he was overcome by feelings of humiliation, impotence, rage and disgust.

"Let's have dinner in the *Milord* this evening," he announced, when at last she picked up.

"Aren't you busy?"

"No, from now on I will be unencumbered with responsibilities. I'm through with them."

Angela's silence seemed to him eloquent. "I see. You must have expected this, mustn't you?"

"It's one thing to expect it, but it's quite different when it actually happens. There's always a crumb of hope."

"Come on," Angela said, trying to rise above these thoughts. "Tonight we'll have a fabulous meal, and we'll get a bit drunk, but not too drunk."

"We either get blind drunk or we stay sober."

"Just a bit tipsy then."

"I need to see you, to sleep with you," Soneri said.

He heard Angela laugh gently, and imagined her face. That was what it meant for them to really know each other.

"We'll do that. If there's anything positive about your profession, it's that every so often it brings us closer together."

The commissario felt relieved, a sensation that stayed with him even when Juvara informed him that Capuozzo had called a press conference to announce that all pending cases had been solved. A sinister ring of dealers, who brought in their drugs via an ingenious but savage abuse of dogs, had been smashed, even if this, regrettably, had not prevented a quantity of white heroin getting into circulation and causing some deaths, including that of the mayor. Laudadio, Petrillo and a group of foreigners had been arrested as leaders of the organisation. Petrillo and other employees of L'Eterna had been charged with concealing the body. The corruption in the City Council, which had led Corbellini to attempt flight from Parma, had been exposed and at the end of the day even the mayor would have been put under investigation.

"It seems everything's been resolved, sir. He even praised us," Juvara said.

"You know the lizard strategy?"

The inspector, surprised and uncomprehending, made no reply. "No, what is it? A film?"

"Doesn't matter. Forget it," Soneri said, and hung up.

He forgot about everything once he was in Alceste's with Angela. They did not want to forego anything. They began with an *antipasto di culatello*, continued with a selection of *tortelli*, followed by a plate of tripe, all washed down with a bottle of Gutturnio. When it came to choosing a dessert wine, they decided a Malvasia was the ideal accompaniment for the *millefoglie* and *sbrisolona*. Alceste tempted them with a *liquore all'erba Luigia* served semi-chilled, and by that stage they were drowning in a euphoria which dispelled all thought.

"Happiness is a chemical fact," Soneri proclaimed.

"Well, if this is the medicine, I'm happy to take it," said Angela, who was now drifting into that twilight zone that precedes inebriation. Her sparkling eyes could not conceal her curiosity. "How do you think it went?" she asked, as they sipped the liqueur. "It's only once you've shared it with me that you'll be able to get it off your chest and come to terms with it in your own way. I know you'll tell me something close to the truth."

The commissario twirled the glass in his fingers, having no idea where to start. "You're entitled to ask me to explain things. Everything began and ended with you."

"I've got nothing to do with it."

"Oh yes you have. Do you remember when you sent me to visit Adelaide because of the mobile ringing down by the river?"

Angela shrugged and laughed. It was a night for light hearts.

"Soon after that, Romagnoli was found dead, but in the early stages it didn't appear that these events were linked. I got the idea that there could be some connection only when I went down to the riverbank and found the paw marks left by dogs. Another dog, Dondolo, Valmarini's bloodhound, helped me understand that many dogs had gone along that track. Romagnoli, the mayor's right-hand man, had been given the task of supplying him with cocaine, but he kept prattling on about dogs, thereby risking revealing facts which no-one was supposed to know. The gang forced Zunarelli, an old friend who shared his passion for hunting dogs, to deal with the problem. He was nearly bankrupt and was being blackmailed. He didn't agonise unduly. All he had to do was work on Romagnoli's madness, and direct him towards the epilogue."

"That could be inducement to suicide aggravated by exploitation of a person infirm of mind."

"Could be, and perhaps it is, but who could ever prove it? In this whole story, there isn't a single killer with a name and address. The killing was carried out by a complex of individuals and circumstances. It's . . ." Perhaps because of the alcohol the commissario struggled to find the word. "It's . . . the context. In this case, the victims felt a noose being tightened around their necks, but were unable to see who they should be fighting. The enemy is legion as well as anonymous, so they end up debating and discussing, but if they launch themselves against any one person, they get nowhere. They're aware of this and feel powerless, or at best incapable of alleviating any pain but their own."

"I don't understand if it's because they could no longer see what's right, or because justice itself is dead."

"What is dead is faith in humankind, and that's altogether worse."

"Carry on."

Soneri took another sip of his *erba Luigia*. "Following the trail of the dogs, I arrived at Zunarelli's place in San Vitale, the vital link between the camorra drug trafficking and politics. I am almost certain that much of the profit drawn from the drugs trade was invested in companies in Parma, perhaps even in those belonging to Ugolini, the unquestioned leader of the Right. He had a member of the gang on his premises. There's no doubt that some of the profits were invested in L'Eterna, which now runs the racket in graveyards both here and in Campania. They had devised a perfect mechanism which only faltered because of something totally unforeseen, in keeping with an unprovable law in which Bergossi places total trust: chance."

"Apart from Romagnoli's role as courier, I see it all now. A dog runs off, or rebels, following its instinct for freedom. It's significant that it was an animal and not a man who got free of slavery. If you think about it, he's the only one in the whole story to do so."

"Very true. An untamed force, as happens in the myths we used to believe in. Anyway, this dog gave us a glimpse of the wickedness of using a living creature as a means to an end, a disposable receptacle for drugs. Money before all else. The camorra makes loads of cash and with its money it can buy anything it likes. It takes over companies thanks to frontmen like our *Avvocato* Righetti, brings in Parma's spineless businessmen and sets up a respectable little empire which is protected from investigation by politicians, among others. Corbellini was no longer answerable to his electors but to those potentates, giving them a free hand to despoil the city. Our government is run by a super-class spurred on by pure self-interest. And what do we do? Can you tell me? We arrest Petrillo and Laudadio, a couple of councillors and some small fry from the lower ranks."

"But was the mayor killed or did he simply remove himself?" Angela asked, attempting to bring the discussion back to the investigation, even if she was aware that the conversation had been diverted towards more general considerations.

"I think they got rid of him because they were afraid he'd speak out. He was out of control, but no-one will ever succeed in proving it. He'd been on drugs for some time, and it'll always be possible to say it was an accident, or that he chose that kind of heroin out of a desire for novelty. He was a weak man and they struck at his fragility. At best, the authorities will charge some foreign dealers, and might even pull in Bonaldi."

"A story of murder without murderers: one man frozen to death, one suicide and a highly suspicious overdose."

"I told you who the murderer was, the context, but you can't arrest a context. You might aim for reform, but it's long-term, perhaps futile, work. In any case, it's not a police matter."

"It's hard."

"It's hard to observe something rotten, to smell the stench and be unable to do anything about it except spray some deodorant. Capuozzo is spraying deodorant, and at the end of the day I'm doing the same. Can you imagine how it weighs me down to be doing the same kind of work as Capuozzo?"

"It's important that we realise how wrong all this is. That's already something, isn't it?" Angela said.

"It's already something," Soneri agreed, semi-seriously.

They went out into the mist and embraced each other. The commissario attempted to convince himself that reality was Angela's body. That was the only way he could believe he was living in a just world.

VALERIO VARESI is a journalist with *La Repubblica*. *The Lizard Stategy* is the fifth in a series of crime novels featuring Commissario Soneri, now the protagonist of one of Italy's most popular television dramas. *River of Shadows* and *The Dark Valley* were both shortlisted for the Crime Writers' Association International Dagger.

JOSEPH FARRELL is professor of Italian at the University of Strathclyde. He is the distinguished translator of novels by Leonardo Sciascia and Vincenzo Consolo, and plays by the Nobel Laureate Dario Fo. His book about Robert Louis Stevenson in Samoa was published by MacLehose Press in 2017.

Valerio Varesi

RIVER OF SHADOWS

Translated from the Italian by Joseph Farrell

A relentless deluge lashes the Po Valley, and the river itself swells beyond its limits. A barge breaks free of its moorings and drifts erratically downstream; when it finally runs aground its seasoned pilot is nowhere to be found. The following day, an elderly man of the same surname falls from the window of a nearby hospital.

Commissario Soneri, scornful of his superiors' scepticism, is convinced the two incidents are linked. Stonewalled by the bargemen who make their living along the riverbank, he scours the floodplain for clues. As the waters begin to ebb, the river yields up its secrets: tales of past brutality, bitter rivalry and revenge.

MACLEHOSE PRESS

www.maclehosepress.com
Subscribe to our quarterly newsletter

Valerio Varesi

THE DARK VALLEY

Translated from the Italian by Joseph Farrell

Commissario Soneri returns to his roots for a hard-earned holiday, a few days mushrooming on the slopes of Montelupo. The isolated village of his birth relies on a salame factory founded by Palmiro Rodolfi, and now run by his son, Paride.

On arrival, Soneri is greeted by anxious rumours about the factory's solvency and the younger Rodolfi's whereabouts. Soon afterwards, a body is found in the woods. In the shadow of Montelupo, the carabinieri prepare to apprehend their chief suspect – an ageing woodsman who defended the same mountains from the S.S. during the war.

MACLEHOSE PRESS

www.maclehosepress.com
Subscribe to our quarterly newsletter

Valerio Varesi

GOLD, FRANKINCENSE AND DUST

Translated from the Italian by Joseph Farrell

Parma. A multi-vehicle pile-up on the autostrada. In the chaos, the burned body of a young woman is found at the side of the road. But she didn't die in a car crash.

Commissario Soneri takes on the case, a welcome distraction from his troubled love life. The dead woman is identified as Nina Iliescu, a beautiful, enigmatic Romanian, whose life in Italy has left little trace, aside from a string of wealthy lovers from Italian high society.

Even Soneri is irresistibly drawn to Nina: a victim whose charms could not protect her from the perils of immigrant life. But her worshippers are an unappetising congregation — was Nina a sacrificial lamb, or a devilish temptress?

MACLEHOSE PRESS

www.maclehosepress.com
Subscribe to our quarterly newsletter